'Holy S***, this book is a stone-cold classic of the genre; the strongest start to a series I've seen in years'
Tony Kent

'An authentic and compelling thriller. Highly recommended'
Mark Dawson

'An incredible piece of work. Great storytelling, pacy and written with such a sense of place'
Chris MacDonald

'Compelling from beginning to end ... a top-draw thriller!'
John Barlow

'A powerful and gripping story of organised crime and police corruption sparked by an ancient family feud. DS Max Craigie is a fantastic creation. I hope we get much more of him'
Howard Linskey

'When it comes to police procedure, this man's the real deal. An explosive opening to an exciting new series'
Paul Gitsham

'If you want to know how the police really do it, you'd be mad to miss this'
Claire Seeber

'A taut, fast-paced, and original thriller. DS Max Craigie is set to become a classic detective in Scottish Noir'
Michael Wood

'An utterly compelling start to a new series. Neil Lancaster is going places and I'm going to be following!'
Rebecca Bradley

Neil Lancaster is the No.1 digital bestselling author of the Tom Novak series. His latest novel, *Dead Man's Grave*, was longlisted for the 2021 William McIlvanney Prize for Best Scottish Crime Book of the Year. He served as a military policeman and worked as a detective for the Metropolitan Police, investigating serious crimes in the capital and beyond. As a covert policing specialist, he used a variety of tactics to obtain evidence against murderers, human traffickers, drug dealers and fraudsters.

He now lives in the Scottish Highlands, writes crime and thriller novels and works as a broadcaster on true crime documentaries. He is a key expert on two Sky Crime TV series, *Meet, Marry, Murder* and *Made for Murder*.

🐦 /@neillancaster66
📘 /@NeilLancasterCrime
www.neillancastercrime.co.uk

Also by Neil Lancaster

Going Dark
Going Rogue
Going Back

NEIL LANCASTER

DEAD MAN'S GRAVE

ONE PLACE. MANY STORIES

HQ
An imprint of HarperCollins*Publishers* Ltd
1 London Bridge Street
London SE1 9GF

www.harpercollins.co.uk

HarperCollins*Publishers* Ltd
1st Floor, Watermarque Building, Ringsend Road
Dublin 4, Ireland

This hardback edition 2021
1
First published in Great Britain by
HQ, an imprint of HarperCollins*Publishers* Ltd 2021

Copyright © Neil Lancaster 2021

Neil Lancaster asserts the moral right to be
identified as the author of this work.
A catalogue record for this book is
available from the British Library.

ISBN: 9780008517120

MIX
Paper from
responsible sources
FSC C007454
FSC
www.fsc.org

Dedicated to John Fisher.
24th January 1941 – 24th January 2021.
Lived a life in the Antipodes, but always a Scot.

Your story, told over a good malt whisky, of a young policeman's search for his family history sparked the story which follows.
I wish you could have read it.

The deil's awa the deil's awa,
The deil's awa wi' the Exciseman,
He's danc'd awa he's danc'd awa
He's danc'd awa wi' the Exciseman.
Robert Burns 1792

1

Tam Hardie was now sure. He had found the place. He felt a swell of emotion in his chest as he surveyed the dense tangle of bracken, gorse and brambles that covered the low wall of the cemetery. The only evidence of a chapel was a few scattered heaps of granite blocks surrounding the grassy broch. The landscape was sweeping, panoramic and bleak. The sea was not quite visible behind the incoming haar, which crept closer by the second. As it swirled, he could just make out wind farms in the surrounding fields, lying motionless in the still air.

He had read some mentions of the disused burial ground on the web, but it had taken a lot of driving around the barren landscape as well as asking the locals at the inn in Dunbeath before he had managed to find it.

He picked out the creased black-and-white photograph from his Barbour jacket pocket and looked again at the old image that he had studied many times over the years. As a younger man, he had given it scant attention but age and the reality of one's mortality have a way of making you more nostalgic for the past. Tam felt a rush of excitement. The undergrowth was thicker and taller, and the wall was a little shorter and more dilapidated, but Tam was certain. This was the burial ground his grandfather had once told him about.

He walked quickly, wheezing heavily in the late afternoon chill as the cold mist began to creep across the landscape from the North Sea. He shivered as the damp, clammy air bit at his exposed skin. His chest burned and he coughed, deep wracking hacks that made his head swim. Wiping his mouth with his handkerchief, he tried to ignore the spots of blood on the white fabric. Something made him shudder, and it wasn't just the haar dropping the air temperature, as it always did. He looked over his shoulder, back towards his Range Rover. Was that a noise, he wondered? He stood there for a long moment staring into the distance, but nothing moved. He shivered, surprised at the slight nip of nerves that began to form in his stomach. Shaking his head, he moved on, determined to face whatever lay in that graveyard.

Tam picked his phone out of his pocket, and noting the faltering signal, called his eldest son, Tam Junior.

'Pa, you okay, man? The boys were wondering where you'd gone.'

'I'm fine, boy, I'm fine. I think I've found it, like.'

'Seriously?'

'I'm walking to the burial ground now. It's the one, no doubt about it and if the grave is there, it'll be plain as the nose on your face.'

'Well, take care. You shouldn't be out on your own.'

'Ach quit your blethering. Has that bastard Turkish Joe called yet?'

'Aye. He wants thirty on the key, though.'

'Well, the cheeky bastard can piss off. I'm no paying thirty grand a kilo and who else is going to take it?'

'I said, man. He got a little pissed off when I told him.'

'He'll see sense. Right, I'm gonna check this shite-hole out. I'll speak later.' He hung up without waiting for a reply.

2

The rusted gate creaked arthritically as he eased it open. The noise disturbed a murder of crows that had been nestling in the brush, causing Tam to flinch. 'Bastard craws,' he spat, his heart thumping in his chest. There was something about this place.

He edged forward a little at a time through the wildly overgrown shrubs and weeds, his muscles complaining with the effort. 'Bollocks to being this old,' he muttered under his breath. He had been fearsomely strong in his younger years, a gifted boxer and an even more lethal brawler. No one came out on top of a square go with Tam Hardie, or at least that's what all the folk in his tenement used to say.

Breathing heavily, his head spinning, he forced his way through the thorny shrubs, wincing as the gorse spikes pierced his hands. Most of the headstones were broken and battered but several jutted out from the undergrowth, with fading inscriptions caused by the centuries of relentless weather. The place reeked of age and long-forgotten history.

The haar swirled around him and he wondered if this was a fool's errand after all. He shivered, once more, this time with that inescapable feeling of someone walking over his grave. It was, he had to admit, appropriate. His well-honed antennae quivered as he looked around him, but he saw nothing. Tam wasn't used to fear, so he forced it down before it took hold.

His attention shifted as his eyes moved to a gravestone that stood proudly erect a few metres ahead of him, its inscription still fairly clear. Quickening his pace, he missed his footing and his boot caught the corner of something hard and flat that was almost entirely covered by weeds and thick moss. 'Shite,' he hissed as he fell to the damp earth in a painful heap, cracking his knee on the edge of a flat, partially concealed gravestone. Still muttering suppressed oaths, feeling suddenly a little guilty about blaspheming on consecrated ground, he looked at the memorial with renewed interest. Unlike the other more exposed and upright stones, the word 'Grave' was still clearly and crisply edged, almost as if the mason had only recently finished with his hammer and chisel.

With rising excitement, he got to his feet and began to scrape the thick moss from the large, flat granite surface. He pulled his old clasp knife from his Barbour pocket, extended the worn blade and began hacking away at the vegetation.

After a couple of minutes of furious scraping and chopping, his work was done. Tam Hardie stood, a mix of apprehension and excitement beginning to take hold as he saw the six words that his grandfather had assured him would be there.

This Grave Never to be Opened

There were no names, no dates, nothing beyond that foreboding statement. His breathing quickened painfully as he tried to suck in the damp air. This was the place. Without a doubt, this was it.

He cleared more of the moss and muck away from the smooth granite, exposing the inscription and removing the trailing bramble fronds from the surface. When it was bare, he stood and stared. The weight of history sat heavily on his shoulders as he thought about what legend had always said would be within that grave. He tapped the heavy granite with his knife, noting that it was solid, unmoving and embedded into the damp sod beneath.

The nasty prickling sensation between Tam's shoulder blades returned, and something in the instinctive part of his brain told him that he was no longer alone. As he was just about to turn, a soft, almost whispered voice spoke behind him.

'They said someone would come.'

He spun around, knife raised. A small, familiar figure was facing him, staring with deep, sunken eyes. The bedraggled man was hunched over awkwardly with one hand inside his jacket. Tam's instincts flared. This meant only one thing. The man wore heavy boots and had a filthy old Mackintosh draped over his bony shoulders.

'Jesus, you almost gave me a heart attack. What the hell are you doing here?' Tam blurted out, his heart thumping, his hand gripping the knife.

'Who are you, mind?' the smaller man said in a quiet voice.

'I, son, am Tam Hardie, and you'd not be staring like that at me if you knew who the hell I am,' he said, brandishing the knife that was still in his hand, but feeling a strange sense of dread in response to the much smaller, slighter man. It was his eyes, dark and unfathomable and empty of even a trace of fear. And that wasn't something Tam was used to. Tam knew, instinctively that the stranger meant him harm. Gripping the knife even tighter, he raised it up, menacingly – the worn tip pointing unerringly towards the man. 'Whatever you're thinking of doing, pal, I'd advise against it. I've killed many men over the years, and you don't scare me even a wee bit.' Even as the words left his lips, he knew that they weren't quite true.

The man smiled, just slightly, showing no trace of fear. His lips pursed, his eyes twinkling and yet somehow vague and empty.

'Aye, they always said a Hardie would come, eventually.' He reached inside his coat, and something long and metallic glinted as he pulled the grimy fabric to one side.

'You can join your ancestors, Hardie, and you'll burn with them.'

2

Detective Sergeant Max Craigie yawned deeply, scratching at his shaved scalp, feeling the stubble bristle against his fingers as he stared blankly at his computer terminal in the open-plan office at the headquarters of the Serious Organised Crime team at Gartcosh. He was really tired after a 4 a.m. start that morning. The team had crashed through the doors of a suspected Glasgow stash-house after an informant had tipped them off that a large quantity of high-grade heroin was hidden there.

This had been Max's first major job since joining the team six months ago after transferring in from the Met Police. So, he felt a little prickle of embarrassment as he sat in the office, staring at but not seeing the words on his computer monitor. The rest of the team had tried to hide their smiles at his obvious discomfort, and a mild stream of piss-taking had already gently begun as they all sat round clutching mugs of tea. This had been a resource-heavy operation utilising the firearms teams, specialist method of entry teams and licensed search officers. They'd spent several hours tearing the flat to pieces, but not a trace of any heroin was found. In fact, the place was totally empty, not a stick of furniture, not a single sock. It was like it had been professionally deep-cleaned ready for a new tenant.

'Nice job, Max. Breakfast rules apply after sending us through a door to an empty house. You got me out of my warm bed for that pile of shite. Who was the snout on this one? Bloody cockney cops coming up here and dragging us out of our beds.' The voice from an adjacent desk was heavy with sarcasm, but at the same time, a touch of understanding. Every cop had smashed through the wrong door at one time or another.

Max sighed, once more, as he laughed off the jibe with a forced smile. He had wanted his first job to go well, but it looked like 'Cookie', the informant, had been a little late with his information.

Whilst a newbie to the team, he wasn't a beginner in policing. He had fifteen years' service, until recently all in London where he had been pretty successful, making detective after only four years and being posted to the elite Flying Squad only five years after that. It had all been going well until one particular job had gone all wrong. His head swam as it jolted back to that day, two years ago, the image of the sawn-off shotgun swinging in his direction, held by the panic-stricken masked raider. Max remembered as if it was yesterday. The look of pure, unadulterated panic in the eyes of the gunman from behind the skull-emblazoned mask as he brought the shotgun to bear on Max. He remembered the Glock 17 bucking in his hands as he double-tapped the gunman, centre mass, and he had dropped like a stone.

A loud and brash voice bawled across the office dragged Max from his reverie. 'Max, what the fuck? You told me this was a sure thing.' Max looked up from his desk to see the portly, balding figure of Detective Inspector Ross Fraser, his face flushed with anger as he limped across the office. His suit was rumpled and clearly hadn't been to a dry-cleaners for some time, if the stain on the lapel was anything to go by.

'You okay, Guvnor?' Max said, smiling at Fraser's worn and unpolished Oxford shoes. Sartorial elegance was not at the top of Ross Fraser's priority list.

'No, I am fucking not, and none of that cockney Met "Guvnor" shite, either.' He mimed quotation marks with his fingers. 'You're in Police Scotland now, no Sweeney bollocks in here, pal.'

'You look sore, Ross,' Max said, smiling. Despite his angry demeanour, Ross Fraser was a good-humoured and kind-hearted man, who had welcomed Max to the team with open arms. It was probably because they were both Highlanders, had both served in the Black Watch a few years apart, and were both fans of Ross County FC. Max was originally from the Black Isle, just north of Inverness, and Ross was from Dingwall, a few miles away. It was a series of small coincidences, but they had helped strike a chord of friendship between them.

'Sore as a bastard, man. It's the pissing gout shite again. Chat in my office?' He winced as he limped towards the glass-walled office in the middle of the open-plan space, dotted with desks where all the other members of the Serious Organised Crime team sat beavering away.

'Too much fine living, Guv. Didn't Henry the Eighth have gout? All that port and venison.'

'Piss off and bring me a tea. We need to chat.' DI Fraser limped inside his glass sanctuary without looking backwards.

Max smiled to himself as he fixed a couple of teas. Ross was full of bluster and bullshit, but he and Max had hit it off immediately. Despite the pugnacious manner, Ross was a highly talented detective, with a long history littered with successes against the major criminal groups that their team was operating against.

Max's posting direct from the Met to the Serious Organised Crime team was unusual, as most transferring detectives would have been put straight into a main office somewhere dealing with volume and routine crimes. A phone call from Max's old boss in London had let them know of his skills and experience. It made total sense to get him working in this area, owing to his training in surveillance, informant handling and firearms. Max didn't feel too flattered by this, realising that it was most likely a simple fact of saving money by not having to put someone else through long and difficult training courses with a high attrition rate.

He'd quickly settled into his new work and was enjoying being in Scotland and away from his life as DS Max Craigie in London. DS Craigie, the officer being investigated for shooting an armed criminal. He'd needed a fresh challenge, and the opportunity to work in Scotland had seemed to him to be exactly that.

'Tea, two sugars, Guv, although with your gout, maybe a bit less sugar would be in order.'

'Don't you start, you cheeky twat. Having a mere two sugars is a nod to health, especially now that Mrs Fraser has bloody stopped me smoking. Why did this job blow out then? Intel was that Turkish Joe had laid up ten kilos of pure smack in that flat. Is Cookie being a dodgy bastard?'

'They're all dodgy bastards. Goes with the turf.'

'Aye, well that's true. He'd been reliable up until now. He was bang on with the snide pawnbroker. We recovered a whole stack of nicked watches from that job.'

'I've called him. He's just as mystified as us. He says it was definitely there three days ago and it was being stashed there until Turkish Joe could offload it somewhere.'

'This is why I need you in here. As far as I can see the only person who could take on that amount of gear is Hardie and his family.'

Max shrugged.

'How long have you been with us?' Ross sipped his tea, screwing his face up slightly. 'Shite tea, by the way. You need more practice.'

'Six months, or so?'

'Settling in?'

'Aye, it's fine.'

'Not missing London?'

'Nope. Glad to be back in Scotland after all these years.'

'Heard from Katie?'

'Aye, sometimes, but we've agreed to not talk for a while. You know, space and that.'

'Is that a problem?'

Max shrugged. 'Just the way it is, Guv. I didn't want to stay in London and she didn't want to come, not at the moment, anyway. Maybe in the future.'

'Ah well, you can be a single gadabout now, lucky boy. Wives always give it you in the bloody neck; take Mrs Fraser, for instance. I wish the old bint would throw me out.'

'That's definitely not true. And Katie didn't throw me out, but you knew that already,' said Max, refusing to bite.

'Bloody is true, drives me up the wall,' said Ross, scowling at the framed picture of his wife on his desk, with what Max could see was affection. Despite the bumptiousness, Ross was devoted to his wife and kids.

'Is the shooting inquiry all finished?'

'I thought so. Inquest jury returned a lawful killing verdict, CPS ruled no evidence against me and IOPC ruled it all legit.'

'But?' Ross asked, his eyebrows raised.

'Family have applied for a judicial review of the findings, bringing up all sorts of shite.'

'Jeez, that's crap, man. When will they let it drop?'

'They're clinging on to the fact that in my notes I said I shot twice, but the weapon exam showed that I shot three times. As far as I can remember it was only two, but, you know, human brain is a funny thing.'

'I read something about this. You know, extreme stress messing with recall?'

'That's true, but it's enough for an anti-police set of solicitors to keep pushing. Not much I can do about it, just have to let it play out. Two shots or three, the bloke had a loaded sawn-off that he was swinging towards me and it was all captured on CCTV.' Max affected an air of nonchalance, but couldn't help the familiar feeling of dread that began to creep into his chest as he talked about the incident. It was palpable, like a knot of flesh.

'You okay?'

Max said nothing, just raised his eyebrows waiting for his boss to continue. A mix of an incident in Afghanistan years ago and the shooting in London had left their mark on Max and Ross knew it. He was feeling better, however, and the dreams were less frequent now, especially since he'd quit drinking. The silence hung in the brightly lit office, the tension tangible.

Max eventually broke. 'I'm all good, Ross. I want to work hard and stay as busy as I can.'

'Well, since I've a shit-ton of work for you . . . Do you know about the Hardie family?'

'I've heard about them, of course. Glasgow based, but influence all over, main suppliers of heroin and cocaine through the country. Father is Tam and he has his three boys, Tam Junior, Frankie and Davie, all up to their eyes in organised crime. As I understand it, they're mad, ruthless bastards who control most of the drugs in Scotland. No one can get up to anything more than a bit of shoplifting unless Old Man Hardie gives the go-ahead.'

'That's about the size of it. Tam is an old man now, but still rules the family and all their employees with a rod of iron, supported by his eldest boy, Tam Junior. He's properly ruthless and there's nothing he won't do to protect his turf. All hard bastards, boxers and MMA fighters, but also very clever buggers – the boys did well at posh schools. We've never got them for anything serious, and he has enough legitimate business interests now, with pubs, clubs, saunas, et cetera.'

'Okay. So?'

'Old Man Hardie has gone missing. Off the radar completely to the extent that his eldest boy Tam Junior has reported him missing, and it's unprecedented for them to seek out the help of the police.'

'So why?'

'Not sure. I suspect that the manner of his disappearance means they need our resources. He's also sick, as in dying, lung cancer, so it's been designated as high-risk. If they're reporting him missing, then something bad has happened and all we have at the moment is that Pa Hardie went off doing some family history up in the Highlands. We need to grip this. We don't want angry Hardies going mental and shaking down all the scrotes around Scotland. He needs finding, pronto. I'll email the link to the report. Have a good squint at it before you go and see the family.'

'Okay. But why Serious Crime and why me? This is surely a local missing person problem?'

'You'd think so, but – and it pains me to say this – the Hardies have people everywhere, including many police stations. We need a clean skin to see this with fresh eyes and to make sure we aren't missing something. This could be a real opportunity, Max. The Hardies have been a major thorn in our sides for decades and you have no history in Police Scotland, leaving here for the Army, as you did, as a sixteen-year-old. You're an unknown.'

Max shrugged. 'Fair enough.'

'Take Janie with you. Have you worked with her yet?'

'Yeah, a couple of times; she was on the spin. Seems solid enough, quiet mind.'

'Spin? What is this cockney crap you keep coming out with?' Ross said with a sneer.

'Spin as in "spin his drum". You must've heard that before.' Ross shook his head in mock annoyance. Even Scottish cops knew the Met term for searching property was to 'spin a drum'. He continued with a half-smile, 'She's a good cop, very young, an accelerated promotion flyer. Posh bird, like. DC at the moment, but she won't be for long. Who knows, she'll probably be our boss soon enough. She's a bit of an odd fish, and she has had a few problems settling, but I trust her. And her old boss in Vice who's a pal of mine really rated her. Right, cut along, man, get this sorted. A wildly aggrieved bunch of Hardies is the last thing we need.'

'Sure, we'll be on our way soon.'

'Overtime is no issue on this. We need to find out what's happened to the old bugger.'

'We're on it,' Max said, standing up.

'One thing . . .'

Max paused and looked at his boss's red and meaty face. There was concern written all over it. In the short time he had known Ross, he had not seen this expression. It was normally more sarcastic or split with a big grin.

'Don't get close to the Hardies, Max, and don't mention this job to anyone else inside or outside the office. They're properly bad people, so don't let them know anything about you and never drop your guard. There's nothing they won't do if they feel it'll advance their cause.'

3

'Nice neighbourhood,' said Max as the BMW driven by DC Janie Calder swept along the wide, well-kept streets.

'Aye well, they're worth a few quid, these guys,' said Janie.

Janie was in her early twenties, with a well-educated Edinburgh accent. She was lean and fit-looking and was casually dressed in jeans and a polo shirt. She seemed shy, slightly nervous. Max had never really spoken to her before, but he had heard the rumblings on the team. Accelerated promotion officers sometimes attracted a little suspicion, and there were enough dinosaurs in Police Scotland that being young and a woman was probably not helping her cause too much either.

'Have you had much contact with the Hardies?' said Max, yawning.

'Nothing direct, talking to Tam Junior today was the first time I've ever spoken to one of them. Did a little surveillance on the youngest of them when we had a whisper that he was running round tooled up with a gun. He kept losing us, almost as if he knew he was being followed, if you get my drift.' Janie's eyes had a frustrated look in them.

'That bad?'

'Yep. Rumours that they've several cops on the payroll. Nothing confirmed, though.'

'Jeez, and I thought we had problems in the Met.'

'The Hardies are the biggest fishes in Scotland and they've money to burn. They've an arrangement with the Turkish gangs for heroin and they source their cocaine direct from the cartel in Colombia. Old Man Hardie has a grip on all the disco drugs with the Dutch supplying him direct. He apparently takes even the slightest suggestion of disrespect from anyone very personally and if only half the rumours about him are true . . . Apparently, his speciality back in the day was removing large pieces of skin from those who displeased him. Hence his nickname, "Peeler", which I guess is a little ironic. Here's their place now.'

'What about the Hardie boys?' said Max.

'Tam is very much the senior and is being primed to take over. The other two, Davie and Frankie, are enforcers as far as I can tell.'

'Been doing your research,' said Max.

Janie just shrugged, averting her eyes.

The Hardie residence was massive. A huge, modern building overlooking a vast swathe of the South Lanarkshire country-side. They gained entry to the extensive grounds via electric gates that swung open as soon as they approached. There was no need to ring a bell or intercom, so they had clearly been seen on CCTV.

'Looks like they were waiting for us. I assume we look just like cops, then,' said Max.

'I imagine there are cameras all over. I think the Hardies are fairly particular about their security.'

'I'm not surprised. Jesus, would you look at the size of this place.' Max tried not to sound too overawed. The whole property was designed around a central tower with three spurs jutting out in opposite directions. There were few walls; the place seemed to be mainly constructed with glass and steel.

'Yep, built in 2009. The Hardies bought it a few years ago

for a shade under two million quid. Not clear where the money came from, but there's no mortgage, that's for sure.'

Max let out a low whistle, admiring the landscaped gardens as they drove slowly up the smooth tarmac drive. The sun reflected from the large windows at the front.

'Looks like a bloody building society, to me. Still, each to their own,' Max said. He'd never been a fan of the huge, sprawling modern architecture. His recently purchased home was a small two-hundred-year-old stone farm cottage at the end of a rutted track.

'It's hard going, all dead ends and blind alleys, but they've plenty of legitimate businesses and off-shores that, at the moment, are keeping us away from their cash.' She pulled up outside the huge, glossy front door that was at the top of a large set of sweeping stone steps.

'Well, let's see where this takes us, then,' said Max, getting out of the car.

The large door swung open noiselessly as they ascended the steps, and a well-built male stepped into the sunlight, his face grim.

'Officers?' he said, with no trace of a smile.

Max and Janie both reached for their warrant cards. 'Yes, I'm DS Max Craigie and this is DC Janie Calder, and you are?' Max left the question hanging, despite the fact that he knew exactly who this was. The family resemblance was remarkable. Tam Hardie Junior. He was casually, if expensively dressed in designer jeans and a Ralph Lauren polo shirt and his wrist glittered with a Rolex. He was tall and beefy, his broken nose and cauliflower ear telling the story of a brawler. In contrast, his light grey and silver-flecked hair was well cut and styled, and he sported a neat goatee beard.

'I'm Tam Hardie. Come in. There's coffee on.' His demeanour was polite and business-like, but it was impossible to hide the concern that was written on his rough features.

The interior of the house was just as impressive as the outside. He led them into a huge, double-height hall with a galleried landing above them and a polished marble floor. He led the way into an enormous, modern kitchen. Acres of granite worktops and state-of-the-art appliances seemed to be everywhere, along with a huge range cooker and well-stocked, glass-doored wine fridge.

Hardie indicated to a line of bar stools next to a vast kitchen island. Max figured that the cost of the granite he was about to lean on was probably equal to about six months' salary.

'Coffee?' Tam said, flatly, his eyebrows raised. There was a delicious aroma of freshly brewed coffee that pervaded the sleek kitchen.

'Sure, thanks,' said Max.

'Very kind. Thank you, Mr Hardie,' said Janie.

'No problem. Your accent is Highland. Am I right, DS Craigie?'

'Aye, Ross-shire.'

'Nice part of the world. My cousin lives there, has a wee garage, and we go up sometimes,' said Hardie.

'It's a good place,' was all that Max said, not wishing to go further down the small talk line.

The big man busied himself before an enormous, professional-looking machine and within a minute two steaming china mugs had been deposited before the detectives.

'Milk and sugar just there,' Hardie said, nodding towards a small earthenware jug and a bowl that contained rustic-looking sugar lumps.

'So, what can you tell us about your father, Mr Hardie?' Max said after taking a sip of the rich, dark brew.

Hardie paused for a second, gathering his thoughts. 'Pa has been very ill, Detective. He has terminal lung cancer and only months left to live. He's been getting reflective about life and had this bee in his bonnet about some old family story. I don't know too much about it, but he's been studying all the genealogy websites and looking for family trees and the like. It had become all-consuming for him. He called it his quest to find out the truth about the family history and "right the wrongs of the past". I'll be honest, I thought he was going a bit doolally with the drugs and all, so I didn't pay too much attention.'

Hardie's accent was not what Max had expected from the son of a rough Scottish gangster with a frightening reputation. In fact, his delivery and tone were more approaching cultured than rough.

'When did you last see him?'

'Day before yesterday. He went off early in the morning saying he was looking for an ancestor's grave somewhere up north, didn't really say where exactly. He called me later that day to say he had found an old graveyard and he thought that it was the one. I heard nothing else after that. I was away from home yesterday on business so I didn't know he hadn't come home. My wife and kids are away in Cyprus at the moment. I just assumed he would be home. Despite being very unwell, he's still independent and gets pissed off if we keep checking up on him.'

'What car was he driving?'

'Range Rover.'

'Know the registration?'

Hardie told them.

'Any ideas where the graveyard was?'

'Other than way up north, no. Like I said, this was very much his thing and he had been getting a wee bit obsessed about it, spending all hours on his computer.'

'Do you have the computer to hand? We could examine it to see where he may have been planning to visit.'

'No. He always took it with him. Wouldn't let anyone else near his precious old laptop.'

Max couldn't help but wonder about this. It was very unlikely that any member of the Hardie family would want police poking around in his computer. Who knows what could be on it?

'Okay, how about his phone?'

'He called us on the same number he's had for years.'

'What time?'

'About 2 p.m. on Monday.'

Max checked his watch. It was just after two, now Wednesday, meaning that Hardie Senior had not been heard from for forty-eight hours.

'Can you be exact about the time? It may be important.'

Hardie sighed and pulled his phone out of his pocket. Scrolling through he said, 'Fourteen-twenty, just a two-minute call on Monday. Exact enough, Detective?' His tone was curt for the first time since they had arrived and Max noted a flash of Hardie's genuine temperament.

'His phone may be the best way of us tracking his movements. Nothing else since then, right?'

'Right,' he said, clearly now bored of having officers in his house.

'What type of phone did he carry?'

'Why is that important?' Hardie was beginning to become impatient.

'Because of the GPS function. If we could discover his passwords, we may be able to track him accurately,' Max said, maintaining his diplomatic approach.

'He didn't like smartphones. Thought that everyone was tracking him or stealing his identity and the like. He had the same Nokia for years.'

'Now I have to ask. Does your father have any enemies?' Max said in an innocent voice.

A slow smile stretched across Hardie's face at the question and he looked down at his polished loafers.

'DS Craigie, my father is an old, sick man, but he has a rich and varied past. He doubtless stepped on a few toes whilst he worked his way up the business ladder. I can't imagine anyone would be stupid enough to challenge him, whether they considered him an enemy or not. You must've experienced situations like this in London, so let's cut the chat, and why don't you just find my father?'

Janie spoke for the first time. 'We'll get straight on it, Mr Hardie. Can we see where he spends his time in the house? There may be some clues as to his whereabouts.'

Hardie turned from Max to Janie and fixed her with a long, searching stare, his ice-blue eyes boring into hers for an uncomfortable amount of time. His voice shifted from flat to patronising. 'No, you may not, my dear. My father is a private man and would not appreciate the police prying into his private affairs. Now we all know that you'll be using telephone intelligence to locate my father, so can we cut the poorly disguised attempts to pry into our lives for ancillary purposes? You need to find my father, or we'll be forced to use our own resources and methods to do so, which may cause unforeseen collateral difficulties for law-enforcement agencies. Do we understand each other?'

Janie opened her mouth to speak, her eyes showing rising anger, but Max pre-empted her outburst. 'Perfectly, Mr Hardie. We'll get right on with it, and we'll call you as soon as we have anything.'

4

'What did you make of that, then?' asked Max as Janie pulled away from the Hardie residence.

'Arrogant.'

'Agreed, but there's no mileage in getting on his wrong side at this stage. His coffee-giving, nice-guy routine didn't last long, did it?'

'No. Not even a little bit. I suspect we are being played.'

'You're probably right, but folk like the Hardies don't involve cops. I think they've hit a brick wall trying to find him, and we're the last resort. They're criminals, not detectives.'

'That's true enough. So how do we play it?'

'We don't tell them anything we're doing until we have something concrete. He's clearly worried about his old man, but we need to be the ones to find him, so we're in control of the situation. When did the phone intelligence department say they'd have the data?'

'Any time, I hope; in fact, it may be ready now.' She plucked her smartphone out of her pocket and unlocked it, passing it to Max as she drove. 'Check my emails. It may be there.'

Max opened the email application on the phone, and sure enough he recognised the telephone intelligence unit email address three emails down from the top.

'It's here, perfect timing.' Max opened the email and zoomed in on the Excel spreadsheet, which gave a long list of call data for the old gang boss's phone. It was a busy line and the phone was clearly in regular use.

'Last call was just as Tam Junior said, fourteen-twenty hours. Tam Senior called Tam Junior, two-minute call.'

'What was the cell site?'

'Hold up, just checking,' said Max, copying and pasting the postcode into the map application on the phone. The map screen scrolled and a red pin dropped.

'So where?' Janie asked.

'Middle of nowhere, a small village called Latheron. On the A9 in Caithness, up towards Thurso. It's difficult to be accurate, but I guess there's only one way to find out.'

'I've a nasty feeling about what you're going to say,' Janie said, resignation in her voice.

'It's a high priority, and it's still early. We have plenty of daylight left. It's mid-summer so in the Highlands it'll be light until midnight, pretty much.'

Janie yawned. 'How long to get there?'

Max pressed the directions tab on the map. 'Less than five hours. Excellent, we'll be there mid-afternoon. I'll call the boss.'

Janie nodded. 'Cool, it's an interesting one this.'

'Hope I'm not ruining your social life,' said Max.

'No big deal, nothing I can't cancel.'

'Think of the money, you'll be on the overtime very soon.'

'Fair enough.'

'Did you notice the little dig from Hardie in there?' said Max, changing the subject.

'Which one?'

'Him flexing his muscles and demonstrating his reach?'

Janie looked questioningly at Max. 'London?'

'Exactly. He was demonstrating that he can find out things about us. It's interesting, he only knew we were coming an hour before we arrived and he used that time to find out about us. His referring to my time in London was just his way of demonstrating that.'

'Jesus.'

'Indeed.'

'So, what does this mean?'

'It means we tread carefully. Very carefully.'

5

The late summer sun beat down across the A9 as Max and Janie travelled north in the BMW. They both marvelled at the stunning scenery of the Cairngorm mountain range as they traversed the roof of the United Kingdom on their way to Caithness, pausing only briefly to refuel and use the bathroom at Inverness.

'You ready?' Max said, handing over a large coffee from the Costa machine in the garage.

'Guess I'm cancelling the date I had, then,' said Janie, reaching for her phone and looking at the screen.

'You had a date? Anyone nice?'

'First-timer, doesn't matter. I'm cancelling right now.' Janie tapped out a message on her phone.

'Done.'

'Blimey, you're ruthless,' said Max.

'I want to know where Old Man Hardie is.'

'Will he be upset?'

'I doubt it. We've never met.'

'Internet dating?'

Janie just smiled, shyly.

'Mystery to me, pal.'

'It's how people meet nowadays, Sarge.'

Max felt a sudden pang of embarrassment, so decided that now was the time to change the subject. 'Only another two and a half hours. You want me to drive the rest of the way?'

'Sure. This is your home turf, right?'

'Almost, just across the Kessock Bridge in a wee while. I grew up on the Black Isle.'

'Nice, remote island life, then. I'm an Edinburgh girl, never been this far north. In fact, I get nervous when the pavement runs out. We always holidayed in Northumberland. I hated it, all wide-open spaces and empty beaches.'

'Proper townie, you. Black Isle isn't actually an isle; it's a peninsula. Three sides surrounded by water.'

'Do you still have family there?'

'Just an elderly aunt. I occasionally go back to visit her when I'm about. It's nice. A big pod of dolphins often visits, at Chanonry Point.'

'Cool. You think we'll find Hardie?'

'Maybe. He's gone somewhere, just need to narrow it down.'

'Aye. It's just I could do with a bit of a successful job at the moment.'

'Why?' said Max, looking at her, curiously.

'It may make the team actually realise that I'm worth having. Some of them aren't exactly welcoming.'

'You know what cops are like, always suspicious of someone with an education. Especially one with a posh private school accent who plays classical music or free-form jazz in the car and obsessively vacuums whatever car she's using.'

'You heard about that?'

'Listening to a difficult string piece or some free-form jazz will always make cops comment, but they like the fact that you leave cars clean. Most of them are bloody slobs.'

'Half the cars are like bloody skips. You like it?'

'What?'

'Jazz?'

'No, sounds like a toddler playing a piano.'

'Philistine,' said Janie.

Max laughed.

'So, that's why people think I'm weird?' she said.

'Well, I wasn't going to say anything,' said Max with a smile.

For the first time that day, Max saw her properly smile back, and it lit her face up.

'More to Scotland than Glasgow and Edinburgh, as you are about to discover. Caithness is very wild and remote,' said Max, keen to move the conversation on.

'Gives me the creeps. Come on, sooner we get there, sooner we can get back to civilisation.'

*

The onwards journey became less interesting. The wild and craggy Munros of the Cairngorms gave way to the sweeping hills of Ross-shire and the remote regions of Sutherland, as they hugged the A9 that snaked along the coastline.

'How much longer?' asked Janie, blearily waking from a slumber and yawning.

'Soon. Just ten minutes from Latheron where the phone lost its signal.'

'Good, I need the loo and my bum is sore.' Janie managed to grimace and chuckle at the same time. 'What's the plan?'

'See when we get there. It's a tiny place and I want to know if anyone saw anything. He's pretty distinctive and he had a flash Range Rover. Highland folk tend to notice things like that, plus we need to look at any graveyards in the local area.'

Latheron was a tiny hamlet, with a few houses dotted either side of the road, a war memorial and an unused post office. Beyond that there was nothing of any note. No shops, no pub, no hotel; in fact, almost nobody to see anywhere.

'Well, this was worth five hours in the car,' Janie said, yawning again. 'You have to wonder what attracted a Glasgow gangster to this blip on the A9.'

'Any churches nearby?' Max asked, his eyes taking in the scene.

'There are a number heading up the coast road, over towards John o'Groats.' She passed the phone to Max who stared intently at the screen.

'It's not tight enough. We need it to be more accurate, so we can close down the search area,' said Max.

'Show me the phone data again,' said Janie.

Max fiddled with the phone before handing it back to Janie.

'No, not up there. The azimuth is all wrong. I don't think he went that way.'

'Azimuth?' Max was confused.

Janie smiled. 'Each cell site tower has at least three or more cell selectors to give three-sixty-degree coverage. They all have identifiers, so if we use the key supplied you can see that the selector Hardie last hit was not pointing that way. He went north up the A9, not up the A99. If he had gone up the A99 he would have hit the north-east-facing azimuth, not the north-west one. Think of the cell tower as the centre of a pie chart. He was somewhere in this sector.' Janie zoomed the map into the zone that covered a huge area north of Latheron.

'Okay, you satisfied? It's still a massive area, with no churches or graveyards on the map, so what do you suggest?'

'We need some local intel, I'd say. Any suggestions on that front? This is more your type of neighbourhood than mine.'

'Pub?' Max smiled broadly. 'You said you needed the loo and there was a small inn we drove past back in Dunbeath.'

'Sounds perfect. I'm hungry.'

*

27

'This place looks terrible,' Janie said, staring at the grey, single-storey building in a large car park. The only indication that it was any form of a hostelry was the decrepit sign in green letters that declared it to be a 'restaurant'.

'It's better than you'd think. I called in here once last year on my way to Thurso when I was going surfing and it was nice enough. Good fish and chips.'

'Well, it would be hard for it to be worse than it looks. It reminds me of a public convenience.'

They got out of the car, the afternoon sun warming their faces and the smell of sea redolent in the air. The distant hum of the North Sea was audible in the silence as they walked to the unprepossessing building. Max realised how hungry he was, having barely eaten anything all day.

Inside, the contrast with the bleak and depressing exterior couldn't have been more obvious. It was warm and welcoming with whitewashed walls and a wood-slatted bar behind which a woman stood, polishing glasses. She smiled brightly as they entered. 'Afternoon, folks, how are we?' Her American accent was as broad as it was unexpected.

'All good thanks. We okay for a late lunch?'

'Sure, have a seat anywhere – we're not exactly busy,' she said.

They took a seat by the window and the waitress appeared almost immediately. 'Drinks?'

'Do you have cranberry juice?' Max asked.

Janie raised an eyebrow at him.

'Sure do, straight or with soda?' the waitress asked.

'With soda,' Max said.

'Ma'am?' She looked at Janie.

'Coke, please.'

'Okay, menu on the blackboard over there. Fish is haddock today, and we have some venison in and we probably have some prawns left if the lunch diners didn't finish them off.' She let forth her beaming smile and headed back to the bar.

'Cranberry juice? You have waterworks problems, Max?'

'I just like it.'

'That's rather progressive of you. I'm used to colleagues going for a pint of heavy.'

'We are on duty, and I don't really drink anyway.'

'Not at all?'

'Not really. At least, not for a while.'

There was a long silence before Janie spoke again. 'I did hear about what happened in London. Guys were talking about it a bit, not to me you understand, but I overheard them.'

'It's not a secret. I shot a guy before he shot me, it was all over the news. I'm the officer referred to as Zulu 43. One of those things.'

'And you discovered that drinking alcohol wasn't the best way of medicating, right?'

'Something like that.'

'Aye, I've learned that lesson too,' Janie said.

'I also really like cranberry juice. Does it bother you – the guys not being overly welcoming?' Max said, trying to move on.

'Not really. Well, maybe a bit,' she said, lowering her eyes.

'It'll be fine, mate. They're mostly all right guys, and you're a good cop. They'll thaw.'

There was a brief pause as the waitress deposited their drinks and they both asked for the fish and chips.

Before the waitress made to leave with their orders, Max smiled his thanks and asked, 'Do you know much about this area?'

'A little. My husband and I run this place together and he's a local boy.'

'Do you know of any old graveyards around here? Like, really old and probably abandoned?'

'Mind if I ask why?'

Max fumbled into his pocket and produced his warrant card. 'I'm DS Max Craigie from Police Scotland in Glasgow; this is DC Janie Calder. We're on an inquiry up here, hence our late lunch stop.'

The waitress stared at the proffered card, and appraised both Max and Janie with renewed interest, her face showing some puzzlement. 'Well, this is a coincidence. A guy came in here asking the same question a couple of days ago. I'm just wondering why Highland graveyards have suddenly got so popular.'

Max and Janie exchanged a look. 'Did you get the name of this man?'

'Can't say I did. Old guy, must've been eighty. Didn't look very well, if I'm honest. He asked my husband about it, but I think it was Willie who gave him directions.'

'Is your husband here now?' asked Janie.

'Sure, he's in the kitchen. I'll take these orders through and ask him to come and see you.' She disappeared out of view via a swing door.

'Nice work,' Janie said, looking directly at Max with her deep blue eyes.

'Pardon?'

'It's no coincidence we're here, is it?'

'Just a hunch, and I'm genuinely hungry.'

'Hmm.' Janie looked at Max with a frown.

'Think about it. Tam Hardie would've driven five hours up from Glasgow, just as we have done. He's searching for an old, disused graveyard. What better place to start your investigations than the local pub? There is basically nothing else here. He called his son at two o'clock, probably after stopping for lunch here, which is conveniently the nearest place.'

'You're smarter than you look, Sarge.'

'Are you saying I look daft, like?'

Janie chuckled, her face a mix of amusement and embarrassment.

A slim man in his early forties wearing a clean white apron approached the table with a smile. He had a bright, open face and piercing dark eyes.

'Afternoon, officers, I'm Duncan Ferguson. I own this place with my wife, Mary, who you've just met. I understand you're asking about a previous customer?'

'Hi, I'm DS Craigie and this is DC Calder.' They both showed their warrant cards. 'I understand that a customer was asking about a local graveyard a couple of days ago?'

His accent was a typical soft Caithnessian. 'Aye, so he did. An elderly guy, in his eighties, I'd say. He was chatting to Willie, one of our regulars, about it.'

'What can you tell me about the customer?'

'Just an old chap. Short hair, Barbour jacket. Hard eyes, mind. He looked like he had seen lots of life, if you understand me.' He spoke softly and thoughtfully.

'Do you know where the graveyard is?'

'Can't say I do. I only came back here a couple of years ago, after living overseas. I've not heard anything like it.'

'That's a shame. Any idea who might know?'

'Sorry, not really, Officer.'

'So, do you think Willie managed to explain it?'

'No idea, I'm afraid. Willie is usually really shy and doesn't like talking to folk. He's a bit of a loner. I'm not sure he's the full shilling, if you understand me. He just comes in here now and again for a pint.'

'Where does Willie stay?'

'I'm not sure – close enough to come here for a drink.'

'Can you describe him?'

'Wee fellow, short and skinny with longish scruffy hair, always in work clothes. Can I ask what this is about?'

'Missing person inquiry, just nosing around a little, but

31

mainly here because we're hungry, and this looks tremendous,' Max said, looking at Mary who had appeared clutching two heaving plates of fish and chips.

'Fresh off the boat this morning, detectives.' Duncan grinned with pride.

6

'Right, let's go find a graveyard, then,' said Janie as they drove slowly through Latheron, their hunger nicely sated.

'Yep. Someone here must know about it, and I'm betting that he will,' Max said, pointing at a man dressed in work clothes depositing a letter into the post box in the centre of the village. He was returning to a battered pick-up truck that had three bales of hay in the rear when Max called out to him from the driver's seat.

'Aye?' he questioned, his face showing no trace of suspicion.

Max pulled over, stepped out of the car and joined him at the side of the road.

He showed his warrant card. 'DS Craigie from the police in Glasgow. I'm looking for an old graveyard around here somewhere. You know of it?' Max's soft Highland lilt seemed to have intensified.

'That'll be Ballachly, just a couple of miles up the road.' His accent was pure Caithness.

'What do you know about it?' asked Max, his face open and friendly.

'Most locals know it. We used to bugger about there as kids, just a ways up the A9. It's a spooky place. All the kids used to tell stories of it being haunted and the like. I've not been there for years and years, though.'

'Can you direct us?' asked Max.

'You have a map on your phone?'

'Sure.' Max produced his smartphone, selected the map function and handed it to the man, who took it and swiped and pinched with his fingers before handing it back, saying, 'I've dropped a pin in the map. You'd never find it, otherwise. We get the odd amateur historian looking for it around here.' He smiled, broadly.

'Thank you, so much. That's perfect,' said Max, grateful for the unexpectedly helpful encounter.

The man laughed, softly. 'I'm not just a farmer, Officer. I also do IT support for a company in Edinburgh. Best of luck.' He smiled before climbing back into his truck and moving off. Silence descended on the deserted village street, once again.

'That was unexpected,' said Janie.

'Highland farmers have had to diversify. It's a tough business to be in.'

'I think your suddenly stronger Highland accent may have helped.' She smiled.

'No idea what you mean, Constable.' Max exaggerated his accent even more as he climbed back into the car and began to head north.

The dropped pin in the map application took them off the A9 northbound of Latheron and onto a bumpy, rutted farm track that the BMW's run-flat tyres bounced uncomfortably on. They headed towards the distant wind farms that stood idle in the fields. The weather was clear and sunny with not even a breath of a wind, unusual in the exposed, sweeping Caithness countryside.

A short left led them alongside a large grassy field that housed a small flock of sheep and an enclosure, bursting with brush and weeds, surrounded by a tumbledown dry-stone wall.

Just in front of them to the side of the road stood a pile of recently baled hay, still tinged green, and a tarpaulin covering some machinery.

'You think that's it? It's not marked on the map, whatsoever,' Max said, staring through the windscreen at the walled area of vegetation.

'It's bang on for the cell site,' said Janie, her eyes taking in the whole scene. 'Place looks a dump.'

'I'm more interested in that,' said Max, staring not at the enclosure but at the tarpaulin.

'Sorry?' Janie said, bemused.

'The tarp. It's covering something big, and I don't think it's been there very long. It's not settled at all and the earth holding it in place has been freshly dug.'

Janie looked at the old, frayed tarpaulin and then at the base. Piles of freshly dug soil held it in place at each corner, weighing it down.

'It's not been windy, it's hardly moved, so if it had been here any length of time it would look very different, especially with the way the wind whistles over these hills from the sea. It's logical, really. Come on, let's check it out,' said Max, smiling at her and opening the door.

'"Crime is common. Logic is rare. Therefore, it is upon the logic rather than upon the crime that you should dwell,"' she said, dryly, as she got out of the car.

'Sorry?' said Max.

'Doyle?'

'Eh?'

'Sir Arthur Conan Doyle, you know, Sherlock Holmes. That's from *The Adventure of the Copper Beeches*. Have you read it?'

'I only read books with exploding helicopters on the front cover,' said Max, shaking his head.

Janie paused, as if thinking for a few moments. 'It's stuff like that which makes everyone think I'm weird, right?'

Max laughed.

He grabbed a corner and pulled it upwards, causing the earth to spill off. He walked, dragging it towards the centre before tossing it over a dark, gleaming car wing. The deep tread pattern became visible as the large wheel was exposed.

'Bingo,' said Max, pulling the tarp over the bonnet, exposing the large grill of the Range Rover.

'That's Hardie's,' Janie said. 'Registration checks out, but who put it under a tarp and why such a crap attempt at hiding? A kid could do better.'

'Whoever killed him, and I suspect they didn't care that he would be found.'

'What?'

'I think Old Man Hardie is no longer with us. And whoever put this tarp over his car, in this very poor effort at hiding it, more than likely killed him. Come on, let's get the rest of it off, make sure he's not inside.'

Together they pulled the rest of the covering from the gleaming, huge SUV. Trying the door handle, Max was surprised when it opened with a reassuring clunk.

'Best glove up,' said Max, a nasty feeling rising in his chest. Whatever had happened to Old Man Hardie, the fact that there had been an attempt to conceal his car, however amateurish, was somewhat ominous.

Janie returned with a couple of pairs of blue nitrile gloves in her hands. Snapping a set into place, she threw the others to Max who slipped them on and pulled the big, heavy door wide open.

'Just a quick check. We'll need forensics up here before we go deep into it. Can't leave any stone unturned. Keys are here on the seat. Even more concerning,' Max said, pointing at the solitary Range Rover key on the plush leather seat. The front and rear cabins were empty and spotlessly clean with no obvious traces of blood. A laptop case lay in the back. Max carefully lifted the flap, seeing a silver flash of the computer inside.

'You going to look at it?'

Max shook his head. 'Nothing we can do now, and even booting it up could wipe it if Old Man Hardie didn't want anyone seeing what's on it. We'll leave it to the tech team.' Max had encountered protected computers too many times to fall into the trap of blithely booting them up. It was all too embarrassing to have to admit that your actions had wiped potential vital evidence from a computer.

'Any sign of a phone?' Janie asked.

'Not here. Let's check the boot.'

Max picked up the key from the driver's seat, then depressed and held the boot release on the fob. There was a deep clunk as the mechanism worked and the boot swung open slowly.

It was empty. Literally devoid of a single item. The pile on the plush carpet showed evidence of having been recently vacuumed and was as immaculate as the rest of the vehicle.

'Looks like the old boy liked a tidy car,' said Max, briefly lifting up the boot floor, revealing nothing other than the polystyrene cut-out compartments that housed the jack and tools required to change a wheel.

'A man after my own heart. This is odd,' said Janie. 'Car parked and badly hidden. For what purpose? Where is Tam Hardie?'

'It doesn't make sense, does it? If someone has kidnapped him, where are the demands and why is the car left here for anyone to find? This is an eighty-grand car. Why not get shot of it properly?' Max pressed the button on the inside of the boot lid and it swung gracefully shut with a soft click. 'Come on, let's go and take a look at the graveyard. I'd better call this in.'

As they walked into the field Max dialled Ross. He answered immediately in his normal gruff fashion.

'What do you know, Max?'

Max filled him in about what they had found and requested

that a forensic team be called and a low loader to remove the vehicle.

'What's your instinct on this one?' Ross asked.

'Honest answer?'

'No, I want you to bloody lie to me, you daft twat. Stop pissing about. I'll give the Major Incident Team the heads-up.'

'Not good, none of it makes sense, so we're going to look at the graveyard and see what we can find. Tam Junior said he was on some quest, his words, so maybe the graveyard will yield something. I'll call you back.'

'Ross okay?' Janie asked.

'Usual charming self. He's dispatching a forensic team and speaking to the MIT. Come on, let's check it out.'

They wordlessly trudged across the fragrant grass, the sheep scattering away as they crossed the hundred metres to the shabby, walled enclosure.

When they arrived at the rusting, ancient-looking, half-open gate, Max suddenly stopped just as Janie reached out to touch it.

'Wait. Before we go in, what do you see?' Max spoke softly, and without any kind of sarcasm.

'Just a rusty old gate leading into an overgrown, walled space with what looks like some broken monuments inside. Why?'

'Look at the gate. It clearly had to be opened with some degree of force by the last person here. Look at all the debris it has pushed inwards.'

There was a pile of leaves, dirt and grass against the inside bottom bar of the gate.

'So, the last person who came in here was probably the first visitor for ages, I guess.'

'Years, I'd say, and the last person was here just a short while ago. The piled leaves and shite haven't been disturbed by wind or rain. I'd say Hardie certainly was in here.'

'What are you a tracker or something?' Janie said.

'A little. I did a course in the Army.'

'I didn't know you were in the Army.'

'Lots you don't know. Anything to see on the inside?'

'No, too dense. What can you see, Crocodile Dundee?'

'There's rough evidence that someone walked in a fairly straight line through the undergrowth. You can see the broken stems of the bracken and brambles. A good few of them have been bent or moved. We should find a new approach path that heads roughly to the middle of the plot. Don't want to trample where he's been, could be evidence of his presence, blood from cuts on the thorns, and the like.'

Max set off walking clockwise around the rough and tumble-down dry-stone, looking into the centre of the graveyard.

'Here, it's mostly soft-stemmed plants from this point inwards, rather than spiky shrubs, so we should be able to get to the centre easier.' Without waiting for an answer Max carefully climbed over the low wall, which despite appearances was solid enough.

'What now?' asked Janie as she joined Max inside the boundary.

'We head to the middle, where the trail Hardie left finished. That's as far as he got in. Anything to be found will be there, and watch out – there are some big old stinging nettles.' Max began to move through the dense vegetation, creating a path that Janie followed, grumbling to herself.

It was hard going, working against the green mass and every few feet they had to feel their way around to avoid tripping on the gravestones, hardly any of which were still upright.

'Shit, this is a seriously old graveyard. I'd like to see the parish records, could be something in them,' Janie said.

'Language, Constable, this is consecrated ground.'

'I didn't have you as a religious man.'

'I'm not, it's bloody old, I'd say. Look, this stone, here.' Max cleared some of the nettles away from one of the few upright stones. The lettering was shallow and only just legible.

'Jeez, 1740.'

'Where's the church?' said Max.

'Destroyed or ruined. There were some old granite blocks just outside and the mound we climbed to get to the back wall was an old broch, I think, which will be really ancient. Lots of the old churches fell down when the communities moved away, particularly around the time of the clearances,' said Janie.

'I see that the history degree wasn't wasted. Come on, not much further.' Max set off again, moving weeds, nettles and six-foot-tall cow parsley out of his way towards where the track stopped just a few feet ahead of them.

A small clearing had been made, presumably by Hardie, beside a prone granite slab on the ground, with deeply edged, crisp lettering still visible, although upside down to them.

They circled the grave and looked at the lettering. Max felt a chill run up his spine as he read the inscription.

This Grave Never to be Opened

'Nice,' Janie said with a mix of sarcasm and seriousness.

'No date, you notice. In fact, nothing beyond that inscription. A bit odd, no?'

'Probably not.' Janie looked thoughtful. 'That inscription, may indicate cholera, or maybe plague. They used to put minimal inscriptions to prevent interest, or descendants opening them.'

Looking at the corner of the stone closest to them, Max noted that there was fresh damage to the granite. A small chunk of it had separated from the main slab and lay about eighteen inches away. Picking up the piece of stone, about the size of a small mobile phone, he matched the broken edge against the gap in the main stone. It fit like a jigsaw puzzle. Max laid it back down again.

He circled the monument, sniffing the air and studying the

surrounding ground. He dropped to his hands and knees and looked at the stone at eye level, examining its surface.

'Can you smell that?' Max said, softly.

'I can just smell dirt, Mr Sniffer Dog,' Janie said.

'Ha ha. Death. The smell of death, Janie.'

Janie sighed before reluctantly, lowering her head closer to the ground and sniffing. 'No, just dirt, with a bit of a boggy smell as well, I guess.'

Max moved slightly away from the grave, looking at the ground, intently, his head bent, watching how the light hit the fronds differently. The grass and soft shrubs had been compacted as if someone had been lying on them.

Max stood suddenly and went to the gravestone. Without a word, he stepped on top of it, feeling the surface of the smooth granite beneath his feet. Shifting his weight from one foot to another, he felt a slight movement in the surface of the stone. Suddenly he stamped down on the stone, violently three times. An eruption of buzzing emanated from the grave and flies swarmed from the crack where the stone met the soft soil.

Janie let out a little yelp. 'What the hell? Where have they come from?'

Max paused, then sighed. 'Hardie is under that stone, and he was killed right here,' Max said in a low, matter-of-fact voice.

'How can you be sure?'

'Can you come up with another theory?'

'No, I guess not, but we can't be positive it's him.'

Rather than answering, Max stepped off the stone and walked around contemplatively. The top end was raised slightly off the surrounding ground and it rocked gently when pressed. Max squatted down on his haunches and dug his fingers into the crack. He gave a cautious pull. The stone moved an inch, rocking, as if it had been inexpertly repositioned.

'It's been removed and replaced very recently. Give me a hand. Let's see if we can lift it enough to sneak a peek,' said Max, standing.

'Are you sure? Like, are we allowed to do this? You know, desecration, and that.' Janie frowned.

'I'm pretty sure we are way past worrying about desecration. Come on, we still have gloves on, and we need to see what's in there,' Max said, smiling reassuringly.

'Just gloves? Hold up, wait there a second and don't do anything until I get back,' said Janie. Without waiting for an answer, she sprinted off, leaped effortlessly over the wall and ran at a surprising pace back towards the car. Max watched her as she reached the BMW, busied herself in the boot and then re-emerged clutching a shoulder bag. She jogged back, leaped over the wall and ditched the bag on the ground next to Max. Her breath rate was only slightly elevated.

'Marathon runner?' Max asked, genuinely impressed at her obvious fitness levels.

'Oh Christ, no, far too much distance for me – that's why cars were invented. Come on, if we're doing this we should at least suit up.' She opened the bag and tossed a forensic oversuit at Max, still in its cellophane wrapper.

Max opened his mouth, but closed it immediately once he realised that his more junior colleague was absolutely correct. They both donned the thin, white paper suits, zipped them up and pulled the hoods over their heads. Janie handed Max some overshoes and a surgical mask.

As they were both now appropriately dressed, Max said, 'Ready?'

'Not really, but come on.'

'You have a torch?'

Janie said nothing but went into her bag and pulled out her smart phone. 'Torch function on here. Like a Girl Guide, Max, I'm always prepared.'

'No wonder you're on accelerated promotion,' said Max, meaning it.

'Not you, as well,' she said, shaking her head.

'What?' said Max.

'Any time I do anything, ever, that could be seen as basic competence, some smart-arse on the team mentions accelerated promotion.'

Max looked at Janie. 'That must be annoying.'

'Just a bit.'

'Okay, I'll not mention it again. I'll try and lift from the edge, deadlift style. You try and get a look with the torch and see if there's anything inside,' said Max, squatting over the loose corner of the stone. He dug his fingers underneath and managed to get a firm grip. Max was a strong man, who regularly lifted weights as part of his boxing training, but he could immediately tell that the stone was going to be seriously heavy. 'You ready?'

'When you are.'

Max lowered his backside to the ground, his back straight, and heaved in a deadlift style feeling immediate movement as the heavy granite began to lift, agonisingly slowly. Max felt his glutes and lower back complain as he pulled upwards, his face contorting with the effort. After a couple of seconds, he felt the stone begin to move. A renewed contraction and Max pulled up, forcing all his weight through his heels, and the stone gave way. Flies swarmed in a cloud as the tiny gap became much larger and daylight disturbed their feast on whatever lay below.

'Jesus Christ,' Janie spat, her voice muffled behind the surgical mask.

'Anything?' grunted Max, his muscles beginning to shake.

'Hold on, I just need to clear all this crap away.' Janie pulled away some disturbed grass and a clod of turf from the edge of the lifted stone, her eyes showing her distaste at the swarming insects that buzzed in a cloud around her.

She squatted and shone the torch into the gap. 'Whatever's in there is about a foot down. Hold on, I can't see without putting my head in the way of the stone. I trust you, Max, but I don't fancy a half-ton bit of granite hitting me on the head.'

'Quick as you like, this is a little heavy,' Max said, the strain evident in his voice. The flies buzzed with renewed vigour as they were drawn to the sweat across his brow.

Janie quickly took her phone and swept at the screen, selecting the camera function. She made sure the flash was operating and pointed it into the grave. A tinny fake camera sound was audible as she snapped away before pulling the camera out and looking at the screen. 'Holy shit, you can drop the stone. I have it recorded.'

Max steadily returned the stone back into place as gently as his complaining muscles would allow and stood exhaling a deep breath of relief.

'What do we have?' he asked.

Janie simply handed the phone over to Max who looked at the screen. Tam Hardie's bloated face and lifeless eyes stared back out of the dark, fly-blown hole.

Max sighed deeply and pulled the mask away from his face, swatting at some flies.

'Let's go back to the car. No sense in sticking around by all these bloody flies. They give me the creeps,' said Max as he handed Janie's phone back to her.

'They're unpleasant, I grant you, but forensic entomology is bloody fascinating, I have to say,' said Janie, looking at the swarming insects.

'Well, that's as may be, but right now they're doing my head in, so can we please bugger off out of here?'

'No stamina, Sarge.'

As they began to retrace their steps Max pulled his own phone from his pocket and dialled.

'Max, tell me some good news.' Ross Fraser's gruff voice filled the silence.

'Sorry, I can't. We need the full works. MIT, a crew with the ability to remove a gravestone and a forensic pathologist. Best get some local uniforms up here too for scene securing. Hardie is dead. I'll email you a map link. They'll all need it to find this place; it's the middle of bloody nowhere.'

'Fuck. In fact, double-fuck, this could be bad. How did he die?' he said.

'No idea. He's under a gravestone in an ancient burial ground by the remains of an old church. Managed to sneak a wee lookie inside and Janie snapped a picture, but it's definitely him, especially bearing in mind his Range Rover is just a few yards away.'

'So, he's been murdered then?'

'Either that or he buried himself to death, and that doesn't seem very likely.'

'Less of the levity, Sergeant. I'll make the calls; just get the scene secure and wait for the MIT. It's their job now. I know one thing, though, this is going to bring trouble to Caithness. There is no way that the Hardies will leave this to law enforcement. They're going to want blood, and plenty of it.'

7

First to arrive were the local officers from the nearby Wick Police Station. They pulled up next to Max and Janie's BMW and a slim, grey-haired, middle-aged sergeant with a less-than-perfect uniform and tired eyes alighted the vehicle, affixing his white-topped cap. He flashed them a weary smile as he approached. A smartly dressed, young uniformed constable got out of the passenger seat and stood, looking at the scene before him.

'Mick McGee, acting inspector for today. What do we have? I got a call from our divisional commander about a murder.'

'DS Craigie and this is my colleague, DC Calder.' Max explained what they had found.

'Shit, that's not good. How the hell did you find it all the way up here?'

'Just inquiries, you know. Are you traffic, as well?'

'Normally I'm roads policing, but I'm also the senior cop on duty for miles about, so I got sent. Glad you're here, pal. Give me an accident to reconstruct and I'm your man. Murders, not so much,' he said with a genuine smile.

'No problem,' said Max.

'Do I need to see the scene?' asked McGee.

'I'd say no, pal, but it's your call. If you could get your guys to cordon it, we can wait for the forensic crime scene manager and the Major Incident Team. I can show you the photographs, if you like. It's not particularly pleasant, though.'

'Nah, I'm good. Just give me the abridged version so I can brief this to the boss,' he said.

'Cool. Myself and Janie entered this scene on a missing person inquiry. Once we realised that someone was probably secreted within a grave, the only interference with the scene was done whilst we were wearing appropriate forensic clothing and only to ensure that life was definitely extinct. My advice is that no one goes back in until the SIO and forensic teams arrive,' said Max.

'I'm happy with that, mate. Glad you found him, and not one of my lot.' He turned to the constable at his side. 'Steve, put some tape over the entrance to the field and let's get another couple of units up here to make sure we keep everyone away, including the bloody sheep. We can make the perimeter the whole field, including the graveyard. Agreed?' He looked at Max for reassurance.

'Perfect. I imagine he's been dead at least a couple of days, judging by the number of flies, but the pathologist will have a better idea.'

'I'll make the call to the control room,' said McGee, reaching for his phone.

'One thing you should know, Mick. The body is a gentleman named Tam Hardie. He's probably the biggest gangster in Scotland, and this is going to be very high-profile. The dead body of a gangster, hidden in a centuries-old grave, will be on the front cover of every newspaper.'

8

A couple more patrol cars arrived at the scene within about forty minutes and McGee sent the officers off to man the cordons that were now in place. He seemed to be a very relaxed sort, genuinely grateful for Max's presence. Due to the remote nature of the area and scant policing resources, it wasn't uncommon for officers to wear multiple hats, hence a traffic specialist turning up at a murder scene.

Max and Janie sat in the BMW, still dressed in their white overalls, the doors open, as the late afternoon breeze wafted in from the North Sea. It was an unseasonably warm period, which this part of north Scotland was definitely not used to. It probably explained why the late Old Man Hardie was decomposing at a fair rate.

Max's phone buzzed in his pocket. 'Hello, Max Craigie?' A light, soft voice asked.

'Yes.'

'Hi, I'm DI Sally Smith, the on-call SIO. We're on our way up to you from Inverness, and I'd just like a heads-up on what's going on there.'

'Sure thing, Boss, no problem,' said Max and he proceeded to give a full account of their actions and involvement.

'A right affair. You okay to hang on there? We'll be about

an hour, I suspect, but I'd like you to walk us through the scene. I've enough officers with me, and some shovels to get us into the grave.'

'Shouldn't be a problem, just need enough pairs of hands to lift the gravestone off. It's not held in place by anything other than gravity.'

'Okay, thanks, Max. Stay put and we'll be there soon.'

*

DI Smith was as good as her word, and fifty-five minutes after her call a small convoy of two cars, a minibus and a liveried CSI van pulled up alongside them. The occupants all got out and began to suit up into their forensic overalls. There was a comforting air of practised efficiency.

DI Smith was an immediately reassuring presence as she jumped out of the car, already thrusting out a hand to Max for a firm shake with a warm smile. Smartly dressed in a business suit, she bristled with confidence and authority and looked younger than Max had imagined.

'Hi, Max, thanks for hanging about for us. I'm Sally; this is Tim, the police search adviser. I thought it probable we'd need PolSA on this job.' She nodded at a smiling sergeant in dark blue cotton overalls with the Police Scotland crest on the sleeve.

'Ma'am,' Max said, returning her smile.

'Sally will do fine. So, what do we have?'

Max went back over their findings and she listened intently, scribbling into an A4 hard-backed book.

'You sure this is Tam Hardie?'

'As I can be.'

The inspector exhaled, puffing her cheeks out as the reality of what she was dealing with became apparent. 'Jesus. That's not good. I've investigated that family's connection to several murders. They won't take this well.'

49

'I think that's why they asked me to look at it rather than the locals.'

'Common approach path to the grave?' she asked, still scribbling, her attention turning back to the immediate matter at hand. Notorious gangster or not, Tam Hardie was still a victim.

'From the rear of the yard opposite the gate, the wall is low and easy to cross and I didn't want to disrupt the route that Hardie or his killer took. Do you have stepping plates with you?'

'Yep, in the CSI van. Bill over there is our crime scenes manager, and he has everything we need.' Sally nodded at a small, stocky man dressed in a forensic suit who was already pulling a mask over his nose and mouth, clearly eager to get moving. Equipment in large plastic boxes was being unloaded and piled alongside camera cases on the rough ground.

'How do you want to play it?' asked Max.

'If you show me and Bill your approach path, the three of us will then move up to the grave and get it photographed before anyone else gets in. We can then get the step plates in place. Once we're happy, we'll bring the PolSA boys and girls in for the heavy lifting. How easy will it be to remove the stone?'

'Half a dozen should be able to do it safely enough. It's pretty heavy, but movable. I managed to pick the edge up so Janie could take the picture.'

'Nice work. Can I see?'

Janie swiped at her phone and handed it over to the detective inspector who looked at it with an expressionless face. 'A bit grotty already with the warm weather. How long do you reckon?'

'I think we can be pretty exact, bearing in mind the call data. Has that been shared with you?' Max said.

'Ross emailed it. Makes sense. I think we can be pretty sure that he died at or around the time his phone dropped off the system. Okay. Bill, Tim with me – let's go and look at this scene.'

*

50

Within an hour, the scene was secured and the controls established. The common-approach step plates were in place and Bill had photographed the whole area in detail, including a videoed walk-through. The scene tape had been affixed more widely and a line of tape had been erected from the entry point to the yard, along the approach path and around the gravesite itself. A uniformed officer had a scene log going and anyone entering or leaving the taped-off area would now be logged.

Six of the PolSA officers, all wearing forensic clothing, stood around the grave in positions ready to remove the heavy, sinister slab of granite.

Sally spoke from behind her surgical mask. 'Okay, folks, one at each corner, one on each side. We walk it sideways over to the cleared point we've designated to deposit the stone. Everyone ready?'

The team got into position and there were nods all round.

'Go for it. Bill, are you recording?'

'Camera is turning,' said Bill, holding a small video camera pointed at the grave.

The six officers all squatted, digging fingers in underneath the stone and pushing into the soft earth, trying to gain traction.

The sergeant spoke. 'Ready?'

More nods.

'On my three, then. One, two, three, lift.' There were muted sounds of exertion as each officer strained and lifted. The stone gave way immediately, moving clear of the rough, dark hole. Flies swarmed angrily in a dark cloud. Totally ignoring the sudden onslaught of insects, the sergeant calmly said, 'And steady now, step.' The team stepped across, taking the stone away from the hole. 'Everyone okay?'

More nods.

'Right, guys, let's get it across.' Efficiently the team moved the large stone to a cleared square of grass. 'And down gently.' As one, the team lowered the stone to the ground.

The grave seemed to yawn, its interior dark and foreboding. The police officers all stood and stared, no one wanting to approach. A chill seemed to descend, as a bruise-coloured cloud moved into the sun's path.

Bill the CSM approached the lip of the hole, his camera raised, with Sally alongside him. Max stepped forward and looked down.

Tam Hardie lay on his back about four feet below, his face swollen and putrid, after the assault of millions of insects. His teeth were exposed in a grimace, his eyes wide open but empty. The smell hit them like a wall, assaulting the nostrils of all who stood surveying the scene. No one moved, retched, or even raised a hand to cover their noses. They were murder squad detectives, and this was their day job. Death was their business.

There was a vivid bloom of black blood that crawled with flies right in the centre of his torso, clearly the site of a terrible abdominal wound. A lifeless mobile phone sat in the centre of his chest. There was a visible straight slice in the fabric of the corpse's shirt. An edged weapon, thought Max. No powder residue, no signs of exit wounds.

'Okay, Max. Thank you for your help, but I think you can leave it to us now. Can you bag your forensic suits, gloves and overshoes and hand them to the productions officer before you leave? He'll need to log them into the register. Once that's done, head off and get your statements to the incident room by tomorrow.'

'How about telling the family?' asked Max, his thoughts turning to the brooding presence of Tam Hardie Junior.

'I've already appointed a family liaison officer who will be on their way to tell the family as we speak. We have to try to keep them onside.'

The look in the detective inspector's eyes was focused and determined. The weight of responsibility of a case like this was huge. Career making or career breaking, this was hers now. Max couldn't help but ponder that this had the capacity to be the biggest and most notorious murder of the year, and it all rested on DI Smith's shoulders. He didn't envy her.

9

Max and Janie were soon away from the murder scene having stripped off their forensic kit, bagged it in self-seal bags and handed it to the taciturn detective who logged the items into his book. It detailed all the many items of evidence, known as 'productions'.

'Want me to drive? No disrespect, but I'm better than you,' said Janie, yawning as they stood by the car.

'You think?'

'Again, no disrespect, but yes, driving is one of my things.' She smiled.

'Then be my guest. I prefer two wheels to four.' Max tossed the keys, which Janie caught.

'DI Smith seems smart,' Janie said.

'She's being careful with retaining the forensic suits. Not everyone does that,' said Max as they pulled away back towards the A9.

'I guess that because this will be a massive, headline-making case she's being all belt and braces. Makes sense to me,' Janie said.

'Certainly does. Plus, you have to factor in the Hardie family. What will they make of this?'

'They'll want retribution, whether that's through the courts or their unofficial methods. I'm knackered. How long back?'

'Same as it took us to get up here,' said Max, looking at the evening sun that was beginning to dip closer to the distant horizon.

'Devastating sarcasm, Detective Sergeant,' Janie said, yawning once more as she drove into the boundary of Latheron.

Max said nothing but chuckled softly as they entered the small village and she reduced her speed.

'I'm hungry and you made me miss my dinner out tonight. This job is ruinous for trying to establish relationships.'

'Now that's most definitely true. Who was the lucky mannie?'

'Who said anything about it being a man?' Janie said, straight-faced, turning to look at Max.

'Sorry, I . . .' Max stuttered, his face flushing.

Janie broke into a grin.

'It was just an internet date, anyway. Strange as it may seem, I'd rather be here right now.'

'Not too many cops say that to me, so I'm flattered, pal.'

Janie said nothing, all her attention on the pavement to the left of the village.

'Come on, I was being nice,' said Max, pretending to be hurt.

'Check out the guy up there on the bench. He looks just like the guy that Duncan described,' said Janie, slowing up and pointing to a small figure who was sitting on a low bench outside the middle house in a row of cottages, set back and above the road and behind railings. Janie slowed some more, eventually drawing up alongside the kerb. Max looked hard at the small man, noting the collar-length tangle of greasy hair and the soiled work clothes. The man raised a can of beer to his lips as he looked directly at Max.

'I think we've found Willie from the pub. Good spot, Janie. Come on, let's have a word,' said Max, opening the door.

'Shouldn't we report this in and wait for the MIT?'

'No time like the present.' Max crossed the pavement and climbed the five steps that led up to the terrace of cottages.

Janie unbuckled her seatbelt with a sigh and followed Max up the steps.

'Willie?' Max said as he approached the seated man.

'Aye, who wants to know?' The man stared into the distance and took another deep draught on the tin of beer.

'Police. I'm DS Craigie; this is DC Calder.' Max produced his warrant card and showed it to the small man, who continued watching the sun begin to dip out of sight.

'I always sit here at sunset. Best view in Latheron – just look at it,' he said, in a soft local accent. His eyes were deeply set, very dark and had something in them that Max couldn't fathom.

'It's a fine view. Can I ask you about the man you gave directions to in the inn in Dunbeath a day or two ago?'

Willie said nothing but simply lifted the can to his lips and drank a little more of the strong lager.

Max looked at Willie's clothing. His blue overalls were frayed and thin at the knees and his boots were worn down so much that the steel of the toecap poked through the battered and scuffed leather. They were spattered with muck and rust stains, as were his trousers. His fingernails were encrusted with dirt as they gripped the can. He looked like he hadn't seen a bath or a shower for many a day.

'Willie?' Max said, softly.

'They always said he would come,' said Willie, with a half-smile that displayed stained and crooked teeth. He looked wistful and satisfied, his eyes still strangely distant.

Max looked again at the reddish-brown marks on Willie's boots, and in that instant, he knew.

He knew for sure that he was looking at Tam Hardie's killer.

10

Max sat on the bench next to Willie with a sigh. 'Ah, Willie, what have you done, man?'

Willie just raised the lager to his mouth and drained the contents, letting forth a contented belch as he crushed the tin in his small hand.

'What had to be done, Sergeant. What had to be done. What I was told to do.'

'Max . . .' began Janie, her face suddenly pale, her eyes widening, but Max winked and gave her a calm look.

'Told you what, Willie?' said Max, his voice soothing.

'The Leitch name. I had to protect it from the bastard Hardies. It was written by my father, and then his father before him. The Leitch name, you understand, no?' Willie Leitch closed his eyes and smiled, just a touch.

'How did he die?' asked Max, quickly miming sending a text message to Janie, who didn't need telling twice and reached into her pocket for her phone. She began to compose a message.

'The same way his great-great-grandfather died.' Willie let out a tiny giggle, a low, throaty cackle. 'Don't you think it's ironic? Hardie gets killed with the Hardie cutlass that killed his ancestor.' He giggled a little more, the sound sticking in his throat and prompting a rasping cough. He spat on the tarmac.

'Is it inside?'

'Aye it is. Will I have to come with you?' He opened his eyes, fully displaying the dark, clouded pools. Max was slightly alarmed to see the expression on the man's features.

It was triumph.

'Yes. You'll have to come with us,' said Max, gently. 'You'll not cause us any problems, no?'

'No, Sergeant. Our quarrel was with Hardie, not you, and that quarrel is now finished. Hardie was a thief and a bastard, and my great-great-grandfather was within his rights in killing him all those years ago. I wasn't going to allow this Hardie the satisfaction of finishing their feud. It dies with him now. My great-great-grandfather told me what to do. They can all rest now.'

Max paused for a moment. 'Best say nothing more, now. Let's sit and enjoy the last of the sun, okay?'

'Aye, you're a good man, Sergeant.' Leitch closed his eyes, a half-smile on his face. He projected utter, serene calm, and it was disconcerting that this small and apparently unthreatening man had, just a day or two ago partially disembowelled Scotland's most feared gang boss.

They all sat there, in silence, the last of the day's sun warming their faces. It was almost peaceful, with the distant whisper of the North Sea just audible on the soft breeze. The absence of wind meant one thing. The midges began to fly, first a few, all drawn to the carbon dioxide being breathed out by the three of them. Max resisted the urge to swat, knowing it would do no good. Willie was oblivious to the tiny insects crawling all over his face.

Two unmarked cars screeched to a halt outside the property and DI Sally Smith and two of her colleagues quickly alighted from the lead car and hurried up the steps and across the tarmac.

'Max?' DI Smith's eyes were confused.

'Sally, this is Willie Leitch. He just confessed to Hardie's murder. He's told us that the weapon used is in the house now. I'm leaving it to one of your guys to make the arrest, preferably one who was not near the grave. He has assured me that he won't cause a problem and I'm sure he's telling the truth.'

Sally nodded to one of her colleagues who approached Willie and gently took hold of his arm and eased him into a standing position. A pair of handcuffs appeared and were secured around the man's wrists. He was compliant, his face relaxed and calm.

The officer led him away to the car, formally arresting and cautioning him as they slowly got him into the back.

Sally turned to Max. 'This was unexpected. How?' she asked.

'Janie saw him, Boss, not me. The landlord at the inn in Dunbeath mentioned Willie was unusually helpful directing Hardie. We drove through and he was here on his bench enjoying a beer. We stopped to speak to him, and he just fessed up.'

'Fessed?' Sally looked slightly puzzled.

'Sorry, confessed.' Max smiled.

'Is he a fruitcake?' Sally asked, incredulous.

'Honest opinion?'

'Of course.'

'A total nutcase. I think you'll have to tread very carefully. I suspect he will be well known to the local health services. He said he was told to do it. He'll need to see a doctor before interview, but I suspect he knew what he was doing. He seems pleased to have satisfied some old family honour, or something.'

Sally exhaled, puffing out her cheeks and considering her options. She looked at her watch, before barking at a tall plain-clothed officer. 'Right, get Leitch to Burnett Road, no way will Wick be able to handle this; we need him in Inverness. It's getting late now. Get him booked in, all clothes forensically bagged, and get the doc along. We'll also need a body map doing for him – fingernail scrapings and clippings, hair samples, DNA, you know the drill. No interviews tonight. By the time we've finished, it'll be well late.'

'No bother, Boss.' The officer – a middle-aged, grizzled-looking detective – nodded.

'Not teaching you to suck eggs, but make sure we get him assessed by the doc for fitness to detain and interview, and be ready to look for an appropriate adult. Last thing we need is the interview getting excluded.'

The officer nodded again, turned and jogged back to the car, getting into the back alongside Leitch, who sat passively, his head slightly bowed, as if in prayer, as the car pulled away.

'You think this seems too easy?' Sally asked.

'Far too easy, but we are where we are. What's happening at the graveyard?'

'Grave is now tented and fully secured. We won't look to recover the victim until the forensic pathologist has been and done his thing. We may get a forensic entomologist along, if I can persuade her to leave the university. The fly larvae may confirm length of time in the ground, not that I think time of death is in question, but belt and braces, eh?'

'Good plan. Despite what Hardie Junior has told us, we can never be sure. I wouldn't trust him to lie straight in bed,' said Max.

'Ain't that the truth. I'm throwing everything at this. We do a half-arsed job and the family will be all over us like a cheap suit.'

'How about this place?' asked Max nodding at the small cottage.

'I think we'll have a very quick walk-through, just in case there are any bodies or severed heads in there, but beyond that I'll have a local uniform guard it until we can get PolSA in tomorrow. May as well do it properly. You want to take a quick look? You have more insight on this, particularly having met the family,' said Sally.

'Sure,' said Max, aware that between the three scenes of the graveyard, Leitch and the cottage, her numbers were getting thin on the ground. Strange as it sounded, Leitch would be treated as a crime scene, as much as the graveyard. He potentially had crucial evidence all over his clothes and body, especially as they didn't look like they'd been changed recently.

'Aye, we can hang about a wee while. He did say that it was ironic that Hardie was killed with the same family cutlass used to kill his great-great-grandfather. If he's telling the truth and it's in there, you'll want it for interview, I assume?'

'Christ, what do we have here, some weird vendetta?'

'It's feeling that way.' Max shrugged and smiled.

'Okay, let's suit up and walk through, literally what we can see on surfaces, nothing too deep. The worst thing we could have now would be that Leitch had someone tied up inside and we hadn't at least had a quick look. Janie, can you be ready with a productions book just in case we decide to take anything?' Sally looked at Janie, smiling.

'No problems, Boss, gets us away from the bloody midges,' Janie said with a resigned smile, swatting at the swarming insects.

They all dressed in forensic suits, overshoes and gloves. As always, one set of kit per scene. The last thing they needed was a later suggestion that any material found inside Leitch's cottage was brought in by them on their clothing.

The cottage was small. Just two rooms on the ground floor, a small sitting room and a compact, old-fashioned galley kitchen with a tiny bathroom leading off it. Max was surprised at how tidy it was. There was so little stuff about inside the place. Leitch clearly had no regard for possessions. There was just a small television, a single armchair and a shelving unit that contained half a dozen or so paperback books. Looking on the wall there was a faded photograph of an impossibly young Leitch dressed in a naval uniform.

'I never had him pegged as a serviceman,' Max said, staring at the portrait.

'I can see it; check how tidy this place is. He looks scruffy but his home is clean and ordered,' Janie said from behind her forensic mask.

'Doesn't make sense to me. Everything seems to be a contradiction,' said Sally.

Max looked across into the kitchen at the small dining table that was laid out with a plate, knife, fork and spoon, all ordered ready for a meal. Max opened the fridge, noting that it was completely empty other than three pre-packaged ready meals and several cans of strong lager.

Sat on the scratched coffee table was a red, leather-bound A4 notebook, worn and battered-looking. The front cover bore no letters or indication as to what it contained, but its position in the centre of the table suggested importance. A blue ballpoint pen lay centrally on top. Max bent down to open it, setting the pen to one side. On the inside of the cover was a scrawled verse in spidery handwriting.

The deil's awa the deil's awa,
The deil's awa wi' the Exciseman,
He's danc'd awa he's danc'd awa
He's danc'd awa wi' the Exciseman.

Max frowned, wondering what the old poem was about.

He began leafing through the pages. A faded envelope was taped to the inside of the cover. It was cracked and yellowed with age, the tape barely fixing it in place. There was a single word written on the envelope in spidery handwriting in fading blue ink: *Leitch.*

The pages of the book were densely packed with a barely legible scrawl that at first glance appeared just to be ramblings. Max only paid limited attention, but certain words jumped off the pages as he leafed through the journal. Quest, feud, Hardie, exciseman, and honour seemed to feature heavily. There were a number of yellowing and faded newspaper clippings, all seemingly journalistic pieces on the Hardie family and their suspected links to organised crime. This was golden, thought Max.

'We have an insight into the mind of Leitch, right here. It's a journal, of some kind. It reeks of paranoia and it looks like he has been waiting for Hardie to turn up for years. Your motive is here, written in Leitch's own hand.'

Sally let out a deep sigh as she looked over Max's shoulder at the book.

'What's the deal with the poem at the front?' she said.

'Burns,' said Janie.

'What, as in Rabbie Burns?' said Max.

'Aye, Burns was an exciseman, you know, early version of customs and excise, about 1790, or so. Not a very good one, I seem to recall reading, and he wrote that poem about it. It's still often sung at folk clubs.' Janie began to tunefully sing a few bars of the poem, before stopping, realising that Max and Sally were both staring at her. 'Strange thing to have in a journal,' said Janie, her cheeks colouring under her mask.

'You're full of surprises,' said Sally. 'Some poor bugger is going to have to sift through and copy that out. Leave it there; I'll have it photographed. What's in the envelope?'

Max lifted the flap and slid out a folded piece of paper, brittle and yellowing. He carefully unfolded it on the table. The paper was cracked and aged, the ink fading, but legible. Max laid it flat on the table and they both read.

Dearest James,

As my life is now drawing to an end, son, so the time has come to pass on the torch that was handed to me by your grandpa, before his death.

Manny year ago, in 1830, your grandpa, Hector Leitch,

was forced to defend our famly from the villan Hardie when I was a wean. A corupt and evil man, working for the English King as a bastad, corupt gager.

Hardie cam for Grandpa Duncan with his navy cutlass with murder in mind, as Grandpa Duncan would not pay his bribe, and Granpa Hector smash him arm with his stick. Hector then finish the bastad Hardie with his own cutlass. Afraid the rope, they hid the body in the old cematry at Ballachly under the grave never to be opened.

The Hardie family are all bastads, but we stoppd them and there bully.

We must ware that Hardie will return, for revenge, James. We must protect the family, boy. For honour, and for what is right. One day, Hardies will return to Caithness, and we must be ready, boy. Hardie remains where he belongs. In Hell.

Go well, James.

I'm proud of you.

Pa.

9th April 1890

'Christ,' was all that Sally said.

Max shrugged. 'A feud from 1830. A feud that could only have been carried on by people with mental illness. The press will go bloody mad for this.'

'You're probably right, but there's nothing we can do about it right now. Leave it all there. We'll get it photographed and ready for interviews. Let's carry on.'

On a small shelf in the corner of the kitchen was an unopened cardboard box of tablets, sitting next to a battered Land Rover key. Max stood the pack so that the label was facing him. It was fairly full and the label bore the name W. Leitch. Both ends were sealed with sticky labels. 'Seen these?' said Max.

'What?' Sally said from behind her mask.

'Risperidone. If my memory serves me well, it's an anti-psychotic. I remember dealing with someone who had schizophrenia who was on them. This pack hasn't been opened and the label is dated a week ago. Hold up, there are two packs here; neither have been opened. Looks like Willie had come off his meds.'

'Oh, Jesus, this is going to be fun to investigate. We need to find out who his keyworker is.' Sally made a note in her book.

Max moved into the bathroom, which just contained a spotlessly clean toilet and bath. A solitary bar of yellow soap sat in a tray on the edge of the bath and a toothbrush sat in a mug on the sink. All abnormally normal. All clean and, it seemed, ready for inspection.

Then Max saw it. The fly in the ointment.

A straight-edged sword lay in the middle of the bathtub. Its blade was heavily stained with dark, dried blood. A few flakes had dropped off and sat there stark against the bright, white porcelain. The whole thing was less than a metre in length and the handle was made of patterned metal.

'Sally?' Max called out, pulling out his phone and taking a snap of the weapon.

Sally and Janie appeared at his shoulder in the tiny space.

'Jesus. Hardie was killed with an antique sword? What are we dealing with, here?' Sally said, her eyes wide. They all stood and stared at the wicked-looking weapon. The pitted and worn blade was dull and lifeless, but the dark, dried blood was indicative of its effectiveness. It had a sweeping knuckle-guard that bore some rust marks, but it was in remarkable condition.

'A cutlass, actually.' Janie's voice pierced the silence.

Sally and Max turned to look at her.

'A naval cutlass. Short straight blade, rolled metal quillon, probably the 1804 boarding cutlass, I'd say, but I'm no expert,' Janie said.

'How the hell do you know that?' Max said.

65

'I did Napoleonic naval battles as part of my history degree. Part of my thesis looked at the weapons of the time. This is a classic example of the boarding cutlass. I've seen one before, at the Kelvingrove museum sword room, but not in as good condition. Have you noticed the initials stamped by the hilt?'

Max leaned forward to get a closer look. 'T.H.' was stamped in the blade, faded but legible.

'Bloody hell. You want to take this in?' Max looked at Sally.

'No. Leave it. I'll get Bill to come down and photograph it in situ. That will do for the time being, but I want CSIs to actually recover and document it. I'm not taking any chances, here. I'm struggling to get my head around this. "T.H."? I'm assuming that we are all now thinking those initials are a little too convenient?'

'Willie did say about it being ironic that Hardie died by his grandfather's sword. Jesus, is this really an ancient feud?' said Max.

'I don't know, but we have the biggest gangster in Scotland murdered, in a weird graveyard with a two-hundred-year-old cutlass. The profile is going to be sky high for this, so we need to keep it tight.'

'Well, I'll say this. I think I'm a decent judge of character, and one thing I'm sure of is that Tam Hardie Junior will not be satisfied with whatever we can offer.' Max paused, searching for the right words. 'He'll want blood. Revenge.'

'It looks like justice won't be too much of a problem, right? This looks open and shut. If we have Leitch locked up within a few hours of them reporting him missing, the Hardies can't complain, can they?' Sally looked calm and resolute.

'Yeah, about that?' Max said his voice even and level.

'Max?' Sally said, a puzzled look on her face.

'Two things. When I asked Leitch if he was going to give us any trouble, he said, and I quote, "Our quarrel was with Hardie." Our, not my.'

'Well, that's not conclusive of anything,' said Sally, her face puzzled, 'but I've a nasty feeling you've something to add?'

Max sighed, and smiled weakly. 'How did Leitch move the stone, get Hardie in it and replace it on his own?'

Realisation dawned on the detective inspector's face. 'Leitch had an accomplice.'

11

Corporal Max Craigie paused briefly and pulled the flexible drinking tube from the top of his day-sack. Jamming it in his mouth he took a long drink of the warm, unpleasant-tasting water. The combination of the stinking forty-five-degree sun and the rubber of the water bladder could ruin even the best quality stuff. He still drank deeply. It was either that or go down from dehydration in a flash.

Spitting out the tube he raised his SA80 and squinted into the optic, surveying the bleak and barren patch of dirt in front of them, leading up to their temporary home at Control Point Salang. He saw nothing more than flies and the skeletal wreck of a destroyed Toyota pick-up.

They hadn't seen any Taliban for days now. It was just too bloody hot for them to be out ambushing British soldiers. His PRR transmitter-receiver crackled in his ear as he watched the stocky form of 'Dippy' scanning the ground in front of them with the Vallon, checking for IEDs that littered this area of Helmand Province. It had been a shit tour, with almost constant mortar attacks on their small base. Thankfully, they only had two more weeks in this godforsaken country, thought Max, as he scanned the points of danger within his arcs of responsibility.

'Hurry up, Dips. I'm busting for a piss.' The broad Glaswegian accent of 'Bones' the medic crackled in Max's ear. They were only five hundred metres from the relative sanctuary of the CP, having only left an hour previously to clear the final stretch of road ahead of the resupply vehicles that were imminent. Dippy's role as lead man was to clear the route for their section as they approached the last few metres. This was always a favourite target of the Taliban. Hit them just as they were getting back to safety. Max almost laughed at the thought. 'Safety?' As if anything was safe here.

He had a sudden prickling sensation between his shoulder blades. Something was wrong. Something was different from before when they had passed by this piece of dust. What was it?

Max wracked his brain for the source of the concern as he watched Dippy continuing to sweep with the detector, moving up to a small banked piece of dirt at the side of an abandoned mud compound.

The donkey. Where was the donkey that had been here earlier, secured against the tumbledown wall? Also, it was so still, and it was too silent. He nudged his pressel on his PRR. 'Switch on, guys, something's not right.' As section commander, it was his responsibility to get the guys back safely, and he had learned not to dismiss these feelings, more accurately known as 'combat indicators'. Something was wrong.

He depressed the pressel. 'Dippy, check every inch, mate. It's not ri—'

The explosion was a deafening, dull crump and the dry, desiccated dirt was instantly thrown skywards, enveloping Dippy in an impenetrable fog. Max's ears rang with the explosion, his face and body blasted with debris.

'Contact, contact IED strike five hundred metres from CP gate. Man down, man down.' Max screamed into his PRR. He rushed towards the clearing dust cloud, already reaching for a field dressing from his webbing, his ears now registering Dippy's sudden, piercing screams.

'Medic!' he screamed into the PRR as he dropped to his knees alongside Dippy whose screams were high and yowling, like an injured animal.

Looking down, he saw that both of Dippy's legs were missing, just below the upper thigh. Not hanging off, not torn. Just gone. Disappeared. Blood fountained from the femoral arteries staining the desert floor almost black. Max unfurled the dressing and clamped it over the wound just as the medic ran up, already reaching for the tourniquets and morphine vials.

'Dippy, man. Stay with me. Look at me, big man, look at me,' said Max, lying on the ground next to his friend, staring into his eyes. Big, fat tears were carving trails down Dippy's dusty cheeks, his russet hair poking out underneath his Kevlar helmet.

'It hurts, man. It hurts like hell, Max!' said Dippy, through clenched teeth, his eyes wide and full of fear. Not fear, terror. Abject, naked terror.

'I'm dying. I'm dying, I can feel it. I'm dying . . . not now . . . not here, man.' Dippy's voice dropped lower and he coughed, painfully.

'Morphine in,' said the voice of the medic to Max's left as he reached across and scrawled the letter 'M' on Dippy's forehead with a felt tip. A warning to others that the powerful painkiller had been administered.

The opioid took effect quickly and Dippy began to breathe more easily, his face relaxing visibly, his eyes losing their focus.

Max pressed on the PRR. 'Barney, you sent the nine-liner yet?' he said to the signaller, referring to the formatted message to ops requesting medevac.

'Yes, mate. It's been received. Help's on the way, coming from the CP and helo is scrambling from Bastion.'

'Roger that,' Max said. 'Dippy man, look at me. Look at me, pal, stay awake. You're gonna go home, man, back to the shite-hole you live in, bud. You're gonna be good, man.' Dippy opened his eyes, and his pinprick pupils were full of confusion as the

medic tried to get a line into his arm to replace the fluids that
were still flowing out of him onto the sand.

'Max . . .'

'Dippy?'

'Max . . .' *His voice dropped an octave and was only just*
above a hoarse whisper.

'Come on, look at me, pal.'

Dippy's eyes glazed and the faraway look became an empty
one. Something changed. A light went out.

*

Max jolted awake with a stifled scream, his heart pounding
in his chest, lathered in a cold sweat, panting heavily. He sat
up in bed in his small farmhouse, terror clutching his insides
with an icy grip.

A cold nose nuzzled against his neck as Nutmeg – his small,
scruffy cockapoo – demonstrated her concern for Max's well-
being, whining slightly.

'It's okay, Nutty. Just a dream, girl,' said Max, soothingly
stroking the dog's tightly curled blonde ears, his breathing
beginning to settle. The dog lay down again, concern in her
intelligent eyes, and rested her muzzle on Max's legs.

Looking at his bedside clock, Max saw that it was 6.20 a.m.
He knew from bitter experience that sleep would not return
after the dream, and Nutmeg was looking at him with an
expectant gaze. She knew what was going to happen. Nutmeg
always knew.

Max threw on his running clothes and headed out to the
front of the small semi-detached cottage at the end of a half-
mile rutted track.

'Come on, girl,' he said, setting off at a fast run, the dog
jogging by his side, with little or no effort.

Max had discovered during his therapy that PTSD struck

people in many different ways, and that for him some things made it better and some things made it worse.

Alcohol made it worse, talking about it didn't help at all and family arguments made it much worse. Running with his dog made it better.

So, he ran hard, with his dog, for a full hour.

And he felt better. Not all better, just a little better.

12

After his run, Max showered, dressed and made himself coffee and toast, then put down a bowl of food for Nutmeg. The morning was warming up nicely, so he took his breakfast and sat at the front of his cottage at the small table. The view, as always, made him feel better. A long, sweeping vista across fields towards the sea. He had moved here six months ago when transferring and positively loved the place. A small single-storey semi-detached farm worker's cottage outside Culross, a pretty village overlooking the Firth of Forth. It was perfect for Max's purposes, being equidistant between Glasgow and Edinburgh, close to his offices at Gartcosh and surrounded by sheep and barley fields.

Nutmeg had come with the cottage, the previous owner having been forced to move into sheltered accommodation. The property had been in great demand, all the other interested parties wanting to put in competing sealed bids, but Max had instantly bonded with Nutmeg. Gladys, the elderly owner, had taken the house off the market as soon as Max had agreed to take Nutmeg on, with the understanding that Max would take her for regular visits at the sheltered housing. They visited Gladys most weeks. She was just content to sit with Nutmeg on her lap for half an hour whilst they chatted and Max made the tea.

Nutmeg was a wonderful companion, who simply stayed home when Max went to work. She would just hang around the large garden, sleep on a bed in the shed and, if she needed company, join Max's neighbours, John and Lynne Fisher and their two dogs, Tess and Murphy. They were a kind couple in their sixties, who looked after a flock of sheep and grew vegetables on the smallholding to the side of their house. It worked perfectly, with Nutmeg being the ideal farm dog, despite never getting the idea of herding sheep. She never strayed, always escorted Max off the premises and was, without fail, there to meet him when he returned.

Max yawned as he looked at his watch, and realised it was almost 9 a.m. He should be making contact to see what, or where, he needed to be. He had eventually got home from Caithness in the early hours of the morning, after dropping Janie at her flat in Edinburgh.

As if on cue, Max's phone rang in his pocket. Looking at the screen, he saw it was Ross.

'Morning,' said Max.

'Is it morning, you lazy bastard? I thought it was practically lunchtime,' barked Ross bumptiously.

'Late one in Caithness, last night. You heard anything from Sally?'

'Aye. Why I'm calling you. The MIT are all full-on. They've the scene at the graveyard, mad boy Leitch at Burnett Road, and his house to look at. They've also found his car, so they need a bit of help. They want you to go with their family liaison officer, as you've already met the Hardies. It's his first FLO job since doing the training and they think it could get tricky. Can you and Janie go with him?'

'Sure. Text me his number and I'll give him a call. How about Leitch?'

74

'Utterly radio-rental, mate. Loop-da-loop. Well known to the Highland mental health team as suffering with schizophrenia and has not been managing his meds well, but something made him flip. He's been telling everyone in the custody suite, all on camera, that he has fulfilled the family honour by killing Hardie. Mental health crash team went to Inverness to section him last night. They've declared him unfit for interview and unfit to be detained at the police station. They're looking for a secure bed to send him to for treatment, so the inquiry continues, just without him.' Ross was not known for being politically correct, but he always got to the nub of the issue at hand.

'No surprises there. Jeez, what a thing, eh?'

'Aye. I just wonder how this will leave the Hardies? The old man was very much the boss, but word is Tam Junior is even more ruthless than his dearly departed pa. You need to make it clear to him that we have this in hand, and he isn't to look to take action himself.'

'I'll give it a shot, but I'm not sure he's the type to listen to advice. How about Leitch's accomplice?' asked Max.

'Yeah, Sally's DCI mentioned that. Apparently, they aren't convinced. Willie Leitch has maintained that it was just him. He even said, and it was recorded on the custody record, "I admit killing Hardie, on my own and with no help." Also, the long and rambling madman journal spells it all out. It's a slam dunk, Max.'

'That's bollocks. How the hell did he move the stone on his own?'

'Well, I have no idea, Detective Sergeant, but as it isn't our job, I suggest we get on with what we have been asked to do, and leave the investigating to the MIT, okay?'

Max sighed, frustration nipping at him. 'Fair enough. I'll go and see Hardie and introduce the FLO.'

'Damn right, man. Then get back here. There's a fuck-ton

of work to do, and I sure as shite ain't doing it.' The phone went dead. Max smiled a little. He liked Ross, but he really needed to work on his personal skills.

Max's phone buzzed in his hand, the number for the FLO flashing up on his screen.

Max ignored it, as a sudden and irresistible urge rose in his chest. He just wanted to hear her voice. He dialled quickly, feeling a small knot of nerves and listened to the dial tone.

'*Hi, it's Katie. Sorry I'm obviously doing something more interesting right now. Leave a message or call back. Or don't. Up to you, byeee!*'

The cheery, soft voice of his wife, tinged with warm tones of Yorkshire, was at once comforting and distressing. Max's stomach lurched. God, he missed her. He missed her so much, he thought, picturing her big smile, infectious laugh and sparkling green eyes.

Shaking his head to clear the sudden fog, he dialled the number for the FLO. It was time to go to work.

13

The FLO wasn't what Max was expecting. Often these officers were fairly young in service, and selected for the ability to be sensitive and understanding. So, the grizzled, middle-aged detective, surrounded by a palpable air of defeat, was a bit of a surprise. He had jumped into the back of their car in a street a couple of minutes away from the Hardie home. The smell of cigarettes and last night's booze came with him. He was munching from a bag of crisps, crumbs falling out of the bag as he settled into the seat. Max caught the angry look from Janie as she watched in the rear-view mirror.

'All right?' he greeted, without even the merest suggestion of enthusiasm.

'Paul?' asked Max.

'Aye, that's me, Paul Johnstone. I've been stiffed with FLO on this shite-show. You'll be Max, right?' His voice was deep and thick with phlegm. He coughed, wetly. His accent was a rough and rapid glottal Clydeside.

'Yep, Max Craigie and this is Janie Calder. How come the Glasgow team is on this? It surely belongs to Inverness?'

'It does, but the murder team are all full-on up north with the scenes and trying to get all the evidence together, so they don't have a FLO to send to the family. Bloody liberty, I'd say; means I'll be up and down the A9 constantly now.'

'I'm sure it won't be for long. Do you know much about the Hardie family?' asked Max, ignoring the man's truculent tone.

'Only by reputation. I'm sure it's all exaggerated – usually is.' He yawned loudly, projecting more cigarette and old whisky fumes to the front of the car.

Max caught Janie's eye with half a smile. 'Well, we met them just yesterday. I'd say we should tread very carefully. The last thing we need is them thinking the police aren't doing their job and deciding to cause us problems.'

'I can't see what they have to moan about. You nicked the fella within a few hours of the report and found the body. I'd say Police Scotland are smelling of roses, right now. They can bury their pa and know that the madman who killed him is caught, even if he's in the nuthouse.'

Max shook his head, just a touch. The man's attitude was beginning to grate.

'Well, we need to be properly professional on this, or you'll have problems. I met Tam Junior yesterday and he's a difficult man, so you had better bring your A game. This murder will be attracting serious press attention, so any loss of confidence from the family and I suspect you'll be firmly in the spotlight.'

Johnstone grunted and began looking at his phone screen. Max bit his tongue, glad that the detective was not one of his people.

The rest of the short journey was undertaken in silence until they were driving up the long sweeping drive to the Hardie residence. 'Nice place,' Johnstone said.

Max turned to him. 'I'll brief them, as I was at the scene and can probably answer any of their questions. Once they're in the picture, I'll hand them over to you and you can explain what your role will be moving forward, okay?' Max's voice was even, but firm. It was a statement, not a request. Johnstone merely shrugged.

Tam Hardie was waiting at the door when Max, Janie and Johnstone ascended the stairs, his face displaying nothing, his eyes flinty hard.

'Thanks for coming, DS Craigie. We were visited last night by an officer who informed us that you'd found our pa, but little else. The rest of my family is inside. Come in.' He was cordially polite, but his voice was bone-dry. There was something in it that Max could not quantify. Was it rage or grief?

Max extended his hand, which Hardie took. It was a firm handshake with none of the trial of strength that Max had expected.

'I'm sorry for your loss, Mr Hardie. This is DC Johnstone, who will be your official liaison between you and the Major Investigation Team.'

Hardie looked with disinterest at Johnstone and merely nodded.

'Come through; the boys are waiting in the kitchen,' he said flatly.

Hardie led them to the familiar kitchen, which had the same aroma of coffee and the same luxurious surroundings as last time, only now there were two other males in the room. Max recognised Davie and Frankie Hardie from intelligence photographs. Both men were almost identical in appearance, lean and tough-looking, with similar-styled neat dark hair, their faces masks of contempt. They looked tough, and they looked mean.

There was an uncomfortable, unquantifiable atmosphere in the room. It was a mix of anger, grief and hostility, but there were no tears. The set jaws, hard eyes and terse body language told their own story. The thick, turgid aura was almost tangible. Max had experienced hostility and anger many times during his career, but this was different. This was malevolent in its intensity. Max realised, with a sudden rush of certainty, that whatever the police could offer the Hardie family, would not be enough. Not by a long way.

'Boys, this is DS Craigie and DC Calder who found Pa, and this is DC Johnstone, who will be our liaison.'

The atmosphere shifted, Frankie and Davie both looking at Tam with obvious respect, almost reverence. There was no doubt who was the boss. None whatsoever.

There was a brief pause.

'So, DS Craigie, what can you tell us?' Tam Hardie said, quietly and politely.

Max cleared his throat and told the story from beginning to end. From their father's journey, stop at the inn in Dunbeath through to finding him in the grave at Ballachly. He then moved on and described Leitch's arrest and the discovery of the murder weapon. He briefly spoke about Leitch's detention and the fact that he would soon be held at a secure facility.

When he finished speaking, a long, impenetrable silence descended on the room and three pairs of eyes bored into Max.

'Do you have any questions?' Max asked, discomfort rising in his chest.

'Just one. The cutlass you found, was it marked in any way?' Tam Hardie Junior asked politely.

'Just the initials T.H. stamped on the blade,' said Max.

'Thank you. We have no other questions for now. Please keep us informed of any developments, DC Johnstone. DS Craigie, DC Calder, thank you for finding our father. We can lay him to rest properly. Now, I'll show you out.' He stood from his kitchen stool, indicating that the meeting was over.

'Can I tell you about my role?' asked Johnstone, handing over a business card.

'No, thank you, Officer. We'll call if we need anything. Now, please, my brothers and I have much to organise.'

*

80

'What was that all about?' asked Janie as she negotiated the drive away from the Hardie residence and back to the road.

'Aye, shite. How am I meant to work with that family?' said Johnstone, his disdain and frustration quickly turning into a hacking, barking cough that projected smoke-laden breath into the front of the car. Janie's nose wrinkled in disgust.

'With difficulty, I'd say,' said Max as they pulled up alongside Johnstone's car in the street.

'DCI will be hating this. Thanks for the introduction; fat lot of good it did. See you later.' Johnstone slammed the door shut and got into his car. Janie drove away.

'He's charismatic,' Janie said, flatly, cracking the window to try to freshen the stale air that Johnstone had left in his wake.

'A real charmer,' Max said.

'I think I know why Hardie didn't ask us any questions,' said Janie, gazing at the road ahead.

'Go on.'

'They know it all, already. They've their own bloody sources,' said Janie, a look of disdain on her face as she pulled to the side of the road.

'Why have we stopped?' asked Max, perplexed.

'Bastard messing my bloody car up,' said Janie, leaning over and grabbing the discarded crisp packet and sweeping a few stray crumbs from the seat. She screwed up the packet, deposited it in a plastic bag and tucked it out of sight.

'You really don't like a messy car, do you?' said Max.

'Not a lot. Anyway, as I was saying, they know everything we know. The only question Hardie had was about the sword, and did you notice one thing?' said Janie as she pulled away from the kerb.

'He said cutlass, not sword.'

'Yep. He knows everything about this case, and it's not yet twenty-four hours old. Someone is feeding him this inquiry, step by step, someone central to it.'

14

Tam Hardie Junior, now just Tam, went to the drinks cabinet and began to finger through the many bottles of old whisky. The worn piece of furniture was incongruous with the rest of the sleek kitchen.

Tam was proud of his collection, assembled over many years. After a minute looking through the bottles his hand fell onto a twenty-five-year-old Lagavulin. This was a rare, limited-edition bottle released on the two-hundred-year anniversary of the distillery. He cracked it open and poured three large measures into crystal tumblers and passed one each to Frankie and Davie who both held their glasses contemplatively, watching their eldest brother, and now head of the family.

'Pa,' Tam said quietly. As one, the brothers raised the glasses to their lips and drained them. There were no tears, no wobbling lips and no outward show of grief, but a crackling and almost electric sense of fury.

The glasses were returned to the granite tabletop and the silence descended on the room, each brother lost in their own moment.

'Davie, what do you know?' said Tam in a flat, low voice, looking at the youngest brother.

'Jack is on board and has a direct link into the murder team.' His voice had a hard edge, and his face was almost still as he spoke.

'He's a wretch. Was there nobody better than him?'

'We have plenty of sources, as you know, but he's the only one with a direct line into the murder team. The DI is straight as a die, apparently. Young bird, wants to get promoted and thinks this case is her ticket. Jack has at least two mates on the team,' Davie said, a trace of a smile on his thin lips.

'So, what of that bastard Leitch?' asked Tam.

'Been sectioned. Pure barmy, as I'm hearing it. He's been transferred to Carstairs.'

'They're taking it seriously then. Did he get interviewed?'

'No. Too mental apparently.'

'Shite. Absolute shite. He's bullshitting them, he knew what he was doing. Stabbed an old man with a cutlass. What evidence is there?'

'A shit-ton. Not been taking meds, I hear.'

'The bastard. We lose our pa, because he can't be arsed taking a tablet.'

No one said anything.

'We have to do something, boys. That bastard keeps breathing in and out and every ned up and down the country will think we're losing our grip, so stay on top of Jack and keep me informed. I want to know everything about Leitch and his family.' Tam rubbed his face, his bristles rasping audibly.

'Aye . . .' Davie hesitated.

'There's something else,' piped up Frankie.

'What?' Tam's eyes swivelled to his younger brother.

'Turkish Joe obviously has his own sources, too. He called to offer his condolences.'

'What? The cheeky bastard. That's him just letting us know he knows, flexing his muscles, the bastard. Did he say anything else?'

'Just that because of the police attention on us the price would have to go up on the skag he's holding,' Frankie said, softly, a little hesitantly.

Tam initially said nothing, his face visibly darkening. 'It's happening already, boys, like I said it would. Pa is dead and the sharks are circling, smelling the blood. Well, I say *no*.' Tam was breathing heavily and his eyes shone with fury. Both brothers were now transfixed on the new head of the family.

'What do you want me to do?' asked Frankie.

'Bring that Turkish prick in. Get hold of him and take him to the farm. I'll deal with him personally. I'm putting the word out. Pa may no longer be here, but the Hardies are and we are worse than ever.'

15

The team members all sat in the conference room at Burnett Road Police Station – the modern, sprawling building on the outskirts of Inverness.

They all looked shattered, having worked almost non-stop since the discovery of Hardie's corpse, and this was the first time they had managed to get together for a briefing. Mis-shaven chins and rumpled shirts told the story of too much work and not enough sleep.

Max and Janie sat at the back of the room. They had been asked to attend to make sure that all their information was shared with the MIT team. They'd had no involvement in the case since leaving the Hardie house the previous morning, and Max had to admit, he was curious where the inquiry currently stood.

Sally Smith cleared her throat and spoke. 'Good morning, folks. Firstly, thank you so much for all your hard work these last couple of days. I'll keep this as quick as possible as I've been warned that the DCC is floating about having come up to see the boss here at Burnett Road. He's being briefed on the murder as he's worried that it may impact on local policing. I want us all out of here before he catches us looking all scruffy and raggy-arsed as we do, okay?'

'Bloody gaffers looking to share glory more like,' said a tired-sounding voice from the back of the room.

'Anyway, it's been a big push but we have broken the back of the major strands of this already. As usual, I'll go round the room and get the main points so we are all on the same page. Firstly, what news from the post-mortem, Phil?' Sally raised her eyebrows and an officer in a rumpled shirt and loosened tie spoke.

'Special PM was done quickly once the forensic pathologist had finished at the gravesite. The victim was terminally ill with stage-four lung cancer. Pathologist thinks he had only months left to live. Cause of death was catastrophic haemorrhaging following a severed aorta, caused by a large, flat, non-serrated blade. He has seen a photo of the cutlass seized from Leitch's place, and has the dimensions, and he's clear that it could have caused the injury. The injury was a through-and-through, as in: in through the abdomen, straight through the aorta and then out of the back. Death would've only taken minutes.' Phil paused for effect.

'Thanks, Phil. So, a single blow only?'

Phil just nodded.

'Time and date of death?' asked Sally, still scribbling furiously away in her red book. A pre-formatted decision log sat open to her side. The mantra of murder inquiries. Record everything. If it isn't written down, it didn't happen.

'Tallies with the time of the last call into Hardie's phone. Blowfly larvae have been preserved for the entomologist, if required,' Phil said, referring to the maggots found, which could be used to estimate how long since a person had died.

'We won't need that yet, unless someone has any other thoughts?'

Bill the CSM spoke up. 'It would be hard to justify the spend on that, bearing in mind the wealth of other evidence.'

'Agreed. Bill, will you talk us through the scene,' Sally said, not looking up.

Bill nodded and pressed a key on a laptop in front of him, lighting the screen on the wall at the head of the table. A photograph of the graveyard appeared, its identifying production number in the bottom corner.

'I think someone has been looking into the history, but as I understand it the burial yard hasn't been used for ages, and correct me if I'm wrong, records were lost in a flood many years ago when the chapel was destroyed. Heavily overgrown, in fact the PolSA team ended up needing strimmers. The fingertip search found a battered old clasp knife in among all the vegetation.' He pressed a key and a picture flashed up of a small, dull-metalled knife with a worn blade extended, nestling in some long grass. 'There's no suggestion forensically that it's been used for anything and it's far too small to be the murder weapon. Maybe it belonged to Hardie, particularly as the grave shows signs of being scraped with a blade to clear it of vegetation.' Bill pressed another key showing the grave, the sinister words emblazoned on the granite surface.

A hush descended on the room, and a few of the room's occupants shifted uncomfortably in their seats. This wasn't supposed to be written on resting-place monuments. A piece of the granite lay to the side of the stone, just as Max remembered it.

'Why that inscription, Boss? I mean surely not opening a grave doesn't need to be said. It's kinda bad form, anyway,' a voice said from the back of the room.

There was a snort of amusement from the other side of the table.

'As I understand, it was used many years ago, either during times of bubonic plague, or possibly cholera,' Sally said, her voice serious.

'Jesus, any risks?' the voice said.

'Apparently not, so don't worry,' said Sally, a small smile on her face.

'You're all ugly enough already; you certainly don't need big pustulating boils on your faces, right?' said Bill, looking around the room and smiling, tiredly. 'Now can I carry on?'

The next slide was an image of the PolSA officers lifting the stone, quickly followed by one of the yawning chasm of the grave. It seemed impenetrably black.

The next slide was lurid in detail and pin-sharp. The bloated corpse of Tam Hardie, on his back, his face waxy, yellow and swollen, his eyes open but empty. The black wound in his midriff seethed with flies. Even in a still photo, you could almost feel the mass of insects feeding on the gore. A mobile phone lay on his chest, it too surrounded by the flies. There were no gasps, no groans; in fact, there was little reaction at all.

'Is there any explanation for the broken piece from the gravestone?' Max spoke for the first time. Several pairs of eyes locked on him, traces of suspicion on their faces. Max was an unknown, and an outsider.

'Damaged when removed by Hardie, probably?' Bill said. 'There are some scrape marks on the underside, so I'd say he used something to prise it up.'

'Could someone lift it on their own? It's a heavy piece of stone, and Leitch is only a skinny wee gadgie?' Max asked, not wanting to press it too hard in an open meeting.

'Well, Leitch's comments in custody were that he did it on his own and we have nothing to disprove that. We can't explore it further until a doctor pronounces him fit to interview, so we can't get near him,' said Sally, her face registering something. Irritation? Or maybe something else. It didn't add up, that was for sure.

'Have we searched his car?' Max asked.

'Yes, PolSA did it. Scrappy old Land Rover Defender. Nothing at all in it.'

'Did it have a jack?' asked Max.

Sally didn't answer, just raised her eyebrows at the blue

uniformed sergeant in the corner of the room who Max recognised as the PolSA team leader.

'I don't think so. It was a right old heap that was practically falling to bits. In fact, I don't even think it had a spare tyre,' he said, looking through a property register.

'Did Leitch have a mobile phone?' asked Max.

'Not that we have found, just an old landline at his house,' Sally said, checking her notebook.

'How about Hardie's computer?'

'Still being worked through, but nothing is jumping out. Mostly research on genealogy websites and local history forums. Certainly, an absence of anything about the family business from what we can see,' said Sally.

Max shrugged. 'Okay.' He smiled.

'Anyway, moving on, Bill?' Sally spoke, clearly eager to change the subject. Max said nothing more.

Bill scrolled through a series of images of the inside of Leitch's premises, which were as he had remembered, but Max wasn't really watching; he was deep in thought about the lack of interest in the concept of an accomplice. Something didn't feel right and Sally's attitude had only exacerbated his concern.

An image of the red journal flashed on the screen.

'This is from Leitch's hand we assume, although we haven't been able to ask him. Jenny, you're going through it. Much to report?' asked Sally, turning to a tired-looking officer in the corner of the room.

'It's really rambling, mostly nonsensical stuff, Boss. Densely packed text about all sorts, but a fairly large section berating the Hardies and calling them a threat to his family. He's obviously been doing research on them, as there were some printouts from Ancestry.com where he had been tracing their family tree. And of course, there's the letter.'

'Aye, I think we've all seen it on the circulated briefing. Looks like it was written by one of Leitch's ancestors in 1890.

We are continuing the research, but there was a William Leitch who died in 1890 in Wick,' said Sally. 'All pretty damning stuff, then. Okay, we are where we are. Next slide, Bill.'

Max looked up as the image of the cutlass flashed on the screen. It was an evil-looking thing, broad of blade, with an iron handle and a wickedly sharp edge. The next photograph was zoomed in on the initials on the blade, a faded but legible 'T.H.'

'This is an 1804 naval boarding cutlass.' Max nodded at Janie, who smiled, as Sally continued talking. 'And we are fairly sure it's the murder weapon. It's gone to the lab along with Leitch's clothing, and all the other recovered samples. We're expecting the DNA results imminently, but I'm confident the blood on Leitch's clothes, hands and the sword will all belong to the victim.' Sally paused to let it sink in, but her tired and weary team seemed to relax at this news, safe in the knowledge that, even with Leitch currently being a patient at a secure hospital, this case would be wrapped up quickly.

'What of the initials?' asked a voice from the back.

'Leitch made comments about Hardie being killed with the weapon that killed his ancestor, so there could be something in that. We are looking into the history of this, but it looks like there was a Tam Hardie in the Navy in the 1800s. We're still digging into it, but the evidence is strong, and we keep developing it,' said Sally.

A silence descended. Murders like this just didn't happen. Centuries-old feuds were not supposed to spill over into the modern day.

'How about Leitch? Where are we now?' Sally asked a slim, fresh-faced officer sitting at the table.

'As we all know, the doctor pronounced Leitch unfit as soon as he got to Burnett Road custody. We managed to get all the forensic samples and recover all his clothes. Mental health crash team came out and sectioned him, on an emergency mental health certificate, for seventy-two hours. He's currently at Carstairs. I have spoken to his care team, and they're certain that he will be further detained, probably for at least the full twenty-eight days, and most likely beyond that. He has dealt with paranoid schizophrenia for some time, but had recently fallen off his meds.'

'Okay, thanks. Paul, how are the family?' Sally said, looking pointedly at DC Johnstone.

'Pretty quiet, Boss. They have very few questions, accept everything I say and are always polite and thankful when I leave.' He coughed wetly.

'How were they at the identification?' asked Sally.

'It was just Tam Junior. He was quiet and restrained, took one look at his father and said, "Aye that's my pa."'

'That's it?'

'Aye. They don't seem to want us there, although they're not rude or obstructive. They just want to bury their pa, as soon as possible. The fiscal has released the body and I think they're preparing a big gangland funeral, you know. Giving the old boy a proper send-off, tomorrow.' Johnstone looked uncomfortable.

'Nothing else?' asked Sally.

'Well, I did as you said and showed them a picture of the cutlass, in case it was a family heirloom. Tam Junior said that whilst he had never seen it before, the old family legend was that it was his great-great-grandpa's and with the initials, and all that, they want it back.'

'So, it looks like Leitch killed Old Man Hardie with his ancestor's cutlass. Jesus, what the hell? Paul, do you think they'll be looking for revenge?' asked Sally.

'I can't see why. The only suspect is secured, and they're just flat, like. Almost unemotional. I can't work them out.'

'Did they mention any vendetta of any type?' Sally asked.

'No.'

91

'Did you ask them?'

'Aye, of course. They said they knew nothing about it.'

'Do you believe them?'

Johnstone just shrugged, his face an almost bored display of ambivalence.

'Have you made it clear that we are dealing with this; we have the suspect locked up and a wealth of evidence and that they have to, I repeat, have to, keep out of it?'

'Aye, I've told them.'

'How did they respond?'

A hint of a smile crossed the detective's big face. 'I can tell you exactly what Tam Hardie said, ma'am. "We have absolute confidence in the fine officers of Police Scotland to investigate our father's murder." Those were his exact words. I recorded them in the FLO log,' he said, proffering the booklet.

DI Sally Smith just closed her eyes and exhaled.

'Okay, guys. Thank you all so much for your sterling efforts. It's been a real beast of a few days, but we have all the crucial stuff captured. Finish up anything urgent, then get yourselves home, see your families and back here in the morning. I know we all think this is slam dunk, but let's not relax. Push on and get this tight, and hopefully Leitch will be well enough at some point. Thank you again.' Sally stayed sitting at the table as the team all filed out, most yawning and clearly ready for a few hours at home. It was often the way when a murder broke. A massive push, long hours to secure the essential evidence that would be lost otherwise. Then a brief pause to recharge before getting back to it.

As the team began filing out, the atmosphere in the room suddenly changed. Two uniformed officers entered, all smiles and nods at the departing tired-looking officers. The area chief superintendent nodded at Sally, his eyes swivelling to indicate that someone of importance was following him. Immediately behind him was a lean officer, with thinning red hair and with rank insignia on his epaulettes that indicated he was a deputy chief constable. His name badge read 'DCC Geoff Caldwell'.

'Morning, sir,' said Sally, rising to her feet.

'Don't get up, please, just a flying visit to say hello, and offer my thanks for the team's hard work,' said the DCC, a wide smile splitting his face showing white, straight teeth, which looked a little too white and straight.

'Sir, can I introduce DS Craigie and DC Calder, who've been assisting us from Serious Organised Crime?' Sally nodded at Max and Janie who remained seated at the table.

The DCC looked at Max and Janie in turn, and his smile widened as he stepped forward and shook each of their hands. 'I've been briefed by the area commander, and of course your own DCS about what you did, guys. I have to say I have rarely heard of a better and more instinctive bit of police work. Hopefully nipped this in the bud before things got much worse. Who knows what Leitch was capable of? If any commendation recommendations come across my desk, they'll most certainly get my endorsement. First-class stuff.' He nodded, in what seemed a sincere fashion. Geoff Caldwell was certainly something of a charmer.

'No problem, sir, but thanks anyway,' said Max.

'Sally, when you've finished up here, can you pop up to the chief super's office, just for ten minutes, okay? I want to be sure I have it all, as I've a bloody community reassurance meeting tomorrow, and I want to be ready,' he said, grimacing slightly.

'Of course, sir,' Sally said.

'Once again, great stuff all round.' He nodded, turned and left the room flanked by the chief superintendent.

'Nice bit of smoke-blowing there. Right, I really need to finish this, before I go and see the boss again.' Sally lowered her head back to her policy log and began scratching away with her pen.

After a few seconds, she looked up to see Max and Janie still sitting watching her write.

'Max?' she questioned, stifling a yawn of her own, a slight look of frustration on her face.

'Are you sure about all this?' he asked, politely.

'Sorry, I don't follow,' she said, although her face didn't reflect this.

'Leitch couldn't have moved that stone and deposited a corpse under it, and I think you know this.'

'Working theory is that he could have lifted it, as you did, and wedged something under it to keep it up. There is no evidence of a third party. No fingerprints, no tyre tracks beyond Leitch's Defender and Hardie's Range Rover. No extraneous footmarks, nothing.'

Max sat more upright and squared his shoulders a little. 'I lifted that with some significant effort, and only by eighteen inches, and I'm probably a fair bit stronger than Leitch. I just don't buy it. I'm also totally unconvinced that the Hardies will leave this here.'

Sally sighed again and rubbed her tired-looking eyes. 'Max, we have almost wrapped this case up. Leitch has confessed, the evidence is all over him or written in his crazy journal and whatever happens, he's either in Carstairs for life on a hospital order, or prison. The job is finished and the detective chief superintendent wants it put to bed. The family are happy with where we are and what we have done.'

'Even if it's all nonsense?'

'That's enough. I'm very grateful for your help and actions in this case, but that's it. I'm under instructions to clear it up. We have our result; it's finished. Am I understood?' Her red-rimmed eyes flashed with sudden emotion and Max could detect the conflict within them. Sally knew. She knew it wasn't finished, not by a long way.

16

Yusuf Tekin was in serious pain in the centre of a rough wooden barn, his hands tightly handcuffed and secured to a stout wooden beam by a length of rusting chain that looked like it had been in place for years. He was scared. In fact, Yusuf Tekin was terrified, which was not an emotion he often experienced. He was more used to inflicting terror than receiving it, certainly since he became the head of a successful heroin importation gang.

His side ached where the stun gun had been jammed and thousands of volts had flowed into his body, temporarily paralysing him. He hadn't even seen his attackers when he left the restaurant in Glasgow in the early hours of the previous evening, much the worse for drink. He had been hooded, thrown into a van, and now, several hours later, he was almost suspended by his wrists, with only enough slack in the chain to allow him to stand on tiptoes before the cuffs bit into the raw, bruised skin of his wrists and hands.

The smell of urine was sharp in his nostrils, as he had been secured for several hours, suspended and not released to pee. In fact, he hadn't seen a single soul since his incarceration began. It had been a simple snatch, a drive from the city centre of about an hour, and now he was in this stinking barn, with no actual idea where he was.

So, yes. Yusuf Tekin was absolutely terrified.

The barn door swung open, suddenly, the bright morning sunshine assaulting his eyes.

'Who's there?' His voice cracked with dehydration. They had to know that he wasn't someone to be messed with. He had a fearsome reputation in Glasgow and wider Scotland.

'I said who's there? You are making a big mistake. My people won't take this. Show yourselves. You clearly have no idea who you're dealing with,' he croaked, hoping that he sounded more in control than he actually felt. His wrists were burning, the pain becoming almost unbearable. 'Uncuff me now, and let me go, and I'll not seek retribution.' The words died in his throat. The tall, lean figure of Tam Hardie strode into the barn flanked by Frankie and Davie Hardie, worryingly all dressed in new-looking overalls and wearing blue surgical gloves. Tam Hardie's eyes blazed with fury, his jaw tight.

'Tam, what the—' His garbled response was brutally cut short by a forceful, open-handed blow to the side of his head, rocking it sideways with a noise like a pistol shot. His head exploded with pain and he let out a cry, from shock as much as from hurt.

'Think you can use my father's death to put your prices up, eh, Turkish Joe?' He followed the rapid words with a vicious punch, which caught the drug dealer square on the nose. The cartilage and bones crunched as Yusuf's nose disintegrated, his head snapping backwards again. He knew all the Hardie boys were boxers, and the overhand punch was devastating in accuracy and power. Yusuf let out a howl of agony that was almost animalistic.

The three Hardies just stood and watched as he whimpered, a long line of bloody snot falling from his nose.

'You remember my father's nickname, Joe, right?' Tam said, in a low, even voice.

Yusuf swallowed a sob before shaking his head blearily, the terror now gripping his insides like a vice. He remembered well enough, as did anyone in the Glasgow underworld. Tam 'Peeler' Hardie's calling card was a thing of legend that struck fear into the criminal world.

'Well, my pa was feared throughout the country, and for good reason. It's unfortunate for you, Joe, that you're going to be the evidence that the Hardies are not only alive and well, but they're bloody worse than ever.'

As if by an unspoken command, the younger Hardie brother marched forward and tore off Yusuf's shirt buttons, exposing his protruding stomach and flabby chest. He yelped in fear, any pretence or attempt at assertiveness now gone.

Tam Hardie reached into his overalls pocket and produced a bright yellow box cutter. He extended the small, angular blade with a flick of his thumb. He smiled, as Yusuf began to scream, the chain clinking as he tried to back away. He only managed to move the few inches that the now taut chain allowed. Apart from the trace of a smile, the look on Tam's face was blank and unfathomable.

'Hold him,' he barked at his younger brothers, who as one grabbed a foot each of the thrashing Yusuf. They pulled sharply and he fell, but only as far as the chain would allow. His shoulders jerked as his bodyweight almost pulled them from their sockets. He couldn't move. The pain was terrible and he screamed like a howling wolf. It felt like his hands would be pulled clean off, and part of him almost wished they would.

'I'm sending a message. It's just unfortunate that you have to be the messenger. Everyone will know that the Hardies aren't finished. Quite the opposite. The Hardies are here, and we are stronger than ever.' The gang leader's voice was low, calm and even, but his hard, flinty eyes told a different story.

Tam's hand thrust forward, the box cutter glinting in the early sunlight.

'No, please. Please, I'll pay you anything. I'll never try anything again, please, please,' Yusuf babbled, spit flying from his mouth, terror gripping him like a vice.

Yusuf's scream was ear-splitting as the wickedly sharp blade carved a large square in the exposed flesh of his wobbling abdomen. Hardie worked at the bucking and thrashing flesh as he ripped it from the yellow fat that lay beneath. The pain was indescribable as Tam tore the square of skin from the stomach, leaving the bloody gore exposed underneath. Yusuf screamed, once more, long and full of loathing.

The blade flashed up towards Yusuf's neck. Strangely there was no pain as the knife bit into his flesh and was drawn sharply, left to right. In fact, the pain went, to be replaced with something else.

Warmth and peace, closely followed by a dark, inky blackness.

17

A classic gangland funeral – that's what it was.

The funeral cortege was impressive. The hearse was pulled along the busy Cumbernauld Road at a slow, mournful pace, by two large, coal-black shire horses, bedecked with black plumes mounted on their massive heads. A solitary police motorcyclist preceded the parade, the bike's blue lights flashing as it led the way in the bright, mid-morning sunshine. Two top-hatted and frock-coated carriage drivers sat at the front of the hearse and skilfully steered it off the main road towards the cemetery. A long line of cars and limousines followed behind as they approached the gates of Riddrie Park Cemetery on the East End of Glasgow.

The pavement each side of the white gateposts was lined by hundreds of mourners, all immaculately dressed in their best gangster finery. Dark suits, leather jackets, bootlace ties, patent leather shoes and sunglasses among the menfolk. The women wore new-looking dark dresses and jackets, black fascinators or hats. There was even a flash of mink and fox fur among the older women present, despite the warm sunshine.

Heads were bowed respectfully as the hearse carrying the body of Tam Hardie swung through the gates and headed into the graveyard. The gleaming black coffin was surrounded by bouquets of flowers, topped with a floral display that simply read 'Peeler'. A gruesome reminder of the coffin's occupant.

The cortege briefly paused as it entered the cemetery and the Hardie brothers alighted from the lead limousine, also bedecked with a multitude of floral tributes. They walked slowly to the front of the hearse. Each brother was dressed identically in a simple dark suit, black silk tie and white pocket square, sunglasses shielding their eyes.

They formed up, side by side, heads bowed for a brief moment as the lead funeral director, an old family friend with a top hat and cane, walked to the front. As he set off at a slow, rhythmic pace in the direction of the family plot where Tam Hardie's wife lay, the whole cortege began to move again, in total silence, apart from the clip-clop of the shire horses' metal-clad hooves.

The remaining mourners all fell in behind the hearse, walking forwards, slowly and solemnly, heads bowed, towards the final resting place of Tam Hardie.

*

'Fuck me, anyone would think this was a Hollywood gangster set. Look at the state of them,' DI Ross Fraser barked between chews of the greasy-looking meat pie that he clutched in his hand. They were all watching the video screen mounted on the wall in the office of the Serious Organised Crime Team, at Gartcosh.

'I think it's what they would refer to as a "good do", Boss,' said Max as he looked at the live feed, from one of the cameras that had been secreted at several locations throughout the graveyard. They had decided that it was a gathering not to be missed.

The previous night the technical support team had covertly accessed the cemetery and hidden a number of cameras on trees, in buildings and on lamp posts. They had considered hiding a surveillance team in the grounds but had rejected this on the basis that no one would want to get caught in the process of observing the largest gathering of the Scottish underworld in many years.

The cameras were all working beautifully, focusing in on the hundreds of mourners gathering around as the coffin was lowered into the yawning grave.

'Zoom in on camera four, Janie,' said Ross, looking intently at the screen.

Janie worked a computer mouse and the camera went full screen and zoomed in on the Hardie brothers, all standing graveside watching their father's coffin disappear into the ground. There were no tears, just blank and emotionless faces behind dark sunglasses.

'Pan left, who's that there – dark suit, dark tie?' Ross said.

'Doesn't help me, Boss; you may need to narrow it down,' said Janie.

'Big nugget back there, next to the ugly, fat wifie bint with the stupid fox around her neck.' Ross stopped chewing his pie and swallowed, clearly concerned that his sexist rant could be misconstrued.

'So eloquent, Inspector,' Janie said, smiling as she zoomed in on a square-shouldered man with buzz-cut grey hair, wearing a dark, silk-lapelled suit. The camera was so clear that you could see the long thin scar on the man's cheek.

'Shit. That's Driller Jock. Enforcer for hire and a right bastard. Not long out of Saughton for GBH. Drilled a poor little bastard's kneecaps out after he forgot to pay for some skag he owed. I didn't have him as being close to the Hardies, but he's almost graveside.' Ross puffed out his cheeks. 'It's like a who's who of Scottish crime.'

'Not just Scottish, either. Zoom in on the big black guy stood a row back to the left,' said Max.

'Who's that?' Ross asked.

'Eustace Fielding, also known as "AK" as his weapon of choice is an AK-47. He's the top man in the MDK posse in Tottenham. He had most of the skag dealing sewn up in London and was running loads of kids who were county-lining the product to all the home counties and several of the coastal towns. I had no idea he was buying from the Hardies. The Met'll be interested in this down south, and that always results in a bit of quid pro quo. He's a very bad man.' Max whistled.

Ross finished eating and they all watched as the funeral party began to break up, some of the mourners returning to their cars, many pausing to commiserate with each of the brothers in turn. Small knots of individuals began to mingle for furtive conversations among the gravestones.

'Where's the wake?' asked Janie.

'Back at their place. No chance of getting a camera in there; it's like Fort Knox,' said Ross, glancing at his watch. 'I've a meeting with the chief super in a wee while. Can you finish up here, Max? We need stills and screen-grabs of any meets of interest, then feed those into Sally Smith's team, ready to be used in the Leitch trial as unused material. Copy to our intel team as well for dissemination where it's required. That's pretty much it, for us. There's a new job that's going to be a real bastard – Albanian trafficking gang, and I think it's coming our way.'

'No bother,' said Max his face fixed on the screen as Ross turned and left the office, muttering to himself and limping slightly.

They continued staring wordlessly at the screens as a long line of mourners remained behind to pay their respects to the new head of the Hardie crime empire. This was a funeral to be seen at, to be able to say you were there and to make sure that Hardie knew that you were.

After about twenty minutes, the line of rough-looking mourners had dried to a few stragglers.

'Shall I start winding this up?' Janie asked.

'Give it a few minutes more,' said Max his eyes on a tall, lean man who was standing away from a small remaining knot of mourners all paying their respects to Tam Hardie. There was something about the man. He was fairly unremarkable. Slim, possibly going to seed a little with a small pot belly. Not classically tough-looking like the other body-builder types who were currently fawning over Tam Hardie. He wore a plain, dark suit, had greying hair swept across his head and thick-framed glasses.

'Zoom in on the mannie to the left of Hardie, stood on his own, swept-over hair and glasses.'

Janie moved the camera and zoomed in on the man. He had forgettable features, everything in proportion, no scars, no blemishes, and no facial hair. It was how he carried himself. He stood there, a much smaller man than the bull-necked, shaven-headed mobsters who were all around, but he had a kind of seedy nonchalance. As Janie zoomed in further, he seemed to be looking into the lens of the hidden camera. His eyes were flat and dove-grey behind the spectacles and projected nothing. Simply nothing.

'Keep the camera on him. I want to see if we can put him to a car,' said Max.

'Recognise him?'

'I'm not sure, but there is something about him.'

'He looks a little familiar to me, but I'm not the greatest with faces,' said Janie, zooming in even further, with a confused frown. 'I'm sure I've seen him before. I just for the life of me can't remember where,' she added.

The group of mourners left Tam Hardie, and the innocuous man approached him. There were no smiles and no acknowledgements. This wasn't paying condolences; this was business.

Hardie nodded at him and they began to talk. Hardie was in full flow, the anger palpable as his jaw worked up and down and the man just looked on, impassively.

The innocuous man looked at Tam Hardie and said a few

words. Max had no idea what he said, but whatever it was it seemed to satisfy Tam, who extended a hand and they shook, briefly. Hardie then strode off, not looking back, all business, once again.

Max wracked his brain, trying to pin down what it was about the man that was bothering him. 'Can you crop that encounter between Hardie and that guy and send it to me and also get a few full-face stills of him?'

'Sure thing, Sarge,' Janie said, tapping at the keys.

'Janie?'

'Yeah?'

'If you call me Sarge again I'm going to put you back on traffic duty.' Max smiled.

Janie stopped typing and turned to face Max, open-mouthed.

'Joke, carry on,' Max said, still smiling.

Max's phone buzzed in his pocket. Looking at the display he saw it was Ross. 'Ross?'

'Turkish Joe has been murdered. They've just found him off Sauchiehall Street, neck slit and his gut skinned.'

'Jesus, when?'

'Within the last twenty-four hours. MIT 4 are taking it,' said Ross, his voice flat.

'What do they want from us?' asked Max, nodding at Janie.

'Nothing,' said Ross.

'What? This is obviously linked to Hardie's death.'

There was a long pause. 'They aren't convinced. Being chalked as a gangland hit. Let's face it, Turkish Joe had enemies,' said Ross.

'What? They know Old Man Hardie's nickname was "Peeler", as in peel people's skin off, right? We all knew Turkish Joe's been selling skag to Hardie. This is a message, Ross. A message to the underworld that the Hardies are still running the streets. This won't end here.' Max was surprised to hear the strength of feeling in his own voice.

'I'm sure you're right, but I've just been with the chief super and he wants us on the trafficking job. I've made my feelings clear, but he wouldn't discuss it. The job is being taken by MIT 4. It's nothing to do with us.'

'This is madness. The Hardies are going to keep killing unless we stop them, and it's all being swept under the carpet.'

'Fortunately, this isn't your concern. We hand all our intel over to the MIT for the Hardie murder and we move on. You and Janie need to get back to Burnett Road again. Take them all the surveillance footage from today and sign the production labels for the cutlass and stuff you seized. It's all back from the lab, tested positive for Hardie's blood. Job's a slam dunk and they want it all sorted and put away until Leitch is out of the nuthouse. Half of their team are helping on the Turkish Joe murder. We tidy the loose ends up, then I want you back here tomorrow for the trafficking job, okay?'

'This is nuts. Why are we on a trafficking job, when we have rampaging Hardies running around Scotland?'

'That's enough. Just get on with it and I'll see you in the morning.' Ross hung up.

Max felt a little sorry for his DI, who was clearly under pressure from above, but it didn't feel right. None of it felt right.

'Janie?'

'Yeah?'

'Can you get all the footage ready to go? We need to head north again, and make sure you have the clip of the man speaking to Hardie. There's someone I want to show it to,' said Max.

'Sure. Give me ten minutes to cancel the date I had rearranged from the last time you messed up my social life.'

'Sorry, but what can I do?'

'Nothing, it's cool. I want to get this job done properly, and I'm not so fussed, anyway.' Janie picked out her mobile and clicked at the keys, composing a brief message.

'Done, I'm all yours,' she said, smiling.

Max had a feeling that the interaction between the stranger and Hardie was important, and he had an inkling of an idea as to who could help him work it out.

The Hardies were on a mission. He could feel it in his gut.

18

Sally Smith was typing furiously at her computer when Max and Janie arrived at Burnett Road, just over three hours later in an otherwise empty open-plan office.

'Quiet here, Sally. Hi by the way,' said Max as they walked into the office.

She smiled, tiredly. 'Aye. Lost most of my team to a drug war murder in Glasgow. Turkish dealer got bloody skinned alive and his throat cut.' She shook her head.

'I heard. Any links to Hardie?' Max asked.

'Other than the flaying of the unfortunate Joe, no. Intelligence reports in from a couple of well-placed inform- ants are convinced it's a new gang trying to take over from the Hardies,' she said, and the tone of her voice suggested she wasn't so sure.

'You happy with that?'

'What, losing most of my team when I have the murder of the biggest gangster in Scotland to finish up? No!' she said, shaking her head.

Max opened his mouth ready to offer an opinion, but then closed it again. There really was no point, so he asked another question instead. 'Are you all wrapped up?'

'Pretty much. Weapon only has Leitch's prints on it and the blood on it is Hardie's. Blood all over his clothes and hands all belongs to Hardie, as well. Plus, a confession of sorts. The psychiatrist tells us Leitch was delusional, that he was fulfilling some old family legacy. His rambling journal seems to confirm all this. He won't be fit for some time. It could end up as a hospital order, but we're ready if he's declared fit.'

'Well, that's good, I guess.'

'As good as I could hope for. Family seem fine; I understand you had surveillance on the funeral?'

'Aye, it's all here,' said Max, handing over a disc.

'Cool, I'll have it looked over.' She smiled. 'Meg over there is finishing the productions off.' She pointed to a harassed-looking officer in the corner of the office surrounded by boxes and bags. 'I think you need to sign a few things if that's okay?'

'Sure thing.' Max paused. 'But do you mind if I ask a question?'

'If you're trying to query why we aren't looking into an accomplice, can I say no? Other than that, fire away.'

'Who was the original occupant of the grave?'

'Well, theory is that it could possibly be an ancestor of Hardie's. There are skeletal bones that hadn't been officially buried, in that there was no coffin. There were also some remains inside the remnants of an old coffin. We have sent samples away for possible DNA extraction, but that will take some time, particularly as the bones are really degraded. It doesn't help that there was some serious flooding in the area many years ago, which not only destroyed the records and the chapel, but has also damaged the remains. And we have another problem,' Sally said.

'Can I guess?' said Max.

'Go on.' Sally smiled, tiredly.

'The Hardie boys won't consent to comparison DNA samples?'

'Correct. We have post-arrest samples for Frankie, but we can't compare that unless he's suspected of the crime, which, of course he isn't. We had a bullshit letter from the solicitor when we asked, giving a myriad of reasons, none of which made any sense.'

'Any clues on where the cutlass came from?' asked Janie.

'Leitch claimed it was Hardie's ancestor's, and the initials obviously bear that out. We have dug out old records that a Tam Hardie was born in Caithness in 1795 and later joined the Royal Navy. He left in 1829 where he found work as an exciseman. Apparently, he was quite successful in seizing and collecting duty on whisky from illicit stills at the time, until he disappeared without trace in 1830. Records are limited from what we can see, and it's unclear what happened to him. Working theory is that Tam Hardie's great-great-grandpa was murdered and secreted in that grave in 1830.'

'Jeez, so it sounds like Leitch could've been telling the truth?'

'Well, his version of the truth, but we have nothing to confirm it, and in reality, it makes no particular difference. Leitch's motive is driven by his condition.'

'Do the Hardies know?' asked Max.

'What do you think?' Her face told him that the Hardies knew it all, whether or not they had been officially told.

'Are you comfortable with all of this?'

Sally just stared at Max with a look that spoke volumes.

'Not even a little bit. Not even a little, tiny bit. It stinks to high heaven, but I'm only a DI and I've been told to turn my attention elsewhere. This job is done, as far as the management are concerned.'

19

'Do you fancy a cup of tea before we head back south?' Max asked Janie as she pulled out of Burnett Road and back into the busy early-afternoon Inverness traffic.

'Sure, why not.'

'Well, it's only that I haven't seen my Auntie Elspeth for ages, and she's only fifteen minutes from here.'

'Auntie Elspeth? That's a sweet name,' Janie said as she drove along the busy road.

'I wouldn't let her hear you say that. She's a force of nature. She's the only family I have left, so I like to check in on her now and again. She's great; you'll like her.'

'What happened to your parents?' asked Janie.

'Five years ago, a car accident,' said Max, his face impassive, but feeling the familiar jolt of loss.

'I'm sorry. It must've been terrible.'

'Not great. How about your family?'

'Looks like we have something in common, Max. My parents died when I was twelve."

'Jesus. You win the sad story contest. I'm sorry. At least I had lots of years with mine. How did they die?'

'Mum died of cancer. My dad was much older than her and he died within six months of her passing. They said heart attack, but we all know it was a broken heart.'

There was a long pause and something passed between them in the silent car. Something in common.

'I'm sorry to hear that. It must've been horrible,' said Max.

'Is what it is. I'm okay, but it probably made me a little weird, you know. Made me throw myself into studying and education, rather than thinking too hard about stuff and having friends, and the like.'

'Well, you do have a nice clean car.'

'Piss off, Craigie.'

Max chuckled. 'So, who brought you up?'

'I was raised by my rather unpleasant aunt in Edinburgh when I wasn't at boarding school. I don't think I had the same relationship with her as you have with Auntie Elspeth.'

'Do you not see her now?'

'Well, no, she's dead.'

'Oh, sorry.'

'No, it's fine. She was a real nasty bastard who hated kids, but she was rich enough to keep me out of the way in boarding schools so she could be off gallivanting. School was a blessed release from her.'

'So, what family do you have?'

'None.'

'What, none at all?'

'Nope. I was an only child. My mum was an only child and my dad just had his evil sister. It's just me,' said Janie, flatly and without emotion.

'Blimey, so genuinely, no wonder you're a bit weird,' said Max smiling.

'Takes one to know one, Sarge,' said Janie, looking straight ahead with the hint of a smile.

They drove over the Kessock Bridge and along the A9 for a few miles before turning off onto the Black Isle or '*Eilean Dubh*' as the brown heritage sign proclaimed.

'You grew up here?' asked Janie.

'Aye, just a few miles from here. We're passing my old primary school now,' said Max as they drove through a small village called Munlochy.

'Cute,' said Janie, looking at the stone cottages.

'It was a terrific place to grow up. Beaches, mountain bikes and all that stuff. I used to climb in the Cairngorms at the weekends, a kids' paradise,' Max said, smiling.

'I'll take your word for it.'

As they passed into a small village called Avoch, Max checked the tide time app on his phone. 'She lives just here, but she won't be in. The tide has just turned, and she'll be looking for dolphins. Carry on through to Chanonry Point.'

'Dolphins, what, like Flipper?'

'Yeah, they'll probably be coming in now. Elspeth's part of the conservation team.'

'Cool, I've never seen a dolphin for real.'

They drove for another ten minutes along the coastal road pulling in at a car park at the end of a peninsula beside a large, white lighthouse.

'How do you know she'll be here?' said Janie.

'She'll be here. Can you bring your iPad?'

'Why?'

'You never know, may come in handy.' Max set off towards the sea.

It was only a five-minute walk, and the weather was beautiful. A soft breeze wafted over the firth, the sea as still as glass. They continued walking towards a small knot of people at the far end of the peninsula close to the sea, who were staring out through binoculars, or long-lensed cameras.

'There's Elspeth,' said Max, pointing at a slight, white-haired lady with her eye glued to a tripod-mounted monocular pointed at the sea. As they approached, a large, grey fin broke the still surface of the water, followed by the flick of a tail as a dolphin dived below the surface.

'Wow, did you see that?' squealed Janie, immediately followed by another yelp as another appeared, leaping this time, tossing a salmon high in the air as it soared fully out of the water, returning with a huge splash.

'Oh my God!' gasped Janie, her eyes wide.

Max approached Elspeth, and rather than speaking, he gently laid his hand on her shoulder. She turned, revealing a worn, but kindly face, with warm, twinkling eyes.

'Max,' Elspeth cried, and threw her arms around his neck, hugging him tight. 'You should've said you were coming. The dolphins are putting on a lovely show today. Now, how's that lovely wife of yours?' Her voice was soft and carrying the Highland lilt.

'We're apart at the moment. You know this. She's in St Albans, and I'm up here,' said Max, reddening.

'Bloody daft if you ask me. You two are marvellous together. The sooner you get her up here, the better,' she chided.

'I know, but it's complicated. Anyway, let's move the conversation away from my relationship woes, Auntie E.' Max felt his heart lurch at the mention of his wife. Katie and Elspeth adored each other. God how he missed his wife, he thought, momentarily sad.

'You're punching well above your weight with her. You'll never do better, you know, so be nice and get her back.' She looked at him with the expression of a stern head teacher.

Pushing the thoughts away and rapidly changing the subject, Max looked Elspeth straight in the face. 'Just a flying visit, up here on a work thing. This is Janie, a colleague.' He nodded at Janie, who smiled, shyly.

'Hi.' She grinned. 'Wonderful dolphins. I've never seen them in the wild like this.'

Elspeth looked at Janie intently, watching her lips as she spoke. 'I watch them all the time, dear. We name them and tell them apart from their fin marks and other body scars. Beautiful creatures.' She smiled, and her eyes twinkled with pride.

Max looked at Janie. 'Auntie Elspeth is deaf. Make sure you're facing her when you speak.'

'Thanks, you could have warned me,' she replied, a little embarrassment creeping into her expression.

'Ach, Max always forgets to tell everyone, my dear, don't fret. Tea? I've a Thermos.'

'Thank you, that would be lovely,' said Janie, scowling at Max, who just snorted.

'So, what brings you up here?' Elspeth asked, pouring a mug of tea from a flask.

'Just had to pop to Inverness for a work thing. How's life?' asked Max.

'Better than the alternative, dear. Spending time watching my wee pals, here. We've catalogued a good few new ones, and some have returned this season that we haven't seen for years.'

'Keeps you busy, right?' Max smiled at his aunt.

'For sure, for sure. What would I do otherwise?'

'Auntie Elspeth, can you look at something for me?'

'Of course, darling, what is it?'

'If I show you a video clip can you see if you can lip-read what the people are saying?'

'You cheeky sod,' whispered Janie.

'I can try,' Elspeth said, reaching for the spectacles that were secured around her neck on a chain and popping them on her nose.

Max took a small SD card from his pocket and slotted it into a lightning port adapter. He handed it to Janie, who gave him a sarcastic smile and plugged it in. The image soon came up of Tam Hardie talking to the innocuous-looking man.

Elspeth stared intently at Hardie's mouth as it moved up and down, his face darkened in anger. 'Such terrible language. He doesn't seem nice at all.'

'What does he say?'

'Well, I'm not sure I want to repeat it. Glaswegian, is he?'

'Elspeth, don't pretend to be a prude – you can swear like a trooper when the mood takes you. Come on, what does he say?'

Elspeth smiled, mischievously. 'I rarely swear. Now let's look at this bastard video. I'm pretty sure he says, "I want every one of the bastards dead. Each and every one of them, and I don't care how much it costs." But it's not always easy to understand a Weegie.' The old lady paused to look at Max, concern on her face. 'He seems nasty. I hope you're being careful.'

'It's all fine. What about the other man?'

'Replay it,' she said, adjusting her spectacles. Max pressed replay and the images began to move again.

She stared intently, her lips moving, just fractionally.

'What does he say?'

'He is a little easier to read. "Of course, Tam. I'll speak to my contacts." How strange. What do you think he's talking about?'

Janie looked at Max, her eyes wide. 'Bloody hell.'

Max shrugged, a resigned look on his face. 'I need to speak to Ross.'

*

As Max and Janie sped south on the A9 back towards Glasgow, Ross Fraser's voice reverberated over the speakers.

'You did what?'

'I had a lip-reader look at the clip of Hardie speaking to that bloke. He said what I just told you,' said Max as he drove.

'And who the fuck gave you authority to do that, man? Jesus, how many times do you have to be told to leave a job alone?' His voice boomed and crackled with static.

'But it's accurate. Hardie is clearing up. He wants the remaining family dead. We need to move on this or there will be more dead bodies. I said this isn't going to end and you know I'm right.' Max remained ostensibly calm, yet he could feel the frustration rising.

'And where did you find a pissing forensic lip-reader, and how is it paid for? Why are you buggering around with intelligence products, and showing it to unvetted lip-readers? This could get you bang in the shit, man,' Ross almost shouted.

'Does it really matter? It's accurate, Hardie said those words and whoever he said them to has agreed to take the job. We need to identify who he is, and we need to be escalating this and starting a disruption job. We need to issue Osman warnings to all of Leitch's relatives and we need to do it now.'

'That's enough. I've fucking just about had it with you. I always try to protect you, but the DCS has ordered me off this job, and you're going behind my back. If the MIT want to investigate this, they can, but it's not ours. Who did you use?'

'My Aunt Elspeth. She's deaf and is a lip-rea—'

The speakers almost exploded out of the dash. 'Your Auntie fucking Elspeth? Max, what the hell are you doing? Are you actively trying to get suspended, or worse?'

Max said nothing. The silence was almost palpable over the airwaves as the A9 passed them by. Max turned to Janie, and incredibly, smiled.

'Right. In my office, in the bastarding morning, and stay off this bastard job.' Ross hung up.

'Well, that went well,' said Janie, flatly.

Max shrugged, a resigned look on his face. 'I'm going home. Can you take the car back and pick me up in the morning?'

'Sure, but what are you going to do?'

'You heard Ross. I'm going to see him in the morning and take a bollocking. It sounds like pressure from above, but I don't like it. It all feels wrong. Why are they refusing to see what is plain in front of their noses? I need something to eat, and I need to go for a run with my dog.'

'You probably need to let this go. It isn't our job and MIT 4 have it in hand,' said Janie.

Max just sighed and shook his head as they drove on.

20

The dream jolted Max awake again just before 6 a.m. The same dream as always, Dippy's eyes glazing as the last flicker of life left his ruined body. Max woke with another muffled gasp of fear, followed by sorrow, followed by self-loathing. Self-loathing and sorrow that he, somehow, had been responsible for his friend's death. Max lay there in a muck sweat.

'It's okay, Nutmeg, just the dream again, girl,' he said, calming his worried dog by tickling her curly ears. She stared at him, a mix of love and concern in her dark brown eyes, her tail thumping rhythmically. 'Run?' said Max in a lighter voice. Nutmeg's ears pricked up and she let out a half-muffled bark of excitement.

Max smiled, and scratched the dog's chin. 'Come on then,' he said, throwing the duvet back and getting out of bed. Nutmeg leaped after him, her tail thrashing, wildly. Max quickly dressed, swallowed a glass of water and headed out of the glazed doors. He paused, as he always did, to take in the sweeping fields that ran down to the firth. A soft mist hung in the lower fields giving a slight chill to the air, but already Max could tell that it was going to be another beautiful day. 'Come on, girl, let's get moving,' Max said to Nutmeg as he jogged off at a decent pace, heading up the hill and into the forest behind him.

He ran hard for forty-five minutes, pausing at his usual tree to perform four sets of pull-ups, each set to failure. He was pleased to see that he equalled his personal best of twenty-six repetitions. Even as he approached his fortieth birthday, Max still ran several times a week and boxed at a gym in Glasgow when he could. He had a small gym in his garage where he did punch-bag circuits, speed-ball work and weight training when the mood took him, not that it often did. He preferred to stay quick and agile, and to rely on his natural, genetic strength, rather than to use weights to build excess muscle.

Arriving back at the cottage, he drank more water before showering and preparing coffee and scrambled eggs, which he sat to eat outside on his deck.

Pulling his phone from his pocket, he opened up Facebook, something he rarely did. He searched for and clicked on his wife's page. There were no updates, but he just sat and looked at her profile picture, her twinkling eyes, straight nose and choppy hair. His stomach ached, and he longed to speak to her, to tell her he still loved her and to hold her tight. He knew it was too soon. They had agreed not to speak for a while, after an argument during their last call. 'I need to miss you, Max. I need to know if we are right together, and only by being apart can I work that out,' she had said. It still hurt.

He moved away from her profile and quickly scrolled his own newsfeed. There wasn't much on it. He stopped scrolling when he came across the post from the *Press and Journal*, the local newspaper that covered the Black Isle and beyond. Shock hit Max like a thunderbolt as he read the headline.

CAITHNESS LANDLORD, 52, KILLED IN MYSTERY HORROR CRASH AT NOTORIOUS BERRIEDALE BRAES

A picture of Duncan Ferguson, the landlord of the inn in Dunbeath, looked from the page at him. It was a family shot of him and his wife, Mary, both beaming at the camera.

Max opened the article with a sick feeling of anticipation, his heart pounding in his chest. This just couldn't be a coincidence. In a few days, two people who had been in that tiny, backwater inn were dead. Max didn't really believe in coincidences, certainly not ones like this.

He stared at the picture of a mangled Ford Focus at the foot of a cliff at Berriedale Braes, a series of notorious hairpin bends on the A9 at one hundred and fifty metres above sea level. Apparently, the car had crashed through the barrier and fallen down the high cliff smashing onto the rocks below. No other cars were thought to be involved, but it was unclear how Duncan's car had managed to smash through the barrier so easily. A full inquiry was underway by Roads Policing at Dingwall, and police were appealing for witnesses who were asked to contact Sergeant McGee on 101. Recognition flashed in Max's mind as he saw the name, but he couldn't place where he knew it from.

Max sighed and scrubbed his face with his palms. What the hell was happening? He needed to know more, but he realised if he went through official channels it would create more problems, particularly bearing in mind yesterday's reaction by Ross and Sally.

He sipped his coffee and laid his hand on Nutmeg's head. Her tail began to wag as he stroked her. Max made an immediate decision and grabbed his phone and dialled.

'I'm still pissed off at you,' said Ross, his tone not reflecting his opening statement. Clearly a night's sleep had softened his boss's demeanour.

'I know, sorry. Can I take a day's annual leave today? Something's come up I could do with sorting,' said Max, keeping his voice light and even.

'That's the best thing you have said for days, pal. I could do with a day of not seeing your fucking mug. In fact, take a bastarding fortnight off and give me a break.' He chuckled down the line. This was typical Ross. He blew up and raged, then almost immediately got over it.

'Just a day, that's all I need.'

'Yes, but promise me you'll stay well away from the Hardies. Last thing we need is your size tens stomping all over the place. I can't take getting bawled out by the DCS for the fourth day running. My career prospects are shite, anyway.'

'Sure thing, thanks.' Max hung up and then quickly composed a message to Janie. *Don't bother picking me up. I've taken the day off. See you tomorrow.*

Janie replied almost immediately. *I hope you're not doing anything daft.*

Max smiled and replied, *As if.* He wasn't planning on doing anything stupid, but this was a lead he just had to pursue. He just couldn't understand why obvious leads were being ignored, and he knew that some answers were out there.

Max stood up and looked at Nutmeg's adoring face as she sat, her tail like a rapid metronome, clearly expecting something.

'Sorry, girl, I have to go out. Go and see John and Lynne.' Nutmeg's head cocked, understanding on her face at the mention of her second family.

'Go on, off you go, John and Lynne.' Max pointed towards next door, and Nutmeg turned and trotted off.

Max went back into the house and to the cupboard in the hall. Opening the door, he pulled out his motorcycle gear, a textile Rukka jacket and trousers, and lifted his helmet down. He quickly pulled the kit on, left the house and went to the garage. His pride and joy sat inside, a KTM Adventure. A big, brutish bike designed to cross continents in comfort and at speed. Max had bought it just the previous year and had not long come back from a long trip across Europe on it.

Throwing his leg over the machine, he gunned the big, thirteen hundred cc engine and pulled away, down the drive and onto the road that headed north. Riding his bike made him feel free, especially on a day as beautiful as this, and he soon felt the stresses leach away from him. Along with his dog, and physical exercise, riding his KTM was his antidote to the dark spectre of his PTSD. It worked so well it should have been available on prescription, thought Max, as he roared north, towards the wild, open spaces of the Scottish Highlands.

*

Max rode for over four hours, at a steady pace, taking great comfort as the congested traffic of the motorways and main roads gave way to the much quieter A9 that traversed the rolling Perthshire countryside. This soon gave way to the steep and craggy Grampian and Cairngorm mountain ranges. The sky was an unrelenting blue as he ascended the Slochd Munro before descending into the capital of the Highlands. He paused briefly to refuel before setting off again, soon finding himself in the wide-open spaces of Caithness, as he hugged the coastline heading towards his destination: Berriedale Braes. Max had driven along this road countless times and knew that it had been the scene of many accidents. The braes dropped from almost five hundred metres to sea level with a number of challenging bends, the worst of which was at about a hundred and fifty metres by the Berriedale Braes viewpoint that looked out across the North Sea, with a huge drop the other side of the barrier.

Max pulled into the viewpoint slip road and put the KTM on its stand. He removed his helmet and put it on the tank, wiping the sweat from his brow. The temperature had risen now, and was nudging at least twenty degrees, which was not at all common in this part of Scotland. He removed his jacket and draped it over the bike. After opening the pannier, he pulled out a bottle of water and took a deep drink.

Max walked out onto the A9, noting grimly the yellow witness board that boldly asked, 'Accident. Witness Appeal'. The date was below along with a direct-dial number. Max walked down to the apex of the hairpin, keeping to the side of the road, noting that there were no skid marks, which struck him as odd. He walked to the new section of road barrier that had been bolted into place. There were still traces of debris on the road and verge by the replaced section of barrier, which stood out all new and shiny against the tarnished sections either side. Max stepped over the barrier and headed along to where the bank dipped away sharply.

He squatted at the join where the new barrier was bolted to the old. Some sharp metal fragments were scattered around the support post, the same colour as the old barrier, although with a different, almost rough quality. He picked up a piece, about four inches long. It didn't look right. It was almost like a fractured shard of glass. Max frowned, turning the piece of metal over in his hand. He tried to flex it, but it didn't budge, even a bit. It felt stiff and brittle. Standing, he tucked it in his pocket and stared out at the sea in front of him.

He imagined for a moment Duncan's car smashing through the barrier and disappearing over into the expanse, tumbling down the almost sheer drop and smashing into the rocks below. He wouldn't have stood a chance. The questions seethed in Max's head. Duncan Ferguson was a local boy, so would have driven this road multiple times. Had he been drinking? How had he breached the barrier?

Walking back to his bike he took his phone and called the number on the witness board.

'Hello, Roads Policing, Sergeant McGee,' a cheery Highland-accented voice replied.

'Hi, DS Max Craigie, Serious Crime from Glasgow. Are you investigating the fatal accident at Berriedale?' Max got straight to the point.

'I am. I take it you're the same Max Craigie who was at the graveyard the other day?'

Realisation hit Max. Sergeant McGee was the acting inspector from the murder scene.

'Of course, my memory. Sorry, Mick, it's been a busy old day. Are you at Dingwall?'

'No, I'm at Wick at the moment. I've just finished the vehicle inspection and I'm writing a few bits up,' he said.

'Great, can I pop and see you? I'm close by, just a few things I'd like to ask your opinion on.'

'Sure thing, man, come on up. I'll have the kettle on, but why are murder squad interested?' Sergeant McGee asked, without suspicion.

'Could just be a coincidence. Is the wreckage somewhere nearby?'

'Aye, it's at Sweeney's place in Wick. Not much of it left, mate. More like a busted brolly than a bloody Ford Focus.' He chuckled.

'Thanks, I'll see you soon.'

'I'm going nowhere, pal. Well not until 4 p.m., anyway, then I'm off.'

'Thanks, see you in a wee while,' said Max and he hung up.

He looked out towards the deep blue North Sea. None of this felt right. In fact, it all felt very wrong.

21

The journey to Wick only took about half an hour and very soon Max was sitting in a shabby office in the police station opposite the cheery uniformed Sergeant Mick McGee.

'What's murder squad's interest in this then?' he said with mild curiosity as he handed him a chipped mug of tea.

'Just a coincidence I'd like to iron out. The murder suspect for the graveyard death was in Duncan Ferguson's inn on the day of the murder and I'm just curious about the circumstances,' said Max. He wanted to play it down, but give enough to spike the officer's interest.

'Aye well, a funny business that. Scotland's biggest gang boss killed in an ancient graveyard. No one could believe it. Up here, normally not so much happens.'

'Anything unusual about the car?'

'Well, we haven't even found half of the bloody thing, it was in such a state. That's what tumbling five hundred feet will do to a car. So far as we can tell, no obvious faults, but then, we haven't even found all of the brake assemblies, so we could never really be sure.'

'How do you think the accident happened?' asked Max.

'Difficult to be sure. There were no skid marks, which I'm

not so happy about, but that could indicate brake failure. He hit the barriers at a fast enough speed to break through them, which is surprising, since they're supposed to be speed rated and from what I can see, they should've held the car. The W-pattern Flexbeam barriers are pretty good. You don't often see them fail, certainly not with a medium-sized family car.'

'Any ideas on why the barriers failed?'

'God knows, mate, maybe they're getting a bit old and brittle,' said Mick.

'Can I see the photos?' asked Max, sipping his weak tea.

Mick sat back in his chair for a moment. Eventually he opened a drawer in his desk and tossed across a small photograph album. Max flicked through photos of the accident scene. They showed the road layout, the broken safety barriers and then the destroyed Ford at the bottom of the expanse. It was almost totally reduced to its individual components, such was the extent of the damage.

'Look at number seven.'

Max saw a picture of the bent and buckled crash barrier that seemed to have sprung open where it joined the post. The next image was of the bolt fixings that should have secured the pressed steel to the post. The bolt holes had clearly failed, the metal almost shattered where immense forces had ripped the barrier from its fixings.

'This shouldn't have happened. Even at a hundred mph, they shouldn't have failed like this. These barriers have flexibility built into them so they absorb impact. These fixings look like they've shattered. The manufacturers are inspecting and will be preparing a report for the fiscal, but to me it looks like the metal failed. Shouldn't have happened, but seems like a fault.'

'Could someone have done something to the metal to make them fail?' asked Max, feeling the excitement begin to gnaw at his insides.

'I can't see how, or why for that matter.'

'Maybe not,' said Max, wondering if he meant it.

'I mean why would someone do that? I can't think of a reason and how could they know that someone would hit exactly that portion of the barrier?'

'I guess,' said Max, turning the idea over in his mind.

'If someone had interfered with those barriers, somehow knowing that Mr Ferguson would hit the barrier at that precise point and speed, it would have to be the most brilliantly conceived murder ever. The whole idea is ridiculous, right?'

22

Max thanked Mick McGee and left on his bike, turning it all over once more as he headed south. He was missing something that was hidden somewhere in Caithness, but try as he might, he couldn't put his finger on it.

The image of the gravestone flashed up in his mind and something tripped.

He suddenly braked and pulled to the side of the road. Pulling his phone from his pocket he did an internet search for Sweeney's garage in Wick. Memorising the address, he turned the KTM round and accelerated off.

Five minutes later he pulled up outside a small gated yard. 'Sweeney's' was emblazoned in a banner sign across the chain-link fence. Max stowed his helmet and walked through the open gate towards a wide-open roller shutter door. A BMW was suspended on a hydraulic lift and an overall-clad middle-aged man was underneath it, struggling with a brake calliper. He whistled tunelessly in time with the tinny radio that blared out in the corner of the untidy garage.

'Hello,' said Max, causing the mechanic to jump.

'Jesus, scared the crap outta me,' the man exclaimed.

'Sorry, I'm DS Craigie from the police. Is the car wreck

still here from the Berriedale head crash?' Max proffered his warrant card, which the man looked at briefly.

'Aye, over in the corner, what's left of it. I thought you boys had finished with it? Leastways, that's what Mick McGee said. I was going to be taking it to the crusher soon.' His face was smeared with grease, and a cigarette dangled from his lips.

'Just a quick look; won't be long,' said Max.

'Help yourself, man. I need to finish this bugger, before I go to the pub. Hot day like this, a man needs a beer.' He turned back to his brake calliper and continued working.

The Focus could barely be referred to as a car anymore, but rather as a large lump of twisted metal surrounded by a series of other twisted components.

Max searched the wreck until he found what he was looking for. The hatchback had been torn off the main body of the car, and lay dented and smashed against the wall. The boot space yawned open and most of the carpet had been torn away exposing the bare metal. Max looked inside the space, seeing that the space-saver spare wheel was miraculously still bolted into the compartment. Quickly, Max turned the retaining nut that held the wheel in place. Unexpectedly it moved without force and within a few moments, Max was pulling the small wheel out and depositing it on the ground. Looking in the compartment he saw the scissor jack tucked inside.

He took out his phone and snapped several pictures of the jack. He looked closely at the jacking plate, and straight away saw what he was expecting. There were traces of granite dust on the top, and some down in the deep groove that was designed to slot into the jacking point.

Looking on the base plate, he saw that it was encrusted with peaty mud.

Duncan had been the accomplice, and he had helped Leitch jack the gravestone up and hide Hardie inside. He had no doubt, and forensic testing of the dust and the soil would prove it.

But Duncan was dead. How had he died? There was only one answer. He had been murdered.

He dialled quickly. 'DI Smith,' Sally Smith answered.

'Sally, it's Max Craigie. I'm at Sweeney's garage in Wick. I need someone to come here as soon as possible for a forensic retrieval. There is a Ford Focus that belonged to Duncan Ferguson from the inn in Dunbeath. The jack in the car contains forensic evidence that will prove he was involved in this murder, or at least in hiding the body, afterwards.'

'What?' She sounded astounded.

'The jack in the rear of his car has granite dust on the top and is encrusted with mud on the bottom. They jacked the gravestone up, Sally. The bottom of the stone was marked, and the corner had broken off. They used the scissor jack from Duncan's car to lift the stone. It's the only plausible explanation.'

'Max, Duncan is dead. He died in a car accident.'

'I know. I've just been speaking to the accident investigator. There are loads of questions. I think he was murdered.' Max started to get the feeling that he was missing something again.

'As I understand, it was attributed to excess speed.'

'Sally, no way, it can't have been. Someone interfered with the barrier and I'm sure it can be proved. There is no way the metal should've failed like that. This is the Hardies. They're clearing up, looking for revenge. We have to take this seriously. It's not just about Leitch anymore.'

'Can you package it and bring it in?'

'No, I'm on my motorbike, and I'm on leave today,' Max said already expecting the follow-up.

'If you're on leave, why are you investigating this? I understood your team was off the case,' Sally said, without any trace of anger.

'Just something I wanted to clear up. I was out for a road trip and wanted to have a pry. I had a feeling that a car jack may have lifted the stone and when I heard Duncan had crashed, it didn't seem right. I thought I'd check,' said Max.

'Well, I expect you may find yourself in a little warm water once the management hear. Not from me, though; in fact I'm impressed. Half of my lot aren't even aware they have access to their own initiative.'

'Yeah, I imagine Ross Fraser will go doolally.'

'Ross blows hot and cold. He'll forgive you and I'll butter him up. Okay, stay there. I'll get someone there from Wick as soon as possible. I'll send someone up from Burnett Road tomorrow to collect it and get it to the lab. We have soil and stone samples, so I assume it'll be an easy match,' she said, and Max could hear the sound of her scribbling on her pad. If it isn't written down, it didn't happen.

Sally was as good as her word and within fifteen minutes a marked car arrived driven by a young constable, who came into the yard carrying a bag of packaging materials.

'DS Craigie?' he said.

'Aye, that's me, thanks for coming,' said Max, smiling at the young officer who looked like he had barely started shaving. He probably joined Police Scotland with dreams of the big city, and yet found himself in the small town of Wick at the very top of the country.

'Are you thinking this is a murder, Sarge? I went to the scene of the crash. It was awful. First dead body I've seen, like.' His accent had the sing-song quality of one of the islands, most likely Orkney.

'I'm not thinking anything, mate. Just making sure we secure all the evidence,' said Max.

Within a few more minutes the entire polystyrene housing containing the jack, brace and locking wheel nut was fully bagged and secure in a self-seal bag. This was perfect, as any soil or dust would remain in the cut-outs, making it easy for the scientists when it all got to the lab.

'What's your name, pal?' asked Max.

'PC Anderson, Sarge,' he said, a little shyly, before adding, 'Pete.'

'Okay, Pete, can you take it back to Wick and book it in? Someone will be up from Burnett Road tomorrow. You'll need to make a statement, okay?'

'Sure thing,' he said eagerly as he deposited the bag in the back of his patrol car.

'Thanks, mate,' said Max as the young man got back into his car and drove off.

Max nodded at Sweeney as he left the yard and climbed back on his bike. He wanted to go home, but he wasn't going just yet. There was something else he needed to do, and he wasn't looking forward to it even a little bit.

23

Max pulled his bike over outside the inn in Dunbeath, a slightly sick feeling in his stomach at the thought of what he had to do. Surprisingly, the inn was open. Max wasn't at all sure what he would find once he went inside.

A solitary young female bartender sat on a stool and looked up from a newspaper when Max walked in.

'Afternoon, what can I get you?' she said brightly, a wide smile on her face. Her accent was local and as soft as pouring cream.

'I'd love a cranberry and soda,' said Max.

'I think we have that, not that we are often asked for it around here. Hold on.' She disappeared out of sight for a moment before coming up clutching a glass bottle full of the wine-coloured liquid. She made his drink and set it down in front of Max.

She headed off in the direction of the kitchen.

'Is Mary here?' asked Max at her retreating back.

The bartender paused, appraising Max for a moment. 'I'm taking it that the fact that you're asking means you know she lost her husband very recently?' Her tone was not accusatory, more curious.

'Aye, I do know. I'm a policeman, my name is Max Craigie and I saw Mary and Duncan a few days ago. I'd like to ask a couple of questions that relate to his passing,' said Max, flashing his warrant card.

'Well, I'll let her know you're here.'

Max sipped his drink while he waited, relishing the cool and dry taste. He did miss a beer now and again and he still had several bottles of whisky back at home, almost as a test. He had come to learn that alcohol really didn't mix with PTSD. One drink always led to another. After a few he would feel the darkness begin to cloud his thoughts again and then he would dream. It was the dreams, above all, that had made him stop drinking.

'DS Craigie?' an American accent stopped Max's daydream and all thoughts of beer and whisky disappeared.

Max looked up and saw Mary Ferguson. She had aged markedly since he had seen her just a couple of days ago.

'Hi, Mary, can we talk a minute?'

'Sure, let's sit over there.' She pointed to a small table in the far corner of the room.

They both moved over to the table and sat in silence for a few moments. Mary's face was puffy and her eyes were red-rimmed.

'I'm so sorry for your loss. I only heard this morning when I saw it in the P and J,' said Max, gently.

Mary stared down at the table, a solitary tear brimming in her eye and then carving a path down her cheek.

'Is it okay if I ask you a couple of questions?'

'Yes. Sergeant McGee has been to see me, but I really don't know how it happened. I heard it was at Berriedale Braes. I didn't even know he was going there, but he had been a little weird since all the business at the graveyard. It was such a shock to him.'

'I can understand. Do you know where he might've been going? He was southbound on the A9.'

'I've no idea. He hadn't been drinking. All he said was he had to go and see someone. I'm a little confused by it all. He's driven that road many times, and he knows it well. He never drove fast; I always teased him for being a boring driver.'

'Was the car all in order?'

'Had it serviced a couple of weeks back, clean bill of health. I just don't know what to think. How could this happen? How could he just smash through the barrier? I thought they were put there to stop this?' She wiped her eyes.

'Sergeant McGee is looking into all that. Hopefully he'll have some answers. When did you last see Willie Leitch?'

'The day he spoke to the stranger who was killed at the graveyard. I still can't believe Willie did that. I mean, I knew he had his demons, but I never thought he was dangerous. Duncan always tried to help him out, and make sure he took his medication and had his meals. Duncan tried to stop him drinking so much,' she said, her eyes full of pain.

Something clicked in Max's head. Mary's description of Willie and her husband's relationship did not align with the account given by her husband.

'How well did your husband know Willie Leitch?'

Mary's eyes took on a puzzled look. 'Duncan didn't say?'

'Say what?' asked Max, his insides contracting.

'Willie Leitch was my husband's cousin.'

24

'Cousins? Sorry I had no idea,' said Max, trying to not let the surprise register on his face.

'Yeah, I assumed that he would've said when he spoke to you the other day, or at least the murder squad detective who came to see him after they arrested Willie,' said Mary with a frown.

'No. He said nothing. Are Willie's parents still about?'

'No, both dead for some time.'

'How about Duncan's?'

'No, both died a few years ago,' she said, her red-rimmed eyes taking on a confused look.

'Any siblings?'

'Willie or Duncan?'

'Either,' said Max.

'Willie has a sister, somewhere, I've no idea where, though. They weren't close and she left Scotland years ago. Duncan has an older brother in Spain, Bruce, but we haven't seen him for a while. I think that's it for family. What's this about?'

'Oh, probably nothing. Did you and Duncan have children?'

'No. We were too busy travelling around. It was never important to us, to be honest.'

'Did Willie have kids?'

'He has an ex-wife, but they didn't have kids. They split shortly after Willie left the Navy and came back to Scotland. I don't know where she lives.'

Max realised that now was probably not the time to push further with Mary. He didn't want to layer worry or fear on top of her grief.

'Thanks. That's cleared some things up, but I had better go. Do you have support around?' asked Max.

'Hettie is helping me, and my folks in America are wanting me to go home, but I don't know yet. It's all too soon.' Her chin began to wobble and fresh tears brimmed and sparkled in her eyes. 'I just can't believe he's gone.' Her shoulders began to heave. She screwed her eyes tight and sat back in her chair, raising both hands to her face.

Hettie, who had been watching them talk rushed over. 'Come on now, darling, I'll take you out the back. I did say that we shouldn't be opening, didn't I? I'm sure the officer can come another time,' she said, shooting Max a disapproving look.

'Of course. I'm sorry, I'll go now.' Plucking a business card out of his wallet he set it down on the table. 'Call me, if I can help.' Max kept his face blank, yet couldn't help but notice a rising sense of foreboding. This wasn't finished. Not by a long way.

He laid a five-pound note on the table and left.

*

'Duncan Ferguson and Willie Leitch are cousins,' Max said, without preamble when Sally answered the phone. He paced back and forth in the car park outside the inn.

'What?' said Sally Smith, incredulity in her voice.

'I just spoke to Mary Ferguson. She thought that we knew.'

'Jesus, how didn't we find this out? One of my team spoke

to Ferguson just after we nicked Willie, but he said nothing about that. I had marked him up for a further visit, but with everything else we haven't had the staff, and now I've lost most of the team to the Turkish Joe murder. It doesn't necessarily mean anything sinister, though. The report I've read says it was down to excess speed at a notorious accident black spot.'

'I'm just not buying that. Leitch killed Hardie, and now his cousin, who I'm sure helped Leitch with the body, is dead. It's too much of a coincidence.'

'But how? How could someone engineer Duncan Ferguson smashing through a road barrier? Who could organise that at short notice?'

'The Hardie family are multi-millionaires. They could easily have organised it. Did Ross tell you about the funeral and what we think Hardie said?'

Sally was ominously quiet for a brief moment. 'I did hear about it. Ross wasn't too happy that you showed it to your aunt, and I have to say, I can see his point. It's hardly how we should treat sensitive evidence, is it? It's unfortunate that others also know about it, and they haven't taken it well.'

Max couldn't really see how he could answer this question without getting angry, so he chose to say nothing, as he leaned against his KTM, suddenly feeling weary. Sally clearly took his silence as encouragement to continue.

'Detective Chief Superintendent White isn't overly happy, either. I think some waves may be washing your way soon. You're probably best staying away from this case. Don't get me wrong, I appreciate your help, but I'm not sure my appreciation is shared across the murder squad management. They want this all wrapped up, and think you're meddling where you're not required.' Sally's tone was soft and, he had to admit, kind. He really had no idea what to say, so in line with the best advice to someone where problems are stacking up against him, he said nothing.

'Well, I've said my piece. Take care. You're a good cop, and I'd hate to see you getting in the proverbial over this,' said Sally, as if lecturing an errant schoolboy.

There was a brief pause, before Max spoke. 'I appreciate your advice.' He hung up.

25

Willie Leitch sat in the day room on a plastic, high-backed chair at Carstairs Hospital, an open novel on his lap. His keyworker had just finished a long chat with him about his medication requirements and the ins and outs of his treatment. Willie didn't really give a shite, though. It was all over, as far as he was concerned. Job done. The bastard Hardie was now burning with his ancestors.

He was proud of his actions, proud that he had satisfied what the voices had told him. He had no choice, did he? The man had to die and the only regret Willie had was that he didn't have the opportunity to kill more of them. He chuckled at the thought, and the voice in his head, although a little muffled because of the medication, assured him that he had done well. His ancestors were proud of him.

Willie picked up his novel and tried to read, but he just couldn't concentrate on the words. It was like there was a fog clouding his eyes and mind that stopped anything from making sense. He hated the drugs, but if he didn't take them voluntarily, they'd just hold him down and force him.

There were only two others in the room, neither paying him any attention. The little guy with the shaved head was doing a puzzle and the huge man called Graham from the room next door was sitting in his chair, staring at the wall in front of him, rocking gently. A slight trail of drool had escaped the corner of his mouth and was carving a path down his chin.

Willie didn't belong here, but he knew that he was probably here for good. He knew that he had been unwell and that he had got worse after he'd stopped taking his medication. The bloody stuff was just ruining him and turning him into a vegetable. He was glad he'd stopped taking it, and found the strength to do what the voice had told him. His old ancestor telling him, when he'd seen Hardie in the pub. Willie giggled thinking about it.

A slight feeling of unease began to seep through the cloud, at first just a mix of anxiety and the drug-induced fog. A feeling of impending doom, maybe, that made him shake his head to try to clear it. These bloody drugs were awful. A creeping sensation began to nip at his feet and rise further into his body. Something was wrong. The voices in his head had been pushed back and were nothing more than a distant and inaudible muttering that he found unsettling. They were barely even there, and for once, Willie missed them. They'd tell him what to do.

A shadow fell across Willie as he continued to stare at his book, the words still not going in. He looked up and saw Graham looming over him, just a foot away, an unfathomable look on his face. His unfocused eyes were empty of any emotion.

'Graham?' Willie began to speak, but the words died in his mouth. He listened in his head for the reassuring presence of the voice, but there was only silence. Looking in the day room, he saw that only the small man with the puzzle was there, and he was paying no attention. The keyworker was nowhere to be seen.

A slow smile spread across Graham's face, showing discoloured, broken teeth. There was not a trace of mirth in that smile, nor was there any malice.

Graham's huge fist thumped with no great force and little malice into Willie's chest. There was no immediate pain. What was Graham doing?

Looking down, Willie saw blood blooming from a small hole in his white shirt, then the pain arrived. A sharp, all-encompassing agony and the feeling that his entire chest was caving in. He opened his mouth to scream, but Graham leaped forward and clamped a giant fist over his mouth, his free hand pounding at Willie's chest, each blow thrusting the sharpened toothbrush deep into his heart.

26

Max was in his garage, dressed in a singlet and shorts with sparring gloves on his fists, working at the big, heavy bag that was suspended from a joist above. He jabbed and punched, varying his attack and utilising his footwork and head movement, imagining that the heavy leather was an opponent.

Max had boxed ever since childhood, starting at the gym in Inverness as a ten-year-old. He had done well, winning lots of bouts as he grew up, and he could possibly have made something of himself in the sport. He loved the challenge, the combative element and the primeval nature of it. He had continued in the Army, winning the combined services middle-weight belt at one time, before Afghanistan got in the way.

His shaved head was beaded with large droplets of sweat as he moved, pounding relentlessly at the bag. As always, the more he jabbed and uppercutted, the more exhaustion nipped at him, and the better he felt. Nutmeg stood at the doorway to the garage, a look of concerned interest on her face.

Suddenly Nutmeg looked away from Max's exertions, hearing a car coming up the long drive. She tore off barking furiously, ready to defend the homestead, in her typical fashion. Max looked out of the garage door to see Janie's blue BMW pulling up at the front of the house. The muffled notes of a complex jazz piece were audible from within the car.

She opened the door, which halted the music, and stepped out to be met by the wildly excited Nutmeg, tail thrashing as she greeted the newcomer. Everyone got this treatment from Nutmeg. She didn't discriminate; she loved everyone. Max took a towel and slung it around his neck and went out to meet her, swigging from a large water bottle.

'Morning, Sarge,' she said, a half-smile on her face.

'Sorry, just been working out,' he said, removing his gloves.

'Glad to hear it, bearing in mind how sweaty you are.'

'What was that terrible music that was playing?'

'Ornette Coleman, the daddy of free jazz,' said Janie.

'A right racket, as my old dad used to say about me listening to The Cure,' said Max as they walked back into his garage.

'Nice,' she said, looking with genuine interest at the heavy bag, speed ball, squat rack with Olympic bar and long row of dumbbells. 'This must've cost you a fortune,' she said.

'Cheaper than a gym membership, and I don't have to talk to people,' said Max, his breath now returning to normal.

'Do you compete?' she asked.

'Not for a while. I did a fair bit, particularly in the Army.'

'What weight?'

'Middleweight. I'm a bit heavier, now, though.'

Janie stepped into the garage, and suddenly, explosively swivelled her hips and executed an expert spinning reverse kick, sending the bag flying back on its chain.

'Impressive. Taekwondo?' asked Max.

'Muay Thai,' she said, completely composed.

'I'm glad you're wearing your gutties, rather than heels, or you'd have wrecked my bag,' he said, pointing at her Converses. 'Remind me not to piss you off. Coffee?'

'Cool. Love your dog by the way. What's her name?'

'Nutmeg,' said Max, with a slight trace of embarrassment. 'And, before you ask, yes, it is a girly name, and a cockapoo is a girly breed, but she came with the house.'

'Whoa, defensive, and what's with the gender stereotypes? Is this another example of the rampant patriarchy repressing women with constant micro aggressions? Is this what it has come to in Police Scotland?' Her face was suddenly serious.

Max paused for a second, a little concern creeping in.

Janie sniggered and her face broke into a broad grin, of a type that Max hadn't yet seen on her face. 'Sorry, I'm messing with you. I like how you took her on, and she's a cool wee dog.'

'Jeepers, you had me going for a moment. I'm in the shit enough, right now. I don't need sexism allegations.'

'Yeah, about that. I overheard your name being mentioned a few times. I'm not sure it was all complimentary.' Janie's face was serious again.

Max sighed. 'What have you heard?'

'Just rumblings, and rumours. You want to tell me?'

Max told Janie everything, the whole lot, the car accident and Duncan's previously undeclared relationship with Leitch.

'What? They don't see the link? Two of the people in that graveyard are now dead in questionable circumstances and they just want to shelve this case?'

'Seems so.' Max shrugged.

'Do you think the Hardies are somehow influencing the case?' Janie sounded shocked.

'I'm saying nothing. Come on, I'll make you a coffee. I'll get a quick shower and we'll get to the office. I may as well face whatever music I have to face.'

*

When Max and Janie walked into the office, it was clear that something was going on. There were knots of officers chatting conspiratorially around desks and it was obvious that the rumour mill was in full flow.

Ross was ensconced in his glass office, a phone clamped to

144

his ear, his face brick-red as he talked. Something was most definitely happening, and the atmosphere strongly suggested that it was not good news.

'What's going on?' Janie asked Nick – a young officer sitting at a desk, his face concentrating on his screen.

'You not heard?' he said, cocking his head to look at them both.

'It seems not,' said Janie.

Max could feel the tension rising in his gut.

'Willie Leitch is dead. Murdered. One of the other patients at Carstairs stabbed him last night,' he said in a matter-of-fact voice.

'Jesus, who stabbed him?'

'Graham Connolly, nutjob who went down a load of years ago for a double murder in Dundee, a proper psycho. Utterly bonkers he is. Just attacked Leitch in the day room when the supervising staff member had popped out for a pee. Stabbed with a sharpened toothbrush multiple times straight to the heart.'

'Any link to the Hardies?'

'I've been researching since the early hours when we got called in, and I can't find anything. He's always attacking others, but normally just fists and feet. This was an execution.'

Max's stomach dropped. Three people who had been in the graveyard on that fateful day were now dead. Three people.

'You all got called in?'

'Aye, about three in the morning, trying to get a drop on the intel, but seems like the narrative is that Connolly was heavily paranoid and this was just a random attack. Told the nurse that Leitch was a demon or some such shite.' Nick yawned.

'Is everyone buying this?' Janie asked.

Nick sniggered without mirth. 'Are they hell. Evidence is what it is, though.' He shrugged.

'Max, in here, now,' boomed the voice of Ross Fraser who

145

had suddenly appeared from his office. He looked fuming, and his face was beetroot purple. His tie was loose at his neck and he had a ketchup stain on his off-white shirt.

'What's the deal with Leitch? Are we looking at the Hardies for it?' asked Max as Ross shut the door.

'What the fucking fuck are you playing at?' said Ross. His jaw set firm.

'Specifically?' Max asked, not wanting to give anything away.

'Well, how about interfering with evidence from a fatal crash without authority for a start? Then there is showing highly sensitive surveillance product from a proactive policing operation to your Auntie fucking Elspeth. How about those two for starters? And whilst I'm on it, how about going straight to a grieving widow of a fatal car crash, when it should've been the FLO going?'

'The accident is not an accident. No one is taking seriously the threat that the Hardies are presenting. Duncan was murdered, I'm certain of it, and now Leitch is dead. Can't you see? This is the Hardies exacting their revenge, just like the video clip I showed to my expert lip-reading aunt proves.' Max spoke quietly, but firmly.

'I've just got off the phone from Detective Chief Superintendent White, and, to put it not too finely, he's pissing incandescent with rage mainly because he's getting a whole heap of shite rolling downhill from his boss, and it's landing on his desk. He thinks you're a loose cannon, and he's considering suspending you for breach of confidentiality, computer misuse and perverting the course of justice. He's giving me shit about my lack of supervision of you, and he's on his way down here right bloody now. I suggest you sit quietly, nod politely and take whatever shit he's intending on doling out, okay?'

'Someone has to stop Tam Hardie. Hasn't Turkish Joe's murder shown what he's capable of? He peeled the skin off the man, just to establish himself as the new leader of the Hardies.'

'No proof of that. Intelligence is that it's another gang.'

'You don't believe that for a second.'

'When are you going to learn that this is none of our, or more specifically your bastarding business? We do as we're fucking told, not go off on crusades. Jesus, I used to look forward to getting out of the bloody house to escape the missus and come to work. Now I'm considering taking leave because Mrs Fraser's moaning is easier to deal with than the shite you keep bringing to my bloody door.'

Ross opened his mouth to continue his tirade of abuse but was halted by the door opening and Detective Chief Superintendent White striding into the room, a blank look on his face. Max and Ross rose to their feet.

'Sit down, both of you. DS Craigie, I have to say I'm a little disturbed by the reports I'm receiving from a number of sources about your conduct over the last few days. Now the way you and DC Calder identified Hardie's burial site was commendable, but I'm really a little perplexed about your actions since then. Max, this isn't your inquiry, and whilst everyone is appreciative of your efforts, the reports I have are troubling. Can you explain why you think what you've been doing is a good idea?'

He was a big man dressed in a well-tailored suit, with a booming voice and a cultivated air of authority.

'I apologise, sir, but before I answer, what exactly is being alleged here?'

'No allegations, I'd just like to know why you've been doing what you've been doing, that's all. I'm getting significant pressure from those above me who believe you've gone rogue. This is a complex investigation, and your actions could compromise it. You understand that, surely.' His tone was soft, and almost sympathetic, but there was something else there. He was clearly under some pressure.

Max decided that being a little cagey was perhaps the wisest option. 'Sir, am I being investigated for disciplinary purposes? If so, I should really be served a regulation twelve notice of investigation, and am I to require federation representation?'

'Max, we really don't want it to come to that. You're a great cop, with a terrific reputation, but you can't be acting like this. It could compromise the investigation. Now, please, just stay out of it. Those above me are concerned that you're not acting professionally.'

'Sir. It is my belief that the desire to resolve this case is blinding some people to the evidence that the Hardie family have killed Duncan Ferguson and now Willie Leitch. It seems these matters aren't being properly investigated. There are other members of the Leitch family who I'm concerned are at risk, right now.' Max's voice was low and respectful, but each word almost seemed to make the detective chief superintendent flinch.

Something flashed in White's eyes. He looked down at his notebook and then let out a sigh, his voice changing to a concerned tone. 'Max, you're a great officer, a real asset to the force, but those above me are concerned that your mental health may be having an impact on your decision-making. They've raised your issues following matters in London and the fact that you withdrew from occupational health interviews after the shooting. This is making them nervous.'

'That's a private matter, sir,' Max said, feeling the darkness begin to creep into his vision. It always happened like this – a creeping, cold darkness that was invisible, but very real. He felt his cheeks begin to flush and the anger that had been absent for some time start to rise.

Ross spoke for the first time since the meeting began. 'Pal, just listen to the boss; no one wants to screw you over, but you can't go blasting about Scotland on a private crusade. You must know this.' Ross's usual bumptiousness had gone, to be replaced with a sympathetic, softer tone. Max felt his anger rise even more. Every bastard was against him here, but he kept his lips tightly pursed and his head lowered.

'Sorry, but I'm ordered to refer you to occupational health,' said White. 'And that referral is mandatory. As of this moment, you are on sick leave until you've been assessed. I believe that your judgement is impaired. Go home, Max, take some time and come back when you're ready and refreshed, and once you've seen OH, okay? Ross, make sure he gets home safely.'

Max felt the darkness rise, a hot anger. His fists were clenched so tightly that he felt his nails bite into his palms. He took in a slow, deep breath, as his counsellor had once made him practise. Strangely, it was one of the few useful things he took from therapy.

As quickly as the darkness had risen, it subsided to be replaced with a sense of calm. Max smiled. 'Well, if I am mental, there's no harm in me saying the following, sir. Fuck you.'

27

Max and Janie didn't speak for some time on the thirty-minute journey from Gartcosh back to Max's place in Culross. Max didn't even moan about Janie's odd choice of music. He just let the mellow jazz wash over him, lost in his thoughts as he stared out of the window, part of him regretting his lambasting of the most senior detective in the homicide command.

'You okay?' asked Janie as they pulled up outside his cottage.

'Couldn't be better, mate,' he said, aware of the irony in his voice. 'For once, your music choice is welcome.'

'What are you going to do?'

'Meaning?' Max asked, turning to her.

'Just that? What are you going to do? Occupational health and that?'

'I'll see them, I guess, if they make the appointment, but that won't be for some time. If they're anything like the Met, they'll have one counsellor for the whole of Police Scotland,' said Max, shrugging.

'You'd be right. A friend of mine got really sick after being shot at. That and her dad dying and she was in a mess. Took months to get an appointment. You're not even sick.'

'I think that's probably the intention. Put me before

Professional Standards, and it's out of their hands, you know, mandatory timescales, supervised by outside agencies, and federation support. Mandatory occupational health could take months and all they have to do is make a touchy-feely phone call to me once a week. Keeps me out of everyone's hair. This whole thing will be over before I'm back.'

'Can you fight this?'

'Maybe, but it'll take too long.'

'You think they're that threatened by you?'

'Think about it. The Hardies have a direct line into the investigation. They never ask anything of their FLO, because they get it direct from their sources. Ferguson gets killed in very questionable circumstances just before Leitch gets murdered. I'm the only one shouting about it, and they want it to go away.'

'But why?' Janie sounded genuinely puzzled.

'The Hardies want to kill every remaining Leitch. That's the only thing that will satisfy a blood feud like this, and I'm getting in the way. Careful they don't start to think you are, because there's no telling what they'll do. Hardie clearly has enough clout to alter the course of a murder inquiry. That means one thing: whoever they have on their team is senior. Really senior. This is corruption and I have no idea how high it goes.'

'Shit.' Janie's eyes widened. 'I knew something fishy was going on, but I thought it was just laziness, you know. Low-hanging fruit and that. What are you going to do?'

'Janie. It's probably best you stay away from me. You have a terrific career ahead of you, despite being a little odd, and associating with me, right now, could ruin that.' Max made an attempt at a smile.

'You don't know me very well, do you – even if you're the only member of the team to make any effort to actually get to know me?'

'I guess not.'

151

'When I joined the job, I always had one thing uppermost in my mind. Whatever happened, whoever was involved, I would never do anything I wasn't happy with, morally or legally. I want to help. You're a good man, and you don't deserve this. Someone in Police Scotland is happy to let people die. That's just fundamentally wrong, on every level. Whatever you need, I'm here for you.'

'Thanks, I appreciate you more than you realise, and I promise, I don't think you're weird. Well not that weird, anyway.' Max forced a smile.

'So, what do we need?'

'I need to find out who the conduit is.'

Janie looked quizzically at Max.

'There will be a link between Hardie and his bent cops. Usually an ex-cop, probably sacked or possibly retired under a cloud. He will be the link between the cops and the Hardies. It may even be that the bent cops won't know who they're working for and possibly the Hardies won't know the identities of the bent cops. We find the conduit; we have somewhere to start.'

'Any ideas?'

'Maybe, but it's a long shot. See if you can inveigle yourself into the team drinks when the MIT have one. Find out who the pissheads are on the MIT and, if they're Freemasons, all the better.'

'That might be difficult. No one invites me anywhere. They think I'm a posh, stuck-up bird – you know that.'

'Good point, well made, although not true. Well, not all of it.'

'Too kind. Anything else I can do?'

'Yes, Duncan Ferguson has a brother in Spain. Can you discreetly find out as much about him as possible?'

'Sure. Anything else?'

'Willie Leitch had a sister somewhere, and an ex-wife. I'd like to know where they are.'

'Okay.'

'Thanks. I can't tell you how much it means to have someone on my side.'

'No problem. You take care, right?'

'Sure thing, but you don't have to do this. I can fight my own battles.'

'Yeah, I do. Now piss off, Sarge,' said Janie, a broad smile on her face.

Max laughed and got out of the car, which moved off as soon as he slammed the door.

Then he felt it, a shiver that shot up his spine as the lizard part of his brain told him something wasn't right. A combat indicator, but what was it?

Then he realised: where was Nutmeg? She always came out to meet any car, without fail. Where the hell was she?

'Nutmeg?' he called out and followed it with a whistle. He felt the panic begin to nip at him as he ran up to the front door of the house. Trying the handle, he found it to be locked tight, which was to be expected. The house seemed to be secure, but it didn't seem right. He jogged up to where she often slept during the day, but her bed was empty, just her favourite toy, a squeaky pig, lying on it. He unlocked the door and ran into the house, calling, 'Nutmeg,' as he did. She was nowhere to be seen.

He ran next door and banged on John and Lynne's door. Barking erupted from inside as Tess and Murphy ran to the door, eager to greet him. The door opened, Lynne looking at him quizzically, and the two dogs bolted out rushing around him. Tess was an elderly, shaggy-haired blonde Labradoodle, who serenely sniffed his hand before offering a paw, hoping clearly for a treat.

'You okay, Max?' she said, her face puzzled at the alarm in Max's eyes.

'Is Nutmeg here?'

'Aye, love, she's asleep in the lounge. Something spooked

her earlier and she wanted to come in,' she said. 'Nutmeg,' she called.

Nutmeg came trotting along the hall, breaking into a deliriously happy sprint and physically leaping into Max's arms, licking him in sheer delight, her tail wildly thrashing.

'What spooked her?' Max asked, once he had managed to calm Nutmeg down.

'I've no idea; she just came running in with the boys, and didn't want to leave. Not like her at all. Normally she's watching for you from about four-thirty.'

'Has anyone been up here, today?'

'A small white car came about two. I didn't pay too much attention, to be honest, but Nutmeg was going crazy. Now I come to think of it, it was just after that when she came to us. She hasn't been out since, which is strange, right enough.' Lynne's face creased with confusion.

'Ah well, no harm. Thanks, Lynne,' said Max a knot of concern beginning to form in his stomach. 'Come on, Nutmeg, dinnertime.' And the small dog, fully emboldened now Max was back, rocketed out of the house ahead of him, her thoughts focused on her stomach.

Max went to the garage and tipped some kibble into Nutmeg's bowl, that she delightedly began tucking into. As she ate, Max walked the perimeter of the property, checking all the windows were secure. Max was careful about home security after all his years living in London. Burglaries were not common in Culross, but they did happen with the close proximities of the cities, even if the majority of the crimes were theft of garden equipment or farm vehicles.

Max couldn't shake the feeling that something didn't add up. There were no packages, and there was no mail, so who was the visitor? Making an instant decision, Max set off down the track to the road three hundred metres away, Nutmeg trotting at his heels.

Reaching the bottom, he crossed the single-track road and into the steading on the other side. This was a large, open barn that housed several tractors, and various items of farm machinery. The owner, Ewan, was busy working on the engine compartment of an elderly-looking tractor, a spanner in his hand, oil on his face. Ewan's dog, Jim, a big, scruffy collie rushed over to meet Nutmeg. A few sniffs of welcome and they were soon rushing around the steading, playing.

'Ach, ya bastard!' he spat as Max walked into the steading.

'You okay, Ewan?'

'It's this bloody thing. Misfiring like crazy, and I cannae afford to take it in. That thieving Rod Maguire will charge me a fortune just to take a look. You okay?' A smile flashed on his tough, weather-beaten face. Ewan farmed the fields that surrounded Max's place and was a kind and funny man. He often came round for a coffee, and kept him supplied with eggs.

'All good. You still have the cameras covering the machines?'

'Aye, insurance company insist on it ever since I had the brand-new Row-Crop pinched. Forty-five grand that cost me and the buggers only paid me thirty-eight. Insurance is just another word for fraud, I tell ya.' He wiped his face with his cuff.

'Can I take a look?'

'What at?'

'CCTV feed. I had a visitor earlier who really spooked Nutmeg, and I want to see who it was.'

'Anything spooks wee Nutmeg; she's nae farm dog. She's a lassie's dog, you know.' He grinned, reaching into his pocket and pulling out a large smartphone. He scrolled through the screen until he arrived at what he was looking for.

'What time?'

'Around two, or so,' said Max.

Ewan swiped a little more, staring at the screen, intently. 'I've four cameras, one faces the steading entrance, which will catch your track, perfectly. They all back up to a cloud server which

I can easily access from my phone. Quite handy when I want to keep an eye on my machines. Here.' He smiled, handing the phone over, with a touch of pride. Despite appearances, Ewan was a real gadget man, and he had actually studied engineering at university before taking over the family farm. He sometimes used agricultural modelling to plan his planting schedules, much to the chagrin of his farming colleagues.

Max took the large Samsung to see a full screen showing the entrance to his track in perfect, high-definition clarity.

'Jesus, this is good. Must've cost a fortune,' Max said.

'Cheap as chips, man, more than covered by lower premiums, and it's all tax deductible.' Ewan smiled. 'You can scroll through at extended speeds, easy enough, and it's motion sensitive, so it'll be easy to find.'

It took only a minute until the clock tripped round to just after 2 p.m., and a small white Mercedes turned into the track, its number plate clearly displayed. It was a new, sporty-looking A-Class, with low-profile tyres, spoilers and skirts.

'Flash bugger's car that,' Ewan said. 'AMG, isn't it? I bet your crap, rutted track rattled some fillings with that suspension.'

'Aye,' said Max, the knot in his stomach telling him that the visitor wasn't right and didn't belong.

The car soon reappeared, the motion-sensitive function of the camera making it appear almost immediately, but the time stamps showed it was ten minutes. As the car edged out and turned away from the track, Max paused the footage. The driver was clearly visible. He took in the dark side-swept hair, thick-rimmed spectacles and worn, lined face. Max's heart jumped. It was the same man he had seen talking to Tam Hardie at the funeral. Why had he been up to Max's house? It wasn't a comfortable thought.

'Can I get a copy of all this? Screen shots and the like?' asked Max.

'I can do better than that. I'll email you the log-in link.

Doesn't hurt me to have more eyes watching my tractors. Is everything okay?' Ewan said with genuine concern.

'I'm fine, pal, I just like to know who's visiting my house and this bastard upset Nutmeg.'

'Can't have that, right? I'd best get on; this tractor isn't going to fix itself.'

28

Back in the house, Max checked each room and window, studying all the locks for any sign of intrusion. He found nothing. The house was as secure as he had left it earlier that day. So that left two options. It was an attempt to speak to Max, or it was reconnaissance. If it was the second, then it meant they would be back. This was not a covert visit; whoever it was didn't care about being seen by neighbours, and Max was certain that he would have had a cover story, if challenged. If it was a recce, the next visit would be sneakier. Max was both alarmed and excited at the same time. One thing was certain: the visitor clearly knew that Max would not be in, and the bust-up at Gartcosh was public enough for word to have reached him.

This was a worry, but at the same time, it offered an opportunity. Max had loads of experience of surveillance, had covertly followed the worst villains in the UK, so having someone try to follow him, record him or monitor him didn't faze him even a little bit.

Max grabbed his phone and dialled.

'Missing me already?' said Janie.

'More than life itself. Can you do me a favour?'

'You know I can. Didn't we just have this discussion?'

'I'll send you a screen grab of a car and an image of its driver, who was, coincidentally, the guy we saw at Hardie's funeral.' Max told her what had happened.

'Wow, good to have paranoid neighbours, but not so good to have Hardie's man at your place.'

'No. Tell no one. We don't know who's feeding them this shit.'

'Sure, but for goodness' sake, be careful. Maybe move away for a bit?'

'No chance. They don't know what I know, and this gives me opportunities. Can you check on the car, and try and get an ID on the driver? Be as discreet as possible; use any backdoor methods you can to get the checks done. Keep my name well out of it.'

'Yeah, that's no problem. I've a nice way of doing checks that won't flag in the normal way. We used them on a Vice job I led a while back where they suspected a bent cop was involved. Anything else?'

'Not right now, thanks. Call me when you have something. If I don't answer it's because I'm on my motorbike, popping out to the shops for a wee while.'

'Don't do anything stupid,' Janie said, sounding worried.

'Just shopping, I promise. Speak soon.' Max hung up. He swiped and clicked at his screen for a few moments before sending two screen shots of the CCTV footage. One of the vehicle with the registration shown, the other zoomed in on the driver.

Max went to the cupboard and grabbed his motorcycle gear. 'Come on, Nutmeg, let's go and see Tess and Murphy.'

29

Max parked his bike in a multi-storey car park right under the CCTV camera and chained it with the heavy lock to a post. There was no chance he was parking it in the grimy side street next to the security shop.

He pushed the door open and a bell chimed somewhere in the back. A small wiry man wearing a head torch was looking over a pair of half-moon spectacles at Max, whilst simultaneously holding a circuit board. The shop was small and grimy and stank of scorched solder, coffee and cigarettes. The glass-fronted shelves on the walls housed a variety of security and surveillance equipment. Overt and covert CCTV, and wireless alarm systems all jostled for space with a bewildering number of locks, padlocks and security lights. This was an old-school security shop, not slick or flash, but effective and operational, designed for professionals.

'Help you, pal?' the man asked, his voice pure Glasgow.

'I hope so. I'm looking for a bug sweeper?' asked Max.

'I've a few. What type?'

'I'm not sure. What do you have?' Max said with a shrug.

'I have fairly basic ones that will do a job as long as you can isolate all the extraneous RF or GSM transmitters. Basically, it'll detect anything that's emitting a signal, so you'd need to switch off your own Wi-Fi, radio, telly and phones et cetera before you scan. It'll then pick up anything that's transmitting a signal. That do you?'

'That sounds good. How much?'

'Cheap as chips, man. Fifty-four quid for this.' He went to a display case on the counter and took out a blister pack. The unit looked like an old-fashioned walkie-talkie with a short, stubby antennae and a hand-held wand for sweeping.

'Does it detect RF and GSM?'

'Certainly will, whether it's using 2G, 3G or 4G. Cameras, transmitters, whatever. If it's transmitting on RF or GSM it'll detect it. Key is, man, to make sure it's searching in a silent environment. Leave your own phone on and it'll detect that, rather than unwanted signals. You get me?'

'Sure, great. I'll take it. I also want covert surveillance cameras. I want it to use GSM and I need to be able to view it on my phone,' said Max.

'Sure, we have loads, Chief. What are you looking to achieve?'

'I want two doors covered, and I want an interior camera in case any bad guys get in.'

'Best plan is wireless with integrated GSM. This one here can either be initiated by a doorbell press or if the IR beam is tripped. It gives you a full screenshot of whoever's ugly mug has just pressed the doorbell and we can set it to begin recording on up to four linked devices. You can then follow any scrote in your gaff just by the controls in the app on your phone. They all have battery backup in case some nasty bastard cuts the power. A simple battery lasts ages because it only activates if someone presses the bell, and then it only keeps recording if they cross the infrared beam. Gives you full coverage and reasonable night vision.' He held up a shrink-wrapped box, with camera images on it.

'How is it concealed?'

'External cameras are pinheads – so easy to hide. Internals are small as well. You have a wired-in smoke detector in the relevant room?'

'Aye,' said Max.

'Then I'd suggest one of these.' He picked another packet from the shelf. Another blister pack containing what at first glance appeared to be a smoke detector. 'Cameras in these bad boys will link in to the system, and can be panned and tilted remotely, even with your phone controls. A couple of these and you can cover most of your gaff. It's even a smoke detector.' He laughed.

'How do they get to my phone?'

'Via an app. They just all transmit back to the control unit, which has the SIM in and is fired off to your phone. Piece of piss, Chief,' he said, positively buzzing with energy. Here was a man who clearly enjoyed his work.

'Okay, how much for two smoke detectors and the camera kit?'

'Smoke detectors are eighty quid each and the camera kit – with base unit, SIM and external cameras – is two-twenty. Tell you what, bud, four hundred for the lot and I'll throw in the bug finder.'

'Fine. Last thing: do you have any GSM trackers?'

'You setting up a detective agency?' he asked, a big smile on his face.

'Something like that,' replied Max.

'I've a load, mate, but to be honest, you can't do better than this. Trakmaster 900, strong magnetic connector, long battery life and accessed by a simple app on iOS or Android. Gives real-time updates with a map overlay. Only forty quid.'

'Excellent. I'll take the lot.'

'Pleasure doing business with you, Chief.'

Max walked the ten minutes back to his bike, his purchases snug in a backpack. He needed to get his car from the offices at Gartcosh at some point, but for the moment he felt secure on the KTM. Anyone wanting to follow him would have significant difficulties. The thought of being followed tripped something in his subconscious, his mind flashing back to his visitor earlier that day.

On a whim, Max went into the backpack and pulled out the bug sweeper. He ripped the packaging off and snapped the two AA batteries into the slot, clicking the cover back into place. He switched the unit on, watching the lights dance as it powered up. Max pulled out his phone and switched it to flight-safe mode. He didn't need a false activation. He uncoiled the magnetic field probe, turning the instrument over in his hands. He adjusted the sensitivity down until the lights settled. He then pressed the scan switch and began to sweep the probe across the frame of the bike. The lights danced as it hit upon the alarm unit but settled as soon as he moved away. Nothing there. He then passed it along the seat pad. Nothing. He swept down to the engine compartment, moving the probe across to the skid-plate, a rugged piece of metal designed to guard the engine from debris when it was ridden off-road. The lights danced wildly.

Max sat back on his heels, a wry smile spreading across his face. No doubt now as to the intentions of his earlier visitor at the cottage. They were worried about him and were clearly threatened by him to the extent that they had put a tracker on his motorbike, probably on the basis that they wouldn't be able to follow him effectively. That felt like a cop's trick, but it also felt lazy and risky. No decent cop deploying a tracking kit would brazenly drive up to the house to plant it. Not a chance.

Max pulled out his phone and switched the torch function on, shining it behind the skid-plate. He could clearly see the small rugged plastic tracker, the dull shine of the magnet connectors visible. Max managed to slide his fingers in and pull the unit towards him until he felt the magnets give way.

He turned it over in his fingers, looking at the simple design: black plastic and firm magnets. It was not too dissimilar from the one he had purchased, just a little more expensive. One thing was for sure, with the brand name 'Winnes' embossed on the plastic, it was not police-issue. Max had deployed trackers on vehicles on many occasions, and they had never looked like this. This thing was a commercial, off-the-shelf piece of kit probably intended for use to help recovery of stolen cars and bikes.

He was about to smash the tracker to pieces when he had a second thought. He knew about the device, but they didn't know he knew. That offered tactical possibilities that may become useful. He was glad that his desire for his precious motorbike not to be stolen had meant he had parked it in a secure car park rather than outside the shop.

Max slotted the tracker back onto the reverse of the skid-plate, feeling it snap as the magnets clicked into place.

Max stood and tucked the scanner into his bag, unlocked the bike and climbed on. The time was coming for Max to turn the tables and go on the offensive. He fired the powerful thirteen hundred cc engine, and rode off feeling strangely uplifted, despite being on questionable sick leave and riding a motorbike that was being tracked. He felt like something was about to change.

*

Arriving back home, Max was reassured to see Nutmeg waiting for him at the bottom of the track, her tail gyrating with glee as Max turned onto the rutted surface. She raced up to him and made a huge fuss when he dismounted the machine.

Max locked the KTM back in the garage and went inside the house, his mind returning to the advice of the man in the security shop. He turned his phone off and flicked the switch, killing all the electrics in the house. He figured this was the best way of isolating any extraneous magnetic fields or any other electrical signal, whether RF, Wi-Fi or GSM. Pulling out his new scanner, he swept the entire house, making sure he covered all likely hiding places for bugs or cameras. Returning to the garage, he passed the wand over the skid-plate on the KTM, the blinking lights reassuring him that the scanner was still working.

Once satisfied he returned to the house and reconnected his home to the electrical grid.

Max smiled to himself. There was some serious badness going on out there at the moment, but his house would be secure. Any visitors coming, and he'd know about it.

Resolve gripped him. He may be on sick leave, but he wasn't stopping. He wasn't going to stop until he'd brought the whole bloody lot of them down.

30

Jack Slattery stood outside the Saracen Head smoking a cigarette and waiting nervously for the call he had been told to expect. The pub had been busy, as one would expect on a warm Friday evening and the place was bouncing with revellers ready for a big weekend. It was the first weekend of the football season and Celtic were home the next day.

He had gone for a little livener in the historic old pub just over the road from the Barrowland Ballroom before meeting Tam Hardie. A couple of pints, each with a chaser, was just what he needed. He had barely listened to the old pisshead at the bar proudly tell him some of the history including that of the old witch's skull in a glass case over the bar. He knew it already. Slattery knew all about the Glasgow pubs, big drinker as he was. It was his fondness for a beer or a dram that had landed him in trouble, and eventually got him slung from the police. In with the wrong crowd, or as it was now, the right crowd. The Hardie family paid him well for his information, and he was keen that this would continue now that the old man had passed on.

On the surface, Slattery was a private investigator and ex-cop, but in reality, he only worked for the Hardies. He offered a service that they needed, being the ability to get inside information on current investigations from his small stable of tame cops who were always happy to exchange for a few beers, a night with one of Hardie's hookers, or a few quid. Slattery could be really persuasive, and his skill was the ability to exert pressure on those who had allowed themselves to be corrupted. He was still nervous, though. The late Hardie Senior was a scary bastard, but Tam Junior was even more imposing, as Turkish Joe had recently found out.

Slattery's phone buzzed in his pocket. He looked at the message on his screen. *1 min.* Davie Hardie didn't waste words.

Slattery threw his fag on the wet pavement and ground it with his shoe. He pushed his glasses back up his nose, which was slick with a light sheen of nervous sweat.

A large Mercedes pulled up alongside the kerb, and the intimidating form of Davie Hardie jumped out of the passenger seat. Opening the rear door, he nodded at Slattery, and simply said, 'In.'

'Jack, how you doing?' Tam Hardie sat on the plush white leather in the back of the big car, dressed casually but immaculately in designer jeans, polished loafers and an expensive-looking leather jacket over a tailored shirt.

'I'm good, Tam.' He offered his hand, which was studiously ignored as the Mercedes moved off.

'What do you know, Jack?'

'About?' Slattery asked, his voice nervous.

'What do you think, man? The investigation. What do the teams know, where are we? I know my old man would pay you a retainer every month, but I need some good reasons for paying you any more of my kids' inheritance.' His voice was low and even, the menace unmistakable. Tam Hardie was overpoweringly intimidating, if anything, worse than his father. His eyes were locked on Slattery's, and they were flat and emotionless in the sodium street lights as the big car glided along the grey street.

'All going smoothly,' Slattery said. 'The SIO Sally Smith has been told to wrap it up quickly and move on to the next one, as you wanted.'

'That's something. We wouldn't have got justice from the police on this one, no bloody way. I want them to forget all about it, so we're free to finish it as I see fit. How about Leitch's unfortunate passing?'

'Again, not being linked to you. Big Graham Connolly is a damned lunatic anyway, always causing problems in Carstairs. He was delighted to make a few quid for his family on the outside, and he was never getting out anyway, so no worries there.' Slattery was relieved that he had managed to find someone with a contact among the staff there. A simple word in the right ear, and all they had to do was point big, crazy Graham in Leitch's direction.

'Glad to hear it. The bastard can burn in hell, as far as I'm concerned,' growled Hardie, hate shining in his eyes. 'I read about the car crash that took out Ferguson. That was good work. I won't ask how you managed it, but will there be any problems with the follow-up investigation?' Hardie's show of approval amounted to a small nod of his head.

'I don't think so, although Max Craigie nearly screwed that up by getting a bit crusader cop on us. He's trying to convince all and sundry that the crash and the deaths are linked. We thought we'd managed to keep it from Sally Smith that Leitch and Ferguson were cousins because it was one of my people who went to see them and failed to report it back. Unfortunately, that interfering bastard, Craigie, went all rogue. I have enough influence to keep him out of the way, and I'm making arrangements about some of the physical evidence. They may find one or two key pieces going missing, if you get my drift.' Slattery chuckled, nervously.

'Good, you're earning your money. Now how about the remaining family members?'

'You still set on that? Leitch and his cousin are out of the game, now, and they were the only two involved in the death of your pa.'

'Those bastards started this. They started it in 1830, so we're going to finish it. Any blood relatives I want to know about, and fast. I want the word out that we're still running things and are not to be messed about. Any suggestion that we're weakening and every bastard will be thinking they can have a pop at us.' Hardie's face was set firm and unmoving.

'He has an ex-wife but no kids we know of, as yet. He has no surviving parents and only one sister. I'm not sure where she lives, probably married with a different surname, but I'll find her.'

'Do it and have her watched, establish a routine. You know the drill. How about Duncan Ferguson's family?'

'He has a Yank wife who's still at the inn in Dunbeath. No kids.'

'Only blood relatives. No innocents. I want this to get out, and I want folk to know that we just go after blood. Fuck with my family and I destroy your whole bloodline. That's the Hardie way, from now. That Leitch bastard started it with his blood feud. Does Ferguson have siblings?'

'A brother.'

'Where?'

'Spain, apparently. I have people over there looking for him, but he's proving hard to find, for some reason.'

'What's his name?'

'Bruce Ferguson. As I say, he's an ex-pat in Spain, probably sunning himself in the Costas.'

'How about the funerals?'

'Well, fiscal has released Ferguson's body, and the funeral is very soon. Leitch's body won't be released for a while, yet, whilst they decide what to do with Mad Graham.'

'Will Bruce Ferguson be at the funeral?'

'He's been told about it. You want us to move on him then?' Slattery asked.

'Let me think about that.'

'No bother. We'll get a look at him, at least.'

Hardie nodded, gravely. 'Get back to me as soon as you hear. I'm going after them, but not just yet. Things need to calm down and the police need to move on to other things. Maybe have them watched for a while, sort out the routines.'

'Well, you achieved that with Turkish Joe. That's decimated their strength on your pa's murder team, so that was an unexpected benefit,' Slattery said.

'Not unexpected at all.' Hardie surprised Slattery by showing his teeth in a wolfish smile. 'Anything you perceive as a risk?'

'Just Craigie, really, but they've forced him off the team and onto sick leave, pending occupational health assessment. Keeps him well out of the way, although I'm not sure he's the type. Told the DCS to fuck off, so I heard,' said Slattery.

'Well watch Craigie carefully. Last thing we need is a rogue cop on our backs. Make sure you've something on the bastard.'

'Already on it. I went to his place earlier to check it out. I've put a tracker on his bike; apparently he goes everywhere on it.'

'Good work, man. How did you manage that?'

'Just playing the double-glazing salesman ready with brochures in case anyone was about. Had to give his little twat of a dog a good kick up the arse, though. The bastard wouldn't leave me alone.'

Hardie paused a moment, as if assessing his options. 'Find out about his family though. Just the info, no move yet. I'd like some leverage to keep the bastard at bay, okay?'

'Sure, but if he starts getting too close?'

'You know the answer to that question,' said Hardie in a flat voice.

31

Janie walked into the open-plan office at Gartcosh, her eyes down, not wanting to draw any attention from her colleagues, knowing that the gossiping and rumours would be flying about Max, and, most probably her. Rumours flew around police teams like wildfire at an almost digital pace. Janie often thought that high-speed computers could barely match it, and a confrontation between a DCS and a DS during which one told the other to 'fuck himself' would be halfway around the force, by now. She wanted no part of it.

'Look out, boys, here comes Fast-Track Fannie. How's the mental patient? Did he kill anyone on the way back?' the bawdy, strongly accented voice of Danny, one of the senior DCs on the team rang out across the office, to be accompanied by some chuckling and guffaws from the other officers, all sitting in front of their computer terminals. Danny was middle-aged, with short, wiry grey hair and was seriously overweight, his stomach so vast that his chinos could barely contain it, and she feared that if his trouser button popped, it would take someone's eye out.

'Very funny, Danny. Max is fine, just in case you were wondering,' said Janie, shaking her head as she sat at her

171

desk which, unfortunately, was directly opposite and attached to his, leaving barely three feet separating them.

'Aye well, just saying, Fan, bloke's a bloody liability, shooting people in London, then coming up here to go bloody doolally, eh?' A big grin stretched over his face that Janie would have described as 'punchable'.

'Whatever, Danny. I've work to do, you know. You may want to try it,' she said without looking at the man's stupid, fat face.

'Calm down, Princess, just because you're destined for greatness doesn't mean you can get all snooty with me. I've socks older than you, sweet-cheeks.' Danny swigged from a large bottle of Irn-Bru, and belched with relish.

'Maybe change them sometimes then, Dan, if you can reach your feet,' blurted out Janie, her cheeks glowing hot with anger and embarrassment.

There were guffaws around the office at Janie's barbed comments.

'Touché, Danny, one nil to Fannie,' came a voice from across the room.

'Cheeky bloody mare, no bloody respect. Too much time hanging with Loopy Max. You need to work with a real man,' said Danny, his face a shade of purple.

'Aye right, if you find one, let me know, yeah?' said Janie, standing up, and shaking her head, her stomach tight, her face red.

'Oh, pal, you're getting fair roasted here. She's brutal today,' came a voice from behind Danny.

Danny span around to the source. 'Shut your geggie, man, this daft bint—'

Quick as a flash, whilst his head was turned, Janie reached forward and flicked the top of the Irn-Bru bottle, sending it toppling into the big man's lap, depositing half a litre of bright orange, sticky liquid over him.

'Whoops,' said Janie, walking away as Danny leaped to his

feet, cursing. The office exploded into raucous hysterics as Danny batted at his crutch trying to brush the iridescent orange liquid away.

A new voice bellowed across the office, 'Will you bunch of apes shut up? Some of us are trying to bloody work in here. Janie, my office,' boomed Ross.

Janie's stomach lurched as she walked into Ross's glass cubicle in the centre of the open-plan space, expecting a major bollocking, but his face was split with a broad grin when she entered.

'I saw all of that. Good work, Danny is a bloody oaf, and he asked for it.' Ross chuckled.

'Accident,' said Janie, shrugging.

'Aye, right, anyway, never mind. He'll whinge, but he'll get over it. You okay?'

'Aye, I'm fine.'

'Do those buggers get you down?'

'No.'

'Sure?'

'I'm a big girl, Boss. I don't need to be babysat.'

'I can see that. Anyway, Max okay?'

'He's pissed off, but he's fine.'

'What do you think about it?'

'What?'

'You know what I mean.'

Janie sighed. 'I think that some folk aren't willing to see what's in front of them, but it's not my place to query that,' said Janie, her face impassive.

'Nail on the head. Not our place. We have new work to do on a trafficking job that's going to be busy when it gets going. I want you to review all the surveillance product we have. I'll have it sent to your laptop. You can do it from home, if you'd like to get out of the office, but it needs doing, okay?'

Janie looked through the glass wall, at the still-muttering

Danny who was now wiping at his stained chinos with a paper towel and glowering at her, his face florid and flushed with anger. 'Aye, I'll do that, then.'

'Excellent, cut along,' said Ross, turning his attention to his screen.

Janie stood as if to leave.

'Janie?'

'Yes?'

'Keep an eye on Max. He's a good guy and he may need a pal who isn't his boss, yeah?'

'Okay.' Janie left the office, went to her desk without looking at Danny who was still chuntering and giving her daggers, picked up her bag and left the office.

She went up to the first floor to an empty room where she found a terminal and logged on. She used an unconventional route into the PNC to check out the registration of the Mercedes that had been at Max's place, noting the details on a scrap of paper. She then ran the results through an open-source database, and up popped an image of the driver. Familiarity nipped at her as she looked at the photograph. The thick glasses, swept hair, and lean yet lined face was just very familiar. More so than that, she was sure that she'd met him.

Janie's phone buzzed on the table in front of her. It was a message from a friend of hers who was on the MIT and it contained a name and an address in Perth. Janie nodded in satisfaction. She needed to get this information to Max, but she urgently needed to bottom out who the mystery man in the Mercedes was. It was going to take some work to get all the information, but she knew where to begin. She went into her bag and pulled out a bottle of water and an apple which she bit into. This was a break; in fact, this was a big break. She took a swig from the water bottle and attacked the keyboard.

*

Janie sat back staring unbelievingly at the screen in front of her. She couldn't believe what her research had revealed. This was it. She picked up her phone and dialled. It went to voicemail.

'Damn.' She flicked through the files and images from that brothel raid a few years ago. It was definitely him. She dialled again.

'Janie?' said Max.

'You okay?'

'Yeah, I'm good. Just had my phone off, briefly.'

'Cool. I've checked the car out. Merc AMG A-Class, registered to JTS Security Consultants at a PO Box address. No reports on it, and from what I can see, no checks and nothing on intelligence systems. It's clean, unlike the owner.'

'I'm listening.'

'I did some digging and JTS Security Consultants are registered with the Security Industry Authority and the only member is one Jack Slattery. He's also the only director on Companies House databases. No website or social media presence.'

'I know you're saving the best till last, so stop teasing and hit me with it.'

'Jack Slattery is an ex-cop. He was a DS in Police Scotland, a legacy Strathclyde officer, who found himself in some shit over missing payments to informants. One of his people alleged that Slattery had top-sliced part of his reward money after information he had given led to the recovery of a serious amount of drugs. He was ready to make a full complaint, but then, somehow, changed his mind, just as the procurator fiscal was about to charge Slattery with corrupt practice. Want to know something else?' said Janie, her voice suddenly serious.

'Yes, but your tone suggests that I may not like it.'

'The informant wound up in Glasgow Royal Infirmary with two broken legs, and a large flap of skin removed from each of his arse cheeks. Also, it seemed he had developed memory problems, because he claimed he had made the whole Slattery business up and the PF withdrew the charges.'

'Shit.'

'PIRC weren't happy, so went after Slattery for failing to adhere to informant handling guidelines, but he threw his cards in before he went to a hearing. I guess he could see the writing on the wall.'

'Is that everything?'

'Nope.'

'What, there's more?'

'There is. I thought I recognised him, and it turned out that I have met him before.'

'Christ, when?'

'When I was on Vice. We raided a lap dancing club that was a front for a full-on brothel. The whole upstairs was a knocking shop where the girls took the clients who weren't satisfied with a bit of naked jiggling and wanted a happy ending. One of the working girls was an informant of mine and tipped us off about it. Slattery, although he didn't use that name, was in one of the upstairs rooms being entertained by my informant. We closed the place down and prosecuted the owner, but let the punters go. Fortunately, we got photographs of all of them and the working girls first. I found one of Slattery, who was calling himself George Smith.'

'Well, that's a helpful coincidence. The dirty bastard, eh?'

'A sleazy bugger – that much I do recall.'

'Well, there's our conduit, then. He's obviously working for Hardie, now.'

'It would seem so, and the intel was that the brothel was a Hardie-owned business, although we never got to the bottom of that. Why was he at your house?'

'The bastard put a lump on my bike.'

'Bloody hell. What are you going to do about it?'

'For now, I'm leaving it where it is. He doesn't know I know it's there, and that gives me the upper hand. I can play dirty, as well. The problem with technical surveillance kit comes with over-reliance. It's useful but it'll never replace the mark-one human eyeball. Slattery will be relying on it, so that presents opportunities.'

'If you say so. I wouldn't be happy.'

'I'm not overjoyed by it, but it's better I use it to our advantage. We now have a place to start with tracking down our dirty cops.'

'I guess so. You sure you don't want to call this in? Maybe get Professional Standards to look at it?'

'If I'm honest, apart from you and maybe Ross, I have no idea who else I can trust. The Hardies have their claws in at a high enough level to get me out of the way, and until I know more, I'm keeping this to just us.'

Janie let out a big rush of breath. 'This wasn't what I was expecting. It's dangerous stuff.'

'It is what it is. Anything on the families of Leitch and Ferguson?'

'Sister has been traced, literally in the last few minutes by the MIT. I managed to find out from a pal on the team. Her name is Elizabeth Phillips, now. Lives in Perth, a divorced social worker, no kids. No contact with Willie Leitch for a number of years.'

'Has she been warned?'

'I don't know, but I doubt it, bearing in mind the attitude of management. I only discovered it a wee while ago. Seems Elizabeth fell out with her brother a long time ago. She blames him for their parents' untimely deaths and says that it was only a matter of time until he either died or killed someone. She didn't expect them to both happen so close to each other, was the comment I heard. Apparently, she won't be coming to any funerals.'

Max paused a moment. 'We have to tell her. We have to

warn her and maybe get her out of the way. If the MIT know where she is, so do the Hardies. Can you get her address?'

'I can, but what if she refuses to go anywhere? We can't force her and we'd be doing this off-books.'

'I'll take that risk. I'm not willing to let any innocents get hurt, without at least trying. Get me the address, and I'll go and visit her. Maybe I can persuade her to move out for a wee while, just whilst we sort this out.'

'I'll get the address, but I'm coming with you. Seeing a weirdo like you pitch up may freak her out.'

'Charming. Can you do this soon?'

'How about first thing tomorrow morning? Ross is giving me carte blanche to be out of the office. There is sod all happening at the moment, despite the apparent urgency of the trafficking job.'

'Great, see you here before work, okay?'

'No bother – about six-thirty.'

'How about Duncan's brother?'

'MIT can't find him anywhere. Mary knows he lives in Spain but only has an email address for him. She's emailed him about the funeral, which is the day after tomorrow up in Caithness. She had a one-line acknowledgement, that's all. Seems a bit of a mystery.'

'Well, if the MIT FLO can't find him, I imagine the Hardies are unable to, either. Okay, I'll see you in the morning.' Max hung up.

Janie sat back in her chair, satisfied and determined. She wondered about Ross's words to her earlier about getting out of the office. Was he keeping her away, or was she being given an opportunity? Whose side was Ross on?

Her mind whirled with it all, but she decided that she was going to trust her gut.

32

A cold, wet nose began to nuzzle Max's hand. Nutmeg stared up at him intently, with that look he knew well.

'Come on then, dinnertime.' Max mixed up Nutmeg's kibble with a little wet food and placed it down. The dog dived in, enthusiastically.

Max yawned deeply, then realised that the strange gnawing feeling in his stomach wasn't the stress of the previous events. It was hunger.

He stretched his arms high above his head, trying to ease the tension from his muscles. As he turned towards the fireplace, his eyes fell on the photograph of Katie. It was a picture of her in the snow in France on a ski holiday they had taken a few years ago. Her mouth was open in a big smile, her eyes sparkling and her hair dishevelled. She looked happy and beautiful. A wave of sadness and longing swept over him again. He shook his head, trying to exorcise the feelings from his mind. Not now, he was too busy and there was too much at stake.

He opened the old larder cupboard, finding very little of interest other than a tin of baked beans. Some slightly suspect-looking bread was at the bottom of the bread bin. Max sighed. He popped the bread in the toaster and tipped the beans in a saucepan. Two minutes later he was tucking into beans on toast with a pile of mature cheddar on top, beginning to ooze nicely as it melted. Food of the gods, thought Max as he ate, washing it down with a glass of chilled cranberry juice from the fridge. He really did like the taste of the juice, but a small part of him yearned for a long, cold beer. He could picture the glass, full to the brim with the amber liquid, the bubbles lazily circling to a foamy head. He could almost imagine the condensation chilling his fingers as he lifted the drink to his mouth, then the soothing, cold liquid sliding down his throat.

He missed beer a lot, but one always led to another, then another, which always led to the darkness and inevitably the dreams. He wanted Katie back in his life, and that was never going to happen if he was drinking again.

His phone buzzed, dragging his thoughts away from alcohol, the number showing 'withheld'.

'Hello?' Max said, suspicion in his voice.

'Max, it's Sally Smith. You okay to speak?'

'Aye, crack on.'

'There was nothing on that jack from Ferguson's car,' she said without preamble.

'What?' Max said, astounded.

'Well, a little bit of oily muck on the bottom, and a touch of chalk dust on the top. Nothing that would suggest it had been to Ballachly. CSI have taken samples, but no way it's come from the cemetery. Sorry.'

Max sighed and massaged his temples. Someone had got to it at Wick; there was no other explanation.

'That's not possible. It was clearly peaty soil, and I'm certain that it was granite dust. Who collected it?' Max said.

'I'm only telling you this out of courtesy. It looks like you were mistaken, but it was still a good shout. We're continuing with the theory that Leitch was alone. We have to work with the evidence, and that's what the evidence is showing us. Now you're on sick leave, maybe just leave this thing alone, now, right?'

Max opened his mouth to argue, but then realised it was probably pointless. His thoughts turned to the photograph of the scissor jack on his phone. It wouldn't be conclusive proof, but it would be something. He decided not to mention it, in case Sally told her bosses and it got back to the Hardies. For now, he needed to stay off the radar.

'Aye, maybe. I'll be off now, just eating.'

'Look after yourself. Don't let the job take over your life.' Sally's voice was kind, and Max believed she meant it.

'Thanks.' Max hung up.

He put his plate down, suddenly not hungry anymore. He stood, walked to the sideboard where a solitary bottle of whisky sat. It was a good bottle. An old Macallan single malt that Ewan had given him as a thank you for a whole day he had spent cutting logs with him. He uncorked it and poured a large measure into a heavy tumbler. He raised the glass and inhaled the deep, smoky, peaty aroma, causing a visceral rush of memories. He paused a second, staring wistfully at the amber liquid and his hand trembled, almost imperceptibly. An anaesthetic maybe. One wouldn't hurt after the few days he had experienced, surely? It was totally forgivable and Katie would understand. He closed his eyes, and inhaled deeply again, his lips touching the glass.

Nutmeg's cold nose nudged his trailing hand and made him jump spilling a little of the liquid onto his hand. She stared at him intently, and Max felt sure that her adoring gaze had an edge of disapproval.

'Jesus, Nutty, what are you, my mother?' he said, caressing the little dog's ear.

'You're right, girl, not now.' Max set the glass back down on the sideboard and picked up his cranberry juice, drinking the rest of it in one.

33

Elizabeth Phillips's house was in a tidy residential street in Craigie, a well-kept and pleasant-looking area west of Perth. The houses were semi-detached and looked to be circa 1930s in style. All the front gardens had been turned into driveways, on which sat predominantly upmarket cars.

'Shall I make some obvious references about how you ought to live in Craigie, DS Craigie?' Janie asked as she drove down the road.

'Can you imagine the post office confusion? Nice area though, looks like Elizabeth Phillips did okay for herself,' said Max with a yawn. He was still dog-tired, having once again woken up just before 4 a.m. with the dream.

'Aye. Nice cars as well. Here's her place coming up on the right, Mondeo on the drive,' said Janie.

Max said nothing. His eyes were fixed on an Audi that was parked on the nearside of the street ahead of them, exhaust fumes billowing from the rear.

'Drive past, Janie.'

'Why?'

'I don't like the look of that Audi. Dark windows, engine on, shitty spoiler. Looks like a wanker's car, and it doesn't fit the street,' said Max, the tension in his voice becoming more obvious. 'Carry on past, and don't look at them.'

'Max?' said Janie, questioningly.

'Just drive past, nice and steady, and pull up onto the drive there, about five doors along, opposite Elizabeth's house.' Max pointed at a well-kept house with an empty drive that was big enough for several cars.

As they passed the Audi on their nearside, Max flipped down the sunshade and looked in the vanity mirror. Two men sat in the car, both youngish-looking with short hair and a nasty, tough look about them. One thing was for sure, they weren't cops. They had no awareness of their surroundings, only had eyes for one thing. Elizabeth Phillips's bright red front door.

'Max, are you sure? The occupiers may not want us on their drive.'

'I'm betting they're away. No cars on the drive, all windows shut tight despite the weather, curtains open, no lights and the lawn needs cutting. I want to keep an eye on the Audi for a minute before we knock. There's something about them. They look like a couple of scumbags.'

'Skills, Sarge,' Janie said admiringly as she pulled onto the drive.

'Kill the engine.' Max pressed the switch and the window wound down. He adjusted the side mirror until he had a good view of the Audi, its engine still belching diesel fumes. Max looked the vehicle over and noted low-profile tyres and after-market skirts. It definitely didn't fit this tidy, suburban street. Max checked his watch. Eight a.m. 'Can you keep a watch on Elizabeth's front door? I'll watch the Audi. Do you have any safety kit with you?'

'Unfortunately not,' said Janie.

'No bother. Eyes on, yeah?'

'You sure about this?' said Janie.

'Just a feeling. You have a radio with you?'

'No, it's back at the office along with my baton, cuffs and PAVA spray.'

'Never mind, keep watching.'

They sat there for a few moments in total silence, locked onto their respective targets.

'Stand by,' Janie said. 'Premises door opening, female leaving, now turning to lock the door.' Max quickly glanced and saw a slim, grey-haired woman at the red door.

'Now, Audi door opening,' Max said. 'Two men getting out, shit, both wearing knuckle-dusters. They're going to bloody beat her to death. Move, it's on now. They're going to take her out,' Max shouted, his door already opening. He leaped from the car, sprinting across the road.

Elizabeth Phillips's face turned from confusion to shock and then to terror, as realisation began to dawn on her.

Max ran to intercept the two thugs, one much bigger than the other, who were halfway across the tarmac, just twenty yards from Elizabeth Phillips. They both remained fixated on the woman frozen on her path. Max's mind was in overdrive now, knowing that one blow with a knuckle-duster could easily be fatal. He moved fast and soon closed the distance, hearing the reassuring sound of Janie's trainers on the tarmac behind him.

The two attackers, just ahead of Max, reached the pavement in front of Elizabeth's house. The larger of the two suddenly heard Max's footsteps and began to turn, almost in slow motion. Max didn't give the big, shaven-headed monster a moment to react, but swung out viciously with his foot, kicking hard into the back of the man's knee joint. He grunted and collapsed, hitting the ground with a thump. But he rolled quickly and almost bounced straight back up to his feet, facing Max, brass-covered knuckles held up in a fighting stance. His eyes were small and piggy, his face full of hate and aggression. 'You're gonna pay for that, you bastard,' he growled in a thick accent.

His friend, a much smaller man with the same shaven head and lean physique, spun to face Max from his position, a few feet in front of the bigger man. He raised his fists in front of him, both knuckles glinting with the metallic shine of brass. The look on his face was a mix of hatred and fear.

'Come on then, you bastard,' the smaller man snarled. His stance and guard were solid, so he clearly knew how to box.

Max looked briefly at Elizabeth Phillips, who was frozen, her mouth open, and her eyes wide with shock. 'Liz, get inside the house now,' shouted Max, immediately turning his attention back to the attackers.

'Not turned out like you thought, eh boys?' Max said, his voice calm, a half-smile on his face. 'Thought you could just come and beat this poor lady to death, right? No chance, boys, not gonna happen,' said Max, his own fists raised, ready. He felt a strange calm descend on him. He'd been fighting all his life, knew what to do, wasn't scared. There were two of them, both fixated on Max, both having clearly discounted the threat posed by the slim, almost slight form of Janie.

That was a mistake, as the smaller man discovered, when Janie appeared from out of his sight line and delivered a powerful and accurate Muay Thai shin-kick straight into his thigh, smashing into the peroneal nerve on the outside of the muscle. He yelped in pain, and his leg buckled as he stumbled around to face Janie, his brass-knuckled hand moving to the source of the pain.

'Ouch, that's gotta hurt,' said Max.

Janie's face was set in grim satisfaction, her hands up in a fighting stance, her weight distributed on the balls of her feet, ready for what came next.

The bigger man flew at Max, throwing a telegraphed haymaker punch, which Max easily dodged, feeling the wind of the huge fist whistle past his ear. Max stepped to one side and delivered a vicious punch into the big man's ribs. He yelped and doubled over, rocking backwards at the force of the blow.

Max glanced over at Janie, just as she spun and executed an almost textbook reverse kick that smashed into the small man's midriff, sending him backwards, his face suddenly registering that things weren't going as expected.

'You need any help, Max?' she said as she took her stance again, her eyes not moving from her opponent.

'No, I'm fine,' said Max, just as the huge man rushed at him, driving his shoulder into Max's midriff, the air rushing out of him. Max let himself fall to the pavement and wrapped his arm around the man's massive neck, gripping tight. A huge fist shot out blindly, the brass knuckle catching Max a glancing blow on the side of the head. The pain was sudden and sharp. Max realised that if the big brute caught him properly with one of those flailing fists, then it was game over.

As another punch flashed towards him, he tightened his grip on the man's neck, and tucked his head down, feeling the blow collide into his shoulder, but with no real force. He shifted his body and managed to snag the massive arm in between his legs and wrapped it tight in a classic joint lock. He tightened his grip on the man's neck, but it was like fighting a raging bull, Max only just managing to cling on to him, realising that he needed to end this now. He squeezed his legs tight, feeling the arm begin to hyper-extend in a way it wasn't supposed to. The big man screamed in pain as Max extended it further, the tendons and bones straining. His opponent flexed his enormous bicep, with a roar of fury, and Max's leg grip began to fail. Max clung on, fear beginning to bite. If he got free, then Max was in trouble.

He risked a glance at Janie, who at that exact moment was delivering a whip-crack of a roundhouse kick, that connected with the side of the smaller man's head, rocking it sideways.

Max breathed hard with the exertion of trying to restrain the still-bucking and thrashing man. He looked again at Janie, who finished off her opponent with a devastating front kick to the groin. He collapsed on the pavement, and without a backwards glance, Janie ran straight to Max. She paused, waited for the right moment, then her right foot whipped out, catching the big man in the side, right in his kidney. He let out a muffled yelp of pain, and his arm relaxed.

Max jerked his legs, and the big man's arm gave way with a horrible crunch of bone and sinew. There was a scream of agony as the joint failed.

Game over.

Suddenly a dark van screeched to a halt on the road beside them. The driver jumped out, clutching an automatic pistol, pointed directly at Max. The passenger dived out and jogged towards the Audi.

The van driver spoke. 'Let him go now,' he barked. Max released the whimpering man and got to his feet. The big man rolled over, clutching his ruined elbow, moaning in agony.

Max watched as the other man dived into the Audi, gunned the engine and drove off. The newcomer looked at Janie and said, 'One move from you, bitch, and I'll shoot both of you. Get up, you two bloody clowns, and get in the van.' His voice was calm and in control. The two meathead attackers staggered to their feet and did as they were told, the one Janie had kicked barely able to walk.

Max looked the newcomer directly in the eye, and amazed himself by smiling at him, his heart still racing. He was smaller in build than the others, and not as physically imposing, but his eyes were blue and cold.

'We are both police officers, shit-for-brains. What you gonna do, shoot cops in the street? Tam will go doolally, pal. You should've sent someone more competent than these morons. Steroids have made them stupid.' Max smiled again, his voice calm and even.

'Shut up, or I'll put a bullet in you both,' he snarled.

'See, I don't think you will, pal. Tam Hardie has paid you and your dull mates to take out this innocent lady, not shoot cops on the street. That will cause a shitstorm that he doesn't want. The whole world will be looking for you, and Tam will be furious. But you know this, which is why you haven't shot us, yet.' Max let out a snort of laughter.

'You're a dead man,' he growled, whilst backing into the van and closing the door, the engine still running. 'I'll see you again, pal.' The van sped off in the same direction as the Audi. The whole incident had taken just over a minute. The street remained quiet.

Max looked behind him, to see Janie, her arms around Elizabeth Phillips who was sobbing into her shoulder. Janie caught Max's eye, disbelief on her face as he walked up to the pair, rubbing the lump that was forming on the back of his head.

'Hi, Elizabeth, I'm DS Max Craigie, and this is DC Janie Calder. We're both cops. You're safe now.' Max showed his warrant card and she looked at it, confused.

She seemed stunned, her face white as a sheet and her eyes wide. 'What just happened?' She was small and petite and you could see the similarity between her and her late brother.

'You okay, Liz?' A voice came from the attached house next door. A stocky man in a dressing gown stood on the drive.

Max and Janie both held up their warrant cards.

'Police, sir, all in hand,' Max said.

'Liz?' the man repeated.

'I'm okay now, police are here.' She managed a wan smile, but her voice was still shaky.

Reassured, the man nodded and returned indoors. But almost immediately he appeared at the window, cup in hand, to watch the unfolding drama.

'Unfortunately, those guys wanted to hurt you, but you're safe for the moment,' Max said to Elizabeth.

The words seemed to hit her like a hammer blow. 'Me? Why me? What did I do?'

'Let's go inside. We need to be quick. You're not safe here, these people could come back.'

As they walked towards the house, Max looked at Janie, his mind whirling at what had just happened. He said nothing, but simply nodded and she gave a half-smile in return. She had pulled his arse out of the fire, of that there was no doubt.

34

Max, Janie and Elizabeth sat in the comfortable lounge, clutching mugs of tea. The walls were all covered with water-colours, either Highland scenes, or softer coastal vistas.

Elizabeth was a small woman, her grey hair neatly cut and styled. She was smartly dressed and wore little jewellery. She was clearly terrified.

'So, who the hell were they, and why were they after me?' Elizabeth said, her accent still bearing the trace of Caithness.

'I think it's to do with Willie. The man he killed was a serious criminal who's now seeking retribution, ridiculous as that sounds,' Max said.

'That can't be possible, I haven't seen Willie for at least ten years.' She opened her mouth to speak again, but paused, and looked at the window, her bottom lip trembling and tears brimming in her eyes. She got to her feet. 'Excuse me a moment,' she said, and left the room.

'Think she's okay?' said Janie.

'She's shocked. Bound to be, right?'

'What do we do?'

'Just give her a minute.'

Two minutes later, Elizabeth came back into the room, her face pink and damp. She sat down, composed herself, and took a deep breath. 'Willie and I had a really troubled relationship,' she said at last. 'He was fine for the few years he was in the Navy, but then he got discharged and started smoking drugs that led to his illness. Why would they come after me?' Her eyes brimmed with tears that spilled onto her cheeks. Max could see this was not something she ever envisaged intruding on her comfortable life.

'Is it just you here?' asked Max.

'Yes. I split from my husband five years ago.'

'No kids?'

'No.'

'Look. I know this is hard to understand, but we have reason to believe that you are at risk. We just need to make sure you stay safe. Is there anywhere else you can go whilst we're sorting this out?' asked Max, gently. They needed her somewhere untraceable, but Max wasn't convinced that witness protection would make her safe.

'I've a good friend in Suffolk. She lives in Southwold in the countryside. I often take holidays with her. I was going to go fairly soon anyway, so I could just bring it forward a week.' She dabbed at her eyes with a tissue.

'Who knows that you go there?' asked Janie.

'Not many folk. She was an old friend from my art class a few years ago. We kept in touch after she moved and I stay with her most years. We just paint together – the light is so lovely down there.'

'Are you connected on social media?'

'I don't do social media at all. I don't like it, so no.'

'Do folk at work know where you go?'

'Not really, I tend to keep myself to myself, especially since getting divorced. I like my own company, you see. I don't socialise with people at work much. They probably think I'm just a sad and bitter divorcee.'

'Can you go to your friend's place, Liz? Just until we sort this out?'

'I imagine so. She's always badgering me to come more. It would be nice to see her and I don't want to stay here on my own.'

'Okay, then, can you pack a bag?'

'What, right away?'

'Afraid so. You'd be safer as far away as possible. Just till we get this sorted.'

'But what will you do?'

'We're going to get to the bottom of this, I promise,' Max said, hoping that it was true.

'Okay. I'll go and pack. Shall I give you my mobile number, in case there are developments?'

'I think it would be better if you didn't take your mobile with you. People can use it to track you. Maybe leave it here.' A sudden thought hit Max. 'Or perhaps leave it with me and I'll look after it for you?'

Liz looked puzzled. 'Why would you look after it? It's only a cheap thing, years old.'

'Just in case. If you urgently need anything from it, you can call me and I can retrieve any messages and the like. If it's here, it's no use to anyone,' said Max.

'Okay. I don't have a code for it,' she said, handing over the scratched old Nokia. 'I'll go and pack, then I'll set off.' She left the room, her face full of confusion.

'Why the phone?' asked Janie.

'If she takes it, she'll use it and then it could be game over. Also, us having it may present an opportunity. In fact, you keep hold of it, okay?' said Max, handing it over.

Janie frowned. 'This is a shit situation.'

'In one way, yes. In another, it's just what the doctor ordered.

192

She's now out of the way and safe, leaving just Bruce Ferguson to worry about, and as he seems to be the Scarlet Pimpernel, I'm less concerned.'

'So what next?'

'We see Elizabeth safely off and we keep this to ourselves. If they know that she's fled, the pressure for us to reveal where she's gone will be difficult to resist, particularly for you. She's safe now, but when they report back, they'll assume it's us. You may want to find somewhere else to stay for a while.'

'Really? You think that's necessary?'

'Well, the Hardies aren't going to take it well, but they won't want to kill any cops either. The van driver with the gun only had eyes for me, and the other two had bigger concerns. I don't think you'll be recognised, but they may well make an assumption. Maybe best thing is for you to go back to work and see what rumours are floating about.'

'I can see the value in that. What are you going to do?'

'All of the relatives are safe now, with Elizabeth on her way to a secret location and Bruce Ferguson being the impossible-to-find man. Unless I'm missing something, they're the only surviving relatives of either Willie Leitch or Duncan Ferguson.'

'As far as I can see, yes.'

'It's Duncan Ferguson's funeral tomorrow, and I intend to go.'

'That seems risky. What if you're spotted?'

'I'll stay out of the way, but I need to be there. We don't know if Bruce Ferguson will show, or not, and I'm concerned that Hardie will want to harm him. I want to be there to prevent it.'

'Fair enough, but I want to come. You'll need some support.'

'That'd be great, I could do with another set of eyes and ears up there. Can you get out of the office without being noticed?'

'Sure, there's nothing much going on, and I can just book out on an inquiry. I have a witness that I've been putting off seeing in Inverness, anyway. What are you thinking?' asked Janie.

'The time has come to go after some of the low-hanging fruit,' Max said, smiling.

'Good call, we used to do this on Vice all the time: take out the smaller pimps so that the traffickers would come out into the open.'

'Glad we're on the same page. Someone caused Duncan to go over that cliff, and then someone at Wick Police Station ruined the evidence. We find them, the bigger fish might start to make mistakes and then we bring this whole thing crashing down.'

'I think it could work. We can't just let these bastards run riot.'

'Janie?' said Max, his voice low.

'Aye?'

'Thanks. I was beginning to flag there. That bloke was bloody strong.'

'No worries,' she said, a glimmer of a smile forming.

'Maybe I need to take up Muay Thai.'

'If you think you can handle it. You did well, though; he was a bloody monster.'

'Aye, but if you weren't there, he'd have broken away, and then I'd have been screwed. Thanks, I'll not forget that you had my back.'

Their eyes met, and something passed between them.

'Forget about it. Forget about the fact that an eight-stone girly rescued you from the big nasty mannie.'

Max chuckled. 'Janie?'

'Yeah?'

'Piss off.'

35

Jack Slattery sat in the café in one of the less salubrious parts of Glasgow. He twirled his packet of cigarettes in his hand, turning the half-empty pack between his fingers, desperate for a smoke. The message had come from the youngest Hardie that they needed to meet urgently, so here he was, a thick cup of tea at his elbow and a slightly sick feeling in his stomach. It had been much easier with the old man, who had more of a sense about keeping the cops at bay by being a little subtle when required. The new Tam Hardie seemed to have no such reticence. Frankly, the guy was insane in his desire to leave the shadow of his old man. The body count was getting higher every day.

He had passed on Willie's sister's address to Hardie last night, once he had received it from one of his contacts on the team. He had heard nothing about that yet, but he imagined that the outlook for the lady wasn't good. Hardie was using his own people in Perth for the job, so he was thankful for that, at least. Nothing would come back to him on that one.

The door of the café banged open and Davie Hardie swooped in, a furious look on his face.

'Outside, now,' he barked, jerking his thumb at the open door.

Slattery's heart leaped into his mouth. What the hell was going on? He jumped to his feet and followed Davie out of the door where the large, luxurious Mercedes sat adjacent to the pavement, the rear door open.

Trying not to tremble, Slattery climbed into the car, where Tam Hardie sat, his face dark with barely concealed fury.

'I thought Max Craigie was off the case?' Hardie said in a low growl.

'He is. He's on enforced sick leave.'

'So, tell me this then: how, when my men go to deal with the Leitch bitch, does Craigie show up and stop them from taking her out?'

'What?'

'Aye, he appeared out of nowhere and smashes one of their elbows and batters the other. My man had to rush in and rescue them. Cool as a cucumber, the bastard was.' Hardie's eyes flashed with fury.

'Is Craigie dead?'

'Of course he isn't dead. You think I'm stupid enough to have a cop shot in broad daylight? What am I paying you for? I thought you had him tracked.'

'The tracker hasn't moved. The motorbike was the only vehicle at his house when I was there.'

'Need to watch him closer, then.'

'Tam, he lives in the middle of nowhere. No way could I watch him normally, even with loads of extra guys. Plus, he's ex-Met Flying Squad, always switched on.'

Hardie almost growled in frustration. A vein throbbed at the side of his head. 'We need to warn this bastard off, and properly. What family does he have?'

'Estranged wife who lives in Hertfordshire and an elderly aunt who lives on the Black Isle.'

'Is that it? No kids?'

'No.'

'You have their addresses?'

'I'm working on that.'

'Let me know as soon as you have them, okay? I'll send the bastard a message he won't be able to ignore. I want this job done, and soon. Meaning the remaining relatives dead and buried. I don't care if it looks like suicide, or if they have to get shot in the bastard head. You understand?'

'Aye, of course,' Slattery almost mumbled like a schoolboy in front of a head teacher.

'Do you know where the bitch sister could've gone?'

'No idea. MIT only had that address. She's got no social media presence, and just seems to live a quiet life.'

'So, we've lost her?'

'I have her phone number, and I can probably get someone to cell-site it.'

'Get it done. When's the funeral for Ferguson?'

'Tomorrow morning, up at Wick cemetery,' replied Slattery.

'Are you going?'

'I'll be up there, but it's a real small do, so I'll stay out of the way. One of my contacts has a solid reason to be there. He'll report back on the brother, if he turns up.'

'What's the plan?'

'If he has a car, I'll get a tracker slipped on it so we can follow him to a suitable spot. If he's flown in, closest airport with scheduled flights will be Edinburgh or Glasgow, so there'll be plenty of opportunities.'

'Okay. Will you do it?' asked Hardie, his face impassive.

'Me?' Slattery sounded shocked.

'Aye, you. Who else? You'll be up there. Follow him back down and when you get a chance shoot him. You need to start earning your retainer. Do this, and there will be a big bonus in it for you.'

Slattery sighed and rubbed his face. 'I've never shot anyone before, Tam.'

'First time for everything, and anyway, Duncan Ferguson's death was set up by you, right? You'd still be going down for murder, if the police caught you. Imagine that, an ex-cop getting life in Saughton or Barlinnie. Jack-boy, you're as much a part of this as any of us, so you bloody need to prove your worth. Or I could find someone else, and I can't imagine I'd want you running around with everything you know about my operation, right? Life would be, shall we say, precarious? Yes, precarious, for you, outside my team.' Hardie showed his white, capped teeth in a smile that was as insincere as it was terrifying.

Slattery said nothing, just breathed deeply, trying to regain control of his nerves. He realised he had no choice.

'Aye, I'll do it.'

'Of course, you'll do it. Give him the piece, Davie.'

A hand snaked around the seat from the front, clutching a small revolver. Nervously, Slattery took the dark, new-looking weapon, feeling the cold of the metal against his sweaty hand.

'Smith and Wesson snub-nose thirty-eight revolver. You fired one before?' Davie piped up from the front of the car.

'I was firearms trained, but always used Glocks,' Slattery said, his nerves dissipating as he turned the weapon in his hand and felt the tingle of power begin to nip. This always happened when he took hold of a gun and imagined its latent power. Even as a cop, he used to get a buzz holstering his pistol. He smiled, just a little. 'I can handle it, no worries.'

'Good man. Revolver is perfect. Never jams, and don't leave spent cases behind. Find the opportunity and do it quick, pal. One in the head, two in the chest, as we all like to say and then chuck the thing in the sea. Okay?'

'What about the body?'

'It's bloody Caithness. There are a million places to hide a body, so get him hid. You're an ex-cop, hide it where you wouldn't find it. Car can be lost later on, let's face it. I know a few scrap dealers who can crush it into a cube.'

'I'll get on it. I'll have someone up there to help me, if necessary.'

'Can you trust him?'

'Oh yeah, he's in it up to his ears already.'

'Will Ferguson be missed?'

'I can't find anything about him. He left Caithness as a young man and never returned, but I'm sure someone will be looking for him. With the other people who've died recently, it may cause a stir,' Jack said, quietly.

'You aren't my only route into the police, trust me. You're just the person I avail myself of most often. You don't survive in our line of business without gaining influence, and my late pa got all his ducks in a row many years ago.

'Now what about the loose end down south?'

'You're still keen on that?'

'Of course, I am. How many times? No bloody loose ends, anywhere.' Hardie's face flushed red.

'I'm still looking into it. I have a contact, and together with your man down there, we should be able to sort it,' Slattery said, his voice catching, just a touch.

'You still need me to sort that out as well? Fuck's sake, Jack, I'm not sure what you're for anymore. Find the information out quickly and get back to me. I want this sorted. Now get out of the bloody car and get to work.'

Slattery stepped onto the pavement and the big car roared off. He pulled a cigarette out of the battered packet and lit it with a shaking hand, his heart sinking at how far he had fallen. He inhaled deeply, relishing the hit as the nicotine bit. Not that long ago, he was just running errands, giving simple bits of intelligence from police sources, and staying in Old Man Hardie's good books for a nice little retainer. Tam had changed all that, and he was now planning the murders of innocents. He was in too far, he couldn't back out, and frankly, he needed the money.

He looked at his reflection in a shop window and saw a seedy middle-aged man. All of a sudden, he loathed himself. His hand went to the pistol tucked in his bulging waistband and as he touched cold metal, he felt a surge of resolve.

He'd bloody do it. He had no choice but to do whatever Hardie wanted, for a good price, then take the money and run. Away from Scotland, away from the UK. He was bloody sick of it. He'd make his money, and then he was off.

36

Max got up early the next day, poured a coffee down his throat and was soon kitted up and on his KTM heading towards the offices at Gartcosh. It felt like a sensible idea to put the tracker still hidden on the skid-plate at a new location on the map. He hoped it meant they wouldn't be looking for him at the funeral.

He pulled into the yard, still mostly deserted because the daytime workers had yet to arrive. He parked his bike in a distant corner out of sight. He went to his Vauxhall that was still parked up and threw his bag and bike kit in the boot. He was dressed simply, in plain dark chinos, a white shirt and a dark tie in his back pocket, ready for mixing with the mourners at the funeral.

As he was settling into his seat his phone buzzed. It was Ross.

'Ross?'

'Max. Welfare check. You okay?' Ross's rough voice had a softness to it that wasn't normal.

'Fine, why?' said Max, suspiciously.

'You're a legend in your own lunchtime at the moment, pal. Word's got out about you telling DCS White to copulate with himself. I have to say, it was quite funny, despite how career-threatening it could be. Genuinely, mate, I'm enquiring as to your welfare.'

'I'm honestly fine,' was all that Max was willing to say. His lack of trust was now widespread, and even included a man he considered a friend.

'Aye, well. The OH referral has been made, and you'll get a call sometime in the next millennium. In the meantime, I'd chill out in whatever foul and depraved way you see fit, but stay out of the case, yeah?'

'Aye,' was all that Max could bring himself to say.

'Shite, man, you're hard work. We're supposed to be pals,' said Ross, concern in his voice.

'I just can't talk right now. Speak later, yeah?'

'Aye, but no more sticking your beak in, right? I may be able to keep the shite away from you, but interfere any further, and I won't. Clear?'

'As a bell. Listen, I have to go.' Max hung up.

He sat for a few moments, staring out of the window, lost in thought and wondering who he could trust. No one, he decided, as he started the Vauxhall, engaged the gears, and drove off.

Within a few minutes, he was once more heading north from one end of the country to the other, a full five hours away.

He dialled Janie on the hands-free function on the car's steering wheel.

'Early bird, Sarge?' she said, and he was surprised to hear sleep in her voice.

'Not on your way? Funeral starts at eleven. Good morning by the way.'

'Unlike you, I like to prepare. Ross was so impressed by my diligence at going to see the trafficking victim in Inverness that he authorised a hotel, so I could see her first thing. He thinks that I'm a shining example of victim care. I'm about to head downstairs for a big breakfast and I'll see you in Wick. What's the plan, by the way?'

202

'Burial is at eleven at Wick Burial Ground, opposite the retail park. I'll meet you there. Are you dressed for a funeral?'

'Well, I have that option with me, if you mean dark trousers and a white shirt.' She yawned.

'Excellent, we'll look like waiters for the wake. I'll see you at eleven. Enjoy breakfast.'

Max smiled, as he drove north, surprised at the warmth he felt for Janie, who was fast becoming a friend. Things were going well, despite the seriousness of the situation. Max was sick of being on the back foot. It was time to go on the offensive.

*

It was just a small cortege that swept into the cemetery. A single undertaker's car came behind the hearse that contained Duncan Ferguson's coffin and a couple of floral tributes. Half a dozen cars followed them into the large, sprawling graveyard. They paused, briefly at the entrance, before the top-hatted undertaker alighted from the hearse and walked the cortege in, cane in hand.

The plot for Duncan was close to the leading edge of the cemetery and Max and Janie watched from the retail park opposite as the party formed up around the grave. The coffin was lowered in, as the vicar, resplendent in full cassock, read from a Bible.

Max looked at the scene with a long-lensed camera, zooming in on all the guests in turn. He paused at the tall form of Sergeant Mick McGee, the fatal accident investigator from Wick, who he'd seen arrive in a Ford earlier. It wouldn't be unusual for the lead investigator in a fatal accident to be at a funeral, but Max wanted to document the guests in any case. He paused on the weeping Mary, surrounded on both sides by an older couple who had to be her parents. Then Max focused on a small, wiry man with a deep tan and short, greying hair.

He zoomed in close on his face and the resemblance to his brother was significant. This was certainly Bruce Ferguson. He was tough-looking, possibly in his mid-forties, with a military bearing, and an unmistakable air of confidence about him. He looked formidable, despite his comparatively small stature.

'We seem to be the funeral squad at the moment, and bearing in mind I'd never been to one before working with you, I'm starting to worry, especially as we've now done two recently,' said Janie, taking in the scene.

'Valuable intelligence sources, Constable. Next stop weddings, christenings and bar mitzvahs.'

'I may ask for a transfer; it's getting bloody depressing.'

'Hold on, party's breaking up,' said Max, pointing at the now dispersing group. There were the usual knots of people who held back, but Max focused the camera on McGee, who spoke briefly with Mary and then in turn to Bruce Ferguson, a sympathetic look on his face, before heading back to the car park.

Rather than walk straight to the Focus that Max had observed him arriving in, Mick walked slowly, eyes swivelling, along the line of cars.

'He looks suspicious. Glad he's on roads policing and not Serious Crime,' said Janie.

Max said nothing, just snapped away with the camera.

Suddenly, McGee dropped to his haunches by a small Ford and began to affect tying a shoelace, whilst his head swivelled in each direction.

'Could he look any more suspicious? Tell me you're getting this,' said Janie.

McGee reached into his pocket and his hand went up to the wheel arch of the Ford, fiddled inside for a few moments and then was withdrawn. He stood and walked purposefully towards his Focus, climbed in and drove away.

'I may be wrong, but that looked very much to me like McGee just lumped up that car,' said Janie.

'This is what happens when you go after dirty cops: they know the dirty tricks we play. Lucky for us he isn't very good, the dirty, corrupt bastard.'

'So, we have our first confirmed dirty cop. Now what?'

'Can you take your car and head back down to Latheron and find somewhere to hole up out of the way? Be ready when I call you to switch on Elizabeth Phillips's phone. It's only an old thing, so doesn't have GPS, but as long as it hits the mast that covers Latheron we're good. They'll assume Lizzie is at Willie's gaff, if they're cell-siting the phone. I'd like to know if they have that capacity. Just get yourself somewhere with a line of sight on Willie's place. Take the camera, okay?'

'You think they'll be cell-siting her phone?'

'It's what I'd do.'

'What are you going to do?'

'I'm off to pay my respects to Mary Ferguson and speak to Bruce. We have to warn him and I don't like him having a tracker on the car.'

'I hope you're going to be suitably respectful.'

'I most certainly am. Take care, this is going to be a desperate situation for them. With what they've done so far, there's no telling what they'll do if you get seen.'

'Received. I'll be careful.'

37

Max sat in his car outside the inn in Dunbeath, thinking things over for a moment, when something occurred to him. He pulled out his phone and dialled 101, the general non-emergency number for all police. When the operator answered he asked to be put through to PC Peter Anderson from Wick.

There was a brief pause as the operator connected Max to the officer's Airwave radio.

'PC Anderson, can I help you?' He even sounded young with the faint hiss of static from the radio.

'Hi, Pete, it's DS Craigie. I just wanted to thank you for taking the evidence in from Sweeney's the other day. Really helpful.'

'No bother, Sarge. I was glad to help. Not often I get involved in a murder squad job.' He almost bubbled with enthusiasm.

'No problem booking it all in? It's important that evidential productions are correctly documented,' said Max with a serious tone.

'No problem, in fact Sergeant McGee helped me with the paperwork and he stored it away. I think a murder squad detective came and took it the next day. Is everything okay?' he said, worry creeping into his voice.

'Everything's fine, mate. Thanks again.' Max hung up and considered this new information. It all pointed to McGee, but just who was he taking his orders from? He shook his head and got out, heading for the inn.

It was just as Max remembered it, except this time the room was busy with black-suited mourners, all at the strange gathering known as a wake.

The atmosphere had yet to be loosened by the influence of alcohol, and there were just knots of individuals in hushed conversations, all clutching glasses and looking uncomfortable. Max had been to a few funerals in his time, but these were mainly military, after comrades had been killed in Afghanistan or Iraq. They often ended up as a raucous, drunken celebration of life, rather than the stilted mourning of death. Max felt uncomfortable as he walked to the bar and all eyes turned on him. The dining tables had been lined up alongside each other and were laden with buffet food and a stack of paper plates.

'Hi, DS Craigie, right? What can I get you?'

'Cranberry juice would be good, thanks,' he said.

Hettie produced a bottle, filled a glass with ice and put it on the bar, with a half-smile.

'How much?'

'Nothing, Mary has an open bar,' said Hettie, nodding to where Mary was standing, looking a little stunned, next to her brother-in-law, who was staring at Max with a curious expression.

'How's she doing?' asked Max.

'As well as can be expected. Her folks are over from the US, and she's returning to the States tomorrow for a little while. I'm minding the place whilst she's gone,' said Hettie.

'Maybe it'll help to get away, right?'

'Maybe. You should say hi to Mary. She's mentioned you a few times, she might have some questions.'

'I'd better go and say hi, then,' said Max, smiling.

He took a sip of juice and sauntered over to Mary, who

was in deep conversation with her brother-in-law. Her eyes were still red and puffy, but she had something else in them. Determination.

'Hi, Mary, I just wanted to pop in to offer my condolences,' said Max.

Mary turned to look at him, and the grief and hurt were clear in her eyes.

'Thank you for coming. I didn't see you at the service?' Her voice was hoarse and thick.

'I thought family only, you know? Didn't want to intrude, just wanted to come to say hi.'

'Well, that's very kind of you. Sergeant McGee came to the burial, which was thoughtful of him, but he had to go on duty straight after. He's been really kind; everyone has been,' she said, smiling, wanly.

'Aye, he seems a nice man. Have you been updated about the incident?' asked Max with a straight face.

'Yes. He said that he thinks my husband was driving too fast, or maybe there were brake problems, but they can't find all the bits. I have to say, it's a little confusing.' Her eyes began to moisten.

'With the car being so badly damaged a forensic vehicle examination is always difficult, particularly if vital components are missing.'

Tears started to fall down Mary's face, and her shoulders began to heave. Her mother swooped in, and pulled her close, whispering softly in her ear.

Bruce Ferguson stepped forward, his hand outstretched. 'DS Craigie, I'm Bruce, Duncan's brother. Can we have a minute?' His voice was rich with the tones of Caithness, but softer, presumably after many years away. Max gripped the man's hand. It was firm and rough.

'Aye, sure. Shall we go over here?' Max pointed at a lone table in the far corner of the room.

Both men sat opposite each other, Bruce fixing Max with blazing eyes. They radiated sorrow, but there was something else. A flinty hardness that Max recognised. No doubt about it, Bruce Ferguson had seen much of life.

'It's hot,' said Bruce, peeling off his dark suit jacket, revealing a crisp white short-sleeved shirt. His tie was plain and dark and had been loosened at the collar. His arms were lean and tough-looking, almost like nylon rope, and heavily scarred. On one there was the pink and puckered skin of a significant burn, on the other a long scar with white stitch marks, stark against suntanned flesh. A solitary tattoo was visible at the edge of his sleeve. Max recognised it as the tip of the Fairbairn-Sykes dagger, better known as the commando knife.

'Aye, fair roasting,' said Max, taking a sip of his juice and loosening his own tie. 'Bootneck?' asked Max, nodding at the tattoo, using the slang for Royal Marine Commando.

'A long time ago. I did my twenty-two, but mostly with the SBS at Poole. You look like you've served,' Bruce said, sipping his own beer.

'Black Watch,' said Max.

'Any tours?'

'Aye, Telic and Herrick,' said Max simply, using the operation names for the Iraq and Afghanistan conflicts. 'Yourself?' he added.

'Aye, both and a few more you may not have heard so much about. What is the real story with my brother's death, Max? Mary's telling me that it's looking like an accident, and that wet fart who said hello at the funeral – McGee, was it? – well, he didn't inspire confidence.' His voice was low and soft, but there was an underlying edge that made him a slightly intimidating individual.

Max explained how he had got involved with the case, keeping it brief.

Bruce said nothing for a moment, just looked at Max with

a cool, appraising gaze. Max had seen that look before from a sergeant major who didn't believe the bullshit being spouted by a junior NCO.

'You believe there isn't a link between the two deaths? Honest answer, veteran to veteran, pal, cos I have to tell you, I don't buy it. No way did my brother die by accident.' His voice was still low and calm, but his eyes shone with controlled fury.

'Being straight with you, I have my doubts, but I'm in a minority. I'm still looking into it, but anything I come up with won't be well received.' There was something about Bruce Ferguson that made Max want to trust him.

'How is it that even though Mary told the murder squad cops that Willie and my brother were cousins, they didn't look into it? I can't believe that with the Hardies' reputation, nobody considered the deaths could be linked.'

'I'm not so sure. Look, I'm persona non grata with the murder teams at the moment. I'm on enforced leave,' said Max, aware that he may be saying too much.

'And yet, here you are?' Bruce's eyebrows raised a fraction. A silence hung in the air and even the hubbub of the inn seemed to fade into the background.

'Aye. Here I am,' Max almost whispered.

Bruce said nothing and the uncomfortable silence between them lingered. This was an interview tactic Max had often used himself in the past. Leave an uncomfortable pause in a verbal exchange and someone will soon want to break it.

Max broke first, realising that Bruce Ferguson was not the breaking type.

'I'm here of my own volition, because I have some concerns for your safety. I think the Hardies are seeking some kind of revenge against blood relatives of Willie Leitch. There was an attempted attack on your cousin, Elizabeth, yesterday.' Max immediately realised that he had said too much.

Bruce's face darkened and his eyes narrowed. 'Is Liz okay?'

'She's fine. She's staying with a friend away from Scotland, and she'll be safe there. Me and a colleague intervened and stopped the attack.'

'And the attackers?'

'They escaped, with injuries,' said Max, feeling as if he was walking down a route that he would find it difficult to come back from.

'What are your bosses doing about this?'

Max paused for a moment. This was now a difficult situation, but there was no way he could share his suspicions with Bruce Ferguson. He decided that his only option was to be a little more guarded.

'The usual. Watching hospitals, looking at any associations, and the like,' said Max aware of how unconvincing he sounded.

'And you think these people want to harm me?' Bruce asked, his eyebrows raised in an almost amused expression.

'It's a possibility. These are bad people, and whilst we have no evidence, I'm fairly confident that the Hardies were responsible for the attack on your cousin and they'll be targeting you next. You should take what steps you can to protect yourself. I'd offer you police protection, but with my current status with Police Scotland, I can't.' Max leaned in closer and lowered his voice to a whisper. He really didn't want to be overheard. 'There is every chance that the Hardies' influence stretches into certain areas of the force.'

'Bent cops, you mean?'

Max paused. 'Aye,' he said, eventually. There was a long pause that almost felt like static. Bruce's face remained impassive.

'You don't look surprised,' Max said.

'I can't say that I am. Are you sure that Liz is safe?'

'As I can be. She's staying with a friend from a while ago, who has no social media links. A colleague I trust has checked and she can't find any link, so I don't think the Hardies will, either.'

'That's all I care about, then.'

'Not worried for yourself?'

Bruce's eyes almost lit up a little, and his tough, lined face broke into a wide smile. 'You've no idea about me, have you?'

'Well, you're ex SBS, so I imagine you can take care of yourself.'

'I did spend many years in the SBS, but for the last six years I've been head of security for a very high-profile and very, very rich Russian businessman. I spend all my life surrounded by ex-Spetsnaz bodyguards, in a well-guarded, large property on the side of a mountain in Spain. Every possible security facility is available to me and when I'm working around the world with my principal, I'm always armed. So I'm not scared of a two-bit gangster, even if he could find me, which he won't be able to. You guys couldn't find me, right?'

'True. Other than knowing you were in Spain.'

'I'm rarely in Spain. I'm rarely anywhere for any length of time. Will you answer me one question, honestly?'

'Depends what it is.' Max matched Bruce's smile.

'Did Hardie have my brother killed?' The smile was gone as quickly as it had appeared.

Max paused for a moment. If he said what he wanted to say, there was every possibility that it may introduce another fly into the already contaminated ointment. An ex-special-forces operative, with access to significant resources, could be a problem if he bore a grudge against Hardie.

'Yes. I think Hardie had your brother killed. I also think he tried to have Elizabeth killed and if he gets the chance, I think he will have you killed as well. This is a blood feud, and it dates back nearly two hundred years. There is no way Hardie will rest until he gets satisfaction.'

'I heard about Willie's scrapbook,' said Ferguson, flatly.

'And?' said Max, his eyebrows raised.

'I think "no comment" is as far as I'm willing to go on that front. Certainly, at this stage.'

'What are you going to do now?' asked Max, deciding that he wouldn't get anywhere by trying to press the man.

'If you're wondering, am I going to be safe, the answer is yes. I'm heading south to Glasgow for a flight later on this evening back to Spain. My boss wants me at work, and with what he pays me, who am I to argue?'

'Mind if I check your car over before you head off? With what happened to your brother, I would feel better if I knew it was roadworthy.'

'Be my guest.' He tossed over a single Ford key with an Avis fob. 'Hired Fiesta parked out the front. I'm going to stay here with Mary for a wee bit longer.' He stood, nodded and walked back over to his sister-in-law who was standing in a small knot of mourners, all clutching drinks.

Max headed for the door, pausing by the buffet for a brief second. He pulled out a small sheet of foil from beneath a pile of sandwiches and folded it in half, before leaving the inn and walking into the car park.

38

Max surreptitiously looked about him but saw only the line of parked mourners' cars. There was no sign of McGee's Focus and no other cars that would have served as observation points. Max smiled to himself. As he had predicted, the problem with technological surveillance equipment was that, inevitably, those utilising it placed too much faith in it.

He quickly pressed the key and the indicator lights flashed as Bruce's Fiesta unlocked. Max produced his smartphone and took a quick snap of the car. He made a show of checking it over, inside and out. The boot had a solitary small military-style rucksack in it and nothing else. Squatting down by the wheel arch Max leaned in and felt around with his hand. He found the tracker almost immediately. Reaching into the space by the axle with the torch on his phone switched on, he took a few pictures. Even though this was all off-books, he felt more secure documenting every step. Looking at the image on the phone's screen he could see that the tracker was a carbon copy of the one currently attached to the skid-plate of his KTM back at Gartcosh.

Quickly, Max pulled hard to free the magnets and wrapped it completely in the shiny tinfoil, thereby encasing it in a make-shift Faraday cage. Max imagined it suddenly disappearing on the screen of whoever was monitoring, as the metallic foil blocked the GPS signal from hitting the satellite circumnavigating the globe thousands of miles above them. Max couldn't help but smile.

He pulled his phone from his pocket and dialled Janie.

'Max, all okay?'

'Yeah, all fine. You got eyes on Willie's place?'

'Yep. Nice little spot a hundred metres away. They'll never see me.'

'Cool. Now listen carefully. I want you to wait ten minutes and then switch on Elizabeth Phillips's phone. Make a call to the operator or something, just to make sure it's visible on the net. Be ready to photograph whoever shows up, okay?'

'Sure, what are you going to do?'

'I'll be close by. I've removed the tracker from Bruce's car, so he's safe to travel. He's an interesting character, and to put it mildly, not even slightly concerned about the Hardies. He's ex special forces and current security manager for an oligarch,' said Max.

'Right, so both relatives are as safe as we can make them, which is good, but what next?'

'Now we're going proactive. We're going to pick one of the bastards off. If we present incontrovertible proof that we have a dirty cop, they'll have to listen to us, right?'

'I guess, but this is all new to me. I don't like it.'

'You think I do? We have no idea how deep this corruption runs, but if we do nothing, innocents die, and I'm not letting that happen.' Max instantly regretted his harsh tone. He was tired. 'I'm sorry, it's just getting to me,' he added before Janie could respond.

'Nah, you're all good. Let me know when you're on your way.'

'Thanks, pal.' Max hung up.

He returned into the inn where Bruce and Mary were talking by the bar.

'Car's all good, Bruce,' said Max, handing the key over to him.

'That's good to know. I'm heading off now myself. Thanks for what you're doing, Max. It's good to know there are some good cops out there. I'd appreciate it if you kept me apprised of any developments, or if you think I can offer anything.' He handed a business card over which Max took. It simply bore Bruce's name, an email address and a UK mobile phone number.

'Thanks. Can I just say one thing?'

'Aye, fire away.'

'I really wouldn't be tempted to get involved in this if I was you, mate.'

'Do I look worried about that?'

'No, but I think it's important. You do anything daft, then the focus could easily shift from Hardie to you. Cops like low-hanging fruit, and they'll lock you up as quick as anyone.'

'I've plenty on my plate already. Hardie means nothing to me, and I trust you to do the right thing. I've zero interest in any of that bloody family.' His gaze was penetrating, and Max wasn't sure if he believed him, or not.

'Well, fair enough then. Take care.' The men shook hands.

It was time to bait the hook, thought Max. In fact, it was time to bait a couple of hooks and see who bit.

39

Jack Slattery sat and smoked in his car at the side of the road just outside Wick in Lybster, a little harbour just a few miles away from the funeral wake in Dunbeath. He had been there for a while now. The blue blob on the map screen on his phone had disappeared out of nowhere a few minutes ago. It had just plain vanished. This wasn't good, as the tracker was the only direct link to Ferguson. He checked the tracker on Craigie's motorcycle, and it was stationary at Gartcosh, and hadn't moved since early this morning. He wondered if Craigie was back working. His contacts should have let him know, if that was the case. Still, he couldn't worry about him right now.

He dialled Mick McGee on his phone.

'What's up, Jack?'

'The tracker on the Fiesta just died.'

'What?'

'Don't bloody *what* me. Did you set it right?'

'Aye, stuck it to the axle. It was firm.'

'Well, it's off now. Where are you?'

'Heading south, ten minutes outside Wick. Just started afternoon shift.'

'Well get yourself to the inn and see if the car's still there.'

'On my way. What are you doing?'

'I'm standing by at Lybster. I'm not showing out until he's on the move. No way I can follow without a tracker, not up here. It's too bloody remote.'

'Okay, I'm on my way.'

Slattery hung up, nervousness gripping his insides like a vice. Hardie would go mental if he lost him. Slattery took a final drag on the cigarette, sucking the smoke deep into his lungs, before tossing the stub out of the window.

He couldn't shake the knot of nerves that sat like a lead weight in his gut at the thought of what he was expected to do when the opportunity arose. Mick McGee had sent him a picture of Bruce Ferguson that he had taken at the burial and Slattery had stared hard at the grey hair, tanned face and lean physique. He looked a tough man despite his diminutive stature, and Slattery knew he would have to be quick and ruthless when the time came to pull the trigger. Slattery had never baulked at roughing people up, where necessary, particularly when the odds were heavily stacked in his favour.

His stomach flipped at the prospect, but he was unsure whether it was the physical act of killing or his fear of Hardie that made his hands tremble, as they were now. He'd far rather be a facilitator, who allowed others to do the deed. He wasn't a particularly good fighter, or any type of a hard case, but he always had a leveller to tip the odds in his favour. The pistol at his waistband was a bigger leveller than he had ever had before, and he was surprised to feel a sense of power and excitement at what lay ahead.

His phone buzzed on the dash. Looking at the dial he saw the number of one of his contacts. A DI at force intelligence who had proved very useful over the years.

'Yeah,' Slattery said, bluntly.

'Jack. That number you gave me to keep an eye on has just

gone live. First time since it was switched off yesterday. It just called the top-up service.'

'What? Where?' Slattery's heart leaped at this news. If both Elizabeth Phillips and Ferguson were up here, they may be able to resolve this whole situation in one go.

'Hitting a cell tower just up the A9 from Latheron in Caithness.' The voice was low and hushed.

'Shit, you sure?'

'Aye, not three minutes ago. Still on the network now, and it's receiving some voicemails and texts. They must've been missed calls whilst switched off.'

'Okay, cheers, pal. Keep me informed if it goes off or moves.' The excitement gripped Slattery. So, it looks like she travelled up for the funeral or something. Jesus, this was big.

He quickly composed a text to Davie Hardie.

Leitch's sister's phone just gone live at Latheron. She must be going to his place. Instructions?

The reply came back almost immediately. *Do it.*

He dialled Mick McGee.

'Where are you?' he barked as he jammed the car into gear and moved off, tyres screeching.

'Ten minutes from Dunbeath.'

'Scrub that, get to Latheron. Willie Leitch's sister's phone is hitting the mast there now. I bet she's gone to his house. She may even have keys, being the only living sibling. We need to get hold of her, okay? You can detain her on some bullshit and I can do the necessary,' Slattery yelled over his screaming engine as he roared up the single-track road.

'Shite, this is too heavy for me, man,' McGee almost whimpered.

'I don't want to hear this. Get there, or I'll be telling Hardie you let him down. Fancy that?' Slattery bawled. He slid a fresh cigarette between his lips and lit it, wrestling with the steering wheel with a single hand, his jaw set firm.

40

'Where are you?' said Max into his phone as he drove into Latheron.

'A hundred metres down from Leitch's place, tucked in the small farmyard hidden by some large machinery. I've a decent view through the camera and I'm positive I can't be seen,' said Janie.

'Awesome. I've found a spot with good cover in the centre of the village. Let me know when anyone arrives, and I'll walk in.'

'What are you going to do?'

'Depends who shows up,' said Max, picking up the small tracker he had purchased a few days ago in Glasgow and tucking it in his pocket.

'Okay, stand by, stand by,' said Janie. 'There's a great big Mitsubishi SUV cop car pulling up outside. Driver getting out. Hold up, I'm photographing as well. Yep, it's McGee – he's going up to the front door and knocking.'

'Well, well. They have phone cell sites, as well. That's interesting. Sit tight, and let's see who else shows up.'

'McGee is looking through the front window. Hold up, another vehicle. A silver Renault has pulled onto the side road and tucked into a parking bay.' She read out the registration number.

'Who's driving?'

'Bingo. It's that sleazy bastard Slattery. He's joining McGee up at the house. They're standing chatting and now they're heading to the rear of the terrace. There must be an alley or something along the back.' Janie's voice was tinged with excitement.

'Right. Keep watching, I'm going to Slattery's car now. I think we have a few moments but keep the line open.'

'Be quick.'

Max jumped out of his car and walked briskly towards the main road. It only took thirty seconds before he saw the new model Renault tucked into its parking bay. Keeping his pace even, he walked until he was alongside the rear wheels of the car and then dropped to his knees, affecting tying a shoelace. Checking both ways and seeing no one, he flattened himself down and reached underneath the car, feeling the comforting snap as the magnets attached themselves to the top of the axle. Max stood quickly and walked off at a leisurely pace in the same direction, before turning towards the main road and Janie.

Two minutes later, he was sitting next to her in her vehicle.

'More trackers?'

'Aye. This is one I bought myself. I've still got the one off Bruce Ferguson's car. I have an idea for a nice little distraction on that front.'

'Is anyone not being tracked, right now? It seems like the good guys are being tracked whilst the bad guys are doing the tracking, and simultaneously being tracked,' said Janie, shaking her head.

'Aye, it could get confusing, but accelerated promotion should mean you grasp it easy. The difference is, we know we are being tracked, whereas the bad guys don't know that we know, and don't know that they are, in fact being tracked. Shit, I'm confusing myself.'

'Straightforward stuff, Max, I can't see what you're struggling with. Wait up, they're back.' Janie raised the camera as McGee and Slattery stood out the front, looking up at the property. McGee shrugged his shoulders, whilst Slattery seemed to be speaking sharply at him, his finger jabbing with venom.

'What next?' asked Janie.

'Is Liz's phone still on?'

'Yes, they can't track us accurately on this old crappy Nokia. No GPS.'

'Switch it off. I want to watch what happens.'

Janie powered down the old Nokia and tucked it back in the glove box.

It only took one minute before Slattery received a call, presumably telling him that the phone was now switched off. Max could clearly see the ex-cop's scowl through the zoom lens.

'He looks pissed, but it shows one thing for sure. These bastards have access to all the databases, and all the tools available to the police.'

'Christ, is anyone straight in Police Scotland?'

'We are, Janie. We're doing the right thing, here, but we need to be very careful. Right now, Elizabeth is in hiding, and Bruce is on his way south to Glasgow, and they don't have a clue.'

'They could be watching the airports, I guess,' said Janie.

A leather-clad motorcyclist swept into the farmyard next to Max and Janie and switched off the machine, a sporty-looking Honda. He pulled his helmet off and took a long drink from a water bottle he produced from a tank bag. He looked hot and sweaty and was clearly taking a quick break from touring the Highlands, a common sight on these long, sweeping roads. He paid no attention whatsoever to Max and Janie.

'Maybe, but what are they going to do? Bruce is just an innocent flying to Spain, and anyway, I can probably use this to throw them off the trail,' Max said, holding up the foil-covered GPS tracker he had removed from Bruce's car.

'I take it that isn't your sandwiches,' Janie said.

The rider jumped off the bike and headed towards the hedgerow, behind a steading, clearly looking for somewhere to relieve himself after a long ride.

'Let's put this to good use,' said Max, opening the door and ripping the foil from the tracker. He quickly and without hesitation went to the bike and snapped the tracker in place on the frame concealed by the exhaust pipe.

Max stood and stretched, yawning as the rider returned, arranging his leather trousers.

'All right, pal? Nice day for it,' said Max.

'Lovely day, bit hot though,' the rider said in a strong Yorkshire accent.

'Touring?'

'Yes, mate, doing the North Coast five hundred, and I'm up to John o'Groats now. Roads are beautiful,' he said, throwing his leg over the machine and sparking the engine, the twin exhaust pipes rumbling with the V-twin-engine power.

'Enjoy,' said Max, smiling.

'I will,' he said, slipping the helmet back on and riding off, heading north, carrying the GPS signal away with him.

'That's going to put the cat among the pigeons. I just hope that poor biker doesn't get topped,' said Janie.

'I can't see it. Nothing in it for anyone to kill a total innocent, and anyway, they'll never get close to him the way most of the bikers ride round here. They think it's a bloody racetrack on the NC500. Let's watch for Slattery's reaction. I bet he has an alert set, and I should think the tracker will be hitting a satellite any time soon.'

Almost on cue, Slattery stopped his finger-pointing at McGee, and reached for his phone to look at the screen.

'Boom. Thank you, global positioning satellites. Just look at the pair of them, doing this in plain sight. They're so bloody arrogant, think they're untouchable,' said Max, watching, the camera focused on the pair, as Slattery stared intently at the handset. Max could imagine the head-scratching as the tracker signal had sparked up, as if by magic. Slattery and McGee both looked at the handset, conversing animatedly.

'Right, switch on Liz's phone now, Janie, and start heading south on the A9, quick as you can. I want it to hit the next mast south of here as soon as possible. I'm going back to my car and I'll follow on. I want them to have one going north after the tracker and the other going south after Liz's phone.'

'You're not just a pretty face, Sarge. In fact, you're not even a pretty face, but that's a smart move,' said Janie.

'Got to think on your feet, Constable. Right, get weaving, quick as you can. We need to get that signal heading south. Stay in touch, and we'll meet up in Inverness, okay?' Max didn't wait for an answer. After getting out of the car he walked through the farmyard adjacent to where Slattery and McGee were still conversing, looking at the smartphone, surrounded by a cloud of cigarette smoke.

Once past them, Max emerged on the road and crossed towards a telephone kiosk in the centre of the village, which gave him a good view of McGee's Police Mitsubishi. Slattery was gesticulating north to McGee when he stopped and raised his phone to his ear. Even at fifty metres he could see the confusion on Slattery's face, as he spoke. Clearly the news of the activation of Elizabeth Phillips's mobile phone was arriving and the body language between the two men became even more agitated and confused.

All of a sudden it seemed a decision was made. After much finger-pointing and intense conversation McGee went to his Mitsubishi and roared off southbound onto the A9. Slattery began to jog back towards his car. Max raised his smartphone and set the video recording, capturing the scene before him as the Renault flew past him, heading north. He caught the intense look of concentration on Slattery's face as he drove past, chasing the GPS signal that he would never catch.

Max smiled to himself as he walked back to his car and climbed inside. He dialled Janie.

'All okay?' she asked, the engine noise audible.

'They took the bait. Slattery's heading north after the GPS and McGee's following Liz's signal. I reckon he's ten minutes behind you, but as it's only a cell site he's following he'll never be able to catch up. Leave it an hour to get him well away and then switch off again, okay?' Max said as he set off south at a steady speed. There was no rush, now.

'All good, then. Where are we heading?' asked Janie.

'Head south, turn off into the Black Isle and go to the Allangrange pub in Munlochy. It's nice there, and I'll buy you something to eat. I'm starving.'

'You've no idea how hungry I am, and you owe me food. We're certainly making progress, here. I had no idea that these bent bastards were like this.'

'We're doing okay, but we need to assess where we are, then we go after them. We now have evidence against a bent cop and a bent ex-cop, but that's not enough. I want the whole lot of them. The bent cops and the Hardies.'

'Well, I'm with you. If they can get trackers on cars and cell site intel on phones, then we have no idea what else they could do. I don't want to be part of a corrupt organisation.'

'Me neither. We're bringing them down. All of them.'

41

Slattery drove as fast as the winding roads would allow, a cigarette clamped between his lips, heading north in the wake of the GPS dot that pulsed on the screen of his phone in a cradle on the dash.

No matter how quickly he drove he just couldn't make any ground up between him and the signal. He was a good driver, having completed his police driving training all the way to class one, but it made no difference.

The hands-free phone rang in his car, the display showing the name of his contact at the intelligence unit.

'Please tell me you have good news?' Slattery said without preamble.

'No can do, pal. Signal went off a few minutes ago having just hit a mast in Brora.'

'Shit. Any calls?'

'Nothing. Just handshake pulses all the way down the A9 as it passed masts, but nothing else.'

'Bastard. Hardie'll go nuts. Can you not get the phone intercepted?'

'No chance, man. Way above my pay grade. It's Home Secretary approval for that, and I can't see that daft bint agreeing.'

'Don't get sarky with me. I know there are ways and means. Add it onto a list or something,' barked Slattery.

'There's no way. I'd at least need ACC approval, and you'd need to get it past that eagle-eyed staff officer too. No chance, man.'

'Christ's sake, what are we paying you for? Leave it with me. I may have an angle on this. In the meantime, keep watching.' Slattery hung up, swearing profusely whilst dialling again.

'Jack?' McGee answered.

'Phone's off again.'

'Right. What do you want me to do?'

'Keep going south until Brora, then wait there for an hour. If you don't hear from me, head back north. I don't want you being missed too much.'

'Okay. Anything on the GPS?'

'Aye, he's flying, near to Durness right now. I can't get close to him,' said Slattery.

'Jesus, that's some going. Is he doing the NC five hundred?'

Slattery paused, turning this over in his mind. 'It doesn't make sense, does it? Why do the tourist route straight after the funeral when he lives in Spain? I just can't see it.'

'Well, if he's doing the five hundred, he's bound to stop at Durness or Kinlochbervie.'

'Aye, I guess you're right. Stay put for a wee while, then head north and get back to your patrol area. I'll keep going.' Slattery rang off.

He looked at the screen on his phone, still moving along the coast road heading towards Durness. There was no choice; he would have to call Hardie.

He quickly composed a message as he threw his finished cigarette out of the window.

I need to speak.

The reply was immediate: *Wait five.*

He continued driving for a few minutes before his phone burst into life. The display simply read 'No Caller ID'.

'News?' Tam Hardie's voice growled down the phone.

'Ferguson was at the funeral. McGee chucked a lump on his car and I'm following it now. Looks like he's doing the NC500.'

'What? Don't talk shite, man.'

'Aye. He headed north from Latheron, and I've never got close to him. Went up to John o'Groats and then headed across towards Durness. I'm sticking with him, but he's moving at a hell of a pace.'

'Don't lose him. He can't keep going forever. He'll need fuel or a piss soon.'

'Sure, but there's something else.'

'What?'

'Elizabeth Phillips's phone came online a wee while ago, right by her dead brother's place in Latheron.'

'Was she there?'

'No, McGee and me were there within minutes, but there was no sign of her and the house is still tight since the police locked it up. I don't think anyone has been there. The phone then headed south for a bit but went off line at Brora. I've a man monitoring it. He'll let me know when it's on again,' said Slattery.

'Well get her hooked up, then. Intercept the bitch's calls.' Hardie was terse and dismissive in his tone, as if this was the easiest task.

'My man can't. He doesn't have the right access and it needs at least an ACC to make it happen.'

'That's bollocks. With what I pay, you need to work harder. Leave it with me, I'll make a call, but we need to have a chat after this situation is sorted as to how useful you actually are. I'm not as forgiving as my old man. Now stay with Ferguson and tell me when he's dead.' The beeps in his ear told him that Hardie had gone.

Slattery sighed, as he floored the Renault once more. This

was heavy stuff now. He was being pulled in much further than he would like. He was committed, though. Hardie would have him killed just as easily as he would kill anyone else.

42

Will Harding kissed his mother and jogged out of the front door, wearing his running shorts and Enfield Harriers running vest.

'Be careful out there, honey; roads are busy,' his mum had said, as she stroked his short, braided hair, that sat in cornrows across his scalp.

'I'll be fine. I know to look both ways now,' he had joked. She was a worrier, his mum, but he loved her dearly. It was tough being a parent to a sixteen-year-old boy at the moment, especially in an area like Enfield with its street gangs, but Will stayed clear of them. He wasn't interested in anything but his athletics and couldn't see the attraction in hanging round with the roadmen. It just wasn't his thing. He kept himself to himself, got along just fine. Some of his friends at school had fallen into the gangs, and were always about, with their jewellery, new phones and designer gear, but Will didn't care about any of that stuff, either. He was friendly with them, and mostly they left him alone.

He had competed yesterday, hitting personal bests for eight hundred and fifteen hundred metres and his legs ached a little. He always found that a slow and gentle jog was the best way to ease the kinks out of his muscles before a big stretching session. He then had a mountain of homework to do.

He entered his usual Zen-like state as he picked up the pace before turning into Trent Park. A quick circuit of the park and he was feeling his breathing begin to labour. Already his legs felt better.

After about twenty minutes in the park, he decided that he'd had enough and began to head home. That was when he saw the boy on the mountain bike. He was clearly a roadman, about his own age, but he hadn't noticed him before in Enfield. Enfield was pretty sewn up by the Get Money Gang or GMG, who sold weed and coke. A few of Will's friends had joined them and one or two had ended up in jail, another getting badly stabbed. Will saw the guy on the bike give him a look and put a phone to his ear.

Speeding up a little, Will left the park on his way back home. A slight tingle running down his back at the thought of the look the boy had given him. If he'd returned the screw-face, it wouldn't have ended well.

He felt the prickle of anxiety build as he turned towards home. It only got worse when he glanced back to see the boy on the bike a hundred yards behind him. He was still cycling steadily in the middle of the road, his phone clamped to his ear. Will picked up his pace even more and decided against turning straight into his home road. He didn't want the boy to learn where he lived. He thought back, tried to remember if there had been anything, however slight, that may have made him an enemy. He didn't make enemies, was known for being everyone's friend and keeping out of beefs.

He was running just below his race speed now, and a quick glance over his shoulder revealed that his follower had fallen off, was a good way back and wasn't showing any signs of pursuit. Will breathed a sigh of relief. He was probably imagining it, in any case. All the stories of beefs and postcode wars making him scared, even if he kept well away from them.

He maintained his speed, keen to get back home.

As he rounded the bend on Corby Crescent, he was shocked to see three boys he didn't recognise, blocking the pavement, all dressed in street clothes, on bikes, hooded and sneering. Will stumbled to a halt and almost fell. Glancing over his shoulder he saw the first boy on the pavement cycling towards him at speed. He froze on the spot and time seemed to slow down. Then he felt a vicious shove from behind him and he flew into the low wall in front of the line of terrace houses, falling over it into the garden. Then they were on him, like jackals, kicking and punching as he lay helpless on the rough concrete. Will screamed in terror as he saw the flash of steel. A huge-bladed Rambo-knife was produced from the waistband of one of the boys and was thrust at him, smashing into his abdomen. Strangely, there was no pain, just an impact as the steel passed into his body.

Suddenly there was a new shout that pierced the madness – stronger, older, and full of authority. 'Armed police!' And there were blue strobing lights everywhere and blue-clad police officers brandishing submachine guns. One of his attackers fell, stiff as a plank, with two thin wires embedded in his jacket connected to a baseball-clad cop armed with a bright yellow taser. There was another shout of, 'Taser, taser, taser!' as one of Will's attackers fell to the ground like a felled oak.

Then it was over as quickly as it had begun. A cop came and squatted by Will. 'You're gonna be okay. Stay with me, mate,' the officer said in a kind voice. He produced a white pad and clamped it against Will's abdomen and pressed hard. Will's vision became woozy and the cop's voice indistinct as the coldness began to envelop him, from his feet upwards, seeping into his body.

'I don't want to die, I don't want to die, I don't want to die,

232

I don't want to die,' repeated Will in no more than a whisper, feeling himself on the edge of sleep.

'What's your name, mate?' the kind cop asked.

'W . . . W . . . Will,' he heard himself say, although it didn't sound like his voice.

'Will, mate, stay awake, stay awake. Keep talking to me, Will, ambulance is here.'

Will looked at the cop's face, wide and meaty and split by a kind smile.

He realised that he had passed out when he woke in the back of an ambulance, a drip in his arm and a concerned-looking paramedic attaching sticky pads and wires to his chest. There was a range of competing beeps and tones in the back of the vehicle. Confusion fogged Will's brain. Was he dying? Was this it? Tears brimmed in his eyes as he thought of his family. He so wanted to see them all again.

'You're okay, Will. We're here now. You're in good hands.' She had a soft voice with a funny accent he hadn't heard before.

Will didn't feel very lucky, but managed to say, 'Please can you tell my mum and dad?' and he recited their address, his head swimming.

'Sure thing, love. The cops will do it now. Close your eyes and rest. We'll be at hospital soon.'

Will did as he was told, and slipped into blackness, thinking about his mum's kind, smiling face.

43

Tam Hardie and his brothers sat opposite Jack Slattery at the bar in their deserted Glasgow club just off Sauchiehall Street. A solitary cleaner was mopping the floor and all the house lights were up, casting harsh and raw shafts across the normally dark space. As always, what was a pulsating, buzzing club when open to the public, became a dank and depressing cave when it was closed. No better than a municipal hall, with scuffed walls, filthy windows and the rank smell of stale booze and sweat that permeated the very fabric of the building.

The club was a goldmine, though, and allowed Tam to launder vast quantities of dirty money through the tills during the busy nights. Whilst having the illicit drug trade sewn up in most of Scotland, Tam was also keen to develop legitimate, cash-heavy businesses alongside his irregular streams of income. It let him clean cash from the drugs, whilst pulling in serious bucks legitimately with the door fees and extortionate alcohol prices.

Slattery fidgeted nervously on one of the bar stools, cradling a large glass of whisky in one hand and a cigarette in the other, as Tam levelled him with a piercing stare. He had given a full account of yesterday's activities in Caithness and Hardie was not pleased.

'Did you see Ferguson's car at any time?'

'Not after the funeral, no.'

'So how do you know it was him?'

'I stayed on the network, just never got close to him. It could be that the battery died, or it fell off. McGee isn't experienced at this kind of thing. I needed to stay out of the picture, as you know,' said Slattery, his voice trembling, slightly.

'This is undesirable. Ferguson has been a bastard to find, and we still have no idea where he is. How did you lose him? There were two of you, one of whom was a uniformed copper with a police car, with blue lights and sirens.'

'We had to split when Elizabeth Phillips's phone came online. I thought we could take them both, and with my contacts monitoring her phone, it seemed too good an opportunity to—'

'And because of that decision we lost them both.' Hardie's voice was laced with irritation. 'Leitch's bitch of a sister has disappeared, but we know she's in the UK and we have a number for her. She'll raise her head again, but Ferguson is gone, and no bastard knows the first thing about him. He's like a ghost. None of your people can find him, and none of my contacts in Spain know anything either.'

'McGee got a photo,' Slattery said, meekly.

'Aye, a fat lot of good that'll be. A shite mobile phone photo of him and nothing else. No phone, no address, no vehicles, no bank. His hire car was paid for by a pre-paid and untraceable card and his driving licence is a bullshit address in London. We have nothing, and I don't like it. You need to find him; get onto Interpol, whatever. I don't care, get him found.'

'I'll get the word out.'

'Aye, you bloody better. My patience is running thin, man. What about the bitch?'

'Not sure why she came up. Her phone was in Latheron,

but no sight of her and nothing at Leitch's place. She then headed off south and disappeared again. I don't know if she's back in Perth.'

'She's not been seen and my people have a camera on her place. Fucking idiots couldn't even take a wee woman out. It looks like that Craigie bastard somehow got in the way.'

'Are we sure it was him?' asked Slattery.

'Who else? He and some girl had a right bloody stramash and took out Jimmy Talgarth's boys before they could get the job done. He had to rescue them, said the man was cool as a cucumber and even mentioned my name. Apparently, he almost dared Jimmy to shoot him.'

'Christ,' said Slattery, exhaling, his cheeks puffed out.

'Christ indeed. How come you didn't know he travelled to Perth?'

'I've only a tracker on his bike. He obviously went by car.'

'Not good enough. Get his phone hooked up. Who was he with?'

'I don't know. None of my people do either; didn't even get reported. Craigie isn't even supposed to be working.'

'Right, I want you to tighten up on that bastard. Get his phone intercepted. He's the key to this. We get his phone, we find out where the others are. I want his car tracked and get on his house, whatever it takes. One thing I do know is that when this is all over, that bastard Craigie is dead,' Hardie growled with pure unadulterated hatred.

'I can get cell sites and I can track his car, but I can't intercept his phone. No way, man. It's Home Secretary approval and you can't go near it without the top brass being all over it. I just don't have that reach.'

'Then what use are you to me, then? Right, get him hooked up for cell sites and get a tracker on his car. I need to know where that bastard is twenty-four-seven, get it?'

'Aye, Tam.'

'Looks like I'll have to sort the other thing. A liberty this is, like having a dog and barking myself.'

'But even if you could get the phone added onto an existing intercept authority . . .'

'Well luckily for us, my pa realised the value of having contacts in the police. He realised that by the early planting of an acorn, you may one day grow an oak tree. Now get out of my sight, and when we next speak, you better have some good news.'

Slattery shuffled out of the bar, disconsolately, his head bowed.

'He's a mess, that boy,' Davie said, shaking his massive head in distaste. 'Could be a liability, if he ends up getting dragged in, no telling what he'd do if his arse was on the line.'

'Aye. It's why I wanted him to take care of Ferguson. He shoots someone then he's ours. He's still useful for the moment, but I'm watching him closely – you can be sure of that.'

'So, what you gonna do?' said Frankie, who was smoking a large cigar.

'If that wretch Slattery can't get us intercepts, then I'm reaching out to one of Pa's oak trees. I didn't want to use them unless I had to, but I think it's time I let the bastards know that they're still ours,' said Tam, reaching for his phone.

44

Max was working out in his garage, with Nutmeg staring at him as she normally did, when his phone rang. Looking at the display, surprise hit him. It was Jill Strother, an ex-Met colleague he had served with on the Flying Squad. Max wandered out into the bright, early morning sunlight to answer the call. 'Jill, you old boot, how you doing?' Max said, a smile across his face. Jill had been a good friend, known for her acerbic, and sometimes cutting wit.

'Max, old son. How's it going in Jockland?' she almost shouted in her loud, sing-song cockney accent.

'Couldn't be better, mate,' he found himself saying, despite the desperate situation he currently was in. 'How's London life?'

'Shit, mate. Too much crime, not enough cops. Listen, can I bend your ear? Something's come up at work. I'm a DS on a proactive syndicate at Hendon, now,' she said.

'Sure, but how the hell did you get promoted? Thought you have to be politically correct to climb the ranks,' Max said.

'My talents are finally being recognised, geezer, and about bloody time too. Listen, we had an attack on a young lad yesterday in Enfield. A definite full-on attempted hit. We were following a team of youngsters who run for the head of the

MDK in Tottenham, when they jumped on this young lad out running. Literally, jumped on the poor bugger and horribly stabbed him in the gut. Fortunately, we were running with a firearms team and we took all five of them out across the pavement. Lad is in a really bad way, though, and it's touch and go. He's a proper innocent, as well. A decent kid, top-level athlete and a good student.'

'Isn't that always the case?' said Max.

'Well, I grant you, normally it's bullshit, but in this case it's genuine. Really lovely family as well; poor buggers are devastated.'

Suddenly the gang name 'MDK' flashed in Max's mind. 'MDK, as in Eustace Fielding's crew?' he said, quickly.

'Bingo. Glad to see that the hills and glens haven't pissed your memory up,' Jill boomed down the line.

'That's a big coincidence. I saw him at a gangland funeral just the other day. He was offering condolences to the family of Tam Hardie, head of the Hardie crime family.'

'Blimey, mate, don't you Jocks share anything anymore? Would've been nice if you'd told us.' She sounded a little put out at this piece of information.

'Well, I shared it with the intel unit up here. They were supposed to disseminate. I take it they didn't?' Max made a mental note to check up on this. He had definitely submitted the video footage to the intelligence unit and he wondered how its dissemination had been neglected.

'Nope, not a sausage. Anyway, to get to the point, one of the gang had a message on his phone from Fielding with a photo of this kid and an address in Enfield. Looks like he set it up, but we can't see why. We thought mistaken identity at first, but the message put paid to that. For some reason, Eustace Fielding wanted this poor lad, William Harding, dead, and we can't work out why.'

'So why do you think I can help?'

'Well, as it goes, Max, it turns out that William Harding is adopted. He was taken into care when he was six months old and adopted by a real nice family when he was eighteen months old. His birth mum died a few years later after a heroin overdose.'

'Okay, and?'

'Well, as I say, FLO turned out all his adoption paperwork, and it seems that his dad was a rat who wanted nothing to do with the lad. He made no opposition to adoption, apparently, said that there was no way he could raise a black kid on his own in the wilds of Scotland. I was going to ask you to look into your intelligence systems for us, rather than going through all the rigmarole of force intelligence.'

Max's insides suddenly felt like they were being gripped by an icy fist.

'What was the birth father's name, Jill?'

'Hold up, it's here somewhere.' Max heard the rustling of papers as Jill searched her paperwork, but he knew. Before she even spoke, Max knew.

'Here, you go. Dad's name is William Leitch from Caithness.'

Max took in a deep gulp of air and held it for a moment. His thoughts whirled as he exhaled slowly and evenly. He knew what he had to do.

'Max, have you buggered off already?' Jill's cockney tone tore him back to the present. He looked at his watch. It was still early.

'I'm going to come down to London. I think we need to chat.'

45

Max sat in the lounge at Glasgow airport, deep in thought, a glass of cranberry juice on the table in front of him. He needed to get to London and meet with the team. He had a feeling that the key to this whole situation lay in the stabbing of this innocent young man.

Will Harding was the blood relative of Willie Leitch, and it seemed his death had been ordered by Eustace Fielding, an associate of Hardie. That was no coincidence, and it couldn't be ignored, but he knew that if he reported it into the murder team in Inverness, it would get straight to Hardie and then the opportunity would be lost.

He unboxed the brand-new, cheap smartphone that he had just bought from the electrical shop in the departure lounge and snapped in a new SIM card. The fact that McGee and Slattery were tracing Elizabeth Phillips's phone made using his own phone whilst travelling too much of a risk. He had left it switched on at home, hidden behind a panel in the ceiling in his gym.

He spent a few moments synching the new phone with the camera feed from home and creating a Gmail account with an innocuous address.

He went to a payphone at the edge of the terminal, slotted in his credit card and dialled a number from the half a dozen on a list he had written in a notebook before leaving.

'Hello, Janie Calder.'

'Janie, it's Max. Free to speak?'

'Max? Yes, you okay?'

'Aye, on my way to London, and I've left my phone at home. I have a burner, so take this number down, and don't share with anyone.' Max read the burner number out to Janie.

'A burner – you think that's necessary?'

'I'm saying yes. I also think you should get one as soon as you can.'

'Fine. I'm at home and have a spare phone and I got a free pay-as-you-go with my last upgrade.'

'Great, get it in and send me a message as soon as it's up and running.'

'I'll do it straight away. Why London?'

'Willie Leitch had a son in Enfield.'

'What?' Janie said, sounding incredulous.

'Yeah. Funny how the research on Leitch who's the suspect of one murder and victim of another never turned up that he had another kid, when a births, deaths and marriages search would've revealed it,' Max said sarcastically.

'Just how far does this go? The intelligence team would almost certainly have turned that fact up.'

'I haven't told you the worst bit, yet.'

'You mean it gets worse?'

'Willie Leitch's boy, now called Will Harding, was stabbed yesterday in Enfield in an apparent gang attack. By sheer luck an armed surveillance team was behind the gang for another matter and they intervened. Took out the whole lot of them with tasers. Turns out one of them has a photo and address of the young Will in a message on his phone, that came from Eustace Fielding, head of the MDK.'

'As in the same Eustace Fielding that we saw hugging Tam Hardie just a few days ago?' asked Janie.

'The very same.'

'Shite, I see what you mean. How's the kid?'

'Not good at all. He's in intensive care with a nasty stab wound. Not looking good, I understand.'

'This situation just keeps getting worse. What's next?'

'I'm meeting the DS investigating it. This is a huge lead, but if we go overt, it's inevitable that it'll get to Hardie almost immediately. I'm not taking that risk.'

'Fair enough. Do you want me to do anything?' asked Janie.

'Not right now – just do normal stuff. You working today?'

'Aye, I'm working from home, though, on the laptop reviewing several weeks' worth of surveillance footage on the trafficking job. They can't get a reliable address for the main suspects, so because no one on the team likes me, I've got stiffed with reviewing it all. It's taking bloody ages.'

'I like you, pal. Well, I at least am willing to put up with you,' said Max.

'Only because I keep pulling your arse out of the fire.'

'Anything else happening?'

'Not really, I've not seen much of Ross. He seems to be under pressure.'

Max paused to consider this. He trusted Ross as much as he could in the circumstances, but not enough to bring him on board with his findings. Ross's only option would be to report upwards, and then it would be all over. It was just him and Janie.

'Okay, message me when you have a new number and I'll call you soon.'

'Will do.'

Max pulled out the credit card from the payphone and slotted it back into his wallet. His fingers brushed against Bruce Ferguson's business card. He took it out and stared

243

at the anonymous-looking card. On impulse, he dialled the number on his new phone and waited.

The phone clicked and beeped a couple of times before connecting, using an international calling tone. It rang briefly before it was answered with a curt, 'Yes?'

'Bruce. It's Max Craigie.'

'Hi, Max. All okay?' His tone was calm, yet curious.

'All is okay. I have a new number for a while, so thought I should update you with it.'

'Very kind. Any particular reason you've changed number?'

'Just being careful. I also have a new email address.' Max read it out.

'Noted. Any actual update for me?'

'I'm afraid not. I'm still off the case.'

'And yet you're calling me?'

'Aye, just to make sure you're okay,' said Max.

'There's no need to concern yourself about me. I'm currently on a yacht in the Caribbean with my employer and a detail of bodyguards. Is my cousin okay in Suffolk?'

'As far as I know. Did I tell you she was in Suffolk?'

'You must have done, pal, otherwise how would I know?' There was a touch of amusement in his voice.

'I guess I must have. Anyway, as long as you're okay.'

'Fine. Call me if you need anything.'

'I will, thanks.' Max hung up.

Max stared through the floor-to-ceiling windows at the stationary aircraft, without really seeing them. He was sure that he hadn't told Bruce that his cousin was in Suffolk. In fact, he knew for a fact that he deliberately hadn't. Strangely this didn't cause him any worry, quite the opposite. It seemed that Bruce Ferguson was using his own resources to make sure Elizabeth was safe. In fact, it made him feel much better knowing that Bruce Ferguson was looking out for his cousin.

46

Max sat in a medium-sized office in the middle of what was left of the old police college at Hendon. All that remained were a few low-rise buildings that surrounded the old parade square that Max had once marched on at his passing-out parade, many years ago.

The building housed one of the serious crime syndicates that had arisen out of the latest reorganisation of the investigative functions in the Met Police. Their job was the proactive investigation of serious and organised crime using surveillance and other covert techniques.

Jill sat opposite Max, clutching a mug. She was a tall and lean middle-aged officer, with short, neatly styled hair, casually dressed in jeans and a hooded sweatshirt. Jill and Max had worked together for several years and had always had each other's backs. Max trusted her as much as he trusted anyone. She was a first-class operator, both clever and resourceful. She was also as tough as anyone Max had ever worked with.

'We got word from a snout,' Jill said. 'One of the bit players from MDK was on the side of the angels, as they say and tipped us off that they were planning to collect a number of shooters for "AK" also known as Eustace Fielding. We ran the job over a couple of days with an armed surveillance team, when out of nowhere they leaped on poor young Will Harding. Luckily the team managed to get to them before they properly disembowelled the poor little bugger.' She pointed up at a whiteboard on the wall that showed what looked like a family tree with photographs attached and names below. At the top of the tree the sneering features of Eustace Fielding glared at the camera. Below him was a succession of photos of younger males, all black, all wearing the same sneer. The last photo on the whiteboard had the word 'Victim' in dry-wipe above it. He was a light-skinned, mixed-race boy, about fifteen, with a keen and eager expression, and short braided hair. 'Will Harding' was printed at the bottom of the sheet of paper.

'How's the boy?'

'Very nasty abdominal injury, perforated bowel and major blood loss. He's in an induced coma at the moment, after he went into cardiac arrest. It's touch and go. Parents are maintaining a permanent bedside vigil. He's under armed guard in the ITU at the Royal Free.'

'How did we connect to Fielding?' asked Max.

'One of the gang had a deleted photo of the victim and his address on his WhatsApp feed from a number we suspect is used by Fielding. When we looked at the little twat's phone the picture was in the deleted items recovered from the Cellbrite download. The cocky sod was playing it all coy until we showed him that, then he started blubbing.'

'Has he snitched on AK?'

'No, he wouldn't last five minutes in jail if he did. But if we can put the phone that sent the message in his hand, we are good to go. The question then arises, who tasked AK to get the job done.'

'Have you nicked AK?' asked Max.

'Not yet. We want all our ducks in a row first and we also want to clear up this shit with the Scotland connection.

We haven't a motive at all as to why they wanted to off this young lad, who's as pure as the driven snow, mate.' Jill was a fairly bombastic character, but even she seemed moved by the targeting of an innocent.

'So, what's the plan?'

'Surveillance team is getting behind AK with the intention of putting the offending phone in his hand. Probably with a filmed test call from a covert phone. We'll take him out then, secure in the knowledge he has the phone in his pocket.'

'Well, I think I can help you with a motive, but I have to say, it's really sensitive. If I tell you the whole thing, I'm not sure where it'll end,' said Max, looking at his shoes.

'You wanna give me a hint, mate?' Jill's eyes narrowed.

'It's complicated.' Max sighed and rubbed his face in his hands, the stress of the whole situation suddenly exhausting him.

'Bloody hell. What's going on?' said Jill. Her eyes softened as she looked at Max's face.

'Who's the boss, here?' Max said.

'DI is Rob Cruise, new fella. I don't know much about him.'

'No, I mean, the big boss. I'm going to have to explain everything, and I only want to do it once. If I go through normal channels this will all go horribly wrong.'

'Mate, you're being weird. DCS is Tony Jeffry, you know him from the Squad, right?'

Max's eyebrows shot up in surprise. 'Tony Jeffry, yeah, he was the DCI before you arrived.'

'He's not been here long, got promoted recently. A good bloke, as far as I can tell and his reputation is solid. What's this about?'

'I need to see him. I do know Tony, and you're right, he's a good man, and I trust him. Is he in?'

'I think I've seen him. Hold up.' Jill turned to her computer terminal and looked at the direct messaging. The light shone green beside his name.

'He's in.'

'Can you message him?'

'Really? Is that not a bit weird? I don't know the bloke, and he has a staff officer who usually manages his diary.'

'Just message him now, Jill, and tell him I'm here and can we come and see him.'

'You sure?'

'Dead sure. We go way back.'

Jill turned to her computer and tapped a quick message.

The message turned green indicating it had been read. There was a short pause before the reply came.

Come up now.

47

'Max Craigie, how you doing, mate?' Detective Chief Superintendent Tony Jeffry shook Max's hand warmly, whilst clapping him on the shoulder. He was a compact man, a ball of effusive energy topped by short, silver hair. He was smartly dressed in a blue suit and plain blue tie adorned with the eagle motif of the Flying Squad. He projected energy and vitality as he smiled broadly and pumped Max's hand.

'I'm doing good, Guvnor, but I need to talk to you about the most delicate of situations.'

'I'm taking the fact that Jill is here to indicate that it's to do with the stabbing that the surveillance team intervened in yesterday?'

'You were always astute, Guv, it's why you're a chief super and I'm still a DS,' said Max smiling.

'I take it I'm right?'

'You are.'

'I also have a very nasty feeling that the fact that you're here from another force, and yet I've heard nothing about it in advance, is indicative that your presence is not officially sanctioned. Having said this, it could be you're just here to buy me a pint, in which case, let's get to the Claddagh

Ring right away,' said Tony, talking of the local pub close to the office.

'Unfortunately, it's the first one, Guv.'

'Why am I not surprised?' Tony turned to Jill, his face serious. 'Now, Jill, normally I would tell someone in this situation to sod off and see their own management and do it properly. However, Max and I worked a number of Squad jobs together, and he pulled my arse out of the fire in one very particular incident, so I'm willing to listen. I'll also add that the rumours I hear from another very good friend of mine about some concerning happenings in Police Scotland make me very curious. I love a good bit of gossip, so, go on, sit down and hit me with it.' Tony sat on his chair, pushed it forward and steepled his fingers just under his chin.

Max told him. He told him everything. After he had finished there was a long silence. Eventually Tony let out a sigh.

'Max, why is it that you don't want me to get promoted ever again?' Tony asked with a wry shake of the head.

'I'm sorry, Guv, but I'm not sure where else to turn. The whole investigation is so corrupted that whatever I do up there will go straight back to Hardie. He has enough clout to get cell sites on phones, and clearly has a direct link in at every level of the force,' said Max, grimly.

'And we now have a clear dog in this fight with Eustace Fielding facilitating a hit, which if you're right, was ordered by Hardie. In short, we're involved, and we can take steps to make sure any issues in Scotland do not compromise our investigation.'

'I can prove a fair few things, just not by conventional means.'

'I get that, and that's the problem we have so far. Your surveillance, whilst ingenious, won't be admissible because it wasn't authorised. We can probably use whistle-blower protection to keep you out of the shit, especially as you were doing what you did to protect innocents, but we need to parallel prove, by lawful means, the evidence you've gathered. It's doable, but I can't authorise this myself; I need to push it upstairs.'

Max sighed. He wanted as few sets of eyes on this as possible, but he couldn't do it on his own. 'Who to?' he asked.

'Jeanette Fowler AC Special Ops, but I know her well enough and I'm sure she'll see it our way. Is there anything time-critical from a risk perspective that won't let this wait for a few hours?'

'Well, the people at risk are out of the way, but that can't last forever. Elizabeth Phillips can't stay hiding, although Ferguson seems strangely relaxed about it all,' said Max.

'Okay, let me talk to the AC and see if I can get in to see her. Jill, why don't you take Max for a pint at the Claddagh and I'll join you in a bit?'

'That sounds good to me. I'm gasping,' said Jill.

Max smiled, feeling positive for the first time in days. He felt he was part of a team, once again, ready to take the fight to the bad guys.

*

Max and Jill sat in the pub, a large faux Irish establishment a few minutes from the offices. Jill ordered a cider and Max his normal cranberry juice.

Jill looked at the juice with a raised eyebrow. 'That's not what I expected you to order. Fair to say you've changed, mate. You'd normally be straight in for a pint.'

'Not at the moment. I found that booze doesn't really agree with me. I also really like cranberry juice,' said Max, smiling.

'On a not totally unconnected matter, is there anything new after the shooting?'

Max felt the familiar knot in his stomach at the mention of the incident in London, two years ago. 'Nothing new. Inquest finding was what it was, but public interest lawyers are still pushing. You know how it goes. These things can drag on for years,' Max said, wanting to move the conversation on.

'Hence the juice?'

'Do you know much about the AC?' said Max.

'Only that she came from Manchester and is really well regarded. Loads of experience and managed to root out corruption when she was there. A bit of a tiger, I hear.'

'Not sure if that's good or bad, bearing in mind I've been driving a horse and cart through regs for a few days.' Max took a drink of his cranberry. It was dry and cold.

'Not like you had any choice.'

Max just shrugged and drank his juice. His phone buzzed in his pocket.

There was an email icon on the screen. Opening up the app, he didn't recognise the address, which seemed to be a series of numbers and letters with no recognisable features. No .com or co.uk either. Max frowned, wondering if it was just some spam, but something told him to open it.

There was a simple line of text and then an audio file attachment.

'*The deil's awa wi' the Exciseman,*' read the text. Recognition flashed through Max's mind. He had seen that somewhere before.

Jill must have seen the look on Max's face. 'What is it?'

'I'm not sure. I've been using a burner, but it's a line from a Scottish poem, or something.' He quickly copied and pasted the line into a web browser.

'You Jocks love all that shite, right?'

Max chuckled, still looking at the phone, curious about the audio file, but not wanting to listen to it in Jill's presence.

'Want another cranberry juice? I'll even get an umbrella and sparkler put in it to make it less girly, mate.'

'Sure, why not,' said Max as Jill stood and headed for the bar.

Max returned to the screen on his phone and pressed the audio file icon. He turned the volume low on the phone.

There was a hiss and some clicks and then he heard the voices. Max's eyes opened wide in shock. There was no doubt, it was a phone call of Tam Hardie talking to someone.

Max restarted the clip and held the phone close to his ear. The audio was clear as a bell with minimal interference.

'Slattery?'

'Aye, Tam, I'm here.'

'You find anything?'

'No, Leitch's sister is still nowhere to be found, and Ferguson is fuck knows where.'

'That's not good enough. What about Craigie?'

'His phone signal is still at his place and the tracker on his bike hasn't moved. No one's seen him at work.'

'Who is Craigie working with?'

'He was with Janie Calder, new bird, accelerated promotion type. She's working on another job.'

'Is she helping him?'

'No idea.'

'Jesus. Why am I paying you? Worse than useless. Anyway, shut up and listen. I've done what you should be doing. Intercepts will be up and running on Craigie and Phillips soon. We'll know everything they know and I need you to be ready to act.'

'Christ, how'd you manage that?'

'Shut up, Jack. You still have the item I gave you?'

'It's safe.'

'Well, be ready.'

'What about Leitch's bastard kid in London?'

'All in hand, leave that to me.'

The call abruptly ended.

Jill placed Max's cranberry down in front of him. 'What was that?'

'Nothing. Load of spam nonsense,' said Max, his insides churning, his thoughts on Bruce Ferguson.

48

'From the OP. Stand by, stand by, stand by. Subject one is out of the premises, and is right, right, right, along Stoneleigh Road towards Tottenham High Road, walking casually, not aware and I'll have him in view for two hundred metres, camera is rolling.' Jill Strother wiped the sweat from her eyes and swore under her breath as she sat in the rear of what appeared from the outside to be an electrician's van. Rolls of cable and other tools in a false back at the rear of the load space completed the subterfuge. The front dash was littered with greasy sandwich wrappers, old invoices, a crushed Coke can and a copy of the *Sun*. It was fairly unusual for Jill to be in the OP van, but in this particular case where the objective was the recording of a test call, it made as much sense for her to be in there as anywhere else. The stultifying heat was beginning to make her regret that decision, however.

The van was plain white and as unremarkable as any of the other thousands of vans driving the north London streets at ten in the morning. The inside, however, was a little different. It had a swivel chair and a bank of monitors all showing images captured by the four cameras front, side and rear of the van. Jill took a draught of water from her insulated bottle and cursed the absence of air conditioning. All that tech, and you still had to sweat like this. She would be the subject of much mickey-taking when they almost had to pour her out of the bloody van. Jill tweaked the control for the rear camera and followed the loping gait of Eustace Fielding as he sauntered down the street, looking at the phone he held in his hand.

'Be aware, subject one is holding a mobile in his right hand. Control, now would be a good time for the call,' said Jill into the mic at the control panel.

'All received, be aware, OP, call is going in now,' the booming voice of Terry, the surveillance team controller came over the net.

'From control we have a ringtone our end, be aware.'

Jill watched as Fielding reached for his pocket. 'From OP, subject one is reaching for his pocket, and there's another phone, looking at the handset now, and raising it to his ear. Looks like he's answering.'

There was a brief pause. Fielding pulled the phone away from his ear, a frown on his face, then he pocketed it once again.

'From control, phone answered. We are good to go. Trojan nine four seven, we are now authorised for hard-stop, over to you.'

A new voice came over the airwaves: 'All Trojan units from nine four seven, we are state red, repeat state red. Nine four five, you in position at junction of Stoneleigh with High Road?'

'From nine four five, yes, yes. In position.'

'Nine four seven, we are on Stoneleigh, towards High Road. He's right between us. OP, still have eyeball?'

Jill spoke calmly. 'Yes, yes, subject one approaching junction, distance twenty metres.'

A more urgent voice came on the net. 'Nine four seven, we now have eyeball on subject one; we are going to engage. Nine four five, be aware.'

'Nine four seven, yes, yes, in position.'

'All units, strike, strike!' came the calm, assertive voice of the firearms controller. There was a roar as a big BMW X5 tore past the OP van closing fast on Eustace Fielding as he approached the junction. Suddenly, an officer wearing a chequered baseball cap rounded the corner, a carbine in his shoulder sighted directly at Fielding.

'Armed Police!' he bellowed, the carbine levelled at Fielding's chest. Fielding reacted immediately, turning and sprinting off back the way he had walked, only to be confronted by the BMW, which screeched to a halt and two officers disembarked, using the doors as cover, carbines levelled at Fielding. The multiple shouts of 'Armed Police' were audible in the back of the van. Jill zoomed in on the scene, recording everything.

Fielding suddenly reached into his waistband, a mix of panic and sheer unadulterated rage on his broad face.

'Shit, shit, no,' muttered Jill. A bead of sweat ran down her face and she had to wipe it out of her eyes.

When his hand reappeared, it was holding a pistol. In what seemed to Jill like slow motion his hand raised, the gun pointing at the officers from the BMW.

'From OP, subject armed, subject armed,' she bellowed into the radio.

There was a crack, and Fielding's hand bucked, a shower of sparks bursting from the pistol. There was an immediate response of a series of sharp cracks from the officers' carbines and Fielding fell, like a puppet whose strings had just been cut.

There was a moment of total silence, and then things went crazy on the radio. 'Man down, man down! Suspect one has engaged firearms officers and is down. Paramedic required, urgently,' bellowed one of the firearms officers, the stress evident in his voice.

Jill focused the camera in as the firearms officers switched roles and sprinted forward to try to save Fielding, who moments earlier had been trying to kill them.

A crowd was already beginning to form as the officers worked on Fielding, one of them performing chest compressions. The bystanders all had their arms extended, phones in hands, as they recorded the unfolding drama before them.

Jill was relieved to see the green uniforms of the paramedics, who had been monitoring the operation by radio, arrive at the scene and take over from the firearms cops.

Within ten minutes there were emergency vehicles everywhere and a rapidly swelling crowd of onlookers being ushered back by uniformed officers. They were stretching blue and white scene tape around the area. Even through her camera, Jill could feel the atmosphere change from calm and professional to febrile as the bystanders became more and more aggrieved. She needed to get out of here urgently, or there was every possibility that the van she was currently in would end up in flames.

A few minutes later, the alarm blipped on the van. She looked up at camera one and was relieved to see Doug opening the van door.

'You okay, mate?' he called from the front as he started the engine.

'I am now you're here. I've a feeling it's going to get a little bit lively,' she said, using the crawl hatch to get into the front, and strapping herself into the passenger seat.

'The crowd is getting much bigger, and angrier, by the minute. I just had to walk through them all to get to you. They're saying that the cops have murdered a black man. It's a good job I'm black, or I'm not sure I'd have made it through.' He smiled at Jill, but she could see the stress on his face.

As they drove away from Tottenham High Road, a group of about twenty young men jogged by, most with bandannas pulled over their faces. The whole dynamic one of anger.

'Bloody hell, this is going to be bad,' said Jill, tuning her radio to the local police channel, intending to report the marauding youths. The net was suddenly alive with shouts for assistance and screamed reports of violence.

The paper-thin veneer of peace was about to be tested to its limits.

49

Max and Tony Jeffry sat in the large corner office in one of the upper floors at New Scotland Yard. The room was silent, Max having just finished delivering the briefing to Assistant Commissioner Fowler. He had prepared his document on PowerPoint and included the surveillance footage of Hardie embracing Fielding. Max was thankful that he had retained working copies of the original. He had also included the video clips of Slattery and McGee arriving at Leitch's home and the images of Slattery arriving and leaving his house in the Mercedes. For good measure he had attached the photographs of the scissor jack in the rear of Duncan Ferguson's destroyed Focus at Sweeney's garage. He was thankful that he had saved everything in his cloud storage for easy access before leaving Scotland.

Assistant Commissioner Jeanette Fowler sat silently for a few more moments before speaking, in soft northern tones. 'So, let me get this straight. You haven't approached any of your management about any of this?' She looked at Max over her spectacles, her eyes shining with intelligence. Max had given the same verbal briefing that he had given to Detective Chief Superintendent Tony Jeffry, just the previous day.

'No, ma'am. Once I was removed from the case and put on enforced sick leave I realised that I couldn't trust anyone in Police Scotland. I'm also fairly sure that at least two murders have been facilitated by serving or ex Police Scotland officers and I'm convinced that Hardie intends to use his contacts to kill the surviving relatives of William Leitch, which is also evidenced by the fact that Leitch's birth son is now in intensive care at the Royal Free Hospital.'

Max had decided to leave out all mention of the illegal intercept that had been emailed to him. That would make a complicated situation almost impossible to manage, and would doubtless put Bruce Ferguson in a difficult position in the future.

'Tony, what's your take on this?' AC Fowler turned to Tony Jeffry.

'Ma'am, I know Max from old and I can vouch for him and his integrity without a second's hesitation. It really does seem that Police Scotland is penetrated by a powerful corrupt element. The question is, what do we do about it?'

AC Fowler sighed, a thoughtful look on her face. 'One thing is clear. We have to act, and we have to act fast. Eustace Fielding's family are demanding answers and we were only a whisker away from a full-scale riot after he was shot yesterday. I make it clear that I attach no blame to anyone involved in this operation. I've seen the surveillance and body-worn video footage and I've briefed the community leaders as to their contents. Fielding was clearly shot, after first firing on police and I have relayed that to the interested parties. They're keeping a lid on any disorder, but we'll have to be clear what sits behind this operation, and we can't do that whilst the situation in Scotland remains as it is.'

'Agreed, ma'am. I'm going to take a wild guess. You have an idea?' Tony said, half-smiling.

'Funnily enough, I do. It's a fortunate coincidence that the recently appointed Chief Constable of Police Scotland is a good friend of mine. We served together in GMP and he's a good man whom I would trust with my life. It won't surprise you to learn that he was appointed very much as a new broom after the authority lost faith in the previous incumbent, and there has been a nasty smell of corruption within the organisation. We spoke just a few days ago, and his number-one priority is tackling it. We may be able to come up with a strategy that will satisfy Police Scotland by bringing the Hardie family and the corrupt elements in Police Scotland down.'

'What's in it for us?' asked Tony.

'Well, at this stage we suspect that Hardie had asked the late Eustace Fielding to facilitate the murder of Will Harding, offspring of Willie Leitch, so this gives us a genuine and reasonable interest. We, as in the Met, have an obligation to see that if Hardie did task Fielding with this murder, then he is brought to justice for it. We can't do that without the assistance of Scottish Police, but we can't use normal means of communication, or we may as well just phone Tam Hardie ourselves and tell him what we're planning. So, my suggestion is that you guys go and grab a coffee whilst I phone Chief Constable Chris Macdonald and see what options are open to us.'

50

Max sat in the canteen at Scotland Yard, nursing a lukewarm coffee. Tony had disappeared after receiving a call from the AC. Clearly machinations and plans were afoot, and Max wondered, nervously, what the next play would be.

One thing was for sure, he was in too deep, now. He had planted trackers illegally, carried out surveillance without authority and broken a suspect's elbow without reporting it. He had relocated witnesses without any authority and was now liaising with another force and planning actions without the knowledge of his superiors.

He thought of how this all started, at that bleak grave in Ballachly a few days ago. The grave said that it should never be opened, and because someone had, many people had died. If only Hardie hadn't found that grave. Six victims, and counting. If they didn't stop this, how high would the death toll reach?

He shook his head, sadly, realising that all of this could easily end his career. And then what, or who, was he? He longed for a drink. Just one cold beer would almost be like a tonic now. He rubbed his face, trying to break the train of dark thoughts that were beginning to seep into the corner of his mind.

He dialled a number from memory on his phone, butterflies

in his stomach. Please answer, he thought, almost desperately. The phone diverted straight to voicemail.

'Hi, it's Katie. Sorry I'm obviously doing something more interesting right now. Leave a message or call back. Or don't. Up to you, byeee!'

Max's shoulders sagged. He missed her so much, and she was only an hour away from where he was sitting. He longed to see his wife, to hold her, just for a few moments.

'You okay, mate?' said Tony, appearing suddenly, causing Max to start.

'Yeah, I'm fine, Guv,' he lied.

'We're on. You have a flight booked at 6 p.m. back to Glasgow. Tomorrow morning at eight, call this number and you'll be told where to go.' Tony handed over a slip of paper with a number scrawled on it and continued. 'You'll have to make the same presentation you just made to the AC to your chief constable. He wants to hear it first and be ready to answer a load of questions. Don't hold anything back, Max, not the dodgy surveillance, or slightly illegal tracker deployments, not busting elbows. The AC didn't tell me anything much, but the inference she gave me is that he isn't the slightest bit surprised. We're gonna make this right, for both forces. This situation stops, and it stops right now.'

51

Unsurprisingly the dream hit Max again, waking him in a cold, cloying sweat, with a gasp. Nutmeg showed her usual concern, nuzzling him with a cold nose, her tail thumping, rhythmically.

Max had arrived home at about 9 p.m., only to find the little dog sitting at the bottom of the track, as always. His first action had been to sweep the house for any new electronic devices, but he found nothing. The cameras had been clear, apart from a couple of Nutmeg-initiated recordings. He'd been really tired, so had gone straight to bed, sleeping heavily until the dream dragged him awake.

He was too tired and weary to run, and a little nervous at the forthcoming meeting with the chief. So, he made strong coffee, and just sat, contemplating.

He picked up his phone that he'd retrieved from the garage last night. There were two missed calls from Ross and a voice-mail. Max keyed into his mailbox and listened to Ross's rough Highland brogue.

'Max, you twat, why the fuck aren't you answering my bastarding calls? Even though you're a bloody nugget, I'd like to know that you're not dead. Call me back.'

Max wondered whether to call him back but discounted it;

he could bloody well wait. He then thought about whether to call Janie. Remembering the earlier strange email with the intercepted call, he laid it back down on the coffee table. Picking up his burner, he dialled Janie on the number she had messaged him with just the other day, feeling a little guilty about not keeping her in the loop.

'Firstly, you're an arse for not being in touch until now. Secondly, you're a double-arse for ringing me this early. I'm not an insomniac, like you,' said Janie, her voice gummy with sleep.

'Morning, sorry on both counts, but I have to say that "double-arse" is a tremendous insult. Kudos,' said Max, chuckling.

'Well, it's accurate, DS double-arse. Where are you?' He heard her yawn, extravagantly.

'Home. I've a meeting with someone significant this morning. We may be turning the tide, soon.'

'Sounds intriguing. Care to elaborate?'

'Not yet. You want an update?'

'Of course.'

Max explained what had happened during the arrest of Fielding, and the mysterious message with the poem and audio file.

'Shit, I saw on the news that police had shot someone, and that's a line from the Burns poem that was in Leitch's journal. Blimey. What are you thinking?'

'Ferguson almost certainly knows more about this feud than he let on, and he has access to intelligence product that we'd never get our hands on. I'm also thinking that this is both a curse and a potential opportunity.' Max sipped his coffee, relishing the smooth, strong brew.

'I'm looking for the opportunity, but I can just see the bad sides.'

'Upside is that we know they're doing it, but they don't know that we know. I also think that we need to keep it to ourselves, okay?'

'So, no calls on our normal phones, right?'

'Quite the opposite, Janie. I'm going to call you straight after this on some pretence, just chat to me and sound normal. We need them to think we don't know, okay?'

'Fine.'

'Are you working today?'

'I'm at court this morning, and this afternoon I have more camera footage from the trafficking job to review. Deep joy. I'm getting properly stiffed at the moment. Did you know that I'm being referred to by the twats in the office as "Fast-Track Fannie"?'

'Can't say I did,' said Max, the corners of his mouth twitching and his eyes crinkling, trying desperately not to laugh.

'It's not funny, Sergeant,' said Janie.

'Definitely not. I'll have words when I'm back.'

'Oh great, then I'll be Fast-Track Fannie the grass, instead.'

'How's Ross behaving?'

'Odd. Not as abusive as normal and he doesn't seem to want me going out much. Are we sure about him? With everything that's going on, he's behaving awful strange.'

Max turned this over in his mind for a few moments, not knowing what to make of it. He had hardly thought of Ross since leaving the offices a few days ago, which was really odd, given the circumstances. He thought he trusted him, but in light of recent events, he now had doubts. 'Ask me that question a few days ago, and I'd have said a resounding yes, but with everything that's gone on, I just don't know. Simple answer: beyond you, I don't trust any bugger.'

'Understandable.'

'Just keep your head down. I'll speak to you soon.' Max hung up. He immediately took out his other phone and called Janie again.

'Hi, Max, you okay?'

'Hi, Janie, you working today?'

'Yeah, I'm at court this morning at Glasgow Sheriff's, then office this afternoon. How are you feeling?'

'I'm fine. Fancy meeting for a coffee?'

'Sure, I'll be done by one. Where?'

'Usual place.'

'Nice, I'll buy you a sandwich. Any word on your occupational health appointment?'

'Not yet, as to be expected,' said Max, smiling to himself. Any listener would be learning nothing by this call.

'Okay, well, see you at one, then.'

Max sipped his coffee once more and looked at Nutmeg, who was staring at him intently and hopefully. 'Come on then, let's go for a walk.'

*

It was almost eight by the time Max and Nutmeg returned from the walk in the fields around the house, and the little dog's lolling tongue told the story of an energetic hour spent chasing a tennis ball.

Max dialled the number given to him by Tony, a little knot of nerves in his stomach. It was not often that any officer spoke to the chief constable of a force, especially not in circumstances such as these.

The phone was answered on the third ring.

'Max?' The voice was deep, confident and resonant with a distinct Edinburgh accent.

'Yes,' was all that Max replied.

'I had a long conversation with AC Fowler last night and I think I understand the issues. Can we meet this morning?'

'Of course, sir. When and where?'

'You know the Best Western in Crossford?'

'Aye, only about fifteen minutes away from me.'

'Well, I'm there, room twenty-eight. Can you come now?'

'Sure, I'll get going.'

'Great. One thing: Jeanette said you had prepared a useful PowerPoint briefing. Do you have it?'

'Yes, sir.'

'Bring it, will you?' The phone went dead.

Max went to the cupboard and retrieved his bike jacket and helmet and picked up the SD card that contained the briefing from the mantelpiece.

After going out to the garage, he slid his fingers behind the skid-plate and pulled the tracker off, snapping it onto the side of a dumbbell. Gunning the engine, he rode off sedately down the track. As soon as he hit the road at the bottom, he opened the taps, the engine roared and he sped off. He had a route in mind, which would, should anyone try to follow, leave them simply grasping at thin air. Following an experienced surveillance officer is difficult. Following one on a high-powered motorcycle is impossible.

52

Max parked his bike at the rear of the hotel, tucked well out of sight from the road. It was a typical chain hotel with a glazed door to reception. Max saw a guest leave the hotel from the rear car-park door that was operated with a room card. He smiled and stepped to one side as the guest, a man in a cheap-looking suit, carrying a briefcase, exited, acknowledging Max with a nod. Max entered the hotel and strode, as if he belonged, along the corridor, as always remembering his surveillance training. If you look like you belong, no one will question why you are there. He continued across the worn carpet and turned where an arrow pointed to rooms fifteen to thirty. Following the sign, Max was soon standing outside room twenty-eight. He took a deep breath, aware that he was about to meet the most senior police officer in Scotland, in relation to his own activities, which even his least vocal critic could reasonably call 'questionable'.

Max knocked twice, softly. There was a click and the door opened slowly. Ross Fraser stood there, resplendent in a rumpled blue suit, his red face split with a wide, genuine smile. 'Max Craigie, ya wee bastard. Come on in, the boss is waiting, and he's even got breakfast in, which isn't like him, as he's normally tight as arseholes.'

'I resent that remark, Ross,' rang out the familiar voice of the Chief Constable of Police Scotland.

53

Chief Constable Chris Macdonald handed a steaming mug of coffee across to Max. The table was laden with pastries and a bowl of fruit. Max was surprised to see no bed in the room, just a few armchairs and a desk with a laptop on it. He was even more surprised to see Jill Strother sitting on one of the chairs, a tablet computer in her hand.

'Fancy seeing you here, mate,' she said, grinning widely.

'Well, I'm a little surprised. Anyone want to tell me what's going on? Good morning, sir, by the way,' said Max, confusion swirling around his head. There had obviously been much liaison and planning in the few hours since he briefed AC Fowler.

Chief Constable Macdonald looked at Max with amusement. Max had only ever seen the head of the force on television, although his reputation was solid. He was well fleshed, in his late forties, with short, dark hair. He was dressed in an open-neck shirt with dark suit trousers. His face was lined and creased with laughter lines at the corner of his grey eyes.

'Have a seat. You're probably a bit surprised to see both Ross and Jill here, I imagine.' His voice was rich and smooth.

'A little. Looks like things moved quickly after I left London yesterday.'

'Pretty much. I got the call from Jeanette Fowler yesterday and she was kind enough to give me a very brief overview of what has been happening and how the cases in Scotland and London overlap. I asked for a representative from the inquiry team into the attempted murder in Enfield, hence Jill's presence.'

'Fair enough. I also wasn't expecting to see Ross here, either.'

'Thanks for your support, Max,' said Ross, crumbs from a pastry flying from his mouth, as he managed to chuckle and cough at the same time.

'Well after you bawling me out, and then leaving me flailing under the weight of nauseating shite from DCS White, I really don't know what to think,' said Max, feeling his cheeks begin to flush.

'Perhaps it would help if I explained a little about where we are, and what I want to achieve. But before I do, let me explain why Ross is here. I've known Ross for many years; in fact we were PCs together in Glasgow almost thirty years ago. Part of Ross's responsibilities in his current role has been as a pair of eyes and ears inside the serious and organised crime command. There is nobody in this force I trust more than Ross, okay?' Macdonald said, softly.

'Aye, you can call me DI Golden Bollocks, Craigie,' said Ross, his cheeks bulging with pastry as he chewed furiously. Ross loved nothing more than food, particularly if he hadn't paid for it.

'I understand that, Guvnor, and I've no beef with Ross. For days now, I've been fighting this battle alone, had my motorbike bugged, probably my phone tracked and possibly intercepted and had to stop the murder of an innocent woman. I've been vilified, had my mental health questioned and I'm now wondering just how far the corruption goes in this bloody force. I've been roundly ignored. Just who is in control of Police Scotland, because it doesn't feel like we are?' Max surprised himself at the strength of feeling in his voice.

'I get how you feel, Max. If you give me a chance, maybe I can help you understand.'

Max sat on one of the vacant chairs. 'I'm listening.'

Macdonald sat behind the desk with the open laptop. 'Since I took over Police Scotland, not all that long ago, I've been really concerned about the impact and reach of corruption within our ranks. As you probably know, I was recruited from GMP, to move the force forward after the many problems that were highlighted in gory detail over the past few years. Anything I've tried so far has met obstacles and difficulties and it's probably fair to concede that I haven't made the strides I would have liked. The homicide command, it would appear, is riven with corruption, at many levels, and it seems this extends to senior officer level.'

'With the deepest of respect, sir. No shit, Sherlock.'

'Max ...' began Ross, clearly thinking of remonstrating with Max's insubordination, but he was stopped by a glare from Macdonald.

'I think Max has a point. The fact that this corruption has become so endemic is a poor reflection on all of us. What is important is what we now do about it. Will you work with us on this, Max?'

'Of course. I want them stopped. I joined the police to be one of the good guys,' said Max with feeling.

'We all did. Most of us stayed on that path, but some didn't and together we can stop them.'

'What, just us?'

'We have friends to call upon, which is why Jill is here.'

'Whatever you need from London, mate, you get,' said Jill firmly. 'The AC has promised surveillance, phone work, analysts – anything, mate. West London is bubbling with tension right now, and they want it to stop. We stop it by nicking those who organised the hit on that young lad.'

'Exactly, and between those of us in this room, we have some people we know we can trust. Firstly, Max, can you bring us up to date with this briefing?'

Max pulled out the SD card from his pocket and handed it over to Macdonald, who took it and slotted it into the port on the computer.

Ross shuffled his chair alongside Macdonald, and silently they clicked through the slides, taking in the text, images and video clips. When it was finished, they exchanged a wordless look.

'Shit,' said Ross. 'I didn't realise it was this bad. I know Slattery and I don't like the bastard one little bit, the snidey wee radge.'

'He makes all this possible for Hardie. He's the conduit into the teams. It's the classic tactic that was once rife in the Met,' said Max.

Macdonald stared at Max, a look in his eyes that he couldn't fathom. 'I don't say this lightly,' he said. 'You've done a tremendous job here, under the most terrible circumstances and I'm sorry that we weren't able to prevent this from happening. People are dead who shouldn't be dead because of this corruption and you weren't listened to. What do *you* think we should do?'

Max paused for a second, almost surprised to find a touch of emotion rising in his chest.

'We need some people, Guv. Just a few good people, and then we really take the fight back to them. We go proactive, we go covert, and we bring them down. All of them.'

There was a silence in the room whilst Max's words sunk in.

'Who do you need?' asked Macdonald.

'We need a surveillance team, preferably armed. I suggest a London team, get them up here at a covert location and we use them. We need unrestricted access to phone data, live cell sites and immediate access to any tech. All activity needs to be authorised covertly and not through the usual channels.'

The chief nodded. 'I'll speak to AC Fowler in London, and perhaps, Jill, if you link in, we can raise a team to relocate to Scotland for a short while?' Macdonald looked at Jill who nodded.

'The boss anticipated this possibility, sir. I think a team has been identified, and I'm assured that the Met's telephone intelligence unit is primed to assist with data and cell sites, if required. We have a dog in this fight, after all,' said Jill.

'Excellent. Authority levels you can leave to me, but if London can also liaise with the phone companies, that will be another layer of risk reduced and it would speed things up, massively. Who do you want to be point of contact for the data?'

'Janie Calder. She's trustworthy,' said Max.

'Janie's a little green, and, if I'm honest, a bit odd,' said Ross.

'She's not odd. She's just not being given a chance by some of the bloody Neanderthals in the office. She's smart, resourceful, and more importantly she's proved her worth over the last few days. I want her with us.'

'Consider it done. As she's accelerated promotion, she's due a rotation. I'll have her seconded to a project under my direct control. Not unusual for this to happen,' said Macdonald.

'Who else do we trust enough to bring in on this?' asked Ross.

'Sally Smith, no doubt about it. She has the benefit of knowing the background of the case well and I'm convinced she's straight. She's as frustrated as we are about what is happening,' said Max.

There was another pause in the conversation that was a little uncomfortable. They all knew that a journey was starting that would be difficult and involve going up against colleagues.

'First objectives?' asked the chief.

'Parallel prove by conventional and admissible means all of what Max has uncovered by unconventional means,' said Ross.

'We also need the tracker off Slattery's car, probably replacing it with a new one.'

'Agreed. Any suggestions on tactics moving forward?' asked Macdonald.

'I've a suggestion,' said Max.

'Go on,' said Macdonald.

'Test out their capabilities. We need to know what they know, and then decide who to target first. We look at McGee, then we look at Slattery. Slattery is the conduit in all of this. We get Slattery, we get to the lot of them,' said Max.

54

A few days later

Jack Slattery was driving into Glasgow, just as the evening rush hour had finished, ready to meet a possible new contact. He'd heard a whisper from one of his tame cops that this officer, who worked in covert policing, was 'approachable'. He was just looking for a parking space in the West End of Glasgow, close to the pub where he had been told the man drank, when his phone rang.

'Yeah?' he said as he reversed into the bay.

'Where are you?' said Tam Hardie.

'Just in the West End. What's up?'

'Elizabeth Phillips has called Craigie. They're meeting at seven in Luigi's Wine Bar in Nile Street. Get there now. The cell site for the phones are both in the city close to the place. Does Craigie know you?'

'No, I've never met him.'

'You know what he looks like, though?'

'I've seen a picture.'

'Okay, well get there, now, before they do. You still have the thing with you?'

'No man, it's at home.'

'Ah, fucking hell. Look, just keep an eye on them, and I'll send some boys. Follow them if you need to, but don't let the bastards out of your sight.' Tam hung up.

Slattery drove straight out of the parking space and began to head to Luigi's, which was only ten minutes away.

Sweat began to bead on Slattery's top lip and nerves gripped his stomach. Despite having just put one out, he reached for another cigarette, lighting it with a trembling hand. He didn't like this at all. Craigie was supposed to be really careful, a very shrewd operator. Slattery was glad he'd left the pistol at home, hidden in his shed. He really didn't know if he'd the courage to shoot someone in cold blood, especially not a policeman. He wondered just how Hardie had come by this information. Could Hardie have got an intercept on the phones, already? Jesus, he knew that Hardie had influence, but getting a phone tapped, especially that of a serving cop, was on the next level.

Fortunately, the traffic was light and within a few minutes, he was pulling up just one street away from Luigi's. A short walk and he was pushing the door open into the sleek wine bar. He used to drink in there pretty regularly, finding it a good place to meet contacts. Nice and quiet, with intimate booths covered in white, faux leather.

He went to the bar and ordered a lager and sat in a booth at the rear of the place that gave a good view of both entrances. He sipped his beer and checked his phone. Seeing nothing, he composed a quick WhatsApp to Tam.

I'm here, no sign yet.

The bar wasn't busy, only a few early evening drinkers getting noisy, necking overly expensive designer beers, or flutes of prosecco.

He was staring at his phone, scrolling through the news-feed, when he heard the door swing open. It wasn't Craigie or Phillips, but recognition flashed in his mind when he saw the stunningly beautiful girl sweep into the bar. It was Marta, and she was dressed to kill, as she often was, being one of the most expensive escorts in Glasgow. She used to work in Hardie's prostitution empire but had managed to get away from him and now was a freelancer advertising herself on internet sites. She sashayed up to the bar and sat demurely on a bar stool, her short skirt rising to show an inappropriate amount of tanned thigh. The sight of her long, silky hair, skin-tight top and impossibly high heels almost made him forget why he was here. He quickly realised that he wasn't the only pair of eyes in that bar watching her. Marta had that effect on men.

His phone buzzed in his pocket. He answered.

'You still there?' It was Hardie.

'Aye, no sign.'

'Well, they won't be there. Daft bitch called Craigie back to say she couldn't face it and was going to bed for a while. Said she'd call him back later, then switched off her phone. Stay local in case she changes her mind, okay?'

Slattery looked at the svelte form of Marta and smiled, slowly. 'Sure thing, Tam.'

The line went dead, and Slattery pocketed his phone. He stood and walked over to the bar, where Marta sat, a disappointed look on her face.

'Hello, Marta,' he said, smiling broadly.

Marta looked around, her face lighting up at the sight of Slattery, 'Jack, darling, so lovely to see you again.' She leaped to her feet and threw her arms around his neck.

Slattery returned her embrace, feeling her large breasts squashing against his chest, her sweet perfume overpowering in his nostrils.

'What are you doing here, babe?' she asked, her smile wide, her bright red lips framing white teeth, the front two of which were slightly gapped.

'Oh, you know, just a wee drink. How about you?'

'Supposed to meet a date, but he just call and stand me up,' she said, her bottom lip extended in a charmingly childish way.

'A coincidence, because my appointment has also failed to show. Fancy spending a little time with me?' Slattery was surprised to find himself feeling a bit nervous yet excited at the prospect of a couple of hours in Marta's sparkling company.

'Jack, of course I spend time with you, my favourite client. I just a little hurt you not see me for a long time.' Her Eastern European accent was delightfully sexy.

'Can I buy you another drink?'

'How kind. Champagne, of course,' she said, giggling.

Slattery ordered a bottle of horrifyingly expensive champagne and within a minute they were chinking glasses. He was delighted to feel her small, dainty hand resting on his upper thigh. It was a little strange, he thought. Marta was a whore. An expensive whore, admittedly, but still a whore. Being able to sleep with her was guaranteed, but he still liked to feel this was seduction on his part, that she was genuinely interested in a middle-aged man with spectacles, and a body that was going to seed.

One bottle of champagne led to another. It was so much fun to be laughing and joking with this goddess. She was a bright and intelligent girl, who had escaped a life of poverty in Slovakia, to find a lucrative use for her assets in Glasgow.

'Is your place nearby, darling?' slurred Jack.

'Oh, what you take me for?' She giggled.

'Oh, don't be a tease. You know how much I want you!'

'Well, darling, let's have another drink, then we go back to my place. It only five minute away.' She raised her glass and clinked it with Jack's.

*

Marta had drunkenly staggered with Jack the ten minutes back to her apartment, a small, clean and functional place in the heart of the West End. Within a minute they had been thrashing around on the bed, the room littered with their frantically discarded clothes.

The sex had been quick and torrid, Slattery far too drunk to be anything that could be considered impressive. He was soon snoring in the large, rumpled bed, his spectacles askew on his nose, and his hair falling over his face.

Once Slattery's breathing had become deep and even, Marta disentangled herself from him and went to the small bathroom. Pulling on a short robe she returned to the bedroom and located her phone on the dresser and composed a short message.

Now.

Marta quickly picked up all of Slattery's discarded clothing and folded it neatly on a chair in the corner of the room. Reaching into his jacket pocket, she found his phone and left the bedroom, closing the door softly behind her. She crept to the flat door and opened it.

Janie stood there, smiling, a small laptop computer in her hand. Marta handed the phone over, a big smile on her face. 'Janie, darling,' she whispered. 'It is Samsung. Unlock pattern is a "Z".' She mimed the drawing of the letter in the air. 'Be quick, he may wake up soon, although he normally sleep deep, you know, like pig.' She had a look of distaste on her face.

'I'll just be a minute,' said Janie, squatting on the floor and attaching a cable into the phone. She clicked and pressed a few buttons, and within a minute it was done. She handed the phone back to Marta.

'Thank you so much, Marta,' Janie, whispered, reaching in and hugging her, warmly.

Then she was gone, creeping down the stairs and out into the night.

55

Janie jumped into the unmarked Ford Mondeo, with Max at the wheel.

'All good?' said Max.

'Marta is an absolute diamond. She even knew the unlock code for the phone.'

'Impressive, although I have a feeling that she may have stretched her participating informant status a little in there,' said Max.

'I won't tell if you don't,' said Janie.

'My lips are sealed. After the call from Elizabeth Phillips's phone, Slattery went straight to the wine bar. Surveillance team videoed him going in, and one of the team managed to go in and capture him in there on a bag camera. Your impression of Elizabeth Phillips making a phone call to me must've been good.'

'Not difficult bearing in mind none of them know what she sounds like,' said Janie.

'Fair point.'

'How's the surveillance team?'

'It's like having the cast of *EastEnders* in Glasgow, but they're good. They're keen as mustard, probably because of the over-time they're getting paid by Police Scotland.'

'Everything's gone according to plan. Your tracker has been removed from Slattery's car and replaced by an official one. They've also managed to get a probe in the car – audio only, so we're good to go with Slattery.'

'It's all going a little *too* well,' said Max, frowning.

'Well, with his phone downloaded, and his current and live phone number, we can start the evidential phone work,' Janie said. 'I'm not sure how, but the AC in the Met has sourced me a direct link into the Telephone Investigation Unit in London. We'll be able to get live and real-time updates with no chance of compromise.'

'Excellent.' Max nodded at the digital clock. 'It's nearly 11 p.m. Let's get back to the base and get a look at Slattery's phone, identify the key numbers, and then you can see all the updates. Now this can all go in the evidential chain, we can nail these bastards.'

*

The base was a small self-contained unit in a new industrial estate on the edges of Glasgow. Ross had procured the place remarkably quickly on a short lease, via a covert purchase order, with a cover of being a newly formed double-glazing outfit.

It had several offices and a large open garage space, protected by a roller shutter. It was perfect for their purposes. IT had quickly been installed along with phone lines and a secure storage area for the Met firearms officers to store their guns.

Jill was at the office along with Ross when Max and Janie arrived.

'All go okay?' asked Ross, looking up from his computer.

'Yep. Slattery's phone download is here, and we've put a proper lump on his car in exchange for the one I bought from the spy shop. By the way can I claim expenses for the bloody thing?' Max tossed the SD card, which Ross caught.

'What, your slightly iffy, nay, highly illegal tracker that you attached to a hard-working ex-cop's car? Can you shite. You can whistle for it.'

'Thanks, so kind.'

'Claim an extra couple of hours' overtime.'

'You already owe me shitloads of overtime whilst I was trying to sort out Police Scotland's corrupt element. Oh, and saving poor Elizabeth Phillips from being beaten to death.'

'Oh, quit being the big I am. Let's look at this download,' Ross said, a broad grin on his face. Despite everything that Max had been through, the piss-taking was already in full flow, as it should be. It made him feel like he was back where he belonged, as part of a team.

'Plenty on it,' said Ross, looking at a spreadsheet on his computer.

'Lots of messages, some pictures and lots of call data. It'll take a while to get through.'

'Do we get an analyst?' asked Jill from the corner of the room, also looking at a monitor.

'Not yet,' said Ross.

'I have an intelligence download of the London job. We need to cross-reference the phones we have. So far, the time-line for the stabbing of poor Will Harding is that Eustace gets a message from a burner phone containing the photograph and address of the victim. There are then some calls between Fielding and the unknown number and then the photo goes from Fielding to his man who carries out the attack.'

'What's the number?' asked Ross.

'Ends 451,' she replied.

'Right, that's the last number into Slattery's phone,' said Ross, his spectacles balanced on his nose. 'Slattery also sent a message a wee while after, saying, "I'm here, no sign yet."'

'Bingo. So, whoever has that phone is the man who not only ordered the hit on Harding, but also on Elizabeth Phillips. We put that phone in someone's hands, we have our man,' said Jill.

'We have just one of our men. Whoever has that phone clearly has access to intercept information. When I made that call to Elizabeth Phillips's phone, they knew exactly where we were going to be. A cell site wouldn't take them to the particular bar that I arranged to meet in,' said Max.

'Well, this proves what we suspected. Those bastards are somehow getting intercepts on phones. Jesus Christ,' Ross blasted.

'This isn't just about low-level police corruption. They have everything. This goes to the highest levels of the force.'

'I'll call the chief.' Ross raised his phone and dialled.

'Sir, it's Ross. Progress report.' He then quickly and efficiently briefed the chief constable on the evening's events. After he had finished, he listened for a few moments, and then nodded, as if the chief was standing in front of him. 'We're on it, Boss,' and he hung up. Ross paused, looking at the team, his eyes full of worry. 'You lot get going. It's late. Get some kip, the chief wants to meet us here tomorrow morning at eight. This is much bigger than Hardie.'

56

Chief Constable Macdonald faced the five officers sitting in front of him, a determined look on his face. Max, Janie, Jill, Ross and Sally were all tired and weary, but there was a definite feeling of unity of purpose in the room, despite the lack of sleep.

'Okay, ladies and gents, where are we?' Macdonald asked.

Ross told the chief about the previous night's activity with Slattery and Marta.

'Impressive lady, is Marta,' said Max.

'She certainly is,' said Janie.

The chief constable sighed. 'You've no idea how much persuasion I had to use to convince the surveillance commissioners that using her was proportionate. So on one hand I'm glad we have proved what we suspected, but on the other I'm horrified that somehow, someone in my force could be this corrupt. The ramifications are going to be enormous.'

'It was worth it, sir. We've captured a reasonable amount of data from the download on Slattery's 500 phone. Evidentially it's crucial, as this, linked with the reaction to the call made on Elizabeth Phillips's phone, proves that Slattery is taking orders from the owner of the 451 number, who, it would seem is being fed intercepted phone calls,' said Ross.

'I'm genuinely relieved to hear all this. Who do we think is feeding 451 the intercepted calls?' asked Macdonald.

'The Met TIU are doing sterling service for us, Boss. 451 received a call immediately before calling Slattery from a number ending 786. It's a fair assumption that this is the person passing the intercepts to 451. Predictably all numbers are burners, no data held, no top-up information and no intelligence leads on either,' said Janie.

'Cell sites?' asked Ross.

'451 is central Glasgow and rarely moves. It's a densely populated area, so not much help. 786 has only been switched on intermittently, and on those occasions has been in central Edinburgh,' said Janie, looking at her laptop.

'How about Slattery's phone?' asked Macdonald.

'Matches his movements, perfectly,' Janie said, tapping at her computer.

'We need more than this. Suggestions?' said Macdonald.

'Sir, what is objective number one?' asked Max.

'Guys, there are two equally vital objectives. Destroy the Hardies and bring each and every dirty cop down. We do this by solving these murders, all of them, whether in Caithness, Glasgow or London,' said Macdonald.

'Then we need a trigger incident. We need to chuck a rock in the pond and watch the ripples,' said Max.

'Okay, so what?'

'We arrest McGee.'

'Why McGee? Surely Slattery is the prime target,' said Macdonald.

'Think about it, the download of Slattery's phone gives it all. McGee will doubtless have damning evidence on his phone, and we have a good shot at finding evidence of him organising the crash that killed Duncan Ferguson. We nick McGee, put pressure on him, and who knows where it'll lead. It's also absolutely bound to make a whole heap of ripples that we are now in a position to monitor,' Max said, with conviction.

'Can anyone think of a reason why we don't do this?' asked Macdonald.

'I can only think of another reason to do it,' said Jill from the back of the room.

'We're all ears,' said Max.

'Slattery's car is lumped and probed up. We make a noisy arrest and let the jungle drums start to bang. We then sit and watch the phones and listen to the probe in Slattery's car. I reckon the dodgy bastards will make it easy for us.'

'This makes total sense to me,' said Ross.

'Then we do it tomorrow, travel up north today, get hotels and get him first thing. I have a management board meeting this morning with my DCCs at Tulliallan. I'm going to throw in a few breadcrumbs about an anti-corruption investigation. Janie, be ready to watch the phones after about eleven-thirty, okay?'

'Sure thing, Guvnor,' said Janie.

'Ah, guys, we're hanging with cockneys far too much, but maybe whilst this job is running, Guvnor is just fine,' said Macdonald and everyone laughed.

57

Chief Constable Chris Macdonald stared at his command team of three deputy chief constables, all in uniform, their shoulders bedecked with the rank insignia denoting their lofty status. The only other occupants of the room were the deputy chief officer who wore a well-tailored suit. As a civilian, she held no rank, but was the senior, non-warranted member of the command team, responsible for budgets and corporate strategy. Macdonald's secretary sat, her laptop open, minuting the meeting.

The meeting had been entirely anodyne, up until now, mainly discussing the new corporate messages to be delivered to all staff in a few weeks. He was striving to simplify the strategies that he felt were overcomplicated and difficult for staff to get behind. He was about to throw a metaphorical hand grenade into the room very soon.

'Anything to add, Jean?' He nodded at Jean O'Neill, the DCC with lead for people and professionalism. She shook her head. 'No, I think we're all on board.'

'Alan?' he looked at DCC Alan Jones, a grizzled ex West Midlands detective, with responsibility for crime and operations.

'All seems clear enough to me. Simpler message, easier buy-in, I'd say.'

'Geoff?' he said, smiling at DCC Geoff Caldwell, who was the officer in charge of local policing.

'Absolutely clear as a bell. I'm sure local units will all get their shoulders to the wheel with this. Excellent leadership,' he said in an educated Edinburgh burr.

Macdonald forced a smile. In reality he loathed meetings with these snidey bastards. They'd all throw him under a bus if they got the chance.

'Finally, Lucy?' Macdonald looked at Lucy Ritchie the deputy chief officer.

'All the civilian staff will be completely on board.' She smiled. At least she wasn't after his job, he thought. In fact, Lucy was the only one of the lot he trusted.

'Okay, well that's nearly us, then. Once the graphics are ready, I want this message circulated widely on the internet. In fact, I'll write an all-staffer to accompany it. It's not negotiable, and we need all staff on board, okay?' There were nods all around the table.

'Okay, final thing. I'm looking into the feasibility of running an anti-corruption initiative very soon. I'm really concerned about some reports I'm getting from certain quarters about corruption derailing a number of live inquiries. I have some clean-skins looking at this now, reporting directly to me. I hope to be able to give a more detailed update at the next command team meeting, but for now, just leave it with me.' He stood, shuffling his papers, indicating the meeting was over.

No one else stood. 'Sorry, Chris, can you say that again?' said Jean, her face a mix of puzzlement and annoyance.

'I'm sure you heard me, Jean. It doesn't affect any other functions. I just want to explore the possibility of a new anti-corruption strategy.' He smiled.

'But, as lead for Professional Standards, surely I should be on this?' said Jean, almost struggling for words.

'Nope. This is my project. If it comes to anything, you'll be the first to know. For now, this is merely exploratory. Now if you'll excuse me, I have an appointment.'

'Chris, what the hell is going on?' blurted Alan Jones. 'You can't just run around like a bull in a china shop. This is sensitive stuff, and we're here to offer our expertise. This is no way to lead . . .'

'Alan, maybe it's time to remind you all that I am still the chief. This is my train set, and last time I looked, I make the calls. Now, if you'll excuse me, I've somewhere to be.' Macdonald picked up his files and strode out of the room, leaving the angry voices behind him.

As he walked, he tucked the files under his arm and composed a text to Janie.

Watch the phones.

58

Mick McGee was hungover. Badly, badly hungover. His mouth tasted like the bottom of a parrot's cage (whatever that tasted like) and his tongue was so dry that it stuck to the side of his mouth. He staggered out of bed, swearing as he tripped on a discarded shoe. He blearily made his way to the bathroom, belching as he stood over the grimy and stained porcelain.

He didn't need to check his watch to realise that he was late for work. He had promised himself that he wouldn't get too drunk last night, but his resolve had weakened as he entered the world of drunk-barfly discussions with the other drinkers at the bar of the Crown.

This had been his life for the last six months, ever since his wife had gone. She had just buggered off with the kids, leaving him with nothing but mountains of debt, and a proclivity for drinking far too much. He was an old campaigner, though, and hungover or not, he would always get to work. He looked at his reflection, noting the straw-like hair standing on end, heavy stubble and red-rimmed eyes. He looked dreadful, he had to admit. He stole a glance at his watch, and saw it was close to seven. If he got a wriggle on, he wouldn't be too late, and, sod it, he was in charge, anyway. He'd send Ian, the senior

PC, a message and he could deliver the briefing and get the troops out.

He quickly ran an electric shaver over his face, removing the worst of the stubble. A lightning brush of the teeth and a damp flannel on his unruly hair and he was good to go. He opened up the smeared mirror door of the bathroom cabinet and quickly necked a couple of paracetamol and, for good measure, a couple of ibuprofen.

Despite feeling shockingly unwell, he was starting to cheer up a little. He was due a big payday from Slattery soon, after all his efforts. That would keep every bastard at bay. And best of all, his bitch of a wife wouldn't know about it. He smiled grimly. Ten grand would make any hangover more tolerable.

He located his uniform trousers and pulled his black base layer police top on. He hated these tops. They were fine if you were a buff thirty-year-old, but for a fifty-one-year-old man, with a drink problem and terrible diet, they did no favours. After putting on his shoes, he began to search for his keys, but as often was the case, post piss-up he couldn't immediately find them. Opening the front door, he was unsurprised to see them still in the lock, jangling and swinging, almost mocking him for being such a mess. He shook his head ruefully and slammed the door behind him, heading for his elderly Focus parked on the grim street he had rented a house on. The properties were uniformly ugly, with grey pebbledash frontages, all thrown up at minimal cost to deal with Wick's expanding population.

He blipped the fob and the indicators blinked as the car unlocked. As he opened the door, he realised he wasn't alone. Three casually dressed figures stood watching him, distasteful looks on their faces.

His vision cleared a little, and he recognised one of them. It was Max Craigie, the DS from Serious Crime. He was standing with a slim, young female officer and a smartly dressed officer

293

who spoke in a soft voice. 'Sergeant McGee, I'm DI Sally Smith from the Major Incident Team at Inverness.'

Sergeant Mick McGee's heart lurched, and his legs suddenly felt as if they were made of jelly. Oh shit, he thought, looking at Max Craigie and remembering their encounter a few days ago. There could only be one reason why they were here. Fear gripped him, and he began to breathe deeply, his heart rate accelerating. It was all over. He was screwed.

Max Craigie spoke, his voice firm and resolute. 'Open your boot, Mick.' A requirement, not a question. His insides began to churn. Craigie knew, but how the hell did he know? He began to think of remonstrating, demanding evidence of their grounds to search. But he knew; he just knew.

'Open it now,' Craigie said, a little more strongly.

McGee said nothing, just handed the keys to Craigie, his face falling as he did. His head swam, and he staggered slightly. The younger female officer steadied him. 'Sit on the wall, Sergeant McGee. We're going to search your car. You know the drill,' she said in a well-spoken, light Edinburgh burr.

McGee sat, as instructed, the colour draining from his face, the street beginning to spin.

His heart sank further when he saw Craigie begin to rifle through the contents of his hatchback, the two other officers just staring at him with blank faces. He inwardly cursed his stupidity. Cursed that bastard Slattery. It had all seemed so reasonable when ten grand was mentioned, but not anymore. Why hadn't he just got rid of the bloody thing in his boot? He could have got a new jack from a breaker for a tenner.

Craigie nodded at DI Smith who looked in the boot of the car and shook her head, with a half-smile. Craigie showed her the screen on his phone and she nodded and turned to Mick.

'Oh, Mick, keeping the jack from Duncan's car wasn't a great idea, was it?' Her tone was that of a teacher talking to an errant child.

'It's not the same one,' he said, but there was no force in his words. He was defeated.

'When Max found it in Sweeney's,' she said, 'he took a picture of it on his phone, which I have here. It has the same scratches, even has the dirt from the graveyard. You know we'll prove that this jack belonged to Duncan Ferguson. You stole from a dead man, to cover it all up. You need to tell us everything and you need to tell us right now.'

McGee closed his eyes and tried to think, his head spinning. There was no deal here to be had. If he told them anything, he wouldn't last a day in prison. He knew the reach that these people had. Wherever he was, they'd get him.

'I want a solicitor,' he said, still not looking up, his thoughts on Slattery and those who sat above him.

'You can have a solicitor, Mick. We're going to Burnett Road, now, but before we do, I'm about to direct a PolSA team to rip your house and car to pieces. You need to think about this now, okay? Are we going to find anything?' the woman said.

He knew what they would find, because PolSA teams never missed anything. He cursed his tight-fistedness. It's not like brake callipers were expensive, he could have just bought some.

'I want a solicitor. I'm saying nothing.'

59

Slattery pressed the button to cancel the hands-free call in his Mercedes, his heart pounding in his chest. This wasn't supposed to happen. He would have to tell Hardie. If he didn't tell him and he found out from other sources, then Slattery knew he would catch hell. He pulled over to the side of the road.

He lit a cigarette, inhaling deeply, and dialled.

'Yes.' Hardie's voice was terse and caused a crackle of distortion in the car speakers. It was always like this; he rarely smiled and was always angry.

'It's Jack.'

'What?'

'McGee has been arrested.'

'What? What the fuck for?'

'Murder. A contact at Burnett Road has just seen him getting brought in. Cops are saying that he was part of a conspiracy to murder Duncan Ferguson by setting up the accident. Apparently, they have evidence that he did something to the brakes of the car and interfered with the barrier.'

'How didn't we know this was going to happen?' Hardie's voice almost exploded out of the speakers.

'None of my sources knew about it. Sally Smith and Max

Craigie seem to be at the centre of it, leastways they've brought him in, with some other bird with a cockney accent.'

'Who is she?'

'No idea.' Slattery pulled on his cigarette, nervously.

'Jack, I pay you to know this shit and I don't like the way this is going.'

'I don't know. My man just said that Sally Smith has been taken away from murder teams on some project and Craigie is no longer on sick leave. He doesn't know how. Something is happening, and no one knows what.'

'Craigie, that bastard. He just won't bloody leave it alone, will he? Right, I want you to get to his place, now, and do what we discussed, right? He's in Inverness, so he'll be a while. We need to discredit him.'

'Okay, Tam.'

'What evidence do they have?' asked Hardie.

'Looks like Ferguson used the jack from his car when Leitch called him for help. That's the theory, anyway. Mick was supposed to get rid of the jack when Craigie found it in the wreck. The daft bastard put his own jack in to replace it, which wasn't the worst idea, ever, but then he decided to keep the jack to replace the one from his car. He's such a tight-arse that man.'

'Does he have a lawyer?'

'Still booking him in. Not got to it yet,' said Slattery.

'Right, get Leo Hamilton and tell him I want him at Burnett Road right away, and he'll be representing McGee. I don't care if he has a solicitor coming from elsewhere, we want our man in there. We need the appropriate message getting to the daft bastard. If he grasses, we're all in the shit.'

'He won't grass. He knows the consequences if he does.'

'Damn right. Make sure Leo gives that message to him. What about his family?'

'Wife left him months ago. Took his kids away down to Edinburgh.'

'Right, make sure he gets the message that it's not just him who will suffer.' Tam's voice was pure venom.

'Aye, he knows the score,' said Slattery, his voice low.

'Best he does. No more shite on this job. Get onto your sources, right now and get to the bottom of it.'

60

Max sat in the incident room at Burnett Road Police Station with Sally, both scrawling arrest notes and making witness statements. They had left the PolSA team finishing the search of the vehicle and McGee's property, but had been updated over the phone on what they had recovered. An album of photographs had been emailed to them. The initial assessment was that it was cataclysmic for McGee.

Feeling the buzz in his pocket he reached for his burner mobile and saw it was Janie calling.

'Janie?'

'Slattery just called Hardie, full update given. Looks like there is a source in Burnett Road who let Slattery know, which is bloody perfect. Sounds like your explanation of the evidence, which you delivered in a tediously detailed fashion to the custody sergeant, had the desired effect. There is only one way they could have learned about all that detail, straight from someone who was listening. Were many people in the custody suite?'

'A good half a dozen. Did you capture the call on the probe?'

'Yep, the whole thing. Hardie ordered Slattery to get hold of Leo Hamilton to be his lawyer at the nick, with orders that the consequences of snitching are explained to him, including threats to his family. You got a mention as well. I don't think he likes you. They were talking about visiting your place. Do we need to do anything about that?' Janie sounded concerned.

'No, I have it all in hand. We can view this as an opportunity to gain more evidence,' said Max thankful for the cameras he had installed and the fact that Nutmeg was safely next door.

'Aye, he told Hardie about the jack in the boot, and hinted about evidence of the brake components you found in his shed. I can't believe the daft bastard held on to evidence from the crash. It's all there, conspiracy to murder, conspiracy to defeat the ends of justice. The whole lot, all clear as day recorded and time stamped.'

'Not enough yet, Janie. We need the rest of them, but it's a start.'

'Right, well, Slattery received a call from a mobile just before he called Hardie. I've cell-sited it and I'm confident it was Burnett Road. So, Slattery's source is possibly in that building right now. It's still pinging the same mast, and, in fact it's on a call now.' There was a pause. 'Calling Slattery, predictably it looks like a burner.' Janie read the number out to Max, who scrawled it on his hand in biro.

Max stood up and walked across the sprawling, open-plan office to the window where he stared out seeing the busy morning traffic below him, and further away, the compact city of Inverness. He looked around at each of the officers, all beavering away at their desks, bashing keyboards, or battling with heaped mounds of paperwork. Only two were on phones, one was Paul Johnstone, the FLO.

'Is Slattery on the probe now?'

'No, obviously not in his car,' said Janie. Max could hear the tapping of the keys as she spoke.

'Okay. Let me know when the call finishes,' said Max, not taking his eyes off the heavy form of Johnstone.

'Will do. Hardie has already been in touch with the mystery caller who's sorting the intercepts out, so I suspect they're going to be listening in to anything you're doing or saying,' said Janie.

'Well, best I give them something to listen to, then,' said Max. 'Call me as soon as that call finishes.' Max hung up, looking at Johnstone, who seemed to be in the midst of a difficult phone call. Scowling, he hung up and slammed his handset on the desk.

Max quickly composed a message to Janie. *Still going?*

The reply was immediate: *Yes.*

Max sighed and rubbed his eyes. He was feeling really tired. 'Coffee?' he said to Sally.

'Save my life, Max,' said Sally, putting her own phone down. 'I think we'll be ready for interview soon. Lawyer is waiting at the front, scummy bloke called Leo Hamilton.'

'I heard Hardie has sent him to issue the advice about not grassing. I suspect McGee won't say a thing.' Max relayed what Janie had just told him.

'Do we reveal this in interview?' she asked.

'No way. We keep all this to ourselves until we get Hardie in. We interview McGee just on his movements on the day of the funeral and the evidence we have found at his house,' said Max.

'Agreed. Plenty to be going on.'

'Anything from CSI?' asked Max.

'Yep, there are definitely soil deposits in the base of the jack and some pale dust that could be granite on the top. It'll have to wait for forensic comparison with the samples we took, but I'm pretty confident. Plus, they have lifted both Duncan Ferguson's and McGee's prints from it.'

'Are we confident in the CSI, bearing in mind how far Hardie's influence goes?'

'Aye. The fingerprint expert is an old pal of mine, and we're using a different external lab for the trace material examination.'

Max nodded. 'That's pretty conclusive.'

'Yep. It gets worse for him, as well. The brake components from his shed are definitely from a Focus the same age as Duncan Ferguson's, and we're fairly sure we'll be able to match them with the wreck. You seen the photos from PolSA?' Sally handed an iPad over with a photo slideshow open.

Max swiped through them, taking in the general state of the place, which spoke of a man who had let himself go. He paused in the ramshackle shed where a pair of brake callipers sat on the work bench next to a tall, robust-looking aerosol canister. 'Any ideas what that is?' asked Max.

Sally looked at her A4 red book. 'It's listed as an industrial aerosol CRY-AC3,' she read out. 'Max?'

'Is it liquid nitrogen?'

Sally zoomed in on the photograph. 'Yes. Cryospray – why the hell does he have that?'

'Do we know where the remains of the crash barriers are?' asked Max, looking at the photograph.

'Not yet. We can't find the remnants that McGee claims to have sent to the manufacturers. They have no record of receiving them, which is in itself significant,' said Sally.

'Absence of evidence is not evidence of absence, Sally,' said Max, smiling, but thinking of the shard of the barrier sitting on his kitchen table at home.

'Such an old copper's saying. Actually, scrub that, it's such a smug twat's saying.' Sally grinned. 'We have a mountain of evidence against him,' she added.

'He used this to weaken the barrier fixings,' said Max, with certainty.

'What?' said Sally, her eyebrows shooting upwards. 'How can you possibly know that?'

'Liquid nitrogen freezes bloody anything. I think it's like way below two hundred degrees freezing point. Put that on metal and it makes it shatter. I found a shard of barrier at Berriedale when I drove up there. In fact, I still have it.'

'You think that spray could shatter metal?' Sally said, incredulity in her voice.

'I'm betting it could change the properties enough so that it would shatter on impact rather than flex. I thought it was odd how there were shards of the barrier still there. We need to get PolSA there, fingertip-search and recover every fragment.'

'I'm on it,' said Sally, picking up her phone.

'Anyway, coffee,' said Max, walking up to the window and the fridge, on top of which was a kettle and a number of mugs. He filled the kettle and switched it on.

As he waited for it to boil, he looked out of the window onto the car park two floors below. A solitary smoker stood by the back door, a mobile phone clamped to his ear. Max yawned as he stared at the beefy figure wearing a smart suit. The kettle clicked and Max spooned coffee into two cups and filled them with boiling water. As he splashed milk into one of the cups his eyes wandered down to the figure who finished his phone call and tucked the handset into his pocket. He turned as a uniformed cop jogged out of the door and headed to a waiting marked car. Max could now see who the smoker was. It was Detective Chief Superintendent White, his face screwed up in a scowl as he lit another cigarette and then pulled a phone from a different pocket and dialled.

Max's phone buzzed with a message from Janie.

Call finished just now.

Max stared down at the large figure of DCS White, who was now pacing as he spoke on the phone.

On his burner, Max dialled the number scrawled on his hand, that Janie had read out to him just a few minutes ago, having first hidden his number by preceding it with 141. He hit call and waited, his heart pounding, aware that whoever answered the phone was the link to Hardie.

DCS White stopped talking and lowered the phone clamped to his ear and reached to his pocket. He produced the other phone and scowled.

'Yes?' his gruff voice barked.

'Janet?' said Max in a broad cockney accent.

'Obviously bloody not,' said White, his voice full of irritation.

'Sorry, wrong number, mate,' said Max, and hung up.

A slow smile stretched across Max's face. It was all coming together nicely. They just needed to stir the hornets' nest a little to draw the bigger fish out. He knew what to do. Taking his personal phone, he dialled Ross, imagining the bad guys listening, ready to act.

'Max, how you getting on?'

'All good. McGee is in custody. Lots of evidence at his house. The daft bugger kept the scissor jack from the wrecked car. Fingerprints and what looks like granite dust and soil from the gravesite all over it.'

'Excellent. Has he grassed yet?'

'Not yet, but it's only a matter of time. He knows it's all over, weight of evidence against him. He has to deal.'

'Nice. Any news on the other bent cops?'

'Oh yes, but not over the phone. We know enough to bring the whole house down.'

'Right. When you coming back here?'

'Me and Sally are about to interview McGee, then we'll leave him to stew for a while.'

'Good man. See you later.'

Max hung up. He took his burner out and messaged Janie. *Watch the phones.*

He then used the burner again to call Ross back, a smile spreading across his face.

'Max, what do you really know after that rather performative bullshit call?'

'DCS White is bent as a nine-bob note and I can prove it.'

'Excellent. I knew that bastard was in on it. So, is it him receiving the intercepted calls?'

'No, he doesn't have the clout. There's someone else. Someone really high up. We have the smaller fish, but there's still a big shark in the water, and the net is closing.'

61

The very senior police officer put the phone down from his contact at the intercept room, his heart thumping. He tasted bile at the back of his throat as he tried to digest what he had just heard. Could Craigie know about him? How? He had been so careful, but then his thoughts turned to the calls from Hardie.

He dialled, his fingers trembling.

'Yes,' barked Hardie.

'It's me.'

'What?'

'Craigie has just called Ross Fraser. McGee is bang to rights, apparently, loads of evidence and they think he'll talk. You said you'd sort this.'

'Stop panicking, man. McGee won't say shit. I have a man with him now, Leo Hamilton. He's told him what the ramifications of talking are. He'll stay quiet.'

'He also says he knows who the bent cops are, Tam. How the hell does he know that? I can't get arrested.' His voice trembled.

'Bloody hell, don't piss your pants. I've got it all in hand, as I said. Slattery will take care of things.'

'Craigie has to be stopped. I can't let this happen. It's taken me too long to get where I am. You have to let this feud drop, leave Ferguson and Phillips alone.' He was almost gabbling as he spoke down the phone, spittle flying from his mouth.

'We stop when I say we stop. Now you do your bloody job. Keep us informed if either phone lights up and keep listening to Craigie. You can leave everything else to me.' Hardie hung up.

The senior police officer took a deep, rasping breath and reached into his drawer, coming out with a hip flask. He took a long draught of the whisky, relishing the burn as it washed over his tonsils.

He cursed the day, almost thirty years ago when he'd accepted the two-hundred-pound bribe from Tam Hardie Senior. He almost rejoiced when the old man was murdered, only for his joy to be curtailed when his eldest son called him, leaving him under no illusions that he was still a Hardie asset.

62

Jack Slattery parked his Mercedes at the top of the forestry track that ran behind Craigie's house. He stubbed his cigarette out into the overflowing ashtray. Locking the car, he walked through the dense forest, coming out eventually at the top of the wide lawn that marked the beginning of Craigie's garden. He cursed under his breath as he climbed over the short, wire fence and his foot sank into the deep mud, soaking his sock. Slattery hated the countryside with the permanent stink of shit. He was a city boy through and through.

Keeping to the side of the garden, using the trees as cover, he quickly covered the ground between the fence and the back of the house. He first went to the big garage and lifted the up-and-over door. It wasn't locked and opened with a tortured squeal. Looking inside he saw the big KTM motorcycle and the storage racks, alongside the squat rack, bench and heavy bag.

He checked behind the engine plate and was relieved to see the tracker was still there. He quickly pulled it out, and with a small screwdriver unscrewed the battery plate. Inserting two fresh cells, he pocketed the old ones and refitted the back before snapping the tracker back in place. Shutting the garage door behind him, he negotiated the low wall and came to the back door. Looking about, he was relieved to see no sign of the stupid dog from last time. He hoped the boot up the arse had scared the little rat off.

He tried the door, but it was locked tight. He didn't want to risk going to the front of the property, as he had no idea where the neighbours were. It was madness doing this in daylight, but Hardie had been insistent. Craigie needed sorting and they needed to make sure they stayed one step ahead of the game. They had no idea how he had been reinstated and White couldn't find out as he was being blanked from above.

He quickly snapped nitrile gloves on his hands and a pair of overshoes on his feet before producing a set of picks from his pocket, thankful for the covert entry course he had completed some years ago. The lock was a crappy one-lever mortise, so it only took a second with a torsion bar and a number three pick to get it open. He quickly moved through the house checking each surface for anything of note. A shard of metal on the breakfast bar caught his attention. It was sharp, like a piece of broken glass. He was curious, but couldn't see the value in taking it, so he simply snapped a quick picture with his phone. He took a brief video clip of the living room, before searching the drawers in the coffee table, carefully. He wanted to leave no evidence of his presence and the video clip would help to make sure that everything was as it should be before he left.

He made short work of the house, finding nothing of note, and being meticulous to leave no trace of his presence. He had just one task remaining before he left. Going back into the living room, he pulled the bottom drawer of the coffee table out completely, placing it on the scrubbed wooden floor. From his pocket he pulled out a small self-seal bag that contained a decent hit of white, flaky powder. He smiled as he attached it to the rear of the drawer with a small piece of tape he had already prepared. He slotted the drawer back in place and stood to admire his handiwork. A call into Professional Standards and they would find three grams of Colombian marching powder. It would result in an instant suspension of Detective Sergeant Max Craigie.

63

Max replayed the footage from his phone with an ironic smile. He had been expecting this for some time, hence making sure that Nutmeg was safely ensconced with John and Lynne next door. It was still a shock, however, to see Jack Slattery picking his lock and then searching through his property. He could only admire his tradecraft and systematic approach to the search. He was also thankful for the motion-sensitive cameras covering the front door and interior. He even had good footage of him removing the drawer from the coffee table and taping something to the back of it. Clearly a set-up of some kind.

His feelings were mixed between outrage at the violation of his home, and a kind of satisfaction that another large piece of highly incriminating evidence was in the bag against Slattery and, with the phone traffic, Hardie. The time was drawing close when they would take this whole bloody conspiracy down.

'Max, you ready?' said Sally, a bag of evidence in one hand and her red A4 book in the other.

'Aye, let's get on with it.' And they both filed into the interview where McGee and his solicitor, Leo Hamilton, were waiting. Max was fairly sure what McGee would say, and that the interview probably wouldn't take too long.

*

Max was right.

McGee said nothing. Literally not one word. He didn't even confirm his name or agree whether he understood the caution. There was no prepared statement, not even an acknowledgement of any part of the interview process.

Sally went through every piece of evidence, a step at a time, but McGee just stared at the table. Hamilton said nothing, either, beyond a grandiose and pompous, 'my client wishes to exercise his right to silence. I cordially ask that you respect his decision.' He then clammed up and remained silent for the whole fifty-minute interview.

As they began gathering the evidence ready to finish, Max decided that he needed to make one last point.

'Mick, we are going to see the custody officer now and we'll be presenting evidence to the procurator fiscal. Once we leave this room, any opportunity for you to level with us disappears. Do you understand?'

McGee stared at the table, but Hamilton puffed his chest, his florid face flushed a deeper shade of red.

'Officer, I object to your tone. My client has exercised his rights and I consider any further comment from you to be oppressive. Leave us now. I wish to consult with Mr McGee.'

Max gave the large, well-fleshed solicitor in his expensive suit a tiny smile, then turned and left the room, Sally right behind him.

64

McGee looked up from the table, tears brimming in his eyes, his face crestfallen. He had been a cop for twenty-eight years, and he knew a mountain of evidence when he saw it. It was all over. He was going to jail for the rest of his life.

'I'm screwed, aren't I?' he said, his voice thick with emotion.

'Afraid so.' The solicitor's casual tone was almost like a slap in the face, as he fiddled with his phone, sending a message.

'Is there nothing that can be done?'

'No. Well, unless you decide to deal with the cops, but I've already explained Mr Hardie's view on that. He can get to you easier in jail than if you're out, but more than that, any cooperation with the authorities will be viewed as an act of defiance that would be heavily punished.' Leo stopped typing on his phone and leaned in close, his mouth widening into a broad smile that did not reach his grey, flat eyes. Mick could smell the man's breath in the confined room. It was sour and bitter, with the hint of last night's whisky. 'He knows exactly where your family are, Mick.' Leo's voice was low. 'Monica and the kids – Michael Junior and Annabelle, yes?'

McGee's hands came up to his face, tears brimming and spilling onto his cheeks. He took in a gasp of air. 'Not the kids,

Leo, please not the kids. I don't care about myself. My life is over; I have nothing. Look at me, Leo. I'm an alcoholic, broke and now facing a life term. I'll get thirty years. I'll die in jail. I just want to do right by my kids.' He began to sob, his shoulders heaving, fat tears cascading onto the melamine-topped table.

The solicitor sat back in his chair with insincere concern in his eyes at the shambolic form in front of him. He smiled again, his teeth stained by too much coffee and red wine. There was a long pause before he spoke again, in a gentle, soothing tone. 'Well, there is another option. Mr Hardie wanted me to tell you there is another way, and he promises to look after your kids, with a large cash sum. You're finished, Mick, but you can give your kids a life. Is that worth considering?'

McGee wiped his face, his eyes blood-red, desperation written all over his craggy features.

'What do I have to do?' he said. A cold determination gripped him. He would do what was right for the kids. Nothing else mattered.

65

They all sat in the covert premises, silently watching the PowerPoint presentation on the large screen. No one spoke and everyone looked exhausted.

Chief Constable Macdonald had personally made coffees for everyone from a machine he had brought in ready for the early briefing. He looked at his small team and made eye contact with each and every one of them. He felt a tug of pride.

Ross, Max, Sally, Janie and Jill all looked back, tired but ready, all clutching mugs of strong coffee.

'Thanks, everyone, for all the sterling efforts. There has been an amazing amount of work done so far, and we are close to bringing all this to a resolution. As I understand it, McGee is charged and is remanded to court later this morning. Thank you, Sally and Max, for pulling that together. We have overwhelming evidence of his sabotaging Ferguson's car and how that leads to Slattery. We also have the conversations over the probe between Slattery and Hardie, which I have heard and which are, as far as I see it, damning. We have enough to wrap this up, but we lack one thing. The final nail is the member of this organisation at the highest of levels who clearly is in bed with the Hardies. Any suggestions?'

Max spoke. 'We need to put 786 in his or her hand, Guvnor, and nick them carrying it. He or she only speaks to Hardie. There is no other link between whoever it is and the rest of the organisation. We get the phones, we get them both.'

There was a soft ringtone from the back of the room, and Jill looked up.

'I need to take this, sir,' she said.

Macdonald nodded and Jill moved to the back of the room, the phone clamped to her ear.

Ross cleared his throat and spoke. 'Boss, are you sure you're ready for this? We already have strong evidence against DCS White, a number of other cops from phone links, a serving cop charged with murder, as well as a bent ex-cop who has his finger in pies throughout the force. We've had cops followed, Max has been bugged and his house searched by Slattery and drugs planted. The press will have a field day.'

'Ross, I don't personally *give* a toss about what the press thinks. We can do nothing in Police Scotland whilst it's riddled with corruption. It's only by exorcising this cancer that I can start to rebuild the force that Scotland deserves. I have no interest in being the boss of a force that's being ruined by corruption. No bloody chance. All these sense-less, pointless deaths, each one of them because someone decided to open an ancient grave that somehow rekindled a centuries-dead feud.'

Jill returned to her seat, a look of sorrow on her fine features. She sat down with a deep sigh.

'Jill?' asked Macdonald.

Jill closed her eyes, briefly, in what could have been a silent prayer. 'Will Harding died a few minutes ago at the Royal Free Hospital. His parents were at his bedside.'

A thick silence enveloped the room for a solid thirty seconds.

'So, we now can add a fifteen-year-old innocent to the list,' said Macdonald.

A further silence followed the words that the chief constable had enunciated, sorrow in every syllable.

He spoke once more, his voice strong: 'Right, we go tomorrow. Ross, get whatever resources you need, from wherever you need them, but we stay covert and under the radar. I don't want them knowing we're coming. We all have people we trust. Let's get them in. We finish this, guys, and we finish it tomorrow.'

66

Mick McGee sat in the rear of the prison van, known to all as 'sweatboxes'. It pulled out of the backyard of Burnett Road Police Station and started the short journey to Inverness Sheriff's court. Despair swept over him as the van bumped its way out of the yard and onto Longman Avenue.

He had nowhere to turn, but he was scared. He wasn't a detective, but he knew enough about police procedures and evidence to know that the case against him was overwhelming. Tears sprang into his eyes again at the thought of his kids spending the next thirty years with their daddy in jail.

He knew what he had to do. Leo had told him. Just do it and Hardie would sort out the kids. Pay for their university, whatever, but he knew he could no longer be around. They were all better off without him.

He reached into his mouth and slid out the small, slim fragment of razor blade that was secreted in a fold of plastic, wedged between his cheek and molars. It was only a tiny piece, but it slotted nicely into a notch cut across the end of a biro. Pushing the pen top back on top it left a wickedly sharp blade protruding from the pen. Just a quick slice and it would all be over. Leo had told him how to do it.

McGee felt in his neck, his fingers searching for the pulse point he had felt on many others over the years when checking for a pulse on a collapsed drunk or whatever. Strangely there was no panic, and only a little fear. This was like a way out.

As soon as he had the pulse located, he pressed the blade up to his neck, feeling the wicked sharpness of the sliver of metal. He closed his eyes, offering a small prayer for forgiveness. He wasn't even religious, really, but it just felt appropriate.

Strangely, the pain was almost comforting. A cathartic release from months of internalised and unbearable pain. Just a sharpness, followed by a deep slicing pressure as he dragged the razor down, the fine metal slicing through flesh and then muscle, then finally through the carotid artery. A spurt of bright red blood hit the Perspex in front of him, followed by another, and another and another. Reactively he raised his hand up to the terrible wound, feeling the pulsing warm precious fluid force itself through his fingers.

The smell of copper filled the van as his vision began to fade. The last thing that he heard was the rattling keys in the door and the shouts of the guard in the back of the van. His vision continued to fade and he was only vaguely aware of the guards attempting to stem the blood flow. Too late, thought McGee. Too late now.

His last thoughts were of his kids, Michael and Annabelle and their beautiful faces. As he lost consciousness, a smile spread across his craggy features.

67

The early morning sun shone over the dingy industrial estate in Glasgow. The covert base was full to bursting with cops, some in uniform, some not. Some were armed, others not. There was a palpable air of excitement and anticipation at what they were about to do.

This was a major operation, planned quickly, yet meticulously. Favours had been called in, trusted cops quickly assimilated and a whole team of Met Police Territorial Support Group had travelled up, ready for the rapid-entry incursions into the listed premises. Teams had been formed, key roles assigned and objectives set.

Setting this up in less than twenty-four hours had been a major achievement, particularly as the level of mistrust necessitated that much of Police Scotland were unaware that it was occurring. It was essential that the Hardies and the bent cops knew nothing of what was about to happen, until their doors flew off their hinges and teams of rapid-entry-trained officers stormed their houses.

Chief Constable Macdonald stood at the front of the room after Ross had delivered the briefing. They were ready, and they knew their tasks.

'Ladies and gentlemen.' Macdonald spoke firmly, his voice clear. Everyone instantly hushed. 'Thank you all for coming to assist on this task today. I appreciate that the timing is short and I'm very grateful for our colleagues from London who have forgone sleep to help us this morning.'

'As long as you sign the overtime cheques, Guvnor,' chimed a loud cockney voice from the back. This was followed by soft chuckles and muffled guffaws. Macdonald smiled widely.

'Despite the historic allegations of parsimony against us Scots, I can assure you that all overtime bills will be honoured. Can I just echo Ross's comments that he so eloquently delivered, which is really unusual for DI short-hands, deep-pockets.'

There were a few muffled chuckles at this.

'This is one of the most important operations that my force has undertaken in the last few years. We have a small, but highly damaging organised criminal network that has infiltrated Police Scotland, and I'm determined that we finish them. With your help, we will destroy this network and its corrupt police enablers today. I need you all to do your jobs, to be meticulous, to be systematic, and most of all to be professional. This network is rich, very rich, and any mistakes will be capitalised upon.'

He paused for a moment before continuing, his voice firm. 'Ladies and gentlemen, when I joined the police, many years ago, it was to be one of the good guys. I always wanted to be the one wearing the white hat in the cowboy films when the bad guys wore black. Now that sounds a little corny and trite, but I'm convinced that all good cops serve for the same reasons. To be one of the good guys. Today, we take down those among us who secretly wear black hats. We destroy them, so that Police Scotland can re-emerge as the force for good that I know it is.' Macdonald paused, and in that instant, somehow, he managed to catch every eye in the room.

'Once again, thank you, and good luck.' He paused and nodded at the room, a sense of steely determination in the air.

The groups began to dissipate, all starting to kit up and prepare. Flame-proof overalls were worn, along with NATO protective helmets, and face shields were carried. This was to be a coordinated and meticulously timed hit on a number of addresses with the prime targets being the three Hardie brothers, DCS White and Jack Slattery. The remaining bent cops would be swept up afterwards.

'Nice touch that – from the boss,' said Ross.

'Aye, he can inspire a crowd, that's for sure,' said Max.

'I take it the news of McGee has come your way?'

'Yeah. How the hell did he manage to get a razor in there?'

'Christ knows. PIRC investigators are looking at it as a death in custody and they'll be going over every inch of the footage,' said Ross.

'They won't have any for his consultation with that bent solicitor, Leo Hamilton, will they?'

Ross just shook his head, a sad look on his face.

'The death toll keeps going up, right?' said Max.

'It fucking stops, today,' said Ross, firmly. 'You clear on what you're doing?'

'Yep.'

'Any changes?'

'No. Still home.'

'How about Hardie?'

Max grimaced. 'Still can't really get eyes on his place because of the walls and gates, but we have an OP on the entrance. If he leaves in a car, we'll know.'

'Best we can do. The brothers are both in, as is that bent bastard White, so we're good to go. Shit, it's been a right slog getting this together in a few hours. I'm knackered, man.'

'Gout attack coming your way then, Ross.' Max smiled.

Ross smiled back widely. 'You can go and fuck yourself.

Good luck, try not to chin Slattery.' He offered his hand and they shook, warmly.

'No promises – the bastard frightened my dog.'

Janie appeared at Max's shoulder. 'You ready? Transport's outside.'

'Let's go,' said Max, strapping his body armour into place.

68

The frantic buzzing of the phone on Tam Hardie's bedside table jolted him awake with a start. Blearily he looked at the time. It was only 3.30 a.m.

Immediately recognising the number, he answered. 'What bloody time is this to call, man? It had better be important.'

'Are you at home?' The voice of his senior police contact was full of panic.

'Where else do you think I'd be?'

'Get out. Get out now. You've a whole team of armed police on their way to you.'

'What?'

'I only just heard myself. Somehow, it's been kept secret from the whole senior team. They have a London team with them and have only got trusted officers. It's just fortunate that an old friend from London tipped me off, literally five minutes ago. You have to get out now. Don't use the front gate. There's an OP van on it. You'll need to find another way.'

A cold rage gripped Hardie. 'I pay you to keep me safe, man. You failed, and you'll pay for this. Keep me informed.' Hardie hung up.

Throwing back the bedcovers, he marched over to his

wardrobe and quickly pulled on jeans and a hoodie. Opening a concealed panel at the back of the cupboard he revealed a safe with a digital keypad. He punched in the code and opened the heavy metal door. He grabbed a plain, dark shoulder bag, thankful for his careful instincts. His father had always warned him that one day he would have to run, and the bag contained everything he needed to move and get away fast. Inside was a passport bearing the name Kenneth Mulhern, ten grand in cash and a selection of credit and debit cards in the fake name. Also nestling at the bottom was a Glock 19, two spare clips of ammunition and a burner phone. Shouldering the bag, he jogged downstairs, not turning on any of the lights, and made for the back door. He pulled on a pair of trainers and headed off, at a jog towards the back wall that led onto the street behind.

Within seconds he was over the wall and walking calmly along the quiet street, powering down his normal phone, and sparking up his burner. Quickly he went to the Uber app and requested a mini-cab. He'd soon be out of the way at one of his safe houses. Straight away he dialled Davie from the burner, to warn his brothers, hoping he wasn't too late.

Davie's voice was panic-stricken. 'Tam, police are here, man. Shit, bloody armed cops are here now.' In the background of the call, he heard crashing and banging and screams.

Tam hung up and carried on walking. A dark people carrier pulled up alongside him, driven by an elderly Asian man. The window slid down, 'Uber?' the driver said.

'Aye,' said Tam, climbing in. Once seated he barked his safe house destination to the driver, who set off, wordlessly. Tam opened the back of the burner phone and pulled out the SIM card, tossing it out of the window. He quickly slotted in a new one, and powered the phone back up, his face grim. He dialled again, inwardly fuming with hate in his heart.

'Yes?' Leo Hamilton's sleepy voice answered.

'Davie and Frankie are getting nicked right now. You need to find out where they are and get them out, okay?' he barked.

'Tam, you okay? Where are you?' said Leo, his voice clearer.

'I'm lying low for a while. Call me on this number when you hear anything, okay?'

'Yes, of course.'

Hardie hung up and pocketed his phone, staring straight ahead at the Glasgow streets.

This was all down to Craigie; he knew it. Max Craigie interfering in affairs that didn't concern him.

69

Max, Janie and the TSG team all walked steadily from the liveried Met Police Carrier, commonly known as a 'riot van' to the semi-detached house in the Glasgow suburb where Max assumed Slattery was currently sleeping.

Officers had been outside the premises all night in a covert van, watching to ensure the private detective did not leave without their knowledge. They were an unarmed team, unlike the teams that were at this precise moment about to breach the doors at Davie and Frankie Hardie's houses. There was no current or reliable evidence that Slattery had access to firearms.

'I'll take the back, guys, let you do your rapid-entry thing,' said Max as they approached the property.

'Watch out. You 'tecs ain't used to getting dirty hands near suspects, right?' said a cockney-accented officer called Chas who Max had worked with, years ago. Chas had a large, heavy-looking red enforcer door-ram slung over his shoulder, ready to breach the front door.

'No, mate, I leave it to you knuckle-draggers,' said Max.

Max went to the rear of the property, creeping past Slattery's Mercedes into the back garden by an unlocked gate at the side of the house. The property was in good order, with a pebbledash façade and bay windows shrouded in total darkness. The garden was unkempt and scruffy, with bare earth and tufts of grass visible in the predawn light that was just filtering through the heavy cloud.

Max's radio crackled in his earpiece, and he looked at his watch as the digital numbers clicked around to four-thirty.

'Breaching now,' was the simple message indicating that Slattery's door was about to be propelled inwards.

There was a brief moment of complete and utter silence before the familiar, sudden and terrible rhythmic crashing as the heavy enforcer was smashed into the door. The repeated bangs indicated that the door was resisting the attention of the heavy ram, as was often the case. Max looked up at each window in turn, all of which remained in darkness.

Suddenly, the back door flew open, and Slattery appeared. His hair on end, clad in shorts and a T-shirt, he stood framed by the door, a large revolver in his hand and panic written across his features.

Slattery spotted Max immediately. 'You bastard, Craigie,' he spat, hate in his eyes.

'Drop it, Slattery. You're not stupid; you're not going to shoot me,' Max said, moving towards the panic-stricken private detective.

'Stay there. I'll shoot you,' Slattery said, his face contorted, the gun now pointed at Max. But Max could sense the hesitation, and he knew. He just knew that Slattery didn't have the stomach to shoot him. He was looking at an unmitigated coward. Slattery kept the revolver aimed straight at Max, the barrel quivering slightly, as he stepped from the house, onto the path. 'Move back,' he snarled through gritted teeth.

Max moved back half a step. 'Drop the gun, Slattery. Drop it now and come in like a man. You haven't got the guts to shoot me, you coward,' Max spat.

'You bastard. Hardie is going to gut you alive. He'll peel the skin from your wretched body,' he sneered, and waved the gun at Max, advancing another half a step. Max didn't even move an inch. He stood there, stock-still, staring straight at Slattery, determination gripping him.

The main problem with a pistol is barrel length. Move it just an inch left or right and it's off-target. An even bigger problem is when you get too close to the person you're pointing the gun at. A simple slap is enough to throw it off, which is what Max did. His hand whipped across his body like a flash, connecting with the blued steel of the Smith and Wesson, knocking it sharply off target. The report was deafening and sparks flew out of the barrel as the bullet smashed into a plant pot to the side of Max.

Max instinctively ducked, his hands in front of his face. In an instant, Slattery had reactively swung the pistol back at Max, the butt connecting with his temple. Stars flashed with the sudden impact, knocking him down to his knees. Max felt the immediate flow of warm blood from the wound that the pistol butt had opened.

With a turn of speed, Slattery ran. He took off like a dog out of a trap, sprinting across the scrubby lawn towards the back garden fence, his bare feet covering the ground at a surprising pace.

Reaching for his radio, Max pressed the emergency button on the top. This controlled the airwaves, and sent a distress call out to all nearby officers.

'Suspect running, rear gardens. He's armed,' screamed Max into the radio, as he took off in pursuit. Slattery leaped over the rickety fence at the bottom of the garden like a gymnast, such was his desire to escape.

His head still spinning, Max leaped the fence too, seeing the white-shirted Slattery sprinting along the neighbour's garden towards the side alleyway, which would lead to the road at the end of the row of houses. Max increased his speed, his head beginning to clear, ignoring the blood that was flowing down his face, into his mouth, filling it with the taste of copper. Suddenly a blinding white light flooded the alleyway, as an automatic security light lit up the dark space. He began to gain on the older man who had reached the wrought-iron gate at the end. He reached for it and pulled.

It didn't move. It was locked fast.

With a howl of anger, Slattery turned, almost in slow motion, the pistol swinging up in a slow arc towards the rapidly closing Max.

Max didn't slow, didn't pause, didn't hesitate. All the days of tension, stress and hate rose to the surface in a surge of aggression. He screamed in utter fury and slammed his body into Slattery, driving him into the wrought-iron gate, his hands forcing the pistol away from his body and upwards. The breath rushed out of Slattery, such was the force of the impact. The pistol bucked again, the report deafening as Slattery pulled the trigger. Max pulled his head back, and drove it forward, smashing into the investigator's face, crushing his nose, and shattering his spectacles. Max felt a sharp stab of pain as the metal and glass bit into his forehead. He butted Slattery again, once, twice, then three times. He heard the metallic clatter, as the revolver hit the ground, soon to be followed by the now limp figure of Jack Slattery, who collapsed in an unconscious heap.

Two TSG officers flew into the alley, from behind Max, batons raised and tasers drawn, the laser sights painting dots on the wall.

'Suspect is down. He's down,' said Max into his radio, his voice eerily calm, before following up. 'Might need an ambulance.'

He moved forward and kicked the pistol to one side away from the slack hand, as Slattery groaned and began to shift on the concrete, his eyes opening and looking straight at Max.

He was clearly without a clue as to where he was or what had just happened.

'That's for upsetting my dog, you bastard,' hissed Max. 'Pistol is on the floor, boys, best one of you takes him in.' Max turned, and walked away, his face now a mask of blood, almost iridescent in the harsh LED light of the security spotlight.

70

Chief Constable Chris Macdonald strode confidently into the briefing room at Tulliallan, dressed in an impeccable uniform, to find a barrage of whirring and flashing cameras from the ranks of press photographers and television camera operators. It was late for such a briefing, which probably reflected the amount of work that his officers had been undertaking since the arrests, two days ago.

He walked up to the lectern, and stood in front of the Police Scotland crest that was projected onto a large screen behind him. He looked tired and drawn, but his eyes were bright with vigour.

'Good morning, ladies and gentlemen, thank you for attending this briefing. I will firstly make a statement to you of which copies will be made available. Unfortunately, I'll be unable to answer any questions at the conclusion of this briefing, owing to the sensitive nature of the continuing investigation.' He paused to look at the assembled reporters.

'Two days ago, a covert team of officers from Police Scotland, assisted by a supporting element from the Metropolitan Police carried out a series of arrest operations at addresses across Scotland. This was part of a wider anti-corruption investigation into a small number of police officers, ex police officers and individuals believed to be responsible for obstructing live murder inquiries. Three serving police officers and three other individuals were arrested. They have now been charged with a number of offences and been remanded in custody. I will now read out the detail of the arrests and charges.' Macdonald paused and took a sip from the glass of water in front of him before continuing.

'Detective Chief Superintendent David White aged fifty-two, from serious and organised crime, was charged with misconduct in a public office and attempting to defeat the ends of justice. Detective Inspector Robert Beattie aged forty-nine, from the Force Intelligence Unit, was charged with attempting to defeat the ends of justice and misconduct in a public office. The final serving officer, Sergeant Michael McGee, aged fifty-one, was arrested twenty-four hours previously in connection with the death of Duncan Ferguson at Berriedale Braes last week. Sergeant Michael McGee had been charged with conspiracy to murder, misconduct in a public office and attempting to defeat the ends of justice. Tragically, Sergeant McGee took his own life on his way to Inverness Sheriff's court, the circumstances of which are being investigated by the Police Investigations and Review Commission. Jack Slattery, aged forty-two, a private investigator and former police officer with Police Scotland has been charged with conspiracy to murder, attempted murder of a police officer, attempting to defeat the ends of justice and firearms offences. Two Glasgow brothers, David Hardie, aged thirty-seven and Frank Hardie, aged thirty-nine, were charged with the murder of Yusuf Tekin, conspiracy to murder, attempting to defeat the ends of justice and firearms and drug offences.

'Their brother, Tam Hardie, is currently being urgently sought in connection with the offences, but his whereabouts are unknown. I have a team of officers searching for Tam

Hardie, who should be considered dangerous and should not be approached. The public are asked to be on the lookout for this man, and any sightings should be urgently reported in to police by dialling 999.' A high-definition image of Tam Hardie appeared on the screen, replacing the Police Scotland crest. He almost seemed to sneer down at them. 'This investigation remains live,' Macdonald continued, 'and I anticipate that further arrests will be made in the near future. I am resolute in my determination that a small, but powerful corrupt element within Police Scotland is completely dismantled and the offenders brought to justice. The people of Scotland deserve a police force that is above reproach and I will not rest until any corrupt officers, or those that seek to corrupt police for their own benefit are brought to justice.

'Thank you, ladies and gents, that's all I can give you at the moment. Know this: if you are a corrupt officer, or you are trying to corrupt serving police officers, then my team will find you. You will be caught and you will be jailed.'

Macdonald nodded, picked up his sheet of paper and walked out of the room without a backwards glance, as the reporters began to shout questions and the cameras chattered like a hundred rattle snakes.

71

Max sat in the CID office at Burnett Road next to Janie, both having just watched the chief's press briefing on the wide-screen TV that hung on the wall.

Max's face bore signs of the recent battle with Jack Slattery. His forehead was coloured an interesting shade of blue and black, with the small cut at the centre covered with steri-strips. The cut on his temple was dressed with a simple adhesive dressing, and for once Max was thankful for his absence of hair. He looked like he had done ten rounds with a heavy-weight boxer.

They hadn't been home since the arrests, only snatching an hour or two of sleep on the office floor, after Max's wounds had been treated at the local hospital. He had refused all instructions to go home, intent as he was to see this job through to its conclusion.

The final task had been to gather the remaining evidence from Burnett Road that was still in secure storage after McGee's arrest. They needed to collate all the evidence from the various strands of the inquiry, ready to present to the procurator fiscal in Glasgow, and it had to be done now, irrespective of their fatigue. Trusting someone else to do this just wasn't an option. With Hardie still unaccounted for, they didn't know who could be trusted.

'Well, the chief certainly used the old theatre adage of leaving the audience wanting more, right?' said Janie.

'Aye. Enough to whet appetites, and get everyone looking for Tam Hardie. Any bent cops will be covering their tracks now, though.'

'Worst of them are cleared up,' said Janie, yawning.

It had been a tough couple of days of prisoner processing, gathering evidence, interviewing and completing the paperwork for the procurator fiscal. Most of the key evidence was from the mobile phones that linked McGee to Slattery and then onwards to the Hardies. The phone downloads had been enough for supporting evidence linking Hardie to Eustace Fielding, and then onwards between Slattery and DCS White. DI Beattie had been sunk after leaving enough of a trail to show that he had organised the cell-siting of the phones, together with the records of him talking to Slattery whilst in Caithness on the day of the funeral. Slattery was truly stuffed. Discharging a pistol in the direction of a police officer would only have one outcome. All in all, the case was solid. They just needed Tam Hardie, and, of course, whoever managed to get the intercepts on the phones. They'd drawn a blank on that, so far.

'So, are we happy with the evidence?' asked Janie.

'Phones and Slattery's listening device give it to us on a plate. Also, the grassing being done by Beattie is going to help. I'd say that the five in custody are slam dunk, but this isn't done until Hardie and our final mystery cop are nicked.'

'Aye,' said Janie, standing up and stretching her back.

'Cameras are deployed at all known premises for Hardie, his phone is hooked up. Port warnings are live and we have alerts on his financials. If he uses a phone, calls known associates, goes to any known addresses, or tries to access any of his accounts, he's stuffed. He'll turn up; they always do. Go home and get some sleep. It's a shame we have two cars here, or you could sleep on the way back.'

'You going too?' asked Janie.

'I guess so, most of the paperwork is done. Are you going to court in the morning?'

Janie shook her head. 'Ross said not to bother as the chief has his trusted case-prep team dealing with the paperwork. I know for a fact that two of them are going with the files. All we need to do tomorrow is tighten all the phone downloads and make more copies of the recording from Slattery's car. That's key to the whole thing.' Janie yawned, extravagantly again, unsurprisingly as they hadn't been home for two days straight now.

'It'll wait till tomorrow. Have a lie-in,' Max said.

'Good work, Sarge. That was brave, what you did with Slattery, you know.'

Max just shrugged. 'Get home, mate. We start tracking Hardie properly tomorrow.'

'Yeah. I'm knackered. See you, Max.' Janie smiled, her eyes full of fatigue. She reached over, and gripped his forearm with her hand, a brief moment of affection. 'I'm glad we're working together.' She turned and walked off.

'Drive carefully.'

Max picked up his mug and took a swig of cold tea. He screwed his face and put the mug back on the desk. He felt little satisfaction, because the job wasn't done. Hardie was still out there and so was his biggest asset.

Max's burner phone buzzed in his pocket, and he pulled it out. It was an email from the same mystery account that had sent him the extract of the phone call in London, what felt like days and days ago.

'*He's danc'd awa wi' the Exciseman,*' read the single line of text in the email body.

There was another media clip attached to the message. His heart sank, a huge sense of foreboding sweeping over him. He played the media clip. This was clearly a message from Bruce Ferguson.

It was two screenshots of WhatsApp messages between three telephone numbers that he didn't recognise. One was just an address, the other a photograph of a small, terraced cottage. He recognised both immediately and his blood ran cold.

The first was Katie's home address. The home they had shared together until just six months back. The message was timed three hours ago.

The photograph was of Aunt Elspeth's cottage in Avoch with a line of text below.

Elspeth Craigie's place in Avoch. Anything else you need, just shout. J. The picture was timed just an hour ago.

There was a reply below.

Thx. Speak later, T

A mix of rage and fear flared in Max's gut. His head swam and it felt as if a cog had worked loose in his brain. No, not Katie, not Elspeth. His thoughts flared and the familiar darkness began to cloud his vision as icy rage took hold. He shook his head. He had to focus, had to act.

Max dialled on his burner, aware that the number would be unfamiliar. But he still didn't want to use his phone, not knowing who could be listening. The phone rang, but the tone wasn't familiar; it was a single, long tone.

'Hello?' Katie's warm voice sounded confused.

'Katie, where are you?' Max blurted out.

'Max, what's up? We're not supposed to be speaking – you know, our agreement?'

'Katie, please, where are you and are you okay?'

'I'm fine. I'm on holiday in Greece with Jodie, last-minute girls break. I was going to phone when I got back.'

Max collapsed onto his chair, relief flooding through him.

'How long are you away for?'

'A week. We only got here today. Are you okay? You sound stressed.'

Max paused. 'I'm fine. I just wanted to say hi. Look, I have to go, work thing. Speak soon, okay?' He tried to keep his voice level, despite the turmoil raging within him.

'You sure you're okay?'

'Aye, I'm fine. Have a good time, and say hi to Jodie.'

Max hung up and picked up his normal phone. He opened WhatsApp and dialled Elspeth's number using the video message function. The call failed immediately with three beeps. He tried again. Same result. His stomach began to knot in fear as he quickly typed out a message. She always carried her phone in her hip pocket, ready to feel the buzz of a message or video call. She usually replied immediately, phone messages being one of the things she relied on for staying in contact with friends and family.

Hi Auntie E. Hope you're well. Are the dolphins running at the moment? Someone was asking me as they want to visit Chanonry. This was innocuous enough, to not raise alarm, if someone was watching.

Nothing. There was no response at all. It was almost 7 p.m., and Elspeth rarely went anywhere after supper, preferring to watch TV or read. Max looked at the message. There was just one greyed-out tick, meaning that the message had not got through. Either the phone was out of range of a mast or switched off. Elspeth never switched her phone off, ever, and the signal was good at her house, both 4G and Wi-Fi.

72

Max stared at the phone, willing it to ring or vibrate. It just sat there in his hand, inert, almost mocking him. His mind reeled at the prospect of his aunt being held captive, or worse. She had been a massive part of his life, so far, almost a surrogate parent after Mum and Dad had passed away. His resolve hardened. He would do whatever was necessary to keep her safe.

He picked up the burner and dialled the number for Ferguson.

'I imagined you'd call, Max, but don't ask me how I came across this information. I just wanted to help.' His voice was calm, without a trace of stress or panic.

'Understood. Why are you doing this?'

Ferguson sighed before continuing. 'Max, whilst my name is Ferguson, I'll always be a little bit of a Leitch, too. I'm not going to spend the rest of my life looking out for that bastard Hardie, you understand?'

'Me neither. What is it that you want, Bruce?'

'I want justice. Justice for my brother, and I want the Hardies finished for good. They were evil bastards in the 1800s and they're evil today. They'll never stop. You've got Frankie and Davie, but it's not enough. You have to get Tam and lock him up forever.'

'That's the intention, but first I need to make sure my aunt is safe.' Max tried to keep his tone level, but his voice cracked with emotion.

'Of course. I managed to pick up the new phone number for Hardie, which went live just after you smashed his doors off their hinges. It then travelled north and was last on the network an hour ago hitting a cell mast at Mount Eagle on the Black Isle.'

'My aunt lives close to there.'

'I know, in Avoch, and you're close by, right?' he said, blithely.

'I'm in Inverness, just fifteen minutes away,' said Max.

'That's something, I guess.'

'How do you know all this?'

There was a long silence on the other end of the line. 'I look after a multi-billionaire who among other interests has control of telecommunications suppliers and other tech companies. This affords me access to many databases that may impact on his security or financial interests. I want to help you, not for revenge, or anything like it, but because it's the right thing. You're a good man, a fellow veteran who has been fighting against the odds. I'll do what I can.'

'So why the Rabbie Burns quote?'

'To get your attention. I know what was in poor Willie's journal. He showed me it once, and I told him he was mental. It's unfortunate that I didn't appreciate how right I was. If I had done something, years ago, when he was losing his mind, maybe this silly feud would have stayed dead, and all those people would still be alive. I owe it to everyone who has been hurt, Max. I feel partly responsible.'

'Thanks. So, what can you do for me?' asked Max.

'I can be your eyes and ears. You still haven't rooted out the worst cops yet. I'll be watching, both your phone and his. How does that sound?'

'It's a start.'

341

'It's better than that. We're ahead of him, especially as his bent cop is no longer feeding him cell sites as far as I can see.'

'That's something, I guess.'

'His only other calls were to his solicitor, Leo Hamilton, straight after the raids, and then the ones about your wife and aunt's places. He's switching it off and changing SIMs regularly. I can keep up with that, as I'm watching his handset IMEI number, so I can stay on top unless he ditches the phone. I'll keep monitoring the calls, but one thing: don't trust any bastard in Police Scotland. You've dealt a lot of them a big body blow, but they aren't down yet. There are still plenty of them left, all wanting this to go away. You're the fly in their ointment.'

Max felt a pressure building in his head, a throbbing at the temples. It was a mix of stress and fury gathering pace and getting worse as the enormity of the situation raged in him.

'Right, I'm going now,' said Max, standing up, suddenly resolute. He would do whatever was necessary to bring Hardie down.

'Be careful. Are you willing to be as ruthless as these bastards are?'

'I hear you.'

Bruce was already gone. His guardian angel was looking out for him, which afforded some level of comfort, but essentially, he had to do this alone. Not because of trust issues – he trusted Janie and Ross – but because to have the best chance of saving Elspeth he may have to cross a line that they wouldn't be able to cross. In fact, if he made it official and called in the cops, he wouldn't be allowed anywhere near the case. He'd be kicking his heels at home whilst a massive operation was launched to safeguard Elspeth, and with the leaks not completely plugged in Police Scotland, he wasn't willing to take that risk. The other problem was, whilst Max loved Elspeth, he was realistic enough to realise that she could be irascible and a complete fatalist.

She would be most likely not to want any fuss, and refuse all protection offers, and tell the cops to bugger off.

He picked up his shoulder harness that contained his handcuffs, telescopic baton and PAVA spray and shrugged it on, thankful at least to have some protective equipment. He picked up the car keys and jogged out of the building, his jaw set firm.

73

Max parked the BMW in the car park of the Station House Hotel well away from Elspeth's place. He pulled his jacket on over his PPE harness, locked the car and jogged off towards the rocky shoreline. Jumping over the low wall, he landed on the stony beach. He walked parallel with Elspeth's small, two-bedroomed terraced cottage that was midway along a street of identical properties.

Max's route along the rocky shore took him past Elspeth's road to the rear of the properties, each of which had small, pocket-handkerchief-sized gardens. Max climbed over the wall and walked along the street to the rear of Elspeth's. He walked confidently and normally, as if he belonged, in classic surveillance mode. This was easy for Max, because these small, quaint roads were as familiar to him as anywhere.

The rear of Elspeth's house was obvious, owing to the proliferation of shrubs and bushes that rose from the small, square garden. The amount of greenery that Elspeth had crammed into that small space always amazed Max. A low, blue-painted picket fence with a gate marked the boundary. The low sun glared at the rear of the property, the shrubbery bathing the small garden in dappled shade. A solitary wooden chair was positioned to the left of the glazed rear door, a glass on the arm containing the remnants of Elspeth's regular gin and tonic. Max walked past the gate and turned immediately into the house next door, which was separated from Elspeth's by a tall, panel fence. Max knew that an old guy called Ted lived there who was, almost without fail, three-quarters pissed at the Station House Hotel by this time of the evening.

Max just sat for a few minutes, listening for any sounds of movement from within Elspeth's house, but there was nothing. Just the soft lapping of the waves and the occasional cry of a seagull.

He turned and peeped through a crack in the fence at the back of Elspeth's house. The kitchen was at the rear, with no sign of life and no sounds of cooking or a TV. Despite her deafness, Elspeth would turn the sound on the TV up, and use her hearing aids together with subtitles. She always said it gave her the best experience of watching her favourite programmes. There was no movement at the upstairs bedroom windows, no flickers and no obvious lights. This was unusual.

Max made a decision. He was going in. She could be in there injured or held captive and he couldn't just stay here forever.

Quickly and without hesitation, Max stood and left Ted's garden, turned right and walked into Elspeth's lush, green space. He pulled out his baton from the shoulder harness and unclipped the PAVA, holding the canister in his left hand and the baton in his right.

Slowly he reached out to the doorknob and twisted gently. He wasn't in the least bit surprised to find it open. Elspeth never locked her door; in fact she had no idea where the back-door key even was. Black Islers rarely locked their doors, such was the absence of crime among the population. He silently moved into the kitchen, sniffing the air for anything unusual, but it just smelt like he always remembered. A mix of faint cooking smells, mild disinfectant and a whiff of lavender. It hadn't changed in all the years he'd been visiting this place. He found the smell almost comforting. It made him think for a moment that perhaps everything was okay.

Max moved into the silent hall, agonisingly slowly, and into the small living room, the baton held low, the PAVA extended in front of him, his finger resting on the trigger, ready to spray.

Nothing. Empty and silent again. He checked his watch. It was only 7.30 p.m. Quickly checking the rest of the house, he found it empty, and in its normal, immaculate state with not so much as a rumple on a bedspread, nor a misplaced knick-knack, of which there were many.

Max exhaled, deeply. Surely if there had been any kind of confrontation, there would be evidence of it. He had an uncanny sense at crime scenes, in being able to come up with a reasonable hypothesis as to what had occurred. He searched his mind for that workable hypothesis now.

Nothing had happened here. That didn't mean that something hadn't happened elsewhere. But where was Elspeth?

Almost on cue, there was a noise at the front door, the handle moved and Elspeth walked in, her face flushed, her eyes bright, a large-lensed camera hanging around her neck.

As she entered, her eyes moved up and locked on Max's. She visibly jumped, startled. 'Jesus Christ!' she exclaimed, her mouth wide open with the fright. 'Max, for God's sake. Max, you scared the holy crap out of me.'

Max ran to Elspeth and enveloped her in a hug, overcome with relief at seeing his only living relative.

'What's up, and what happened to your face?' she said, from within his embrace. Max pulled away so she could see him, touching the dressing on his temple.

'Your phone is off. Your phone is never off,' he said, sure that the emotion would be obvious in his voice.

'My battery died. I was at the point and the dolphins were

putting on the display of a lifetime. I just couldn't leave. What's up?' She looked at him quizzically.

'I was concerned. I was at Inverness and wanted to call in, but when I saw your phone was switched off, I got worried.' Max decided that now wasn't the time to mention it. He thought that his chances were better of getting her to relocate for a while if she wasn't aware of the reason. She could be stubborn, so he had to tread carefully.

'Elspeth . . .' Max began but was stopped in his tracks by a knock at the door. His head snapped like a whip to the entrance. A figure was visible through the small glass panel. He was a man in his late forties, wearing blue overalls, with sparse, wispy hair. Vaguely familiar, but Max couldn't place him.

'Who's that?' he asked, looking directly at his aunt, whilst firming his grip on the PAVA.

Elspeth squinted at the door, a perplexed look on her face.

'Och, it's only James H. You know James, from the garage in Fortrose? He looks after my old heap of a car. Wonder what he wants?' Elspeth began to walk towards the door, but something in Max's mind told him that this was wrong. It was all wrong. He tried to remember where he had seen the man before and link it with the name. James H? Garage in Fortrose? Then it came to him in a flash, in a mental picture of the small, scruffy garage he had once visited with Elspeth a few years ago. Hardies' Garage, Fortrose. Tam Hardie's words from their first meeting flooded back to him with a crash. His cousin's garage.

Elspeth pulled the door open. 'James, man. What brings you all the way here?' she said, a smile stretching across her face.

The door exploded inwards after a violent shove from James, and he stepped inside, pushing Elspeth back with a firm palm to the chest. The old woman fell with a cry, hitting the floor with sickening force.

Max dropped the PAVA, realising in a fraction of a second

that to use it in this enclosed space would be just as likely to impact Elspeth. Instead, Max threw himself towards the staircase, body-checking the big man into the wall. He collided with force, smashing into a line of photographs that had been hung on the wall. The man spun and recovered almost immediately, and Max took him in properly for the first time. He was much taller and clearly heavier than Max, and his bent and broken nose bore the hallmarks of a fighter. He was unmistakably a Hardie.

'Bastard,' he spat and launched himself forward. Max side-stepped at the last second, extending a foot over which the big man stumbled. Max sprang back, putting himself between the man and Elspeth, who was writhing around on the tiled floor, trying to stand.

'Elspeth, get out the back and call the police,' Max shouted, his eyes fixed on his attacker. She managed to get up and hobble away into the kitchen, out of sight. Max flicked the extendable baton out with a reassuring click, and a smile extended across his face.

'You messed up, pal. Coming here to attack an old lady. Never thought I'd be here, eh, and you'd have to face someone who'd fight back.' Max flipped the baton, between hands, the dulled steel flashing and drawing James's eyes. 'Imagine the damage this will do when I smash the bastard between your eyes? I'm cracking skulls today, Jim-boy, because I'm feeling pretty angry, and very fucking mean, right now,' said Max, his voice even and low, dripping with menace. He almost willed the bigger man to attack. Max saw it in the man's eyes. Doubt, tinged with fear.

Max switched the baton to his left hand, watching as James's eyes followed it. The big man's eyes swivelled, following the weapon as it moved from side to side. He didn't look sure of himself, and Max could tell just from his stance that the big man was no fighter. Max was correct. The punch when it came was telegraphed with a large backswing, ready to add momentum to a haymaker of a right cross that, had it connected, would have almost taken Max's head off. Max watched the fist approaching with almost a casual interest, moving his head to the left, just as it approached and sailed harmlessly past his ear. The momentum caused the big man to overbalance as the impetus of the punch threw him too far forward, exposing the back of his head to Max. It was just too inviting, so his right hand flashed forward, the baton extended. It smashed hard into the back of James's head. The skin split and blood immediately flowed, and James's hands reflexively reached up to the wound as he gasped in pain. Max drew the baton back again, and smashed it down, full force on the back of James's knee, which collapsed under the weight of the hard, pressed steel. He hit the floor as if his legs had suddenly disappeared, letting out a howl of agony.

Max moved in, already pulling the rigid cuffs from the harness and snapping one on a wrist. He pulled the man to the bannister and secured the other restraint to one of the rails. He didn't resist. All the fight was out of the big man, who just lay there whimpering.

'You okay, Elspeth?' said Max, standing up, but still keeping his eyes on James, who just lay still, groaning.

'Elspeth?' Max repeated. 'We need to call the cops.'

He turned his eyes towards the kitchen, already half-expecting the sight that met him.

Tam Hardie was at the kitchen door, standing directly behind Elspeth, one hand clutching her shoulder, the other hand pointing a Glock directly at Max. Hatred flashed in Hardie's pale blue eyes.

74

'Max fucking Craigie. You've no idea how much trouble you've caused and how much money you've cost me,' he snarled between gritted teeth.

'Leave Elspeth, Hardie. She's nothing to do with this. She's just an old lady. Surely, you've more pride than this. I thought you had old-school values.'

'Shut up. Just shut up.'

'Your old man would be turning in his grave. Elspeth is an innocent. An old lady and an innocent. You remember those rules, right?'

'You take my father's name out of your mouth, or God help me I'll shoot you and the bitch right now.' Hardie's eyes flashed.

'Let her go,' said Max, his voice rising.

'Screw you, Craigie. You just couldn't leave it alone, could you? What are you trying to be, the only straight cop in Scotland?'

'Let her go, and we'll talk.'

'In the lounge, now. Hands where I can see them.' He flicked the barrel of the Glock towards the open door of the small lounge. 'If I even think you're trying something, I'll put a bullet in the bitch,' he said, his voice shaking with anger.

Max raised his hands at shoulder height, hoping to portray a non-threatening figure. Hardie had nothing to lose, and Max had nothing to offer. All he could reasonably hope for was to get Elspeth out of this alive.

Max walked into the small, over-furnished lounge and stopped by the large, wing-backed armchair.

'Sit,' said Hardie, entering the room, the pistol pointed at Elspeth. He pushed her inside, where she stumbled and fell to her knees on the carpet. She didn't make a sound, just glared at the large form of Hardie, looming above her.

'Stay on the floor,' he barked, switching the pistol to point directly at Max, Elspeth already forgotten.

'You just couldn't leave it, could you? Why be the crusader cop, eh?' said Hardie, his voice becoming harder, his eyes getting that fixed, blank look. It was the look of a man preparing to kill. Max just stared directly into Hardie's blazing eyes.

'I can't let you live.'

Max looked away, as if scared, gazing at Elspeth who sat on the floor, her hand up her sleeve, a familiar look on her face. Her hands began to move, almost imperceptibly. Max watched, still affecting fear. Elspeth was signing. Max's heart leaped. Max had learned British Sign Language as a child, spending so much time with Elspeth, and he still was able to hold conversations with her. So, he could read what she was saying. A finger in the air, '*I.*' An upturned hand, '*Have,*' and finally a subtle action with her hand of spraying an aerosol.

'*I have spray,*' she signed once more. It hit Max like a jolt; Elspeth had obviously picked up the PAVA from the floor in the hall. She was about six feet away from Hardie. Well within range.

She signed again. '*In five seconds.*'

'You're a coward, Hardie,' Max said, turning to face him. 'A snake, and your father is rightly rotting in that grave,' he spat, enunciating every word, slowly and steadily forcing the gangster's focus one hundred per cent on him, and not Elspeth.

Hardie laughed nastily. 'I was just going to shoot you in the head, Craigie, but now I'm going to shoot you to pieces, you bast—' At that moment the long stream PAVA spray jetted from the canister that Elspeth was holding and hit him straight in the eyes. The concentrated irritant instantly bit and Hardie let out a howl. With a roar Max rushed at Hardie with his shoulder smashing directly into his kneecaps, in what would have now been called a 'chop tackle' in rugby. Hardie fell in a heap to the floor, a hand clawing at his eyes, whilst the other still clutched the pistol. His attempts to clear the agonising pain and temporary blindness were futile. He roared again, just as Max rolled away, his own eyes stinging, and picked up the poker from the hearth in front of the wood burner. Hardie let out a wild kick from his prone position, which caught Max on the temple. Pain exploded and stars danced across his vision.

Hardie blindly swung the pistol, firing wildly, the bullets burying into the wall above the wood burner. The air filled with the smell of cordite and Max's ears rang. He forced the pain in his head away, his instinct to survive and protect Elspeth stronger than the effects of the blow. His eyes regained their focus, still streaming with the secondary effect of the irritant spray. He turned to see Hardie kneeling, bringing the pistol to bear in his direction. Max swung the poker, catching the hand holding the gun, sending it spinning from Hardie's grip. Max launched himself at the bigger man, landing in a heap on top of him, the poker slipping from his grasp and falling onto the floor. Twisting his arm free, he drove his elbow repeatedly into Hardie's face, feeling the crunch of bone and cartilage under the sharp point of his limb.

Hardie struggled, desperately trying to escape the onslaught, managing to turn his head, deflecting the blows still raining down on his nose, cheeks and mouth. Max barely felt the stab of pain as the blows into Hardie's mouth broke teeth that dug into the exposed flesh. Max kept pounding, again, and again.

Elspeth filtered through the burning rage, firstly her faint voice that he could ignore, then a stronger one he could not.

'Max, that's enough. He's finished. Please don't kill him, not in my home. Max, please. Please stop,' said Elspeth, shock written all over her sweet face, tears running down her cheeks. A faint wail of sirens sounded in the distance, presumably prompted by the gunfire. The noise began to filter through the fog in Max's mind. He stopped, and stood, his face and clothes flecked with blood. He looked down, and the gangster's face was just a mask of exposed flesh and blood.

He turned to his aunt. 'It's okay, Elspeth. It's over, I'm done.'

'Oh, Max,' she said, throwing her arms around his neck and hugging him tightly, sobbing.

Max returned her hug, feeling her heaving shoulders. 'Police on their way, by the sounds of it. Why don't you go and meet them? I need to make sure that Hardie is secure, okay?'

'Thank you. I've no idea why this has happened, but I can see that you came for me.' She rested her hand on his head and left the room.

Max sat on the chair, panting heavily and coming to his senses. Hardie was unmoving but breathing. Max quickly stood again, the rage dissipating, and rolled the big man into the recovery position. He reached into his pockets and pulled out a new-looking iPhone. He swiped and the phone asked for a code. He lifted Hardie's left hand and pressed the thumb to the reader. Nothing. He tried the index finger and this time the phone sparked to life. Max opened the messaging function, seeing that there were no messages. He looked at WhatsApp and saw the familiar number. The mystery bent cop.

Max knew what to do. He dialled a number from his burner, which was answered immediately.

'Max?' the firm voice of Chief Constable Chris Macdonald answered.

'I have Hardie. He went after my aunt in Avoch, but I managed to intervene. Can you get everyone we need here? CSIs and the like. He discharged a firearm multiple times. I've no injuries. Well, no new ones anyway, but he may need a little attention,' said Max, looking down at the destroyed face of Tam Hardie.

'You okay?'

'Aye, I'm fine. I also have a plan to finish this whole thing off. I have to go now, Guvnor. Locals are here, and I have a little explaining to do. Maybe make some calls, eh?'

'Sure. Max?' the chief questioned.

'Yeah?'

'Well done.'

'No bother. One thing. Can you get onto the duty officer at Burnett Road? Hardie will need to go to hospital, but we need this closing down. Nothing can get out. Full incommunicado. No one can know that Hardie is nicked, okay?'

'I'll make it happen.'

'Thanks. I'll need Janie and Ross as well, and maybe one or two others.'

'I'll personally make sure you get whatever you need, with one proviso?'

'Aye?'

'We end this tonight.' The chief ended the call.

75

Max was exhausted. Truly exhausted as he sat in the rear of the control car in a Glasgow suburb, with Ross and Janie up front. Hardie's phone was on his lap, the display switched on. It had been a very quick bit of work by one of the tech gurus to override the fingerprint recognition and leave the phone unlocked.

Hardie was safely secured in a small sub police station after being patched up at hospital. Max's elbow strikes had left him with a large gash, a broken nose and a fractured cheekbone. There was a single custody officer and no other prisoners in the unit that had hastily been opened once Chief Constable Macdonald began throwing his weight around. He was also being kept fully incommunicado. No calls out, no calls in, and definitely no attendance by Leo Hamilton. An independent but security-vetted solicitor had offered legal advice to Hardie, who had vehemently declined it, saying he would wait for his own man.

A story had been leaked to the press about an incident in Avoch that was ongoing and 'domestic in nature'. The lid had to be kept on the whole incident, or the rumours would fly. They had to move fast. If the bent cop knew that Hardie had been arrested, he would be sure to ditch the mobile phone he had been communicating with.

'You ready?' asked Ross.

'I'm knackered, but ready,' said Max, looking at his watch. He was shocked to see that it was almost 7 a.m. He had been awake for almost thirty hours.

'Send it then,' said Ross, picking up his phone and dialling. 'We're sending now, standby, and call us as soon as you have a location.'

Max pressed the green arrow icon in WhatsApp and the message went with the familiar 'pop'.

We need to meet, urgent.

The message bubble showed a single greyed-out tick to indicate that it had been sent, but was yet to be received.

'Think he'll bite?' asked Janie.

'Yep, he doesn't have a lot of choice. I just hope it works,' said Max.

'It'll work. There's no way whoever this is can stay out of touch with Hardie for any length of time.'

Ross's phone buzzed. 'Yeah?' he said, brusquely. There was a pause as he scrawled on a notepad.

'Hitting a mast at Hillhead. Get moving, Janie.'

'Roger that, only ten minutes away,' she said, starting the engine and moving the BMW off.

'Roger that? What are you, SAS?'

'Does it make me sound all tough?'

'Nope, just daft as a brush,' said Ross.

'Tick's still grey, so whoever it is either hasn't seen the message or is choosing to ignore it,' said Max, looking at Hardie's phone.

'They'll look. They have no choice. Who wants an angry Hardie getting impatient? Never know what he'd do,' said Ross.

The car was silent as Janie negotiated the quiet Glasgow streets, heading towards the West End.

Ross's phone buzzed once more. 'Yep?' he barked into the handset, listening and scribbling.

'Azimuth has the handset signal somewhere north of the Hilton hotel, pushing up through the Royal Botanical Gardens and into Kelvinside, medium signal strength so probably within a couple of kilometres,' said Ross. Still scribbling.

Max looked at the map open on his lap. 'The gardens take up most of that area, which only leaves us a small grid of streets north of them in Kelvinside. Can they narrow it further?'

'Doubt it, we have it down to half a dozen streets. I'm calling the boss.' Ross dialled, once again.

'Sir, signal is down to one of a few streets in Kelvinside, message not replied to yet. Aye, that's what I wondered. Yeah, we'll wait for the reply.' Ross hung up. 'As far as he knows, the chief doesn't believe that any of his management team live around there.'

'That means nothing.' Max stared down at the screen and swallowed. 'We've two blue ticks. Message has been seen.' The adrenaline started to blow his debilitating fatigue away. 'We should get the surveillance team on standby, Ross,' he added.

'Go for it, pal. You speak cockney better than me.'

Max snorted before pressing the concealed radio switch pinned to his T-shirt. 'Stand by, stand by. We have unknown subject in receipt of message, currently stationary close to Royal Botanical Gardens in Kelvinside.'

'That's all received by surveillance control. Stand by for plotting,' said a broad cockney accent.

'See, I barely understand the bugger,' said Ross with a grin.

The voice then began to assign each of his units: seven cars and a single motorcycle. Each got a road junction to cover, ready for the subject, whoever it was, to make a move.

'Listen to him. It's like Dick Van Dyke on the streets of Glasgow,' said Ross, chuckling again.

'Someone's writing a message,' said Max, looking at the screen.

357

There was a buzz as the message arrived.

Why?

Max typed out a reply. *Not over the phone, it's urgent.*

There was a long pause, before the screen indicated that someone was typing again.

Seven-thirty, benches outside Kibble Palace in Botanical Gardens. Just you.

Max smiled as he read out the message, 'They've bitten.'

'Half an hour, so he's staying nearby,' said Janie.

'You seem sure he's a man? We don't know that for sure,' said Ross.

'Money where your mouth is, Ross?'

'I'm not taking that bet. I'm not pissing daft,' said Ross.

Max was speedily googling the Botanical Gardens. 'Gardens open at seven. Can we get the surveillance team in, plotting the benches before then?'

'Walls are low, so I'd say yes. You call the team leader on the phone and explain. They're defensively armed. You reckon that's enough?' he asked.

'Should be fine, no suggestion of a threat, is there?' said Max.

'Nah, no threat from this bastard,' said Ross, dialling.

Max nodded, but couldn't shake the feeling that this wasn't over, just yet.

Not by a long way.

76

The weak, early morning Glasgow sun was warming the streets as the gates were unchained and unlocked on the Botanical Gardens by an unsmiling, hi-vis-clad member of staff. He yawned as he let in a jogger and a couple of staff members waiting to go to work. Max, Ross and Janie had hung back as the team scaled the low walls and took up positions surrounding the row of benches. They were outside the long glass building that was the historic greenhouse, at the far west side of the seventy-acre gardens.

Although Max and Janie were both surveillance trained, they had opted to stay back in their car and let the London team take care of this. Once the target turned up, Max would walk through to identify whoever it was and make the arrest. There were multiple entry points, so they decided to let the target enter and settle before moving in. Now they waited, all sipping strong coffees that Ross had bought from an early morning coffee shop.

'Ready for this, Max?' said Ross, sipping his drink.

'Aye. Ready as I'll ever be. I've never nicked a senior cop, but I'm looking forward to it.'

'Well, the chief is staying away. He specifically said he wanted you to bring him or her in.'

359

'Bet's still on offer,' said Janie.

'Sod off,' he said.

'Lone male approaching benches from east side, blue hoodie, blue jeans, black baseball cap pulled low. He's very aware and has his eyes about. Not got a great view of face, but looks to be middle-aged,' said a broad northern accent, over the radio. 'He's pausing by the benches, looking each way and seeming uncomfortable.'

'Sounds like our man,' said Ross.

The northern surveillance officer spoke again. 'He's sitting, on his own, third bench from the entrance to the greenhouse. We have our man. Team move up, block exits, but stay out of sight. Units acknowledge.'

'Go for it, Max. We'll move in as soon as you make the arrest. Surveillance team have your back,' said Ross.

Max said nothing, just got out of the car and crossed to the open gate. He walked through, still carrying his coffee. He felt calm, relieved that this whole situation was about to be finished.

He continued along the broad, tree-lined path towards the Kibble Greenhouse.

The covert earpiece crackled. 'No change, no change. Still sat, same bench, looking at watch,' said a male officer.

Max looked at his own watch. It was seven-thirty-seven and Glasgow was waking up. A jogger loped past, panting heavily.

Max rounded the corner on the path and saw the figure sitting, exactly as described on the bench, not relaxed, staring at the ground, his shoulders hunched. He felt for Hardie's phone and sent the pre-written message.

There in five minutes.

His cap was pulled low down partially obscuring his face, but even with this obstruction, there was no doubt that Ross had been wise not to accept Janie's wager. Almost on cue, he

360

reached into his pocket and pulled out a mobile, scowling at the screen and looking around.

Max pressed the concealed transmit switch in his pocket. 'Backup foot unit, I have the eyeball and a positive on the phone. I now have control. Suspect on the bench and I'm approaching. All units stand by for my signal before moving in,' he said, his lips barely moving.

Max continued, walking confidently straight up to the lone man and sat next to him with a sigh.

The man jumped slightly and looked at Max. He was clearly expecting Tam Hardie. Confusion and recognition flashed on the man's lined face along with irritation at having someone sit close to him. Max recognised him, though. Senior officers loved having their photographs plastered on the force's intranets, and they all competed to get in front of the press cameras at every opportunity. Also, he hadn't forgotten about the praise that this man had heaped on him and Janie, just a few days ago.

Max recognised him all right.

'Excuse me, pal, but can you piss off? I'm meeting someone, and it's important, you know. Sensitive and all that?' said Deputy Chief Constable Geoff Caldwell, looking away, his cultured accent at odds with his bad language. His face was still full of confusion, as if he couldn't work out where he'd seen Max before.

'I don't think I can, Geoff,' said Max.

Caldwell's head snapped back towards Max again, a look of confusion, that was shifting to fear as realisation began to dawn.

'Who you here to meet, Geoff?' asked Max, his voice low and even.

Geoff opened his mouth to remonstrate, but then realisation hit him like a truck and his face fell, arrogance giving way to desolation.

'It's Craigie, isn't it?' he said, his voice trembling, his deep-set eyes wide.

'Aye. That's me, and Hardie isn't coming. He's nicked and in custody in a covert facility, having tried to kill me and my elderly aunt. You sent him to me, and now it's over. You're coming in.'

Caldwell's breathing sped up, his face began to lose colour as he stared around, not seeing the nearby surveillance officers.

'I'm not coming in, not like this,' he said, suddenly rocketing to his feet, reaching into his waistband and producing a revolver. He pointed it straight at Max, the barrel quivering.

Max didn't move. He was utterly exhausted and wasn't even sure his feet would support his weight.

'You're not going to shoot me, Geoff. We both know that.'

'Shut up. I'm not coming in, not like this. I'm not going to jail,' he babbled, spit flying from his lips.

'You're not stupid and you aren't going to shoot me. Shoot me and it's life with a thirty rec. Come in nicely, then it's more likely a ten-stretch. You'll be out in five with a life ahead of you.' Max's voice hadn't altered pitch or tempo. He continued to portray an image of complete calm.

'I'll shoot you!' The pistol remained trained at Max, the barrel wavering as his hand shook.

'There are armed cops everywhere, mate. Shoot me and you get shot.' Max was almost stunned when he felt himself yawning. He pressed the transmit button. 'All units wait. He's not going to shoot,' he said into the concealed mic.

Caldwell just stood there. A look of utter desperation and desolation written across his face. Suddenly he lowered the gun and sat again, the pistol on his lap, the air of murderous rage gone to be replaced by defeat. He let out a deep, forlorn sigh.

'I knew it couldn't go on forever, Max. This day had to come. I once took a bribe from Hardie almost thirty years ago. Then he had me and I was always there for him, no matter how high I progressed. He was always there, waiting and demanding. A word here, a tip-off there, you know how it goes.'

362

'Come in, Geoff. Tell us everything, the lot, man. Cleanse your soul, and the judge will go light on you,' said Max, soothingly.

'It doesn't end with me, you know. This goes further than you could possibly imagine. Hardie was just a thug, but there are others out there who have turned other people in our force and other national organisations. I'm just the tip of the iceberg.' His voice was low, resigned.

Caldwell closed his eyes, tightly, and a solitary tear trickled from the corner and ran slowly down.

'Then tell us about it. Help us bring all of them in.'

'I'm sorry,' he whispered, his eyes still closed.

Before Max could even think of moving, Caldwell reversed the revolver and jammed it under his chin and pulled the trigger. The report was deafening, close as Max was, and the top of Caldwell's head blew off, shooting brain and skull upwards through his cap and depositing blood all over Max's face and hair. A spray of blood and gore splattered across the shining glass of the Kibble Greenhouse. Caldwell was dead even before he slumped against Max's shoulder.

77

Max sat with Ross and Janie in the chief constable's office, all smartly dressed and feeling a little more human after a couple of days at home, plenty of sleep and some decent food.

Following DCC Caldwell's highly public suicide, there had been an absolute whirlwind of activity. Almost forty trusted detectives were urgently formed into a large squad to investigate the whole conspiracy, including the Hardie case and corruption, all supervised by the PIRC. A member of the surveillance team had captured footage of the incident. Corruption at the top of a major police force was a big deal, and it made national and international news. Macdonald had not minced his words at the press conference.

Max and Janie had been sent home as soon as the scene had been dealt with and Caldwell's partially headless corpse removed to the morgue. Max's bloodstained clothing was seized and packaged forensically, and he was given a pair of joggers and a sweatshirt. After a long, hot shower at Gartcosh he had been driven home. He had declined any immediate intervention by counsellors of any type, saying he just wanted to sleep. He had slept for twelve hours straight, in a deep, dreamless state.

Max had remained home the following day, just pottering in the garden, exercising in the garage and taking Nutmeg on a long walk. He needed to be away from the case and to allow his brain to breathe after what it had witnessed over the past few days.

The chief seemed a little hesitant as he welcomed them all into his large office at Tulliallan. He had coffee brought in before he spoke.

'I wanted to see you all together for a few reasons. Firstly, Max . . .' He paused as if forming the words. 'As chief of this force, I want firstly to apologise for the situation that you were forced into. You showed enormous fortitude, and determination to deal with this corruption, and it must've felt like the entire world was against you,' he said, seriously.

'I've had better times in my career, Boss,' said Max, without anger.

'I can imagine, and I can assure you that I've recommended you for the highest awards.'

Max just sat, saying nothing, unable to organise his thoughts. In the last few days, he had been threatened, shot at and had his dearest relative almost killed. There had been too many experiences in too short a time, and he realised that it would take a while to put it into context. No award, medal or certificate would make any difference.

'Of course, my similar thanks go to you, Janie, and of course, Ross. You both acted with utter professionalism. Similar reports have been submitted for recognition.'

'Thanks, but a bottle of malt will do for me,' was all that Ross said, his face straight.

'A quick update on the case, then. Thanks to your efforts with the phones, surveillance, recorded material and emerging witness statements that are all now filtering through, we have enough evidence to completely destroy this network that begins with the Hardie family and ends with the corrupt colleagues. I could explain it to you piecemeal, but the new SIO, DCS Morgan, has provided a detailed briefing document that I will get emailed to you all. Suffice to say, the case is a slam dunk and the PF is more than happy. All concerned are now charged and in custody and will be before the courts.'

'Boss, can I ask just one thing? Why are we here?' said Max, a little tersely.

'To thank you and update you,' he said, unconvincingly.

'With respect, sir, you may need to try a little harder than that. As I for one don't believe you,' said Ross, a touch of humour in his voice.

Macdonald paused and looked at each of them in turn. 'The last words Caldwell spoke to you have raised flags, Max. I don't think the job is yet done, if indeed it will ever be done. I think that there is a wider problem with corruption, not just in Police Scotland, but in other law-enforcement agencies. I don't want to relax just because the Hardies are now a spent force. I want to take this cancer on, and destroy it. In short, I want you three to look into this. I want you to form a new proactive anti-corruption team. I don't want to fight fires anymore, I want to take the fight to the bent cops and force them so far onto the back foot that they become irrelevant.'

'Don't you already have anti-corruption units?' asked Janie.

'I do, and I'm not sure how much I trust them. Well, to be a little clearer, I don't trust all of them, although I accept that there are some good officers there.'

'What, you don't trust the cops going after bad cops, so you want us to look at the cops looking at the bad cops? Jeez I'm confused,' said Max.

'Not just that, Max. Corruption anywhere in Scotland. I want any bent cops to fear us. To fear getting caught, so we will take the fight to them. We will use all the techniques, all the equipment and whatever resources we need.'

Max, Janie and Ross looked at each other, something passing between them. It was trust and, as things currently stood, that was everything they needed.

'I'll think about it,' said Max.

'Me too,' said Janie.

'And me,' said Ross.

78

'Drop me here, Janie,' said Max as Janie was about to turn up Max's track. 'I need to wheel the bin up, and I could do with the exercise.'

'Wow, man, it's beautiful here. Look at that view,' said Janie gazing at the azure blue sky colouring the expanse of sea in the Firth of Forth.

'Aye, soothes my soul. I'd never live in a town again.'

'Would drive me mad, but I have to say, it's very pretty.'

'Horses for courses,' said Max, shrugging.

'Back to domesticity, then, after all these days of fighting monsters, right?'

'Nietzsche, right?'

'Never had you as a philosopher.'

'He who fights with monsters should look to it that he himself does not become a monster. And when you gaze long into an abyss then the abyss also gazes into you. That's right, yes?'

'Jesus bloody Christ, and to think that *I'm* the one everyone takes the piss out of for being bloody weird. Careful, Craigie, or they'll be giving you nicknames and ignoring you in the canteen, soon,' said Janie, laughing.

Max laughed hard, for a full fifteen seconds, tears brimming in his eyes, before continuing, 'Corny as it sounds, it's something I've lived my life by. We have to always be the good guys, or the whole house falls down, right?'

'No argument from me, Max.'

'I'll drive in tomorrow, give you a lie-in. What you thinking about the chief's offer?'

'It's tempting, I have to say. You?'

'Same, I don't know, though. Rubber heelers has never appealed,' said Max, shrugging.

'Rubber heelers?' asked Janie.

'Are you too young to have heard of that?'

'Obviously, Grandpa,' said Janie, smiling.

'Old-school term for internal affairs, or Professional Standards. Cops going after other cops.'

'The way I'm thinking, it's nothing like that. I don't think it's being suggested we go after someone claiming an extra hour's overtime. We're chasing criminals, or as Nietzsche claims, monsters. The fact that they're cops is neither here nor there, they're just bloody crims who need their collars felt, right?'

'I guess,' said Max.

'Anyway, Sarge, piss off. It's date night tonight, and you aren't cocking that up again,' Janie chuckled.

'Janie?'

'Yes?'

'Thanks, pal. You stuck by me and had my back when no one else did. I won't forget that,' said Max, surprised at the touch of emotion he was feeling.

'You're welcome, Sarge, now sod off. I'm required elsewhere.' She punched him lightly and affectionately on the shoulder.

Max laughed as he got out of the car, waving as Janie pulled off in the BMW. He grabbed the blue wheelie bin and began to tug it up the track towards his home. He was looking forward to a workout in the gym and then just sitting in front of the TV, something he hadn't done for some time.

He stopped still in the middle of the drive, his senses alive, despite his bone-wearing fatigue. It suddenly occurred to him that Nutmeg hadn't come down to meet him. He frowned, a tickle of apprehension nipping at him. A combat indicator, once more? But from who, and why? Surely not now, he thought, not after everything that had happened. His synapses began to fire, once again. He instinctively reached for his pocket, suddenly cursing the fact that he'd left his baton in his desk at the office.

He continued, cautiously, until he reached the top of his drive, using a birch tree as cover. As he peeped around the thick trunk, he could see that he had company.

Katie sat on the bench in front of the glass doors at the front of the house, Nutmeg curled up next to her, resting her shaggy blonde head on Katie's leg.

'This is a surprise,' was all that Max could think of to say, as Nutmeg leaped off his wife's lap to joyfully welcome Max home.

'I saw the news, so I took a flight to Glasgow. I was worried,' she said, pointing at her suitcase on the ground next to her.

'You should've asked Lynne to let you in. She has a key,' said Max.

'I was happy here with Nutmeg. I had no idea you lived somewhere so beautiful.'

'I like it. Why are you here?' said Max, his mind whirling with conflicting emotions. He looked at her sparkling green eyes, choppy, dirty blonde hair and wide mouth and he was gripped by a longing for her. For everything to be right between them, again.

'I wanted to see you. We said that we needed to be apart for a while, to see if we wanted to be together. I've missed you. I've missed you a lot,' she said standing.

Max took her in his arms and hugged her tight, smelling her light perfume.

'Can I stay a while?' said Katie, pulling away and looking at Max.

'You can stay forever,' said Max.

They both sat down, next to each other on the bench, their arms entwined, and Nutmeg leaped up and snuggled in between them, looking adoringly at both of them in turn.

'This feels like home,' said Katie, resting her head on Max's shoulder.

'It is. Welcome home.'

Author's note

I feel that I need to explain the motivation for this book as it really does ram home how much a simple spark of an idea can morph into a 100,000-word novel.

It was Christmas 2019 and we were staying in a beautiful huge old house with a load of friends in the depths of the Scottish countryside close to Pitlochry.

After much food and drink, I got chatting to an elderly chap called John Fisher, who had travelled over from Australia to visit family and friends. He was almost eighty, but still had a broad Scottish accent. We got chatting and I learned a little about him. He had been in the police in Scotland in the 1960s for a few years. He was a splendid chap, full of fun and stories, and I also discovered that he was an avid fan of Scottish crime fiction. He told me how much he had enjoyed my books, which was lovely to hear. He then hit me with the fateful words that all authors hear at some point.

'I've a great idea on how to start a book!'

Now, firstly, I don't want to sound ungrateful, but most of us breathe deeply when we hear these words. However, a few whiskies had been consumed so I listened intently.

He proceeded to tell me about the time back in the late

Sixties when in a remote graveyard in Caithness doing a little research for his wife's side of the family, he uncovered this spooky grave that simply bore the inscription: 'This Grave Never to be Opened'. He then followed it up with: 'I reckon that's a pretty good way to start a book, yeah?'

Well, my socks were well and truly knocked off.

The Grave Never to be Opened. What a hook. What a start. My mind began to seethe with ideas, and a couple of days later I began writing, and a number of months later *Dead Man's Grave* was written.

Sadly, John Fisher passed away on his birthday, the 24th January 2021, so he never had the opportunity to read it. But his son in Australia had told him all about it, about his part in the book being born, that Max's neighbour is named in his honour, and that the book is dedicated to him.

So, John, this is for you.

Neil

Acknowledgements

As always, once the words 'the end' are typed under a manuscript it strikes me that things really aren't over. There is still much to do, and as such, there are lots of people who offer so much and help to bring the book to life. So, I have lots of people, who have helped me turn this from an idea through to a book, who deserve my heartfelt thanks.

To my agent, Robbie Guillory. I owe Robbie lots of beers, which this cursed virus has stopped us having. Robbie took a risk on me when a chance discussion about an idea for a book was floated with him. He said, 'I'd love to see it!' Problem was, I hadn't actually written that much of it, beyond an outline and a few thousand words. He took me on anyway, and I feel fortunate to have him in my corner. The world of publishing isn't easy to navigate and we all need someone to bounce ideas off, be a buffer, an adviser and a pal. Robbie is ace.

To my editor Finn at HQ Digital, for loving the story, helping me make it as good as it can possibly be, and seeing the potential of DS Max Craigie and the team.

To everyone else in the HQ family for helping to turn my nonsensical ramblings into something approaching a book that people may actually want to read. You guys rock.

Lots of far more talented writers than me have helped

along the way with ideas, advice and encouragement. I want to namecheck a few.

Tony Parsons, who was generous with his time in helping me conceptualise the basic theme of this book and put the idea into an outline that someone wanted to buy. It kept me focused and it kept me on track.

Denzil Meyrick, Lin Anderson and Ian Rankin for convincing me that the story idea was a good one, you'd never heard of anything like it and that I should definitely write it.

Colin Scott. You know who you are. I couldn't do this without the advice, encouragement, swearing and belly laughs.

To my beautiful wife, Clare, for putting up with me whilst I tap away, occasionally coming out of the office after 40k words and saying, 'I'm not sure this is going to work.' You always nod sympathetically, but you always know that this is just a phase. You're always the first to read any book I write, and your opinion really matters. Your love and support mean everything to me.

My kids, Alec, Richard and Ollie, for not laughing at me for writing my silly stories and being proud that your old man is chasing the dream.

To all my big, mad, raucous and crazy family, all over the world, who read the books and shout out to everyone that they can to read them.

As always, I have to thank the source of all my stories. Twenty-five years in the Metropolitan Police gave me an endless supply of material that I continue to mine for inspiration. The vast majority of the cops out there are putting themselves in harm's way, day in, day out and they do it to protect us, the public.

Of course, to you, the reader, who parts with their hard-earned cash to buy my stories, a big hearty thank you. You're the ones who count.

Neil

If you loved *Dead Man's Grave*, don't miss this exclusive early extract from Book 2 in the Max Craigie series . . .

THE BLOOD TIDE

You get away with murder.

In a remote sea loch on the west coast of Scotland, a fisherman disappears without trace. His remains are never found.

You make people disappear.

A young man jumps from a bridge in Glasgow and falls to his death in the water below. DS Max Craigie uncovers evidence that links both victims. But if he can't find out what cost them their lives, it won't be long before more bodies turn up at the morgue . . .

You come back for revenge.

Soon cracks start to appear in the investigation, and Max's past hurtles back to haunt him. When his loved ones are threatened, he faces a terrifying choice: let the only man he ever feared walk free, or watch his closest friend die . . .

1

The rib chugged steadily, its engine note low, as it nosed into Loch Torridon and on towards the small beach by the road. Jimmy McLeish had left his Toyota pick-up there, trailer still attached, as he often did when he went out fishing or picking up his creels. It wouldn't cause any comment or curiosity, so he should have been relaxed. This wasn't the same, though, and he was anything but relaxed, because his cargo wasn't the usual fish or lobster. This trip was a whole different ballgame.

The night was dark and moonless, with that inky, impenetrable blackness that you only get in the Highlands, far away from light pollution. If it hadn't been for the night vision goggles clamped to Jimmy's face, he would never have been able to navigate his way in past the rocks. Lights tonight would be a mistake, however, particularly with the nature of the cargo that lay in a black bag between his feet. Darkness was his ally.

Jimmy scanned the scene before him, the ghostly green tinge from the goggles bathing the landscape in an unnatural hue. A few dots of light were visible just to the west, where a handful of dwellings dotted the tiny hamlets of Fasag and Torridon, but beyond that the scenery was dark and desolate.

This was his neighbourhood. This wild, bleak, but beautiful coastline was his home.

He took a deep breath and edged the small craft towards the shore of the sea loch, aiming for the tiny single-track road that ran parallel with the edge of the frigid water. He scanned the shore and let out a sigh of relief when he saw the dark shape of his pickup truck, a silhouette against the craggy rock that bordered the road. Another vehicle was parked right behind it, just as he was expecting. Three brief flashes of a torch indicated he was good to go. That was the agreed signal, so Macca, Scally's right-hand man, was there waiting for him. Jimmy gently increased the engine power, and the small rib picked up speed towards the truck.

He knew this area well, having been raised a few miles away in Kyle of Lochalsh, which he accepted, along with the fact he owned a rib and worked as a fisherman, probably made him perfect for this trip.

His task was simply to deliver the cargo to Macca and his job was done. It was childishly simple, so he really shouldn't have been this nervous. He reached into his jacket and pulled out his battered old hip-flask. His hands shook as he unscrewed the cap and took a hefty nip of the peaty whisky, enjoying the warmth as it slid down his throat.

The torch flashed again, three times, as he nosed the boat to the shore, close to the launch trailer he had left when casting off. There was a soft bump as the rib came to a halt on the stony sand and he killed the engine, simultaneously flipping the goggles up on their harness. The sudden silence was absolute. He looked at the shore but saw nothing in the blackness. There was no one there.

He nestled his night vision goggles down to scan the area, the scenery once again bathed in the soft green glow. He had seen the flashes from the shore, he was certain of it, so where the hell was Macca? He jumped off the small boat into the shallows and pulled the rib ashore, feeling the rocky, gravelly surface grip the keel. He quickly jammed a stake into the ground and lashed a line to it.

He looked again at the new vehicle, which was as dark and foreboding as the landscape surrounding them. Where was he? He adjusted the intensifying properties of the goggles, hoping to see something, and the landscape gradually lightened. His eyes followed the loch's shore towards Torridon, where his wife would be at home in front of the fire. More than ever, he regretted the blazing row that they'd had before he left. As always it was about money, or the lack of it. He'd stormed out, giving her no indication of where, or what, he was doing. He hoped that enough cash to pay the outstanding bills and maybe get a nice meal would soften her up. Part of him wished that he could be with her, right now, rather than here in the inky blackness, about to hand over some illicit cargo to the distinctly intimidating Macca. Not for the first time, he wondered if he had made a terrible mistake.

Suddenly a blinding burst of torchlight shone directly on him, immediately overwhelming the image-intensifying properties of the goggles. He gasped and pulled them away from his face. Stars danced in front of his eyes from the sudden assault on his senses and he blinked rapidly, trying to clear his vision. He rubbed his eyes, but the flare remained.

When he opened them, he was once again flooded with bright torchlight from a head torch worn by a huge man. This wasn't the short, stocky Macca.

'Jesus, you almost bloody blinded me,' Jimmy said. 'Who the hell are you? I was expecting Macca.'

'I'm Davie, and this is Callum. Scally sent us. You got the cargo?' The man was tall and muscular, with a pale face and dark hair. His accent was pure Glasgow and there was something about it that Jimmy didn't like. He looked mean, nasty. In fact, he radiated menace.

'Aye, it's here. You got my money?'

'Of course we have, but we need to see the package first,' said Davie, smirking unpleasantly.

'But Scally said cash on delivery,' Jimmy said in a faltering, shaky voice, unsure where this was going.

'Cash on delivery? You hear this, Callum? Mannie here wants paying before we've even seen in the bag.'

The man called Callum stepped forward. He was a full head shorter than Davie and much slimmer, although it was hard to see him properly, the only light sources being Davie's head torch and what looked like a penlight in Callum's hand. 'Oh dear, my friend, is this your first time?' Callum snorted. 'Nobody gets paid before we check the bag, right? Do be a sport and pass it over and we need to get your rib out of the water, pronto. I know this is a little bit of a backwater, but the local constabulary may venture here. Come on, chop-chop.'

Callum surprised Jimmy by having a light, cultured accent that sounded like it came from southern England. Despite his voice, he projected something a little more subtle. Ruthlessness. They seemed to be seasoned professionals, but unlike any criminals Jimmy had encountered before. Anxiety began to nip at him, and he suddenly felt very exposed.

'Aye well,' Jimmy said, 'give us a hand getting the rib hooked up, but we'll leave the bag where it is until we're out of the water.'

'Fair enough. Give Davie your keys and he'll reverse your truck up.'

Jimmy tossed his keys at the big man who caught them and walked unhurriedly to the pick-up.

Jimmy eased the wheeled launch ramp into the water and within a few minutes had the rib secured onto the low trailer. Davie was soon reversing the pickup, with trailer attached, onto the beach. Within a few minutes, Jimmy was using the winch to pull the boat and launch trailer onto the back of the vehicle. Jimmy then spent a few minutes securing the rib with straps, until it was tightly fastened and ready to go.

'Now, old bean. I believe you have something for us?' said Callum. 'Much as we trust you, we'd like to see it before we hand over your fee.'

Jimmy reached into the rib and dragged out the heavy waterproof canoe bag. He heaved it with a grunt onto the stony sand at the side of the truck. Davie quickly unbuckled the bag and reached inside. His head torch lit up the interior with a bright blaze of white light.

'Tiger stamped, Cal,' said Davie, a trace of pleasure in his voice.

'Capital. Sling it in the back of the truck then, Jimmy,' said Callum.

With a growing sense of unease rising in his belly, Jimmy did as he was asked, carefully securing the canoe bag.

He hefted it onto his shoulder. Callum's torch illuminated the back of the truck. It was bathed in bright white light. Jimmy heaved the bag into the load-bed and it landed with a thump, but didn't lie flat.

'Shift it, man. It needs to be out of sight,' said Callum in an oddly effete and simpering voice, which managed to combine insincerity and sarcasm in equal measure.

Jimmy suddenly felt cold. He swallowed, reached in and dragged the bag away from a long object that was stopping it from lying flat. The bright torch beam fell on a pale, white face. Jimmy let out a yelp and leaped back. A dead body stared up at him with sightless eyes. There was a red-rimmed hole, deep and black, in the centre of its forehead. Even in Jimmy's blind panic, he recognised Macca, Scally's right-hand man. His heart raced and bile rose in his throat as the sudden realisation hit him that he was about to be ripped off, or worse.

He turned to look at Davie and Callum as terror thundered

towards him like an express truck. They both stared at him, with unpleasant, yet amused looks on their faces. Davie stepped forward. The head torch beam flooded into Jimmy's face, blinding him.

Dear Reader,

We hope you enjoyed reading this book. If you did, we'd be so appreciative if you left a review. It really helps us and the author to bring more books like this to you.

Here at HQ Digital we are dedicated to publishing fiction that will keep you turning the pages into the early hours. Don't want to miss a thing? To find out more about our books, promotions, discover exclusive content and enter competitions you can keep in touch in the following ways:

JOIN OUR COMMUNITY:

Sign up to our new email newsletter: hyperurl.co/ hqnewsletter

Read our new blog www.hqstories.co.uk

https://twitter.com/HQStories

www.facebook.com/HQStories

BUDDING WRITER?

We're also looking for authors to join the HQ Digital family! Find out more here:

https://www.hqstories.co.uk/want-to-write-for-us/

Thanks for reading, from the HQ Digital team

If you enjoyed *Dead Man's Grave*,
then why not try another gripping
crime thriller from HQ Digital?